" . . . SO, WE BELIEVE GANZ OR NEERA ORDERED THIS LEKKAR KILLED. DO WE KNOW WHY?"

"No," Nogura said, "nor do I particularly care. What I do care about is whether Ganz, or Neera, or whoever, might decide that a better long-term alternative to killing their own people is simply getting rid of Reyes. We need to get him out of there."

"So that we can arrest him again?" Moyer asked.

Nogura eyed her with annoyance. "That's what is usually done with those who've divulged Starfleet secrets, and consorted with the enemy to place Starfleet or Federation personnel and property at risk."

"With all due respect, Admiral," Moyer countered, "we don't know the whole story. Diego Reyes is a lot of things, but a traitor? I find that hard to believe."

Holding up a hand, Nogura shook his head. "I'd like nothing more than to share your doubts, Commander, but at the very least, there are questions to be answered. If nothing else, Reyes is still a convicted criminal, with a prison sentence waiting in the wings if and when all of this insanity finally shakes out. Even if it's decided that he still has to be sent to that penal colony on Earth, it's a better fate than anything Ganz has planned for him."

DON'T MISS THESE OTHER NOVELS IN THE *STAR TREK: VANGUARD* SERIES

Harbinger

by David Mack

Summon the Thunder

by Dayton Ward & Kevin Dilmore

Reap the Whirlwind

by David Mack

Open Secrets

by Dayton Ward

Precipice

by David Mack

Declassified

by Dayton Ward, Kevin Dilmore,
Marco Palmieri, David Mack

STAR TREK®
VANGUARD

WHAT JUDGMENTS COME

DAYTON WARD
& KEVIN DILMORE

Story by
Dayton Ward & Kevin Dilmore
and David Mack

Based upon *Star Trek*
created by Gene Roddenberry

POCKET BOOKS
New York   London   Toronto   Sydney   New Delhi

Pocket Books
A Division of Simon & Schuster, Inc.
1230 Avenue of the Americas
New York, NY 10020

This book is a work of fiction. Names, characters, places, and incidents either are products of the authors' imaginations or are used fictitiously. Any resemblance to actual events or locales or persons, living or dead, is entirely coincidental.

First Pocket Books paperback edition October 2011

POCKET and colophon are registered trademarks of Simon & Schuster, Inc.

For information about special discounts for bulk purchases, please contact Simon & Schuster Special Sales at 1-866-506-1949 or business@simonandschuster.com.

The Simon & Schuster Speakers Bureau can bring authors to your live event. For more information or to book an event, contact the Simon & Schuster Speakers Bureau at 1-866-248-3049 or visit our website at www.simonspeakers.com.

Cover design by Alan Dingman; cover art by Doug Drexler; *U.S.S. Sagittarius* design by Masao Okazaki

Manufactured in the United States of America

10 9 8 7 6 5 4 3 2 1

ISBN 978-1-4516-0863-2
ISBN 978-1-4516-0864-9 (ebook)

For Marco Palmieri and David Mack.
Thanks for inviting us to the party.

WHAT JUDGMENTS COME

PROLOGUE

April 2270

A crisp breeze was cutting across the immense lake, and Tim Pennington shivered at the chill on his nose and cheeks. Stepping onto the wooden dock that extended twenty meters out over the water from the bank, he turned and waved to the pilot of the boat that had transported him three kilometers from the mainland to this small island. The pilot, as he had during the entire journey, feigned interest as he returned the gesture before directing his attention back to the boat's controls. Pennington watched the small craft back away from the dock before turning clockwise until its bow pointed back the way it had come. The boat accelerated across the water and in a handful of seconds disappeared into the layer of fog that had moved in to shroud the lake.

"Have a nice day, mate," Pennington muttered. Now alone on the dock, he jammed his hands deeper into the lined pockets of his jacket. A look to the forest on his right told him that the Caldos sun had already slipped behind the trees. It would be dark soon, nightfall taking with it any residual warmth. He was coming to realize that his jacket was not heavy enough to prevent the bracing, damp cold from reaching his body. A dull ache in his right arm was making itself known, and he reached up to massage his shoulder socket.

Almost makes me miss Vulcan. Almost.

Pennington walked the length of the dock until he reached a set of stairs leading down to a landing that was constructed of a dozen evenly cut and spaced sections of thick wood. Like the dock itself, the landing appeared to have been installed recently.

Scrutinizing the framework of wooden railing running alongside the stairs, he noted that the metallic bolts and clamps used to anchor the support posts were free of rust. He supposed that the builders might have used components that would withstand corrosion for an extended time, but that seemed unlikely, given the tenets upon which the colony on Caldos II had been established, and by which it was continuing to expand.

Originally conceived as a re-creation of Earth's Scottish Highlands from the seventeenth century, the Caldos colony's various structures all were built using construction materials and techniques of the era. The settlement offered numerous modern technological conveniences, though whenever possible such equipment was housed within a traditional façade. Even the weather modification network had been programmed to replicate the climate of the Highlands.

A bit too closely, for my tastes, Pennington decided. Despite any misgivings he might harbor about the local weather, to his practiced eye, the colony was a fine tribute to his homeland, the care and precision with which the re-creation had been realized succeeding in making him yearn for a return to the region of his birth. How many years had passed since his last visit to Earth? Too many, Pennington knew, and indeed he had been making his way in that direction when one of his colleagues at the Federation News Service had made contact, sending via subspace message the information that had led him here.

"Of all the places," he said aloud, though there was no one— not even the party to whom his comment was directed—to hear, "you certainly found yourself a nice little hideaway, didn't you?"

Pennington knew that calling the Caldos colony isolated was a bit extreme, but the star system was outside the established trade routes. Still, it was comfortably within Federation territory and benefited from semiregular Starfleet patrols through the region. Though the settlement was just establishing itself, long-term plans called for a sweeping spaceport that would benefit from both commercial and Starfleet traffic. That facility, according to information Pennington had read, would be constructed more than a hundred kilometers to the south, near the continental coastline, well away from the tranquil colony's population center. For now, though, Caldos II was the perfect location for someone who did not want to be found.

Or who'd been ordered not to be found.

The walk from the dock was easy enough, with the gravel trail charting a winding path through the forest. It took only a moment for Pennington to realize that this section of the woods only partially obscured from view the straight, angular silhouette of a large, single-story building nestled within a small glade. The cabin was constructed from stone and wood, with a sharply sloped roof and a covered porch running along the structure's frontage. As he drew closer, Pennington saw that the cabin's large front window likely afforded its occupant a picturesque view of the lake as framed by the trees. Lights were on inside the house and visible through that window, as well as a few others, and a wisp of thin, light gray smoke drifted upward from the stonework chimney that was the most prominent feature of the cabin's western wall. Stacks of wood lined that wall, each piece cut into serviceable lengths for easy transport through the adjacent door leading into the house. Besides the interior illumination, the only other noticeable clue to the presence of modern technology was a low, muffled hum Pennington heard as he walked closer to the cabin. It seemed to be coming from a small outbuilding situated near the tree line behind the house. A generator, perhaps?

He was half a dozen steps away from the cabin's porch when the front door opened, light pouring out from the structure's warm interior and highlighting the form of a muscled, middle-aged man. His appearance had changed since the last time Pennington had seen him, his thinning black-and gray hair having now grown to a point well past the man's shoulders. A trimmed, salt-and-pepper beard highlighted his face, and the Starfleet uniform he once had worn with much pride was long gone, replaced with loose-fitting, comfortable-looking clothes that Pennington supposed were ideal for the Caldosian climate. What had not changed was the man's expression. His eyes bored into Pennington's, studying and sizing him up, while the rest of his features remained impassive.

"Diego Reyes," the journalist said, unable to suppress the smile he felt forming on his lips, "as I live and breathe."

His expression betraying nothing, Reyes replied, "I'm pretty sure I told the concierge I only wanted maid service on weekends." He said nothing else for several seconds, the silence lingering just long enough to become awkward.

Pennington cleared his throat. "It was a damned chore tracking you down, mate."

"That was sort of the point," Reyes said, moving not the slightest muscle as he continued to regard his unexpected visitor. After a moment, his features softened. "Though I'll admit, it's nice to see a familiar face, even if it has to be yours."

Anxious as to how he felt this meeting might play out, Pennington allowed himself to release a small sigh of relief. "It's good to see you, Commodore."

Reyes held up a hand. "Not for a while, and not anymore. That's all behind me now." He seemed to consider the situation for a moment before reaching the decision to resign himself to Pennington's presence. Stepping back into the cabin, he gestured for the journalist to follow him. "Come on in."

Like the exterior, the inside of the home was a blend of masonry and wood. The wall with the fireplace was composed of elaborate stone work, with decorative, irregularly shaped rock in multiple colors set into a light gray mortar. A mantel above the fireplace looked as though it might have been fashioned from the trunk of a once-mighty tree, cut into the shape of a beam and laid atop a trio of rocks jutting out from the wall at chest level. On either side of the hearth were shelves containing a few dozen books as well as assorted keepsakes, some of which Pennington recognized from Reyes's old office on Starbase 47. The room's furnishings were simple—chairs, tables, a coat tree by the door, a pair of overstuffed recliners near the fireplace. Aside from the notable lack of modern equipment such as a viewscreen or computer terminal, there was one type of memento that was conspicuous in its absence, and that was any sort of photograph. None hung on the walls or occupied space on the shelves or tables.

"Rather cozy, I must say," Pennington offered as he removed his jacket. He hung the garment from an unoccupied hook on the coat tree before turning back to face Reyes, who now regarded him while leaning against the waist-high bar separating the front room from what looked to be a modest yet still well-appointed kitchen. "A bit off the beaten path, though, you know."

Reyes shrugged. "I like it here. It's quiet, and nobody bothers me. Well, almost nobody." Pausing, he stuck his hands in his pants pockets before nodding toward Pennington. "How's the arm?"

It took a moment for the journalist to realize that, without thinking, he had reached up again to massage the mild twinge in his shoulder. "Only aches when it rains. Or it's cold, or damp, or any combination of the three."

"Well, then you're going to love it here," Reyes replied. Pushing himself from the bar, he made his way into the kitchen. "Want a drink?"

"Whatever you're having," Pennington said.

Reyes nodded. "Caldosian whiskey it is, then." Reaching below the bar, he produced a stocky, square bottle made of green glass, and with his left hand extracted the sizable cork from the vessel's neck. "It's a local specialty, and better than anything you'll find anywhere that's not Scotland."

"That good, eh?" Pennington asked, playing the game as he watched Reyes pour some of the bottle's contents into two squat tumblers with thick bases.

"You'll want to eat the glass when you're finished," Reyes said, holding up one of the tumblers and offering it to Pennington.

The journalist offered a nod of thanks as he accepted the drink, then held up the glass in an informal salute. "Cheers, mate." Taking a tentative sip, Pennington braced himself for what he was sure would be the rush of peat-saturated, oversmoked rot-gut as brewed by some local farmhand working with a storage drum hanging over an open fire pit behind his house. To his surprise, the whiskey was smooth and slightly sweet, warming his throat as he swallowed. "Now that's nice," he said, feeling the tingle of the alcohol as he exhaled. Nodding in approval, he tossed back the rest of the glass.

"Go easy with it," Reyes warned. "It's an acquired taste." With that, he downed the contents of his own glass in a single swallow before refilling both glasses. Setting the bottle back on the bar, he retrieved his glass and moved back into the main room. "How'd you find me?"

Pennington shrugged. "It wasn't easy," he replied as he turned and followed Reyes to the pair of recliners positioned before the fireplace. "I had to call in quite a few favors, and even then I ended up owing some people. So far as the whole galaxy seems to be concerned, you ceased to exist the day you left the station."

Nodding without looking away from the fire, Reyes said, "That's the way it was supposed to be." Using a metal poker, he shifted the quartet of smoldering logs around the elevated grate inside the firebox, stirring the embers until hints of new flame appeared from beneath the wood.

"We didn't get a chance to say much that day," Pennington said.

Reyes returned the poker to a stand situated to the left of the firebox. "That was more my fault than yours, I suppose. I've never been big on good-byes. Besides, I was on something of a schedule. There were a lot of people who were pretty anxious to have me away from there as quickly and quietly as possible. I imagine a few of those people are still pretty pissed that I didn't end up at the bottom of a hole somewhere."

"True enough," Pennington replied, "but Admiral Nogura told me he got over it."

The deadpan remark was enough to elicit the first real grin from Reyes since Pennington's arrival, and he even chuckled as he moved to one of the recliners. He motioned for the journalist to have a seat, and the two men sat in silence for a moment, sipping their drinks and staring at the fire. Pennington breathed a sigh of contentment, the effect of the fire on his feet similar to that of the whiskey in his belly.

I could get used to this.

After a moment, his right hand turning his glass in a slow circle as it sat atop his thigh, Reyes said, "Don't take this the wrong way, Tim, but what the hell are you doing here? I know you didn't come all this way for a drink."

"Well," Pennington said, "for what it's worth, I also haven't eaten since breakfast."

Releasing another small laugh, Reyes sipped from his whiskey. "I'll get right on that. Okay, out with it. What really brought you to the ass end of space? To talk to some washed-up relic nobody's going to remember in a hundred years?"

"There are a handful of people who know the truth about what happened out there," Pennington replied, holding up his glass and swirling its contents. "Not much was said about your departure. Top secret, hush-hush and all that. Starfleet and the Federation have washed their hands of you, so I figure now was as good a time as any to try cornering you somewhere and getting you to tell me your side of the story."

Reyes eyed him. "You can read about it in my memoirs. I've got a contract from Broht and Forester sitting on my desk. They want a juicy tell-all book for Christmas."

Laughing at that, Pennington shook his head. "That'd get some Starfleet knickers in a twist, wouldn't it? I'm impressed you even know the name of a major publishing company."

"I got it from one of the books Zeke gave me before I left the station," Reyes replied, waving toward one of the shelves near the fireplace. "The first time, that is. You know, before all that fun I had with the Klingons and Orions."

"Right, that," Pennington said, his gaze settling once again on the fire. "Quite a holiday you had there. You never talked much about that before you left, either."

"I lost the books Zeke gave me," Reyes said, "thanks to those Orion pirates' blowing up my prison transport." He paused, and Pennington wondered if he was recalling the events of what had to have been a most bizarre day, or if his thoughts had turned to his longtime friend, Ezekiel Fisher. "I had to get new copies made," he added after a moment, "just so I could find out how they ended. Bastards." Chuckling again, Reyes finished the whiskey in his glass before rising from his chair and crossing the room to the kitchen. Pennington did not turn to follow his movements, but he did look up when the other man returned to the fireplace, whiskey bottle in one hand and his refilled glass in the other. Without saying anything, Reyes gestured toward Pennington's glass, and the journalist held it up for a refill.

"I figure this might take a while," Reyes said, setting the bottle on a small table positioned between the two recliners before reclaiming his seat.

Pennington shifted in his chair in order to regard the former, now-disgraced Starfleet officer. "As it happens, I have time to kill."

"It's not like they'll ever let you write about it," Reyes said, his gaze drifting to the fire before them. "You try publishing anything, and the best you can hope for is being allowed to retire gracefully to some backwater colony."

"Maybe we could be roommates?" Pennington suggested.

"Not for nothing," Reyes replied, "but I have a shovel and access to a lot of uninhabited forest. You won't be missed. At least, not for a while."

Laughing at that, Pennington said, "Noted." He paused, watching flames lick at one of the logs burning in the fireplace, before adding, "Look, I know there's no way a lot of what happened will be made public, certainly not within our lifetimes and perhaps not ever, but I still want as much of the story as I can pull together, for my own curiosity and maybe even for my sanity. I'd like to think that what we all experienced meant something, even if most people will never really know about it. Does that sound so crazy?"

"No, it doesn't sound crazy at all." Reyes sipped from his glass, saying nothing for a moment, but then he released a sigh that to Pennington's ears sounded more than a bit like resignation.

"All right. What do you want to know?"

THE TAURUS REACH

2268

1

"What do you want to know?"

Tim Pennington had to strain in order to hear the question over the din permeating the *Omari-Ekon*'s main gaming floor. Even standing less than an arm's length from the person he was talking to, he had to shout to be heard.

"I want to know what the hell you're doing here!" Pennington said, then looked around as he realized his voice had carried above the dull roar around him, and likely to ears not belonging to his intended target, Diego Reyes. The last time Pennington had seen him —almost a year ago, now— Reyes had been wearing a Starfleet commodore's uniform, but now the man seemed quite at home in an open-necked dark shirt and pants, over which he wore a black leather jacket. His hair, far more gray than black now, was longer on the sides, though still thinning on top. To Pennington, the former Starfleet officer appeared no different than the other civilian customers taking up space on the gaming floor.

Leaning against the bar, a thin rectangular glass held in his left hand, Reyes paused to scan the faces of nearby patrons, as though trying to verify that he and Pennington were not being overheard. He considered his glass before downing its contents in a single swallow, grimacing at its taste before returning his attention to Pennington. "It's a long story."

"I gathered as much," the journalist replied, taking care now to ensure his voice did not rise above the crowd noise. Still, he tossed glances over both shoulders to check for potential eavesdroppers, but saw no sign of anyone appearing to engage in such activity. Everyone in the room appeared to be focused on the gaming tables, or their meals as they sat at tables or in booths, or the lithe figures of the Orion waitresses as they drifted around and among the patrons. A thin veil of multihued smoke lingered near the ceiling lights, a by-product of the different tobaccos and other noxious substances of which various customers were partaking. Pennington tried not to think about the potential damage being inflicted upon his own lungs at that moment.

The man now standing before Pennington seemed to possess only a superficial resemblance to the Starfleet flag officer he once had been. How much time had passed since they had last spoken? More than a year, the journalist recalled, before Reyes's arrest by Captain Rana Desai and imprisonment while awaiting court-martial. Pennington had missed those proceedings, electing instead to travel to Vulcan with Starbase 47's former assistant chief medical officer, Jabilo M'Benga. The doctor had made the journey while escorting his patient, T'Prynn, who at the time had fallen into a coma following a severe neurological trauma. By the time her condition was treated and she and Pennington left Vulcan on what at best could be described as a circuitous journey back to Vanguard, they had learned of Reyes's trial and conviction, and his sentencing to ten years' confinement at a penal colony back on Earth.

What had come as a shock was their learning of an attack on the *U.S.S. Nowlan,* the transport vessel carrying the disgraced officer to Earth. The ship had been reported destroyed with all hands, so it came as an even greater surprise to subsequently learn that Reyes was alive and in Klingon custody. Further, it appeared that the former Starfleet commodore had provided the captain of the Klingon vessel with sensitive information, ensuring a successful attack on Starbase 47. For reasons that remained a mystery, Reyes had found a way to trade his Klingon hosts for Orions—specifically, the merchant prince Ganz and the crew of the *Omari-Ekon,* where he had been for the past several months. Though the vessel was docked at Vanguard, it remained sovereign Orion territory. As such, Reyes was beyond the grasp of Starfleet regulations and Federation law.

And of course that has somebody's innards in an unholy knot, Pennington mused, thinking of Admiral Heihachiro Nogura, Starbase 47's current commanding officer and the one nursing the biggest headache with respect to the "Reyes situation."

"So, what? Are you hoping to write some award-winning exposé or something?" Reyes asked, holding up his glass and signaling the bartender for a refill.

Pennington shrugged. "The thought had occurred to me, and it goes without saying that it'd be the easiest sale I ever made to my bosses at FNS." Pausing to sip from his drink, he added, "However, I'm afraid I'm not equipped to conduct a decent interview." Upon boarding the *Omari-Ekon,* the journalist was subjected to a thorough search, and as a consequence had been relieved of the handheld recording device he normally used to collect notes and his interviews. It would be returned to him upon his departure, but it was obvious that neither the guards nor their employers wanted anyone making any audio or visual recordings of the ship, its crew, or its patrons. As for his personal inspection prior to entering the gaming floor, while it had not advanced to the point where Pennington might have asked the Orion guard frisking him to at least consider buying him dinner, it had come uncomfortably close.

"Well, then," Reyes said, accepting a new glass of some unidentified green liquor, "it was nice seeing you, Tim. Take care of yourself." He turned as though readying to cut a swath through the crowd milling near the bar, until Pennington reached out and put a hand on his arm.

"What's your bloody hurry, mate? I just got here. After all we've been through together, this is how you're going to treat an old friend?" His comments, delivered in what he hoped were an accusatory fashion, were enough to catch the bartender's attention, and Pennington noted how the Orion strove not to appear as though he might be eavesdropping on their conversation.

Real smooth, wanker. Still, now that he had confirmed he was under surveillance, Pennington knew he would have to be even more careful than he had been to this point.

When Reyes turned back to face Pennington once again, the first signs of irritation had begun to cloud his features. "Just for your future reference, there's a sizable chasm separating casual or professional acquaintances from those I call friend. Now, while you're probably closer to the latter group than the former, don't go pushing your luck."

Pennington offered an uncertain nod. "No problem. Look, I suppose I came here because I wanted to know what happened to you. I wanted to know how a man with your record and reputation could turn his back on everything and everyone he cared about. I can't believe you'd just walk away from all of that, and I sure as hell could never believe you'd do it to partner up with the enemy."

"I'd watch your words here if I were you, Mister Pennington," Reyes said, glancing toward the Orion behind the bar, who was doing his level best to keep his attention on the drinks he was concocting. "There are people skulking about who might not take kindly to some of your views." If he understood what Pennington was trying to do so far as throwing off the bartender's covert observations were concerned, he offered no sign. "As for me turning my back on anything, hopefully you'll recall that I was heading for a penal colony when the ship I was on got blown out from under me. Everything I've done since then has been motivated by simple survival."

His eyes narrowing, Pennington asked, "Does that include collusion with the Klingons?"

Pausing as though to consider his answer, Reyes frowned. "Let's get something straight: the Klingons were planning that raid on the station. I gave them the information they needed to get in and get out without inflicting casualties."

"But what about the security concerns?" Pennington asked, struggling to process what he was hearing. "What if we hadn't been able to get back what they stole from the station?"

"It still wouldn't have been worth anyone getting hurt," Reyes said, biting every word. He reached for his glass and gulped down a substantial portion of its contents, after which he all but slammed his glass down onto the bar. When he spoke again, there was no mistaking the new edge in his voice. "Now, are we done here, Mister Pennington?"

Holding up his hand in a gesture, Pennington cast another glance around them before responding. With the exception of the bartender, who truly was doing a very poor job of feigning disinterest, none of the bar's other patrons appeared to give a damn about anything that did not involve their own drinks or ogling the Orion women serving them.

Damn, this is harder than I thought. It took physical effort for Pennington to keep from repeating his hurried looks around the bar, or otherwise tip off any alert observers that he knew he and Reyes were being watched. "I'm sorry," he said. "I didn't mean to imply anything, but look at it from where I'm standing. Now, I don't for one bloody second believe that you could ever betray Starfleet or the Federation, no matter how disillusioned you might've become with them." When Reyes regarded him with a quizzical expression, he added, "Yeah, I heard about what you said at your court-martial."

Pennington had not been surprised to learn that Reyes had offered no defense for his actions. The commodore had been forced to order Gamma Tauri IV's destruction in order to contain an attack by a group of runaway Shedai sentinels which had wiped out the Federation colony there. An encounter with other Shedai entities on their apparent home planet resulted in the destruction of the entire Jinoteur system. Reyes had violated his orders and given Pennington approval to write an article for the Federation News Service, recounting what he had witnessed firsthand in the Jinoteur system, along with a companion piece detailing the events on Gamma Tauri IV. Pennington was certain that there was much more to the mystery of the Shedai than had been made public. He also knew that what Reyes had allowed him to expose was damaging to the veil of secrecy in which Starfleet had wrapped Starbase 47's true purpose in the Taurus Reach.

"Those records are supposed to be sealed," Reyes countered, lowering his voice so that Pennington could barely hear him above the crowd. "Classified. Top secret, and all that other bullshit."

The journalist nodded. "And they are, but you still have friends, Diego, whether you want to believe that or not. No matter what you might've told those blokes at your trial, you're still you, and the Diego Reyes I know would never betray his oath, no matter how pissed off he might get at the idiots in charge. Doing what's right is part of your DNA. That's why you did what you did and said what you said, and why you allowed me to write what I wrote." He paused, noting that the bartender seemed once again to be hovering too close. Directing his attention to the Orion, he said, "If you're going to keep standing there, at least bring me a decent shot of whiskey. In a clean glass, if it's not too much trouble, mate." The bartender responded with a menacing glower before turning to reach for a rectangular blue glass bottle on one of the shelves behind the bar.

With the Orion now otherwise engaged, at least for a moment, Pennington redirected his gaze to Reyes. "So far as I and a lot of other people are concerned, you're a bloody hero for what you did, but none of that matters when we see you consorting with Klingons and Orion pirates. And to help the Klingons steal Shedai technology from the station? You do understand that to casual observers, you look like a traitor, right?"

His gaze fixed on his own glass, Reyes nodded. "I know what I look like."

"So," Pennington said, stepping closer, "tell me the casual observers are wrong."

Both men stood silent as the bartender returned with Pennington's drink before holding out a beefy jade hand, palm up. It took Pennington a moment to realize the Orion was waiting for payment. "Put it on my tab."

"I'm closing out your tab," the bartender replied. "You'll be leaving soon, and I don't want you skipping out on your bill."

Pennington saw Reyes's expression change as he looked toward the entrance to the gaming floor. "Security's coming," he said, scowling. "You've got about fifteen seconds before they get here. Anything else you want to say before they toss you out on your ass?"

Turning to look toward the door, the reporter saw a pair of burly Orion males heading toward him. They were bare-chested save for the leather bandoliers that crisscrossed their muscled, jade-green torsos, and their heads were shaved bald. Both guards sported an assortment of gold and silver rings, studs, and other piercings on their faces and bodies, and there was no mistaking the disruptor pistols and sheathed knives each Orion wore suspended from the thick leather belt around his waist.

Uh-oh.

Doing his best to appear resigned to his forthcoming departure, Pennington turned back to Reyes. "Guess that's my cue," he said, struggling to maintain his casual demeanor. "Any messages you want me to pass along? Something for Doctor Fisher or the admiral? Hell, if you want, I could even pass on a note to your mother." Though Pennington saw recognition in Reyes's eyes as he spoke that last word, the former commodore's features remained fixed, and he even shrugged before nodding in apparent understanding.

"If you can get word to my mother," Reyes said, "let her know I'll try to send a message soon."

Well, that's bloody insightful, Pennington thought, but kept his musing to himself. What the hell was Reyes's response supposed to mean, anyway? Rather than spend too much time contemplating that question, he instead offered a simple nod. "You got it, mate."

His reply was punctuated by the pressure of a large hand on his shoulder, and he turned to the owner of the hand, one of the Orion security guards, towering over him. The guard's expression was one of controlled disdain, and Pennington was sure that the Orion would happily kill him where he stood with only the slightest provocation.

"Mister Pennington," the guard asked, his voice low and gravelly, as though he had spent the past few hours inhaling some of the pernicious substances people around the bar were smoking, "we've been asked to escort you to the docking port."

"Is that right?" Pennington asked, hoping his words carried

the appropriate level of surprise and annoyance. "What's the problem? I just got here."

The guard leaned closer. "All I know is that I've been ordered to see you off the ship, sir. You can either come willingly, or I'll carry you."

Okay, that's enough, Pennington decided. "All right, mate. No worries. I promise not to make a fuss." Turning back to Reyes, he provided a mock salute. "Cheers, Diego."

Reyes nodded. "Take it easy, Tim." Pennington thought he saw something else, some question or request, in the other man's eyes, but then it was gone as the former Starfleet flag officer signaled with his glass to the bartender. "Hit me, barkeep."

And that's it, then.

As he had promised, Pennington did not make a scene while being escorted to the security guard station near the gaming floor entrance. There, his Orion chaperones stood in silence as he collected his portable recorder and the other odds and ends he had been forced to remove from his pockets for safekeeping. Only one of the guards walked with him to the docking port and collar that served as a connecting gangway between the *Omari-Ekon* and Starbase 47.

"Thanks, but I think I've got it from here," Pennington joked as they reached the *Omari-Ekon*'s docking hatch, knowing full well that the Orion would not venture into the passageway, much less onto the station itself. The guard's sole response was to glare at him, though Pennington was sure he heard a low growl from somewhere at the back of the Orion's throat.

The short stroll through the gangway was followed by a brief inspection at the Starfleet checkpoint inside the docking hatch that served as an entrance to Vanguard, with the two security officers positioned there grateful for the interruption in their otherwise boring assignment. Pennington passed through the checkpoint without difficulty and made his way toward the bank of turbolifts at the far end of the passageway. Dinner at Tom Walker's place, one of the civilian establishments in the station's retail center, Stars Landing, was sounding pretty inviting right about now, followed by a drink or two and then, most likely, bed.

Living life on the edge again, I see.

However mundane his evening schedule was looking, none of those activities would be happening right away, he knew. At least, not until he got past T'Prynn. The Vulcan was waiting for him near the turbolifts, her hands clasped behind her back as she stared at him. She was dressed in a standard female Starfleet officer's duty uniform, the form-fitting one-piece red skirt and tunic working in concert with the polished black boots to accentuate her trim, athletic figure. Her long dark hair was worn in a regulation style, pulled away from her face and secured with a clip at the back of her head, leaving a ponytail to drop between her shoulder blades.

"Lieutenant T'Prynn," he said as he approached her. "What a pleasant surprise, meeting you here."

T'Prynn's initial response was to raise her right eyebrow, though she offered no rebuttal to his comment. Instead, she asked, "Were you successful?"

"I think so," Pennington replied, sticking his hands into his pants pockets. "I managed to slip the code phrase you gave me into our conversation. I don't think the bartender or anyone else who might've been eavesdropping took anything from it." He had no idea why T'Prynn would instruct him to ask Reyes if the man wanted to send a message to his mother, who so far as Pennington knew had died nearly three years earlier. Despite his uncertainty, he had done as the Vulcan intelligence officer asked, the whole reason for his venturing aboard the *Omari-Ekon* being to meet with Reyes and make that request on her behalf. It was obviously a signal of some kind, as had to be the case with Reyes's response. "The commodore said that he'd be in touch with her soon."

Nodding in approval, T'Prynn said, "And you're certain your actions were not understood to be anything more than a casual conversation with Mister Reyes?"

"I don't know about that," the journalist replied. "I mean, I know we were overheard, and there's no way the bartender wasn't a spy for Ganz or one of his lieutenants. However, I was careful with what I said, and the commodore was very guarded."

"Was he under guard, or accompanied by any other escort?" T'Prynn asked.

Pennington shook his head. "No, but I'm sure they're watching every move he makes." Wondering where all of this might be heading, he frowned. "You're not thinking of trying to snatch him off that ship, are you?" Was Reyes's response to the code phrase a call for help? Did he perhaps possess some information T'Prynn sought?

All this cloak and dagger bollocks makes my gut ache.

Rather than answer his question, T'Prynn instead said, "Thank you for your assistance, Mister Pennington. Your efforts are most appreciated."

"Whoa," Pennington said, holding out a hand as the Vulcan turned to leave. "That's it? What the hell did I just do?"

"You provided information that may well prove quite useful," T'Prynn replied. "However, I'm sure you understand that discussing this matter any further risks violating the station's operational security. Now, I must return to my duties, but when you check your station credit account, you'll note that your apartment's rental fee has been paid for the next six months. Consider it a small token of our appreciation for your efforts."

Caught off guard by the intelligence officer's abrupt dismissal, Pennington said, "So, you just used me as a go-between, and now you're paying me off? After all we've been through, that's how you treat me? What if Ganz or his men had decided to drag me into some back room or toss me out an airlock?" *Or worse,* he mused, recalling what his unlikely friend, Cervantes Quinn, had told him about Ganz's treatment of the Sakud Armnoj, one of several accountants employed by the merchant prince. After the crazy—and quite nearly fatal—adventure Quinn and Pennington had undergone to retrieve the insufferable Zakdorn and bring him to Ganz, the Orion had, according to Quinn, "disappeared him with extreme prejudice." Quinn had not elaborated, and Pennington had never quite summoned the will to want to know the details.

"The risk to you was actually quite minimal," T'Prynn

answered. "Neera would not allow Ganz to take any action which might endanger the relative protection their ship receives merely by being docked at the station."

Pennington scowled. "Right, Neera." He recalled what T'Prynn had told him about the truth behind Ganz's organization, and Orion women in general. According to the Vulcan's intelligence-gathering efforts, Neera was the true head behind Ganz's criminal enterprise, allowing her lover to act as its public face while she pulled his strings from a position of relative anonymity. It was a startling revelation, given the common perception of Orion females and their role in the supposedly male-dominated culture. "Something tells me that if she wields that kind of power, she can order the removal of a bothersome journalist without too much trouble."

T'Prynn's eyebrow cocked again. "In that unlikely event, we would have ensured that any funeral expenses were addressed."

Releasing a chuckle, Pennington replied, "Good to know. With friends like you, and all that."

"I really must return to my duties, Mister Pennington," T'Prynn said, once more turning to leave. "Thank you again." She said nothing else as she entered one of the nearby turbolifts, but her eyes met his, and he could swear he caught the faintest hint of a smile tugging at one corner of her mouth just as the lift doors closed. Once she was gone, Pennington stood alone in the corridor, shaking his head in disbelief.

No matter how long he lived, he was certain he never would understand that woman.

2

I must be out of my mind.

Sitting at a quiet table in one corner of the central bar on the *Omari-Ekon*'s gaming floor, Diego Reyes feigned indifference as he sipped his drink and watched the comings and goings of various patrons. Though most of the customers, humans as well as representatives of more species than he had fingers to count, appeared to be civilians—residents of Vanguard or crew members from the different freighters and other transport craft currently docked at the station—Reyes also noted a dozen or so Starfleet uniforms sprinkled among the crowd. No one he saw appeared to be taking any notice of him, but he did not rule out one or more of Ganz's people watching his every move. The Orion merchant prince was not about to let him wander about his ship with anything more than a semblance of freedom and autonomy. Reyes expected even that illusion to vanish the instant Ganz decided there was nothing more to be gained by the presence of a disgraced Starfleet officer who now lived as a fugitive from Federation law.

He had considered surrendering himself, but almost as quickly dismissed the notion. As much as Ganz might not want him on his ship, he likely found the idea of Reyes blathering everything he knew about the inner workings of the *Omari-Ekon* and its crew to Admiral Nogura even less appealing. The former commodore knew how things likely would play out; he would suffer some kind of unfortunate accident or simply disappear altogether without explanation. The chances that Reyes would be able to leave the ship before being captured by Ganz's men and suffering such a fate were slim at best.

Calling for transport would also not be an option. Even if Ganz did not employ sensor-scattering technology as well as transporter inhibitors throughout his ship, Federation regulations prevented such incursions into sovereign territory without the home government's consent. Any attempt to retrieve Reyes, even if he signaled for such an extraction, would create an interstellar incident not needed by the Federation or Starfleet, and least of all Admiral Nogura. Retrieving one wayward fugitive was not worth the political fallout that would result from such brazen action.

So, the trick seems to be making me worth the effort.

That seemed to be the thinking, if what Tim Pennington had conveyed to him was to be believed. It had taken Reyes a moment to comprehend the code phrase the journalist conveyed to him, couched as it was in the question he had asked about Reyes wanting to have messages dispatched to anyone. T'Prynn had managed to get a message to him soon after the *Omari-Ekon*'s return to Vanguard, letting him know that the key phrase was one that might be given to him at some point, should the intelligence officer have need to communicate with him. By asking if he wanted to dispatch a message to his mother, T'Prynn was asking Reyes if he was willing to act as a covert operative on Starfleet's behalf while living aboard the Orion ship. Reyes was sure she would make such a request only if she believed he could provide information unobtainable by other means, and he had hesitated only a moment before offering a response that he knew T'Prynn would interpret as his willingness to collaborate with her. There was no way to know at this point what the Vulcan might be after, and that likely was by design, in order to insulate Reyes as much as possible should his activities be discovered and he was interrogated or even tortured by Ganz's men.

Well, there's something to look forward to. Grunting in approval of his own observation, Reyes punctuated the thought by tossing back the last of the Aldebaran whiskey in his glass, wondering when or if the infernal concoction might take to eating a hole through his stomach lining. He cast one last look around the bar, deciding that no other familiar faces—enemy or ally—were lurking among the crowd, partaking of the gambling tables, the bar, or anything else the gaming floor might have to offer. Reyes inserted his credit chip into the payment slot at the center of the table and allowed the bar's computer to extract from his account the payment for his bar tab. That bit of business concluded, he began making his way across the gaming floor, ignoring the calls from dealers at numerous tables and the suggestive looks and gestures of the various provocatively dressed women, as well as a few men, milling about the room. None of the wares offered by Ganz's legion of vice enablers interested him, for personal as well as practical reasons. The last thing he wanted was to engage in any activity—gambling, drinking to excess, or finding temporary solace in the company of an escort—that might place him in a vulnerable position and provide any sort of leverage for Ganz to exploit. He had enough to worry about without looking for additional trouble.

Trouble, however, had a knack for finding him.

"Human."

The voice, low and measured, came from behind Reyes, and when he turned to face the speaker he found himself staring into the face of an Orion male. Unlike the security guards, who were big and muscled and wore clothing to accent their physiques, this Orion was dressed in a simple if well-tailored suit of a style Reyes had seen favored by Deltan males. Reyes had seen him before, usually talking with employees on the gaming deck, and recalled that his name was Lekkar, an accountant or floor manager or some other sort of administrative cog in the wheel of Ganz's organization. He was not an enforcer or "lieutenant"—his mode of dress suggested a low-level supervisor in the *Omari-Ekon*'s food chain—though it was possible he might be carrying at least one weapon concealed on his person. He probably fancied himself someone of greater importance, if only in his own mind, which might make him dangerous.

Getting cynical in your old age, aren't you?

"Yes?" Reyes asked, keeping his tone casual and doing his best to affect a pleasant demeanor. "I already told the hostess I wouldn't be staying for dinner." As he expected, Lekkar said nothing, though the clenching of his jaw was enough to convey that he did not enjoy being compared to one of the bar's common employees. It was but one of numerous subtle verbal jabs Reyes had employed during his prolonged stay aboard the *Omari-Ekon,* which did little to enhance his stature in the eyes of Ganz and his people, but was enough to offer Reyes some measure of amusement from time to time.

The Orion was standing with his hands clasped behind his back, though Reyes doubted he was actually holding a weapon. Not here, in public on the floor. That would be bad for business. If there was going to be anything untoward taking place, it would happen elsewhere, away from curious eyes.

"You were talking to that Federation journalist," the Orion said, glaring at Reyes.

After Lekkar said nothing else, Reyes prompted him with a gesture. "And?"

"And I want to know what you two were talking about," Lekkar replied.

Reyes shrugged. "I'm not sure how that's any of your business. We're friends, we haven't seen each other in a while, and we were just doing a bit of catching up."

Appearing less than impressed with this answer, the Orion's expression hardened even further. "He's a journalist," he said, his voice barely carrying over the conversations and laughter of nearby patrons.

"Yes, you mentioned that," Reyes said. "Can I go now?"

Any pretense of tolerating the direction this conversation was taking disappeared as Lekkar stepped closer. "No. In fact, I think you need to come with me."

"Where would we be going?" Reyes said, not surprised by this development, but also not liking it. Out here, in front of customers, he was reasonably safe. Once away from the public areas and on their way to some dark room in the depths of the *Omari-Ekon*'s Byzantine network of corridors, Lekkar might well decide to try something more than simply talking to him.

When the Orion spoke this time, there was a definite hint of menace in his voice. "Listen to me, human. You're coming with me, one way or another. Do so willingly, and we may be able to look past any transgressions you may have committed. Force me to engage security, and the consequences will be severe."

"There's just one problem with that," Reyes said, adding a new edge to his own words. "You and I both know you're not in charge of much more than making sure there's booze behind the bar and toilet paper in the bathrooms, neither of which I need right now. So, unless you're acting on behalf of someone with more pull around here, I'll be going now."

As he expected—indeed, as he *hoped*—Reyes felt the pull of a hand on the left sleeve of his jacket just as he was turning away from Lekkar. He felt the Orion's fingers beginning to tighten around his forearm, which was all he needed. Guided by instinct, as much as years of training to the point where such actions were all but reflexive in nature, Reyes whirled back toward Lekkar. He twisted his left arm so that his left hand now found purchase on the Orion's arm, at the same time stepping closer just as he noted his opponent's other hand reaching for something beneath his jacket. Before Lekkar could retrieve whatever weapon he had hidden there, Reyes lashed out with the edge of his other hand, catching the Orion in the throat.

The effect was immediate, as Reyes felt Lekkar's hand loosen its grip on his sleeve as he staggered backward, coughing and reaching for his wounded throat. As he stumbled, something long and shiny fell from his other hand, and Reyes heard the clatter of metal against the deck. Lekkar fell against the bar as well as a brawny Tellarite who was sitting there, dressed in khaki overalls that Reyes recognized as being from one of the civilian transports currently docked at Vanguard. The husky freight-hauler growled his displeasure at Lekkar, who was oblivious to the offense he had caused, occupied as he was with rubbing his throat and trying to catch his breath. Despite his dislike for the Orion, Reyes was happy he had not killed him, as that was not his intention. Making the irritable lackey pause and consider his decision to start a confrontation, along with any other questionable life choices, would be sufficient for the message Reyes wanted to send to other members of Ganz's organization who had to be watching this quarrel.

Seeing the disapproving look on the bartender's face, Reyes held up empty hands to demonstrate he was carrying no weapons. "Self-defense," he said, before pointing to the long, nasty-looking blade with its serrated edge that still lay on the deck near his feet. "He pulled a knife on me." This actually seemed to placate the bartender as he reached for an intercom switch set into the wall behind the bar and spoke into the panel. Reyes could not hear what the Orion was saying, though he guessed someone in a position of authority was being notified. The bartender touched the panel again to deactivate it, then returned to the bar and produced a new glass, which he filled with the same Aldebaran whiskey Reyes had been drinking earlier.

"On the house," the Orion said, gesturing toward Lekkar, who had pulled himself to his feet long enough to make a hasty retreat from the bar. "I never liked him, anyway."

3

In his private office, Ganz looked at the computer display monitor that occupied one corner of his expansive desk, trying to decide whether he preferred it with the rather large hole that now dominated the center of its screen.

"You really should stop doing that," said Neera, Ganz's confidante and lover—and employer—from where she lounged on a sofa positioned along the office's far wall. Dressed in a silky red robe that left her arms and much of her legs exposed, she held a wine goblet in her left hand, while her right toyed with the knot of the robe's belt at her slim waist. "Do you have any idea how much those things cost?"

His mood still foul, Ganz shrugged as he rubbed the knuckles of his right hand, which still stung from the impact of his fist against the computer terminal. "It's therapeutic."

"If it's therapy you want," Neera said, her lips forming a teasing smile, "then you should hire a private counselor."

Ganz indicated the destroyed computer monitor. "This is easier, and I don't have to worry about it repeating anything I say in confidence." The faint aroma of her perfume caught his attention, and he eyed her for a moment as she reclined on the couch. "Besides, I have you for therapy."

"True enough," Neera replied before taking a sip of her wine. "So, what is it that has you so upset?"

Stifling the urge to emit a growl of frustration, Ganz stood up and began to pace the length of the office. "I just reviewed security footage of the gaming deck. Lekkar took it upon himself to confront Reyes."

Neera frowned. "About what?"

"I don't know. That's why I'm having Tonzak bring him up here." The security footage from the gaming deck had not included an audio recording of the exchange between Reyes and Lekkar, though it had with stark clarity captured the physical altercation that had transpired. The visual record showed with certainty that Lekkar had initiated the brief scuffle, but despite his greater age and presumably lesser physical strength, Reyes had brought the skirmish to a quick conclusion with the speed and efficiency Ganz expected from someone with Starfleet close-combat training.

"Lekkar is an opportunist," Neera said, rising from the sofa and adjusting her robe. "No doubt he was attempting to curry favor with you. He's always fancied himself as being more important than he really is."

Ganz nodded. "I know how he feels." The comment earned him a knowing, even approving smile from Neera. "He may be an opportunist, but he's not a complete fool. If he confronted Reyes, then he must have seen or heard something that made him suspicious." Grunting in irritation, he reached up to rub the bridge of his nose. "That insufferable human causes me grief in every manner imaginable. I should have killed him long before now."

"That will come in due course, my lover," Neera said. "For now, we still need him."

Snorting in grudging agreement, Ganz nodded. "I know." Allowing Reyes to seek sanctuary aboard the *Omari-Ekon,* after which he had assisted Ganz in negotiating with Starbase 47's commanding officer, Admiral Nogura, for the ship to be able to dock at Vanguard once again, was an unexpected coup. Sheltered underneath the very large umbrella of protection afforded by the massive space station, Ganz was reasonably certain that his enemies—of which there were many—would not risk Starfleet's wrath by attempting to attack him here. Both he and Neera also knew that Nogura wanted to keep Reyes close, even if Federation laws and Starfleet regulations prevented him from taking any direct action to retrieve him from the Orion ship. It was therefore an odd, symbiotic relationship enjoyed by all involved parties, each dancing around the other and unwilling to take any action that might upset the delicate balance they had established.

"Don't think I haven't considered alternatives to keeping him around," Neera said as she crossed to the small bar set into the wall near the balcony at the back of the office.

Releasing a humorless chuckle, Ganz replied, "You mean like poisoning his food? Pushing him down a turbolift shaft? Having him suffer an unfortunate accident at the hands of one of my less-experienced yet overly eager security guards?" To him, the options for engineering Reyes's demise seemed limitless; the problem was finding the one solution that would not arouse the suspicion—or the ire—of Admiral Nogura.

"Nothing so overt," Neera said, reaching for a wine carafe sitting on the bar and pouring some of its contents into her goblet. "Besides, dead or severely injured, he's of no use to us. There's too much information in that head of his to simply kill him."

Ganz scowled. "There are a multitude of ways in which useful knowledge can be extracted from him."

"Again, too risky," Neera countered. "Though, don't think I haven't considered it. I've even had a few of my best companions try to ply him with their various wares, all to no avail. He's stubborn, even for a human. I never would have thought I'd meet the Earth man who could resist Trianna."

His eyebrow rising in genuine curiosity, Ganz asked, "Trianna? That is impressive." He had sampled for himself the many talents harbored by the enthusiastic young woman, though of course he had never confessed as much to Neera. That Reyes was able to withstand what must have been nothing less than an all-out assault of seduction on Trianna's part spoke very highly of the former Starfleet officer's self-discipline.

Or, it doesn't say much about yours.

"Well," Ganz said, "I had something else in mind. Less subtle actions."

"Nogura won't do anything about Reyes that violates Federation law," Neera replied as she headed back to the sofa, "at least, not so long as Reyes remains healthy." Resuming her place on the plush cushions, she paused to drink from her goblet before returning her attention to Ganz. "However, I have no doubts—and neither should you—that the good admiral will tear this ship apart if he hears even the slightest hint of Reyes being mistreated at our hands."

Once more, Ganz was forced to acknowledge his lover's wisdom. The Federation's various laws and regulations pertaining to the recognition of the sovereign territory of another government were as explicit as they were simple. The sanctity of an independent nation-state was inviolable, with very few exceptions, but one of the key exclusions from those directives was in the case of assault or the unlawful detention of Federation citizens. In the event of such an occurrence, appropriate action to retrieve such persons could be ordered, but only by someone in the highest echelons of the Federation. Ganz did not doubt that Heihachiro Nogura, operating as he was far from the hallowed halls of the Federation Council, had been entrusted with a great deal of autonomous decision-making powers. The admiral would waste no time utilizing them to retrieve Reyes, should Ganz or anyone else aboard the *Omari-Ekon* be so stupid as to provide just cause. For the moment, Diego Reyes would have to be treated as that which he appeared to be: a fugitive from Federation justice who had been granted asylum.

"It galls me to think of the power he holds," Ganz said, shaking his head, "even in his position as a virtual prisoner aboard my ship."

Neera once again regarded him with a sly, knowing smile. "Whose ship?" Rather than answer the teasing question, Ganz crossed to the bar and poured himself a drink. "The point remains. For someone who's supposed to be helpless, Diego Reyes seems to be doing quite well for himself."

"You can't take it so personally," Neera replied. "It's just business, Ganz. Remember that. Reyes is a pawn, and at some point when the game reaches a turning point, he will be sacrificed."

"Fine," Ganz said, mindful to keep his tone from sounding

too much like a challenge to Neera, to her person or her authority, "but promise me that will happen the very microsecond he ceases to provide any value."

The soft touch of Neera's hand on his shoulder was enough by itself to chase some of the pent-up frustration from his body. "When the time comes," she said, her fingers caressing the bare skin of his arm, "you will have free reign to do with him as you please, though I can't promise I won't want to exact my own manner of recompense before I let you have him."

"Sometimes," Ganz said, "I think you say such things merely to agitate me."

Neera's hand traced its way around his arm and across his broad, muscled chest. "Of course. It keeps you interested, *and* motivated."

Turning to face her, Ganz smiled as he took in her mischievous expression. She said nothing more, but what her eyes communicated was unmistakable. He felt a familiar, welcome stirring and moved to take her in his arms, but stopped when Neera placed her hand against his chest.

"First things first, my dear," she said, her voice recovering some of its forthright tone. "Tell your people about Reyes. For now, we need him. They're not to confront him without permission. Start with Lekkar, once Tonzak brings that fool to you."

Ganz considered her directives. "Sooner or later, somebody else is going to see an opening and make a move. They won't all make the same mistakes Lekkar did."

"Then use him as an example to the others," Neera replied. "Leave no doubts as to what will happen if any harm should come to Reyes."

Before he could say anything else, the office's door chime sounded, a quartet of musical notes followed by the click of the intercom system installed in the bulkhead outside Ganz's private chamber.

"*Ganz,*" said a deep male voice, "*this is Tonzak. As you requested, I've brought Lekkar.*"

Looking once more to Neera, Ganz stood silent as she offered one final, resolute nod. "No doubts."

There could be no disagreeing with her, Ganz decided, even if that was what he desired. Her logic, though brutal, was indisputable. Despite his personal feelings for the human, Diego Reyes offered more value so long as he was alive. For now, the unlikely, uneasy alliance in which they all were locked would have to continue.

It was just business.

4

"Ow."

Thomas Blair winced as he looked up at the gymnasium ceiling, his unobstructed view courtesy of the vantage point he currently enjoyed while lying on his back atop the exercise mats covering the floor. From this angle, Blair was able to discern that one of the overhead lighting fixtures was slightly dimmer than its companions.

"Captain, are you all right?" asked a deep voice, before a dark silhouette entered his field of vision and blocked his view. Dressed in red exercise attire, Commander Kamau Mbugua regarded Blair with an expression showing equal parts concern and amusement.

Nodding, Blair replied, "Yeah, I'm fine. Nice throw." Why he had decided that today was a good day to accept his first officer's invitation to practice some hand-to-hand drills was a question he would have to ponder at some point. Mbugua's unarmed combat skills—which included mastery of at least half a dozen different styles of martial arts—were unmatched aboard the *Defiant,* and while Blair had not aspired to defeat his second-in-command, he had figured he might last longer than five seconds once the friendly sparring match got under way.

Nope.

"Sorry about that, Skipper," Mbugua said, holding out his large right hand in a gesture of assistance. "That was more instinct than anything else."

Blair waved away the apology. "My fault, Kamau. That's what I get for trying a straight-on attack right off the bat." He thought he might catch the commander off guard by launching an immediate strike right at the start of the match, but Mbugua had seen and reacted to his captain's movements almost before Blair started moving. His defense was ready even as Blair committed to the tactic, and by the time the captain realized his mistake, he was already being flipped over Mbugua's hip on his way down to the mat.

Seeing the first officer's hand, Blair shook his head. "I'm okay. I think I'm just going to lie here a minute, and collect my thoughts."

"Did somebody call a doctor?" a female voice called out. Mbugua's response was to release a hearty laugh that echoed off the gymnasium walls as Blair raised his head from the mat to see Jane Hamilton, the *Defiant*'s chief medical officer, standing at the room's entrance. Arms crossed, she was leaning against the door frame and eyeing him with no small amount of glee. Rather than a standard duty uniform, the doctor was dressed in gray sweatpants and matching shirt, across the front of which was emblazoned the *Defiant* insignia. Her shoulder-length red hair was dark with perspiration, and there were damp spots on her shirt.

"Good morning, Jane," Blair said, reaching up to scratch the top of his head where his sweat-matted gray hair was at its thinnest. "You're just in time to pronounce me legally dead."

Her gaze shifting to Mbugua, Hamilton asked, "That bad?"

"I've gone up against punching bags that put up a tougher fight," the first officer replied, making no effort to hide his wide grin.

From where he still lay on the mat, Blair asked, "Do they still let ship captains keelhaul people?" Eyeing Hamilton, he added, "This is all your fault, you know." For weeks the doctor had been after him to increase and vary his exercise routine. Though the captain made routine use of the ship's gym and other recreational areas, his duties often prevented him from taking advantage of the facilities as often as he liked. As a result, his last physical had yielded a slight weight gain, in and of itself a recurring problem of Blair's for the past few years. Though lack of time occasionally was at fault, so far as keeping to a regular exercise schedule, he had admitted to Hamilton that he was becoming bored with the routine of his workouts. With his fifty-first birthday approaching later this year, the doctor had suggested trying some new sports or pursuits, and engaging other members of the crew while working toward that goal. Blair had always preferred to exercise in solitude, often while listening to or reviewing the reports and communiqués that always seemed to accumulate on his desk, or which were intended solely for his attention. He received no sympathy from Hamilton, who had provided a good-natured scolding with respect to his solitary habits.

"I suggested you try something new," the doctor said. "I don't recall saying you should let yourself get thrown around the gym."

Blair chuckled. "Captain's prerogative, I suppose. Every crew should see their commanding officer getting his or her butt handed to them once in a while. Keeps things in perspective."

"If the crew sees you exercising," Hamilton countered, "even with everything you've got on your plate, then they might just think they have no excuse, and they'll get out there and work up a little sweat themselves." She gestured in his direction. "Now, get up and continue to perspire in an orderly, proficient, captainly manner, and lose those four kilos before I have to change your diet card again."

Any retort Blair might have given was cut off by the whistle of the ship's intercom system. "*Bridge to Captain Blair,*" said the voice of Ensign Ravishankar Sabapathy, one of the *Defiant*'s communications officers.

"Saved by the bell," Blair said as he pulled himself to his feet and crossed the room to a wall-mounted comm panel and thumbed its activation switch. "Blair here."

"*Sorry to disturb you, Captain,*" Sabapathy said, "*but we're picking up a faint broadcast message that appears to be a distress signal.*"

Frowning at the report, Blair asked, "Any idea who it is?"

"*Yes, sir,*" the ensign replied. "*According to its signature, the signal's source is Tholian. The translator says it's a ship, and that they've been attacked.*"

Blair glanced to his left as Mbugua moved to stand beside him. "Do they know who attacked them?" the first officer asked.

"I don't think so, Commander," said Sabapathy. *"The signal looks to be automated, repeating at regular intervals. It's encrypted, but using an algorithm we've managed to break. Still, it's taking a bit of work to translate the whole thing, and from what we can tell, it's intended for other Tholian ships that might be in the vicinity."*

"Are sensors picking up signs of other Tholian ship traffic?" Blair asked.

The communications officer replied, *"Negative, Captain. So far as we can tell, we're all alone out here."*

Remembering that gamma shift was still on duty, Blair said, "Have Commander Shull take us to Yellow Alert, and change course to intercept the ship. We'll see if there's anything we can do to help."

There was a break before Lieutenant Commander Terry Shull, the gamma shift duty officer, answered, *"I've already had the helm computing an intercept course, Captain. If we accelerate to warp six, we can be there inside of sixteen hours."*

Blair nodded in approval. Of course she would be anticipating his orders. The *Defiant*'s crew did such an exceptional job of anticipating and reacting to his instructions that he often wondered how long they might carry on with their duties before noticing that he had slipped away in the dead of night, bound for a vacation on Argelius or some other fanciful destination. "Do it, and keep me apprised of any new developments."

"Aye, aye, Captain," Shull replied.

Terminating the connection, Blair turned away from the companel to regard Mbugua and Hamilton. "Well," he said, "what do you make of that?"

"Out here?" Mbugua asked. "There's no telling. Could be Klingons, could be pirates, could be somebody else we don't know about yet."

Hamilton said, "We're fairly close to the Tholian border, aren't we?"

"Depending on whom you ask," Blair replied, "and what day of the week it is, and the mood of the captain of whichever Tholian ship you happen to run across on that day." The Tholians, despite being strict and even extreme isolationists, often engaged in the contradictory practice of extending and redefining their territorial boundaries as though fueled by whimsy. The lone exception to this odd policy was in how the Tholians treated the Taurus Reach, which they steadfastly refused to include in their expansion or annexing efforts. Indeed, their only excursions into the region were usually in response to actions by other parties they deemed threatening to their territorial security. Looking to Mbugua, Blair asked, "What about the Klingons?"

The dark-skinned first officer reached up with a towel to wipe perspiration from his bald head before replying, "They've laid claim to a few planets along the Tholian border, but nothing in this immediate area. At least, that's so far as we know from the latest survey and intelligence reports." Klingon activity in this part of the Taurus Reach had been on the rise in recent months, which was but one of the reasons that ships such as the *Defiant* had been re-tasked to the region and placed under the overall command of Starbase 47. The rationale was simple: Despite the fact that all-out war with the Klingons had been avoided, tensions remained elevated between the Empire and the Federation, and one of the potential flashpoints for any hostilities that might break out was the Taurus Reach. Therefore, in addition to conducting security patrols, the *Defiant* and other Starfleet vessels also were charged with visiting and offering expanded protection for the numerous colonies established in the Taurus Reach since the Federation had taken an interest in the area five years earlier. For the most part, all the parties in the area seemed to be keeping to themselves, but that did not rule out the occasional skirmish.

Thomas Blair's gut was telling him this might be something else.

"Let's revisit those reports," Blair said, "and prep a report for transmission back to Vanguard. Admiral Nogura's going to want to know about this."

5

Cervantes Quinn turned from the bar in time to see the fist coming right at his face. In his mind's eye he visualized his opponent's stance in an instant, determining from the arc of the swing and the way he carried his body that the other man was an experienced bar fighter, but woefully lacking in any sort of refined unarmed combat skills. Countering his attack would be child's play.

It was a good theory, Quinn decided. His instincts were sharp—no mean feat considering his present condition. On the other hand, his reflexes were deplorable. In attempting to step into the other man's attack, Quinn instead succeeded only in moving his face into a position better suited to receiving the full force of the punch. He took the strike along the left side of his jaw, the impact of bone against bone snapping his head back. Stars danced before his eyes as he stumbled, his back slamming into the bar behind him.

"Hey!"

The voice was distant and dulled by the bourbon currently doing its best to marinate his brain, and Quinn ignored it, just as he gave little regard to other nearby patrons of Tom Walker's place as they scattered away from the escalating fight. Quinn registered movement in his peripheral vision and raised his left arm in time to block a second attack by his opponent. This time, instincts kicked in and he adjusted his stance as he brought up his right fist, driving it into the other man's abdomen. He was rewarded with a satisfactory grunt of pain, which was repeated when he again slammed his fist into the man's midsection.

"Knock it off! No fighting in here!"

His opponent went limp in his grasp, and Quinn let him fall away just as he sensed someone else closing on him. He looked up in time to see a big, brawny giant lunging at him with arm raised and fist clenched. Like the first man, the newcomer wore a set of worn, dirty beige coveralls. He likely was a shipmate, Quinn figured, and looking none too happy that his friend seemed to be getting his ass kicked by a drunk.

"You should learn to keep your mouth shut, old man," the giant said, his boots thumping along the bar's simulated wooden floor. Quinn, his jaw still smarting, shook his head. Blinking did nothing to bring his eyes back into focus, and instead they split the big man into three as he barreled forward.

Shit.

The muscled freight hauler—all three of him—started to swing his fist. Without any shred of grace, Quinn dropped to one knee and threw a punch straight into the figure dancing in the center of his blurred vision, catching his opponent square in the groin. The result was immediate, with the other man crying out in pain as his legs gave out and he staggered backward before colliding with another of the bar's patrons, who, Quinn saw, was also wearing beige coveralls.

"How many of you are there, anyway?" he grumbled, reaching up to rub his aching jaw.

The new guy scowled. "Just me, boss." Though smaller than his friend, this freighter jockey was stockier, as well as being bald and possessing no neck that Quinn could see. He looked as though he might bench-press cargo containers just to pass the time while enduring the boredom of low-warp transport.

A few drinks earlier, Quinn would have found a way to avoid turning a verbal exchange born of alcohol-induced bravado into a physical altercation. A few drinks before that, he might even have laughed off the antics of the freight haulers, who as far as he could recall were merely enjoying their first night in port after being cooped up inside their ship for weeks or even months.

And a few weeks before that, I wouldn't even be in here.

That was then, Quinn conceded, and this was now, and now he could not care less how the verbal joust had started, or why it had escalated. The fight was all that remained, and for Quinn, that was good enough.

Gesturing toward the newcomer, he made a show of bringing up his hands and assuming a defensive stance. "Okay, big boy. Let's see what you've got."

A hand clamped down on his shoulder, and Quinn jerked his head around to find himself staring into the none-too-pleased expression of Marshall Watts, a member of the kitchen staff who also doubled as one of the bar's unofficial bouncers.

"Sorry, Quinn," Marshall said, his tone one of warning. "Can't let you do that."

The freight hauler did not seem worried by the bouncer's presence. "You saw what he did to my friends." To emphasize his point, he waved one beefy hand to where one of his shipmates still sat on the floor with his hands pressed to his groin. His other friend, the one who had thrown the first punch at Quinn, was leaning against the bar while holding his midsection.

"It's not my fault they fight worse than they dress," Quinn said, pausing to run his tongue along his teeth. None of them felt as though they had been knocked loose. *Well, that's nice.*

His comment got the expected response as the brawny freighter crewman growled something unintelligible before stepping forward.

"Whoa, ace!" Marshall said, holding up his free hand, but the hauler paid no heed.

Quinn jerked his arm free of the bouncer's grip. "Let go of me!" he snapped, keeping his eyes on the other guy as he closed the distance. If there was going to be a fight, there was no way he was giving this idiot a free shot at him. The instant the hauler was close enough, Quinn slammed an uppercut into his jaw, snapping back the other man's head and sending a bolt of pain down the length of Quinn's arm.

What the hell's he got in his mouth? The question screamed in Quinn's mind as he winced and pulled back his hand. *Duranium?*

It was still a good punch, halting his opponent's advance and giving him pause as he staggered to retain his balance. That was enough time for Marshall to move in and grab the other man's right arm and begin the arduous process of dragging the hauler's muscled bulk away from the bar. Quinn was still trying to shake off the ache in his hand when he felt a hand on his collar before he was jerked backward.

"Hey!"

"You're out of here, Quinn," said a female voice, one Quinn recognized as belonging to Allie, one of Tom Walker's lead bartenders.

Twisting himself around, Quinn could not help but smile in appreciation at the bartender, who was wearing maroon leather pants and a matching vest. She wore no shirt beneath the vest so her arms were left bare, and so far as he was concerned, the form-fitting ensemble was doing a fine job of accentuating the curves of her trim, athletic figure.

"Stop staring at my ass," Allie warned, her tone possessing not a hint of her usual humor as she pulled him along through the crowd of onlookers on her way toward the bar's front door.

Doing his best to dredge up some lingering vestige of charm, Quinn replied, "But, it's . . ."

Allie turned to glare at him, holding up her free hand and aiming her forefinger at him. "Finish that sentence and I'll carve out your liver. Whatever's left of it, anyway."

"Come on, babe," Quinn said as she resumed directing him toward the door. "You know I never mean any of the stuff I say. Even the stuff I say when I'm drunk." Frowning, he added, "Which I know is a lot, lately."

"Too much, in fact," Allie replied. "I can't have you in here riling my customers anymore, Quinn." She stopped when she got within arm's reach of the door, and turned to face him. "It seems like all you do anymore is come in here looking to pick a fight."

Holding up a hand, Quinn waved it back the way they had come. "I didn't start that. He hit me first, remember?"

Allie nodded. "Sure, after you insulted his girlfriend. Don't play games with me, Quinn. You knew what you were doing, and what kind of reaction you'd get." She paused, releasing a sigh of disappointment. "Look, I know things have been rough for you since your friend died. I get it, but you can't be using that as an excuse to come in and disrupt my place."

"Your place?" Quinn said, his brow furrowing in confusion. "I thought this was Tom Walker's place?"

Rolling her eyes, Allie replied, "You know what I mean, you idiot. Tom wanted me to throw you out weeks ago, but I kept talking him out of it, because I know you've been hurting, but I can't keep covering for you if all you're going to do is cause trouble. You get that, right?"

"Yeah, I do," Quinn said, reaching up to rub his bruised jaw. "I'm sorry, Allie. It's just . . ." He let the words fade away as thoughts of Bridget McLellan forced their way through the fog clouding his muddled brain. Bridy Mac, his partner, confidante, and lover, had died on a planet with no name—Starfleet might have given it a name by now, but Quinn did not care—sacrificing herself to keep Shedai technology from being acquired by Klingon agents. Everything about her had made Quinn come alive, filling him with a confidence and conviction he had not felt in years. After the second chance he had been given, thanks to the timely assistance of T'Prynn, the enigmatic Vulcan intelligence officer, having Bridy Mac around had only strengthened his resolve to continue the arduous task of reforming and remaking himself. In the aftermath of years wasted on drinking, gambling, carousing, and simply eking out a marginal existence on the fringes of civilized society, partnering with McLellan and doing something that actually mattered had given him a fresh, optimistic outlook on whatever years might remain to him. Her passing had taken with it all of the hope and drive he had worked to accumulate. What was the point? He had done his best to pay whatever penance might be owed for his earlier mistakes and sins, and had come up short. Bridy Mac, the only part of his life that made the rest of it worth a damn, was gone, and so too was his ability to care about whatever might come next.

In short, he reminded himself, *to hell with it. To hell with every last damned bit of it.* He knew that such a cynical stance should not include innocent bystanders and those concerned for his welfare, and it was this errant thought that made him regard Allie with an expression of apology. It was the first time in weeks that he had acknowledged caring about anyone or anything other than where he might acquire his next drink.

Reaching out to grip the doorjamb in an effort to steady himself, Quinn drew a deep breath and tried to blink past the bourbon. "I just miss her, Allie."

"I know you do," Allie said, placing one hand on his arm. "But that's not good enough, not right now." She nodded toward the door. "Go and get yourself cleaned up. Until you do, I don't want to see you around here."

"Come on, Allie," Quinn said, genuine regret taking hold in his alcohol-addled mind, at least for a moment. "You know I'm just a harmless idiot."

"Don't make Tom ban you outright," Allie said, her tone now firmer. "Go sleep it off. I'll check on you when I get out of here, okay?"

Unable to resist one more leering grin, Quinn eyed her with mischief. "Promise?"

Allie's response was to push past him and open the door, after which she prodded him toward the street. "I mean it, Quinn. Not until you clean up your act."

Holding up his hands in mock surrender, Quinn nodded. "Okay, okay. I get the message. You'll be sad when I'm gone, though." The parting comment would have been more effective, he decided, if he had not chosen that moment to trip on the steps leading down from the door to the cobblestone walkway.

"Damn," he muttered. "I hate when that happens."

He turned back to the bar, but Allie was already gone, the door closing behind her as she made her way into the crowd and back to work. His last sight of the comely bartender was of her shapely, leather-clad backside.

Anyone who doubts the existence of a supreme being need only look at that.

Chuckling at his lascivious thought, Quinn cleared his throat as he looked up the street, getting his bearings. Humans and other assorted species, some wearing Starfleet uniforms but many more dressed in civilian attire, were walking past the various storefronts or sitting at tables positioned outside some of the establishments. Stars Landing had its share of bars and restaurants, catering to a wide range of clientele and cuisines, but for Quinn none of them held the charm of Tom Walker's place. Feeling a wave of lightheadedness beginning to wash over him, he considered stumbling his way back to the apartment that had been provided by Commander ch'Nayla on behalf of Starfleet Intelligence for "services rendered." He frowned at that idea, knowing that the suite of empty rooms and their Starfleet-issue furnishings would provide him nothing in the way of solace. It was little more than a place to grab a few hours' sleep and a shower, but it was not a home.

"Guess it's another bar, then," he muttered, the fingers of his right hand fishing into his trouser pocket to retrieve his credit chip. He tried to focus his bourbon-fogged mind long enough to recall his account balance, and decided the best way to verify the state of his funds was while buying another drink.

"Quinn?"

Turning at the unexpected summons, Quinn had to blink several times before the figure walking toward him came into focus. When recognition finally dawned, he could not help offering a broad, toothy grin. "Well, butter my ass and call me a biscuit—if it isn't Timothy Pennington, superhero journalist to the stars and beyond."

"Cervantes Quinn," Pennington replied with a smile, "I'd heard you were dead, or in jail."

Quinn shrugged. "The night's young. How they hangin', newsboy? Still trying to write your own chapter for the history books?"

"I've been looking for you, mate," Pennington replied. "Seems like we're always missing each other these days. If I'm not off following a story, you've been busy doing whatever it is . . . Commander ch'Nayla's having you doing." His expression turned somber. "I just wanted you to know how sorry I was to hear about Bridy Mac, Quinn. I'm truly sorry I didn't get to say that to you before now."

Holding up a hand, Quinn shook his head. "Don't sweat it, ace." Had it really been that long since he and Pennington had last seen one another? Quinn tried to do the arithmetic in his head, but abandoned the notion when the numbers began drifting in and out of the haze clouding his brain. All he knew was that it had been a while—plenty of time for Pennington to show up before now to offer his condolences. He did not know the reasons for the journalist's not being able to find him before today, and the more he considered the issue the less he cared. "These things happen."

Pennington frowned. "I know what she meant to you, Quinn, just as I . . ." He paused, clearing his throat, and Quinn sensed that the journalist was recalling an unpleasant memory. "I know what you're feeling, is all."

"Oh," Quinn replied, "you do? Well, then. Maybe we could just hug each other until the pain goes away." Though he knew the reporter was divorced, there had never been mention of some other lover who might have met some tragic fate. That in itself was an interesting notion, considering the amount of time the two men had spent crammed inside the *Rocinante,* Quinn's late and very much lamented Mancharan starhopper. Of course, now that his thoughts turned to his former ship, they served only to deepen his foul mood.

Thanks for that, Quinn mused. *Jackass.*

His expression darkening further, Pennington cast a glance toward a pair of passersby who had overheard Quinn's comment. "I was thinking you might want to talk about it, maybe over a cup of coffee or something."

"Talking about it means I have to remember it," Quinn countered. "And coffee would only get in the way of my drinking, which helps me forget about it, or at least gives me a break from thinking about it. I like my plan better." It was such a straight-forward idea. Why was it that no one besides him could see its simple beauty? Still, even the bourbon he had consumed could not keep Quinn from asking himself why he was coming down so hard on Pennington. Had the journalist truly done anything to be the target of such ire? Quinn had decided that one of the advantages of not caring about anything was that it liberated him to direct his anger at anyone he chose. That included innocent by-standers, idiots taking up space in his favorite bar, or even the man now standing before him.

Friendly fire's a bitch, ain't it?

Sighing, Pennington said, "Look, Quinn, I'm just trying to make sure you're all right. I know you've been having a rough time of it."

That prompted Quinn to offer a disapproving grunt, and before he realized he was even uttering the words, they seemed to just pour forth from him, unimpeded by any filter he might once have used to parse his comments. "Seems like everybody around here knows how rough I've had it. I'm surrounded by people who want to be my friend. Well, let me tell you something, newsboy: I don't need any friends. Life was easier when I didn't have friends, or didn't give a damn about anybody." Despite the occasional stumbling block, that attitude had served him well for most of his adult life, and returning to that path held a definite appeal.

"That's the booze talking," Pennington snapped, his irritation now evident. Stepping closer, he held out a hand as though reaching for Quinn's arm. "Come on, let's get you someplace where you can catch some sleep."

Before he even realized what he was doing, Quinn was swing-ing. His right fist connected with Pennington's jaw, sending the reporter staggering backward until he stumbled and fell to the faux cobblestone street. Other Stars Landing visitors stopped in their tracks, turning to observe the altercation, and Quinn was sure he heard at least one person using a communicator to sum-mon station security.

"What the bloody hell?" Pennington asked, rolling onto his back and sitting up as he reached to rub his jaw. "Quinn, you damned tosser. What in the name of Satan's codpiece is wrong with you?"

Stepping toward the journalist, Quinn pointed one long finger at him. "Do us both a favor, and just stay the hell away from me. You're better off not associating with a damned loser like me, anyway." He stepped back as Pennington pushed himself to his feet, wincing as he reached once more for his injured jaw.

"You know what, Quinn, you win," Pennington said, brushing dust off his clothes. "You want to wallow in self-pity, that's your choice. Try not to die of liver failure or alcohol poisoning while you're busy feeling sorry for yourself. I'm sure that's just what Bridy Mac would've wanted."

Now genuinely angry, Quinn advanced on Pennington, once more pointing a finger at his face. "You watch your mouth, or next time I'm not pulling my punch."

Holding up his hands in surrender, Pennington shook his head. "Don't worry, Quinn. That's the last you'll hear from me. Call me when you clean up, assuming both of us are still alive. See you 'round, mate." Turning, he walked away without another word, moving past several curious onlookers on his way deeper into Stars Landing. Quinn watched him go, trying to make some sense of what had just happened, and why he had allowed things to deteriorate as they had.

Because you're an idiot, you idiot.

"What the hell are you looking at?" he called to the spectators, some of whom wore expressions of undisguised disapproval, while others seemed to look upon him with pity. "You never seen a drunk making bad decisions before?"

The next of those, Quinn decided, would be where to find his next drink.

6

Tapping his fingers on the polished surface of his desk, Hei-hachiro Nogura studied the image of the *Omari-Ekon* on his office's main viewscreen. The Orion ship, moored at one of Starbase 47's lower docking ports, appeared as innocuous as any of the other vessels that made use of the station's facilities. Nogura knew better. To him, the ship represented nothing less than a tumor requiring excision. Left unchecked, how badly would the vessel and those who worked and played aboard it infect his station and crew?

My, aren't we melodramatic in the morning.

Stifling an urge to yawn—itself a consequence of having been roused from slumber that was already too short and prone to interruption—Nogura reached for the steaming cup of green tea sitting on his desk. As he cradled the cup near his chest and allowed it to warm his hands, he savored its aroma. Its effects were soothing, helping to alleviate the foul mood that had hovered over him since he was awakened. If only solving all of the other problems he faced could be accomplished with such ease.

Turning his attention from the viewscreen to the cadre of officers he had assembled at far too early an hour, he took a first, tentative sip of his tea before asking, "So, what's the story?"

Lieutenant Haniff Jackson, Starbase 47's brawny chief of security, was the first to answer, "At approximately 2240 hours last night, one of our informants observed an altercation between Diego Reyes and one of the *Omari-Ekon*'s Orion employees." Standing near the viewscreen, Jackson consulted the data slate he carried, which appeared small and fragile in his large hands.

"My informant doesn't know what caused the fight, only that it took place shortly after Reyes met with Tim Pennington near the bar in the *Omari-Ekon*'s central gaming hall. By his account, the Orion seemed to be acting in a belligerent manner toward Mister Reyes, before attempting to restrain him from leaving the bar."

"Restrain him?" Nogura repeated, frowning.

Despite his composed bearing, Jackson smiled. "That was his word, Admiral, but based on his report, I don't know if I'd go that far. Apparently, Reyes and the Orion exchanged words, and when Reyes tried to leave, the Orion grabbed him by the arm. Mister Reyes promptly demonstrated the risks that come with such fool-hardy action."

"That sounds like Reyes," said Lieutenant Commander Holly Moyer, Starbase 47's ranking representative of Starfleet's Judge Advocate General Corps, from where she sat in one of the two chairs positioned before Nogura's desk. Recently promoted to her current rank, Moyer at present was standing in as the station's interim JAG liaison until Starfleet decided what to do about replacing Captain Desai, who had departed the station following Nogura's granting her a transfer to an Earth-based posting. While he had been reluctant to approve her request, it had become evident from Desai's conduct and attitude that she harbored no small measure of disapproval of Operation Vanguard's classified nature as well as decisions and actions which had come about as a consequence of maintaining that secrecy. Following Desai's departure, Starfleet had promised a proper replacement for her at the earliest opportunity, and until then Moyer was shouldering a formidable load. So far as Nogura could tell, the commander was adapting to her new responsibilities with aplomb.

"I take it he's okay?" Nogura asked, blowing on his tea to cool it.

Sitting next to Moyer, the station's intelligence officer, Commander Serrosel ch'Nayla, nodded. "Yes, Admiral. Mister Reyes was not further challenged after the incident, and our informants say that, so far, neither Ganz nor any of his people seem interested in pursuing the matter." The Andorian *chan* shifted in his seat as he cleared his throat. "However, it's worth noting that the Orion who initiated the exchange, Lekkar, seems to have gone missing."

Moyer's expression was one of concern. "Does that mean what I think it means?"

From where she stood behind ch'Nayla and to the left of Jackson, Lieutenant T'Prynn replied, "It would not be out of the question for Ganz or his employer, Neera, to sanction the removal of an employee who posed potential security risks." The Vulcan woman's hands were clasped behind her back, her expression passive even as her right eyebrow arched. "It is a proven method of Ganz's when dealing with persons he finds threatening or otherwise undesirable."

Turning in her seat, Moyer said, "A simple 'yes' would've sufficed. So, we believe Ganz or Neera ordered this Lekkar killed. Do we know why?"

"No," Nogura said, "nor do I particularly care. What I do care about is whether Ganz, or Neera, or whoever, might decide that a better long-term alternative to killing their own people is simply getting rid of Reyes. We need to get him out of there."

"So that we can arrest him again?" Moyer asked.

Nogura eyed her with annoyance. "That's what is usually done with those who've divulged Starfleet secrets, and consorted with the enemy to place Starfleet or Federation personnel and property at risk."

"With all due respect, Admiral," Moyer countered, "we don't know the whole story. Diego Reyes is a lot of things, but a traitor? I find that hard to believe."

Holding up a hand, Nogura shook his head. "I'd like nothing more than to share your doubts, Commander, but at the very least, there are questions to be answered. If nothing else, Reyes is still a convicted criminal, with a prison sentence waiting in the wings if and when all of this insanity finally shakes out. Even if it's decided that he still has to be sent to that penal colony on Earth, it's a better fate than anything Ganz has planned for him."

"That goes without saying," Jackson said.

T'Prynn said, "I also do not believe Mister Reyes to be acting in a treasonous manner. I spoke with Tim Pennington following his excursion aboard the *Omari-Ekon,* during which he met with Reyes. Mister Pennington told me that Reyes's actions, particularly his dealings with the Klingons, were guided by the desire to minimize any unnecessary casualties to station personnel."

"He requested sanctuary aboard that Orion ship," Nogura countered. "He gave the Klingons everything they needed to launch a mission of espionage and sabotage against us."

Nodding, the Vulcan replied, "Indeed he did, sir, but as he told Mister Pennington, the Klingons were going to conduct such an operation with or without his assistance. According to him, Reyes only provided information essential to allowing the Klingon-contracted operative the access he needed to carry out his mission with a minimum of collateral damage."

Though he started to retort, Nogura stopped himself and instead considered what he had just heard. Was it possible that Diego Reyes, faced with the possibility of watching helplessly as any number of the personnel he once commanded suffered injury or death at Klingon hands, had chosen the lesser evil, sacrificing any hope for his own freedom and perhaps even his life? Of course, the admiral conceded, but Starfleet and he were a long way from making such a determination. Doing so would require access to Reyes himself.

As though reading Nogura's mind, Jackson asked, "Does this mean we can think about staging an operation to go in and get him?"

Ch'Nayla turned to regard the security chief, his antennae shifting atop his head. "That would not be prudent."

"It also wouldn't be legal," Moyer added. "Admiral, we've been over this. Any attempt to extradite Diego by force would be tantamount to an act of war against the Orions."

Nogura could not help a snort of derision. "Given everything I know about the Orions, they'll bend over backwards to avoid an all-out confrontation with the Federation. They're just as liable to view any 'disagreements' we have with Neera and Ganz as the cost of doing business, and cut their losses." In his experience, such decisions were the norm more often than not for the Orion central government, such as it was. The small, independent state relied heavily on trade with Federation as well as nonaligned worlds, and to a lesser degree with the Klingons, the Tholians, and other upstart adversaries of the major interstellar powers. Nogura was confident that any incident involving a lowly merchant gaming ship—which may or may not be involved in any manner of illicit activities—would suffer only brief, superficial scrutiny before being forgotten in the interests of preserving the façade of peaceful relations with the Federation.

"That may be true, sir," Moyer replied, nodding, "but you'd still be taking a big risk. Going by the book, a court-martial wouldn't be out of the question."

Releasing a small chuckle, Nogura said, "Commander, you don't get to my position and standing in Starfleet without ruffling several sets of feathers along the way. I've been threatened with court-martial no less than a dozen times during my career. So far, there have been no takers." Of course, the duties with which he currently was charged, and the secrets he was responsible for keeping, far outweighed anything he had overseen during his years of service. "Still, your advice and warnings are sound. We will continue to tread carefully." For how long, Nogura was not certain.

"Admiral," ch'Nayla said, "there may be another avenue available to us." He then turned and gestured toward T'Prynn.

The Vulcan stepped closer. "While Mister Pennington's original intentions for visiting the *Omari-Ekon* were legitimate, in that he hoped to meet with Mister Reyes, I co-opted his excursion to the vessel for another purpose. I asked him to relay a specific phrase that was agreed upon by Mister Reyes and myself as a means of determining whether he was agreeable to undertake certain actions on our behalf. Based on his response, he has indicated his willingness to do so."

"You mean spy?" Moyer said, making no effort to hide her disbelief. "For you?"

Nodding, ch'Nayla said, "T'Prynn enlisted Mister Pennington's assistance with my authorization, Commander. It seemed an idea worth exploring, and Mister Reyes's consent does afford us a singular opportunity."

"How in the hell did you get a message to him in the first place?" Jackson asked. "I mean, before his meeting with Pennington."

T'Prynn said, "I exploited a vulnerability in their subspace communications system in order to contact Reyes via the communications panel in his quarters aboard the *Omari-Ekon*."

"They let him have access to the comm system?" Nogura asked.

"It was deactivated and a lockout had been placed on it," T'Prynn replied. "However, that is not an obstacle to someone trained in the circumventing of such measures. I was able to forge an access code long enough for me to have a brief conversation with Mister Reyes. We used this opportunity to set up a means of initiating covert information exchange through the use of go-betweens to be identified at a later time. Our entire conversation lasted less than two minutes."

Nogura pondered what he was hearing, before allowing himself a small smile. "There seems to be no end to your talents, Lieutenant." He had at first been reluctant to grant Commander ch'Nayla's request to retain T'Prynn's services and give her an active role in the Andorian officer's ongoing intelligence efforts. Despite his initial misgivings, there was no discounting T'Prynn's skills, and her knowledge of the key players not only on the station but also on vessels like the *Omari-Ekon* made her a valuable asset. Regulations had required Nogura to mete out punishment and demote her for her disobedience and flouting of Starfleet regulations and protocols. He naturally wondered—if only for a moment—if T'Prynn might cast aside the logic and maturity expected from a Vulcan of her years and seek retribution for her conviction, either against him directly or against the station and its crew. Her own actions, even while acting as a fugitive from Starfleet authority, along with his own instincts, told the admiral that her engaging in any sort of traitorous behavior was an unlikely scenario. By all accounts, official and otherwise, Lieutenant T'Prynn had presented herself as someone for whom the past had been put to rest, and that she was ready to get on with whatever duties she might be assigned. For now, and while operating under ch'Nayla's watchful eye, Nogura was willing to let things play out. "I'm sensing this contact method of yours was of the single-use variety?" he asked.

"That's correct, Admiral," T'Prynn replied. "I was unable to mask my entry into the system. Instead, I made the illicit communication appear as though it was initiated by one of Ganz's lower-level enforcers to a discreet contact off the ship. According to unconfirmed reports, that person is no longer in Ganz's employ."

Frowning, Moyer asked, "Are you saying you set up one of Ganz's men to take the fall for your espionage?"

"I'm saying I deflected attention from Mister Reyes," T'Prynn replied, "thereby preserving his safety for at least a while longer. How long the status quo is maintained will depend entirely on his actions as well as our own."

Though she clearly was uncomfortable with the harsh yet unspoken reality of the likely consequences of T'Prynn's subterfuge, Moyer's only other reaction to the Vulcan's revelation was to draw a deep breath before asking, "What is it that he's supposed to be doing?"

"We need to know where Ganz obtained the Mirdonyae Artifact he gave us," ch'Nayla said. "The only way to get that information is to access the *Omari-Ekon*'s navigational logs."

A silence fell over the room, during which Nogura leaned back in his chair, clasping his hands before him and touching his forefingers to his lips. "Interesting," he said after a moment. As incredible as it had been to discover that Diego Reyes had somehow parlayed his way to sanctuary aboard the Orion's ship, learning that Ganz also had in his possession a twin to the enigmatic object Ming Xiong had brought back with him from

Mirdonyae V was something else altogether. While there appeared to be no evidence that the merchant prince had the slightest notion of the artifact's origin or purpose, or how it fit into the complex tapestry that was mystery of the Shedai, Ganz was no fool. Rather, Neera, Ganz's superior, was no fool. Even without specific knowledge of the artifact itself, she comprehended its value to Starfleet and to Nogura in particular. That, along with the possibility of somehow repatriating Reyes, was the primary reason the admiral had returned the *Omari-Ekon*'s station docking privileges.

"You're kidding," Jackson said, his eyes wide. "We think Ganz might know where those things come from?"

T'Prynn replied, "That, or he can lead us to someone who does. Given what Doctor Marcus and Lieutenant Xiong and the rest of the research team have discovered about the Mirdonyae Artifacts and the power they control, particularly with respect to the Shedai, it is vital that we find the objects' origin before anyone else."

"Agreed," Nogura added. The two artifacts currently were being stored in the Vault, the secret research facility hidden within the bowels of the station and dedicated to studying all aspects of the Shedai and their technology. Each of the artifacts held a Shedai trapped within its crystalline confines. Despite what had been learned about the ancient, all-powerful alien race to this point, the research team had not yet found a way to communicate with the entities contained within the objects. Further, simple guesswork and experimentation without any true understanding of the artifacts had come at an appalling cost. After learning that the team's use of the objects in attempts to make contact with planets suspecting of harboring Shedai technology resulted in the obliteration of eleven worlds, testing on the artifacts had been suspended.

Even the Shedai themselves seemed afraid of the power the things contained, if the attack on Starbase 47 itself by a Shedai entity was any indication. That much, at least, seemed to make sense, given Lieutenant Xiong's theory that the crystals looked to have been constructed by some race, possibly as a weapon to be used against the Shedai. The alien that had attacked the station in an apparent quest to get at the artifacts had wreaked considerable damage, from which Xiong and the Vault team were still recovering. Though much of the exterior repairs to the station were complete, work continued in some areas of the Vault. As for the crew and civilians residing aboard the starbase, the overwhelming majority of whom were unaware of the Shedai's true origins and power, they had resumed their normal schedules, but Nogura knew an air of apprehension remained. Would other Shedai come? There was no way to know the answer to that question, just as there was no easy solution for how the station might deal with another, perhaps larger assault. It was only through the most fortunate stroke of luck that Xiong had figured out how to employ one of the Mirdonyac Artifacts to capture the alien. Since then, it had been learned that each of the crystals was imprisoning up to a dozen of the creatures in similar fashion.

Who knew what other abilities the objects possessed, either individually or working in concert with others of their kind? It was clear they represented something of a threat to the Shedai, which made finding their source and learning more about their capabilities a matter of paramount importance. Even in their most innocuous state, the Mirdonyae Artifacts represented unparalleled power that could not be allowed to fall into the wrong hands.

The main problem with that, Nogura mused with no small amount of cynicism, *is that there's no guarantee ours are the right hands.*

"With all due respect to everyone in the room who outranks me," Jackson said after a moment, "that being everyone, we need to be sure we all understand what we're talking about here. If we get Commo . . . Mister Reyes to help us, and he gets caught, the Orions won't show him anything even remotely resembling mercy."

"He will not be caught," T'Prynn said. "The situation we face here is far more controlled than when we sent Cervantes Quinn and the late Commander McLellan to infiltrate the Orion freighter captured by the Gorn. We will be able to anticipate and react to unforeseen complications with greater speed and resources than what Quinn and McLellan had available on their mission."

Nodding, Nogura replied, "That's certainly true." After an Orion freighter had been damaged by an unknown gravitational anomaly in Gorn space, it was determined that the phenomenon it had encountered had displayed elements of the Jinoteur Pattern, an energy waveform that, when employed in concert with the Taurus Meta-Genome, appeared to be the key to decrypting the massive artificially engineered raw genetic material created by the Shedai. The pattern had received its name from Lieutenant Ming Xiong, who had employed the moniker in reference to the equally enigmatic solar system determined to be the source of the Shedai and all the technology and power the ancient race once commanded. Though it had fueled much of the research and discovery conducted by Operation Vanguard since the top secret project's inception, all traces of the waveform appeared to vanish along with the Jinoteur system itself at the hands of the mysterious entity known as the Shedai Apostate. The powerful alien had engineered the staggering feat as a means of preventing the other surviving members of his race from regaining control over their technology and the immense power it once had given them.

As for the damaged Orion ship, it had been captured for study by a Gorn military vessel. Operating with the clandestine support of the *U.S.S. Endeavour,* Quinn and McLellan attempted to obtain sensor and navigational logs of the anomaly that had crippled the freighter. During their operation they almost lost the valuable data to a Klingon spy who also was pursuing the information. The covert agents ultimately were successful in their mission: preventing the Klingons from obtaining knowledge of the Jinoteur Pattern reading or its source. They also had received information from the Shedai Apostate about the existence of even more of the artifacts, which might be the key to defeating the rest of the astonishing being's race.

If only McLellan had been so lucky on her next assignment, Nogura mused, with no small amount of regret. The retrieval mission had spawned yet another assignment for Quinn and McLellan, with a similar goal of keeping out of Klingon hands not only Shedai technology, but also that of the Tkon, another ancient, long-dead race, and the one responsible for the Mirdonyae Artifacts. It was while carrying out that demanding task that McLellan had given her life in order to preserve the mission objective.

"There's a larger issue," Moyer said. "If the Orions catch him, they'll turn it into a public relations nightmare for us. They'll broadcast whatever show trial they decide to hold for him across subspace, and they'll execute him in front of the entire quadrant."

Jackson added, "The Klingons would provide a clean execution, but not these thugs." He paused, shaking his head. "That's no way for anybody to go."

"Then we should probably take steps to ensure that doesn't happen," ch'Nayla said.

Nogura rose from his chair. "That would be my preference, Commander." Crossing his arms, he began walking the length of his office, aware of his officers turning to watch him. "However, let us make no mistake, if we enlist Mister Reyes in this effort, the priority must be obtaining any and all information that might help us to track the source of the Mirdonyae Artifacts. His safety, as well as any black eye the Orions could give the Federation if they were to capture him, would regrettably have to be viewed as secondary concerns." Halting his pacing, he turned to T'Prynn. "Lieutenant, are you certain he's willing to take on such a risk?"

"I am, Admiral," the Vulcan replied without hesitation. "I believe Diego Reyes to be incapable of shirking his duty, regardless of his current standing."

Nodding in agreement with her assessment, Nogura reached up to stroke his chin. He was no stranger to difficult decisions, and this certainly would not be the first time he issued orders that put people at risk. So, why did this feel different, and for reasons he could not explain?

I'm damned if I know.

"Very well," he said after a moment. "Commander ch'Nayla, Lieutenant T'Prynn: you may proceed."

7

Music filled the evening air over Paradise City.

Ambassador Jetanien stepped from his third-story office onto his small balcony, itself the lone architectural indulgence he had allowed himself when outlining his facility needs to the Corps of Engineers attachment tasked with the building's construction. His vantage point offered him an unobstructed view of the city's main courtyard, and out here the music was loud and vibrant. Not that the song being played necessarily was to his liking—he believed it to be an inventive take on a traditional Tellarite work chantey—but it was a vast improvement over construction noise, shouts of disagreement, or other flavors of cacophony he had grown accustomed to hearing in recent weeks.

Leaning over the balcony railing, Jetanien looked down at the street to find the source of the song. He saw what appeared to be the beginnings of a street party, complete with musicians occupying a small performance stage at the center of the thoroughfare. A pair of block-long rows of dining tables and benches radiated from the stage and down the street, and booths lining the sidewalks offered freshly prepared dishes from the cuisines of a dozen species. A crowd that Jetanien judged to be several hundred strong, representing easily half of the new settlement's population, had already collected in the courtyard to enjoy food and fellowship. The atmosphere in the streets was one of warmth and welcome.

"Happy Great Hope Day!"

Turning at the sound of the voice, Jetanien stepped back into his office to find his administrative attaché, Sergio Moreno, waiting for him. Extending his manus in greeting to the smiling, brown-skinned young human standing near his desk, Jetanien said, "And I do think it will be, Mister Moreno."

Moreno returned the gesture by clasping Jetanien's scaled mitt within his hands. "Are you watching the celebration? I think we're getting a great turnout."

"As this is likely to be the only social event this evening in Paradise City, let alone on all of Nimbus III," Jetanien said, "I would certainly hope so." He added a few clicks of laughter that seemed to cause Moreno's smile to fade. "Don't get me wrong, Sergio. I'm very encouraged by what I see."

"Your plan to create a citywide celebration is being well received, Ambassador," Moreno said as he released Jetanien's manus. "A new holiday we can call our own is not only a great unifier, but a boost to morale after a lot of hard work."

Jetanien felt a small surge of pride upon hearing that. While not overly grand in scope, the street festival to celebrate Great Hope Day had been his idea, and it certainly was something he hoped might succeed enough to continue as an annual event for the colony. He had marked the date on his calendar weeks ago, eyeing it as a means of rewarding the efforts of Paradise City residents for completing construction on the experimental colony's first phase. Events in past weeks, including a few altercations and accusations among the colonists themselves, apparently had begun to take an emotional toll on all involved in the endeavor. Such behavior was not unexpected, of course; it was part of the natural and unavoidable growing pains for the first settlement ever to be shared by citizens of three such disparate political and social entities as the United Federation of Planets and the Klingon and Romulan empires. Despite these and other minor issues, in the end the colonists had persevered, and the results were all around them.

"New holiday?" Jetanien asked. "I appreciate your optimism, Sergio, and I can only hope that it's contagious."

"I'll do my best to spread it," Moreno replied as Jetanien settled onto his *glenget,* a special chair constructed to fit his large, ungainly physique, which allowed him comfortable access to his large stained-wood desk. "Will you be going to the festival yourself?"

"Of course," Jetanien said. "I first have a brief meeting to attend, after which I shall do my level best to . . . what do you humans say? Dance the night away."

Sergio asked, "Then you have time for a few progress reports? Unless you would prefer that I submit them at our morning meeting."

Jetanien twisted his mandible to affect an expression he had learned best approximated a human's smile. "You aren't seeking an excuse to avoid the celebration yourself, are you, Sergio? Surely the smell of the Klingon food isn't enough to keep you off the streets tonight."

The attaché smiled. "No, Ambassador, I'll be going. Actually, I'm waiting for S'anra to arrive so I can accompany her this evening."

Recognizing the name, Jetanien nodded in approval. "And is this your first date with a Romulan, my good man?"

"Oh, no," Sergio replied, though Jetanien noticed the color shift in his face indicating the young man was embarrassed.

"Ah!" the ambassador exclaimed. "So, you make a habit of entertaining Romulan women? And what would your mother say?"

Moreno seemed to trip over his own laughter before replying, "No, Ambassador, I mean that this isn't a date. We're simply immersing ourselves in the idea of 'cultural exchange.' It's actually more of a wager, to be honest."

This piqued Jetanien's curiosity. "How so?"

"We're each going to see who can find the most foods that the other will like," Moreno replied. "I talked one of the vendors into using my grandfather's recipe for chorizo. Very smoky and very spicy. Any Romulan would love it."

Jetanien nodded. "And I trust you know just what you'll be letting yourself in for?"

"Oh, I'm fine with anything but the Andorian dishes,"

Moreno said. "I'm just not into tuber root and cabbage. I need more meat."

The chime to Jetanien's office door sounded, interrupting their discussion. "Come in," he called out, and the door slid aside to reveal an aged Romulan male, his thin white hair neatly trimmed around his pointed ears. Straight bangs all but covered his brow, and his face, deeply lined and wan, contrasted with the ruddy ceremonial robes draping his withered body.

"Senator D'tran," Jetanien said, surprised and happy at the sight of his guest. "Please, join me. My aide was just leaving."

If Moreno was at all surprised by his abrupt dismissal, he did not reveal it through facial expression or body language, a response Jetanien noted as indicating a level of self-control that would befit a successful member of the Diplomatic Corps. Sergio Moreno was the youngest and least experienced of Jetanien's two-member staff on Nimbus III, but the ambassador considered him well suited to the challenges that came with the significant if not historic mission of overseeing the prototype community of Paradise City. The young man's soft-spoken demeanor and amiable, accommodating approach to problem-solving seemed to ingratiate him to the diverse local population, which certainly could benefit from as much social lubrication as Jetanien's office might provide.

"Yes, Senator, I was," Moreno said. "And Happy Great Hope Day to you, sir." When D'tran said nothing, the attaché returned his attention to Jetanien. "Enjoy your evening, Ambassador. Should you need me for any reason, don't hesitate to call."

Jetanien shook his head. "I cannot imagine needing to interrupt your . . . cultural exchange. Please give my best to S'anra."

That prompted D'tran's first words since his arrival. "She is sure to inform you that her duties in my office will start promptly at our usual hour in the morning." His voice was low and raspy with age, lending it an edge of intimidation that evoked a wide-eyed expression from Moreno. "And if she does not inform you, you will inform her." When D'tran's eyes met Jetanien's, it was all the ambassador could do not to laugh.

"Certainly, Senator," Moreno replied, his words tinged with pronounced sincerity. He passed through the doorway, and D'tran waited for the door to close before allowing his smile to widen. "Youth. It is wasted on the young."

Now free to laugh, Jetanien released a string of clicks and chirps as he indicated a chair in front of his desk for the elderly Romulan. "You enjoy that sort of thing, don't you?"

"I'm only sorry I won't be there to see his reaction when S'anra actually *does* mention it," D'tran replied as he settled into one of two upholstered leather armchairs positioned before Jetanien's desk. "She takes her duties quite seriously."

"As do we all," Jetanien said. "And to that end, thank you for joining me this evening. I think it's important for the three of us to make a joint appearance at the festival. I like what that show of unity represents to our population."

A scowl flashed across D'tran's face and faded away just as quickly. "I'm happy to do so, and if our Klingon counterpart had any sense of punctuality, we could get on with this."

"I imagine he'll be along shortly," Jetanien said.

D'tran shrugged. "I believe he's been the last to arrive at nearly every meeting we've ever held."

"I would go so far as to say Lugok has, without exception, been late to each and every meeting, Senator," Jetanien said. "He's very deliberate about it."

"That kind of posturing seems unnecessary at this point in our cooperative efforts," D'tran countered, adjusting his position in his chair.

"You realize that he does this because of you."

"Me?" D'tran looked puzzled. "I don't understand."

"Well," the ambassador said, "you did keep us waiting on this rather forsaken planet for more than three months. Lugok once told me that he was planning to get those three months back from you, minute by minute if necessary, and he seems to be driven by a singular focus. He mentioned having sworn a blood oath to himself on the matter, but at the time I assumed he was joking."

D'tran paused as though mulling over what he had just heard, his expression all but unreadable. The Romulan then offered a slight nod, as though to himself, before shifting once more in his seat. "Lugok is a passionate Klingon, though I fear I'll never be able to predict the targets of his enthusiasm. I exhibited similar exuberance in my younger days, Ambassador, and perhaps it's my penance for that unbridled zeal that I'm here, undertaking this crusade of yours."

Jetanien offered a soft, polite laugh in reply, even if he took issue with his friend's observations. He certainly did not regard his assignment to Nimbus III as retribution for any impetuous behavior in his past. "Come now, Senator. We've had our share of hardships in getting Paradise City established, but surely you now can see that our efforts are bearing very promising fruit."

That he and D'tran along with Klingon ambassador Lugok had successfully negotiated terms for the colony's construction and operation, let alone that they even had won support for their proposal from their respective governments, still seemed almost incomprehensible to Jetanien whenever he allowed himself pause to consider the events of these past months. Extended negotiations, which had stemmed from the trio's first clandestine meeting, were the easy part, he thought. Lugok had already benefited from peaceful coexistence during their shared tenures aboard Starbase 47, and that appreciation for cooperative ventures had continued to grow even in the wake of the Organian Peace Treaty. The two diplomats had used that chemistry to work together in convincing Senator D'tran to secure a Romulan commitment toward the test venture on Nimbus III, their arguments matching the veteran senator's progressive views on diplomatic relations with interstellar powers. That outlook had served D'tran for several decades, dating back to his role in ending the Earth-Romulan War and helping to draft a peace treaty that had remained unbroken during the intervening century.

The subsequent discussions with the diplomats' respective governments that led to the Nimbus III proposal's acceptance were nothing short of landmark, at least in Jetanien's opinion.

However, his counterparts had made him privy to precious few details of those negotiations, offering no insight as to how protracted or heated their talks had been, or what personal favors had been promised or exacted in order to secure the needed support. True to form, Lugok complained about his having to exert additional effort with the Klingon High Council, but Jetanien was painfully aware of his propensity to complain about laying out any effort in general. The closest D'tran ever came to discussing his own process was to say that his fellow senators were long used to his grand ideas, and this one simply must have caught them all in a particularly generous and tolerant mood.

Jetanien found that his own challenges had come not in winning the hearts and minds of Federation Council members, but in doing so from his remote posting aboard Vanguard. Rather than leave the station during a time of unrest in the Taurus Reach, Jetanien had negotiated his proposal chiefly via subspace communications, a medium he detested in comparison to conducting such discussions in person. Travel time to Earth from Vanguard made such a meeting impractical, but at the time he also had been motivated by a desire to negotiate with members of the Orion Syndicate—he hesitated to call them diplomats—for the extradition of Diego Reyes from the *Omari-Ekon,* which according to the most recent status reports remained docked at the station. His efforts on that front had proven futile, even as he gained support from the Federation Council for his Nimbus III proposal.

Since returning to the planet, the colony had been the sole focus of Jetanien's focus and energy. While the plans he had formulated with his fellow diplomats had met with skepticism so far as their content was concerned, he had encountered little resistance to the process by which it would be accomplished. Tenets of the settlement's cooperative foundation and operation as developed by him and his fellow diplomats were approved, with one caveat. Out of concern for security during the proposal's initial discussions, one member of the Federation negotiating team insisted that Nimbus III's location not be discussed openly. In its stead was offered a more inspirational and vague moniker: the Planet of Galactic Peace. To this day, Jetanien remained unsure as to the accuracy of the name, but it had certainly stuck.

With negotiations complete, progress from arid flatlands to habitable colony owed much to the ample resources committed to the project by the governments involved. The central population center's basic infrastructure was constructed by support specialists in a matter of weeks, complete with roadways, utilities, and the beginnings of a hydroponic agriculture facility. All of this was followed by the initial buildings containing living quarters, office space, and storefronts. Even outdoor recreational areas were planned and constructed by engineers from each contributing government. Then there were the transport ships, laden with the first several hundred colonists and the supplies they would need to begin a new life here on Nimbus III, and when a group of those settlers came forward to suggest a name for their shared enclave, Jetanien enthusiastically championed its acceptance among his peers. Thus, Paradise City was born.

"We have come a long way since that fateful first meeting, Jetanien," D'tran said, "and had the spacecraft which initially carried me here only been capable of a faster speed, perhaps Ambassador Lugok might have joined us by now."

Jetanien laughed again. "I'm going to regret mentioning that, aren't I?"

"I will not speak of it again," D'tran countered, holding up his hands in mock surrender. "That said, I may not be as concerned with my own punctuality from this point forward."

"And here I've come to count on Lugok's pettiness as a means of enjoying time with you in private counsel," Jetanien said. "I hope my remarks will not cost me that, either."

D'tran shook his head. "Please ascribe my comments to the protests of an empty stomach. I took the liberty of passing by the food vendors on my way here, and their offerings do look promising. I trust you will be able to find something that suits your particular palate."

"If I've found one common denominator among humanoid species," Jetanien said, "it's a shared amusement surrounding my choices of food and drink. If memory serves, the bond you forged with Lugok started when you chose to sit together upwind of me during our shared meals."

"You may be right," D'tran replied, nodding in agreement. "Perhaps your decision to join him in eating a few Klingon dishes to my disdain warmed his warrior heart to you as well."

"In uncounted ways has food forged alliances that intoxicants keep lubricated," Jetanien said. He had heard that quote somewhere, long ago, but he had forgotten the source. That did not stop him from enjoying and employing it whenever the opportunity presented itself.

"Up to the point that they do not," D'tran replied. "Shall I assume such drink will be offered during the festival as well?"

"It will," Jetanien said, "with instructions already given to vendors that guests are not to be overserved. I had considered barring some of the more potent Romulan beverages, but that seemed to run counter to the event's multicultural spirit. I have to assume our residents will use proper discretion."

Offering a small, derisive laugh, D'tran shook his head. "You may be too generous in your assumptions, my friend. Will the constabulary be a visible presence at the festival?"

"And on the surrounding streets as well."

Jetanien's response seemed to do little to assuage the elderly Romulan's doubts. Representatives of each official state occupied positions within the colony's civil police force, the initiative being yet another attempt at furthering the concept of equality among the colonists. One of Paradise City's greatest hurdles—and one that Jetanien knew would take much more time to forge—was the establishment of a civil code that reflected the best balance between the different cultures the colony represented. Though Jetanien did not want to single out Klingon colonists as one of the main contributors to Paradise City's numerous accounts of social discord, he could not ignore the increasing reports of civil complaints filed by various colonists. Whether made in regard to a dispute over property, perceived threats of personal harm, or incidents of fighting and other violent outbursts, the great majority of incidents shared a common thread of Klingon involvement.

More to assure himself than anything, Jetanien said, "We're bound to experience our share of conflict as we all get accustomed to living with one another."

"The situation is something we need to monitor and to temper should the trend continue," D'tran replied. "Citizens have not been as quick to occupy the city as I had hoped. If this is to work, we need them to live and work together in the colony proper, and not continue to stay segregated in the outlying camps."

Jetanien could not disagree with his friend's contention. "We decided not to force an exodus of the camps, but instead to let volunteers come forward of their own accord. Do we need to set a deadline?"

"Possibly," D'tran replied. "More socialization will help further an appreciation of tolerance. We cannot let them view Paradise City as a place to visit. It must be a place to live."

The door chime sounded again, and when it opened this time it was to reveal a portly Klingon, dressed in an ill-fitting black and gray military uniform.

"Ambassador Lugok, son of Breg," Jetanien said, as though announcing the new arrival to a room full of guests. "Happy Great Hope Day!"

Offering a groan of disdain, Lugok sneered as he shuffled past Jetanien into the room. From the smell of the Klingon's breath and the grimy metal tankard clutched in his right hand, Jetanien surmised that Lugok had commenced his own celebrations earlier than the rest of the ambassadorial team.

"Remind me again what it is we're celebrating?" Lugok asked as he stood beside the unoccupied chair next to where D'tran was seated.

"The completion of the residential facilities within Paradise City, for one thing," Jetanien replied. "We were just discussing incentives to get more of the colonists to move within the city's perimeter. Now that we're able to accommodate all of the colonists, we can set about eliminating the outlying encampments."

"I understand the theory behind your incentives," Lugok said, "but I doubt the Klingon colonists will vacate the camp until they are ordered. Once they occupy the city residences, we'd better prepare for a settling-in period."

D'tran added, "Until they get used to their accommodations?"

"More like until everyone else gets used to the Klingons," Jetanien said.

Lugok laughed. "My people are not as used to such structured living arrangements. They seem to be handling themselves reasonably well in their camp. You might want to consider letting them stay there."

"You speak as though the mere act of bringing them into Paradise City is only asking for trouble," Jetanien said.

A sharp scream from somewhere outside made the ambassador rise from his chair and make his way to the balcony. Down the street, he could see the crowd, which had grown noticeably since he last looked, roiling against itself. More shouts followed as people fled the courtyard, while a handful of others broke from the pack to engage in shoving matches and fistfights.

As D'tran and Lugok joined him on the balcony, Jetanien watched a number of city constables—each wearing distinguishing white jumpsuits—pushing their way into the crowd. One of them was grabbed and hoisted aloft by an enraged Tellarite before being flung to the street. The wail of an alert siren rose above the crowd, which Jetanien knew was a call for more constables to converge on the scene.

Lugok snorted and released a loud belly laugh. "This now concludes Great Hope Day on the Planet of Galactic Peace. We hope you have enjoyed your evening."

"Your humor is ill-timed, Ambassador," Jetanien snapped,

feeling his ire beginning to rise. "This is exactly the sort of problem we're working to prevent."

"Klingons are a proud people, Jetanian," Lugok said. "Forcing them into a peaceful retirement community with their lifelong sworn enemies is not going to be easy."

Jetanien shook his head. "Ordinarily, I'd agree, but they did volunteer to come to this planet, did they not? Besides, responding to a celebration of unification by starting a street riot is not what I would call acting with honor."

"Do not speak to me of honor, Jetanien," Lugok countered, pointing one gloved finger at the Chelon. "Not that it matters to those *petaQ*. You know as well as I do that our test subjects—excuse me, our *colonists*—do not come from the most respected Houses of the Empire."

"Did you empty your prisons to populate Nimbus III, Ambassador?" D'tran asked.

The Klingon paused, eyeing the aged senator with contempt. "Of course not, though many of our colonists volunteered to take part in this 'experiment' as an alternative to prison, or worse. As such, living among us is a shame to their Houses. I wouldn't bother tainting my blade with their blood, but they are here, and we must work with them." Raising his tankard to his lips and scowling at the realization that it was empty, he grunted in irritation. "Now, if you'll excuse me, I'm going down there to see things for myself."

"Now does not seem the appropriate time for us to make an appearance," D'tran offered.

Lugok laughed again. "For the two of you, I agree, but this is my kind of celebration." He turned to leave, but stopped upon seeing the frustration on Jetanien's face, and he adopted a more serious tone. "Do not worry yourself, Jetanien. This little commotion will die out on its own, and if it doesn't, we can always call for a warship to destroy the planet." The smile returned, and he released another deep rumbling laugh that echoed in the office as he made his way to the door and left.

Once the Klingon had departed, Jetanien said, "This is not the most promising of starts for a Great Hope Day tradition."

D'tran placed a hand on his shoulder. "Paradise City is an experiment, my friend, and for many of the colonists, it is a place for second chances. I'd imagine very few of our settlers are coming with unblemished pasts and ignorance of life's less savory quarters. We should show great patience as well as hope."

Jetanien could only wonder how long his own patience might endure.

8

Streaks of multihued light retreated on the viewscreen, settling into distant pinpricks in the dark curtain of space as the *Defiant* dropped out of warp. From where he sat in the captain's chair at the center of the ship's bridge, Thomas Blair regarded the screen, instinctively looking for threats even though reason—and the starship's sensors—told him there was no danger.

"Maintain Yellow Alert," he ordered, rising from his seat and stepping around the helm and navigation console situated before him so that he might have a clear view of the screen. "Okay, let's see it."

"Aye, sir," said Lieutenant T'Lehr, the Vulcan seated at the helm station. Her long fingers played across her console and a moment later the image on the main viewscreen shifted. Instead of empty space, the screen now depicted what Blair recognized as a Tholian vessel.

Or what's left of one, anyway.

From where he stood next to the command chair, Commander Mbugua released a small grunt that Blair recognized as the first officer's normal reaction to something that had interested him. "Somebody didn't like these guys very much, did they?"

Moving to stand so that he could lean against the red railing separating the command well from the upper deck at the front of the bridge, Blair nodded. "That's putting it mildly. T'Lehr, can you magnify the image?"

"Yes, Captain," the helm officer replied, and the view changed yet again to bring the Tholian vessel into sharper focus. Torn metal was now clearly visible, outlined by scorch marks from what Blair figured to be powerful particle-beam weapons. A cloud of debris surrounded the ship, which was dark and drifting without any obvious means of propulsion.

"What are your sensors telling you, Nyn?" Blair asked.

At the science station, Lieutenant Commander Clarissa Nyn bent over her console's hooded sensor viewer. "I'm not picking up any life signs, sir," she replied without looking up from her instruments, her words carrying a soft Dutch accent. "The only power source appears to be an emergency battery, but it's weak. My guess is it'll be exhausted within a day or so." Her attention remained on her instruments throughout her report. It was a habit that Blair had found irritating during the first weeks after Nyn arrived aboard the *Defiant,* replacing his former science officer after her transfer to the *U.S.S. Kongo.* Commander Mbugua was the one who had made him see that Nyn was not being intentionally disrespectful with this practice, but simply very focused on her work. At his recommendation, Blair opted not to mention his peeve, itself a reluctant decision made easier by the fact that Clarissa Nyn was damned good at her job.

Or, you're just getting soft in your old age.

"Just enough to run their comm system and keep sending that message," Mbugua said. "For a while, anyway. Any idea how long the signal's been broadcasting?"

Turning from her station, Nyn stepped closer to the railing, her hands clasped behind her back. "According to sensor readings from the backup power system, I'd have to say somewhere in the neighborhood of two weeks. Three, at the outside."

"Judging by the damage to that ship," Blair added, "the crew had to know they wouldn't survive long enough for anyone to come to their rescue." Turning from the viewscreen, he said, "Nyn, are there any escape pods on that ship, or evidence of any having been launched?"

The science officer nodded. "One escape pod, sir, still in its berth. Whatever happened, the crew didn't have time to make use of it."

Considering this, Blair said, "Any idea who's responsible?"

The likely suspects had already been the topic of much discussion in the hours since Blair's first learning of the distress call, but all of that had been without the aid of any supporting evidence.

"Residual energy signatures don't match Klingon weapons, sir," Nyn said, "but Orion pirate ships have been known to possess disruptors that fit the pattern."

"That's hardly conclusive," Mbugua countered. "Orions have been buying and selling weapons systems for as long as anyone can remember. Besides, this is a bit out of the way, even for Orion pirates."

Blair frowned. "Maybe, but that doesn't mean I'd put it past them, either. Even if it is Orions, the big question is whether they did it on their own, or if they were paid to do somebody else's dirty work." He had read the report of how Orion pirates, contracted by a Klingon agent, had attacked and destroyed the *U.S.S. Nowlan* while the transport ship was on its way to Earth. It had all been part of an elaborate smokescreen to cover their kidnapping and delivery into Klingon custody of Diego Reyes, former commander of Starbase 47, who had been convicted by a Starfleet court-martial and sentenced to a ten-year prison term.

"For what it's worth, sir," Nyn said, "I scanned the ship's cargo hold, or at least what I think was the hold, and found nothing. If they were carrying anything, it's long gone now."

Folding his arms across his chest, Mbugua added, "It's an awfully small ship. I'm not sure what cargo they could be carrying that's worth the risk of coming all the way out here by themselves. Plus, where would they be going? Are there any planets in the vicinity that are likely destinations for a Tholian vessel?"

"None that I've been able to determine, sir," Nyn replied, "though we're not that far from the Tholian border—a day's travel at their vessel's top speed."

"And what about the Klingons?" Blair asked. "We're sure they've not been reported in this area?"

Mbugua said, "I double-checked the latest intelligence reports and didn't find anything new. That said, we're less than a week out from at least two systems with planets known to be under Klingon control: Traelus and Leramin. Both systems are within spitting distance of the Tholian border."

"We've had scattered reports of Tholian ships running surveys of Klingon-occupied systems in the Taurus Reach," Blair added, "particularly those in proximity to their territory." He gestured toward the viewscreen. "Maybe this ship was doing that, and got too close to something that someone else didn't want seen, scanned, or reported."

"That's a lot of theory," Mbugua replied, "without much of anything to back it up."

Blair nodded. "I know, but the more I think about it, the less I believe that pirates, Orion or otherwise, would bother with a ship like that. As you said, it's pretty small to be carrying much in the way of impressive cargo. The fact that it's a Tholian ship in the Taurus Reach makes me think they were checking out something they didn't like, and the big item on that list would be the Klingons."

From the intelligence reports he had read while the *Defiant* was en route to take on this assignment, Blair knew the Tholian government had been none too happy to learn that the Klingon Empire had planted its flag in the Traelus system nearly three years earlier. Of course, that claim had put the Federation on edge, as well, coming as it had following a tense confrontation with the *U.S.S. Sagittarius,* one of the Starfleet vessels assigned to Starbase 47, during an early survey of that area. The system's proximity to Tholian territory was a primary point of contention, with Starfleet tactical analysts concluding that a Klingon base in that region could serve as an effective launching point for military offensives into Tholian space. So far, the Klingons appeared to be uninterested in such action, preferring instead to establish a mining support colony on the system's second planet and take advantage of the world's rich deposits of dilithium and other useful minerals.

"Even if that's true," Nyn said as she reached up to brush aside an errant lock of blond hair, "we still don't have any evidence of Klingon involvement."

Gesturing toward the viewscreen, Blair asked, "Have engineering retrieve some of the debris and give it a complete once-over. Maybe Mister Stevok and his team can find us an additional clue or two as to who's responsible for this attack." If anyone could convince the remnants of the wrecked Tholian ship to divulge any secrets they might hold, it was Stevok, the *Defiant*'s chief engineer. The Vulcan's investigative talents were on a par with his technical skills, which were formidable.

Mbugua replied, "Aye, sir. What do we do in the meantime?"

"Update Vanguard on our latest findings, and carry on with our patrol," Blair said, his attention returning to the viewscreen and the image of the destroyed vessel. "If Admiral Nogura wants us to investigate further, he'll let us know."

Thomas Blair's gut was already telling him exactly what the admiral would say.

9

"Turn your head and say, 'Ahhh.' Oh, wait. I mean, open your mouth and cough. Whatever. I never could get those straight."

Though Reyes thought he detected the hint of a whimsical smile on the face of Ezekiel Fisher, the doctor offered no other hint that he might be joking. Still, Reyes was certain he knew his old friend well enough to sense a scam in the offing, so he decided to play along for a bit and see what might happen. "Any other parts of your job you tend to mix up? Medications, operations, patients, that sort of thing?" He sat in one of two chairs that, along with the small, unadorned table positioned against the wall, comprised the sole furnishings within the drab, windowless office that had been provided by Ganz for Fisher during the doctor's visit to the *Omari-Ekon*.

The doctor shrugged, keeping his attention on the status display of the tricorder he held in his left hand as he waved a medical scanner over Reyes. "I may have slipped up from time to time, but I'm lucky in that I have people who all are willing to cover up for my mistakes."

"That figures," Reyes countered, now certain his friend was playing at something despite his implacable expression. "Wish I'd had them on my staff. I might've been able to avoid all this trouble."

Shaking his head in apparent disagreement, Fisher replied, "I doubt it. Subordinates tend to hold a grudge when you don't remember birthdays, anniversaries, or other special occasions. You always were lousy at that sort of thing."

"That's why I had a yeoman," Reyes said, before pausing to

reconsider his comment. "Come to think of it, I probably forgot her birthday, too."

"And there you go," Fisher said, deactivating the medical scanner and returning it to his tricorder's storage compartment. From where he sat, Reyes had been able to see and interpret the unit's status displays, and he knew that the doctor's scans had found nothing out of the ordinary. Despite some rough days in the early going, Reyes had suffered no lasting effects during his tenure as a guest first of the Klingons and now the Orions.

"So, what's the verdict, Doc?" he asked after a moment, wondering what Fisher's response might be and hoping it at least would be entertaining.

Drawing a breath, the doctor replied, "My scans are inconclusive. It's possible you came into contact with someone who's infected, but so far no symptoms have manifested themselves. I'm going to inoculate you anyway, just to be safe."

Rather than reply, Reyes offered a nod with an expression he hoped would convey the proper level of concern for anyone who might be observing the examination, not the least of whom was the towering, muscled Orion male who had been assigned as Fisher's escort. He stood behind the doctor, blocking the only exit from the office.

"You cannot do that," the sentry said.

Fisher offered the guard an admonishing glare. "Says who?"

The blunt nature of the question seemed to catch the Orion by surprise, and Reyes watched while the guard blinked several times, as though struggling to formulate a reply. "My orders are to prevent you from having any physical contact with this human."

"Son," Fisher said, "you want to live, right?" He crossed his arms, adopting his most disapproving demeanor—the one Reyes knew was reserved for wayward interns and low-ranking Starfleet officers who came to Vanguard's hospital with injuries sustained during a bout of binge drinking at Stars Landing. The expression on the sentry's face was such that Reyes almost laughed, though he was able to maintain his professional decorum.

"Yes," the guard replied after a moment, uncertainty beginning to cloud his stern expression.

Nodding in what Reyes took to be understanding, Fisher replied, "Well, okay then." He indicated Reyes with a wave of his hand. "This man has presented preliminary indications of having been infected, which means he requires a vaccination, the same vaccination I gave you an hour ago. If I miss inoculating even one person on this ship who's come into contact with the contagion, it means that I've wasted a lot of valuable time and medicine vaccinating the rest of you. Get what I'm saying?"

His expression wavering as he appeared to ponder Fisher's words, the sentry finally said, "I will have to verify this with Ganz."

"You do that," Fisher replied, "and while you're at it, remind Mister Ganz that Starfleet regulations state that in the event of any form of potential viral contagion, the station's chief medical officer is required to conduct a thorough inspection of all vessels docked or seeking to dock at this facility. Further, all infected persons aboard any such ship are required to receive the proper vaccinations in order to arrest the possibility of widespread infection." He indicated himself by pointing his thumb at his chest. "Since I'm the chief medical officer, if I don't get to do what regulations require me to do while your ship's docked at our station, the alternative is for you to undock your little ship from our station and be on your merry way. I'm betting Mister Ganz won't be happy when he finds out his having to leave is all your fault, and that's before the fever really takes hold and body parts start falling off people in a day or so."

The guard now eyed both Fisher and Reyes with no small amount of concern. "Body parts?"

Fisher nodded. "Yep. The small, fleshy parts are usually the first to go." Reyes was forced to look away as the doctor made a point of glancing toward the wide belt encircling the sentry's waist. "It's not a pretty sight, let me tell you, but that's Arcturian blood disease for you."

"Arcturian blood disease?" Reyes repeated. He had heard of

the rare disorder once or twice before, but that was the limit of his knowledge on the subject. Still, he sensed the need to help strengthen the obvious falsehood Fisher was attempting to feed the Orion. "You're kidding."

Continuing to play his role, Fisher said, "Wish I was. Somebody brought it aboard. Probably a freight hauler picked it up from one of the colony planets."

"What is this Arcturian blood disease?" the sentry asked, his tone one of skepticism. "I've never heard of it."

"That's okay," Fisher said, and Reyes said nothing more as the doctor turned back to the table and the equipment he had laid out atop its surface. "Not many people know about it." Reaching for his medical kit, he picked up a hypospray and checked its setting. "It has a lot in common with Rigelian fever, and seems to favor humanoids of various species, including humans, Vulcans, and Orions. Tellarites seem immune, but then Tellarites are pretty much immune to almost everything."

Watching Fisher ready the hypospray for use, Reyes silently commended Fisher on the ease with which he was playing this little game of misinformation. The strength of a good lie was in not overselling it, and the doctor's delivery of all the technical-sounding medical mumbo jumbo was just as smooth and polished as when providing an actual, truthful diagnosis. Indeed, Reyes was starting to wonder if the Orion might run from the room in a panic, perhaps to summon a superior or even Ganz himself in order to weigh in on what the guard might well believe was a dangerous viral outbreak aboard the *Omari-Ekon*.

"I didn't think there was a cure," Reyes said, fueling the fires of deception, though still worried about not overdoing it.

Shaking his head, Fisher stepped closer to his friend, his right hand wielding the hypospray. "There wasn't, at least not until six months or so ago. Starfleet Medical was able to synthesize a ryetalyn derivative that works well enough."

"What is ryetalyn?" the Orion asked.

Fisher did not answer before pressing the hypospray to the left side of Reyes's neck as though readying to inject the vaccine into his patient's carotid artery. At the last instant, with his body blocking the guard's view, Fisher changed the alignment of the hypo so that it now rested just below Reyes's jaw before triggering the device's injector mechanism. The tiny office was filled with the hypo's pneumatic hiss as Fisher completed administering the vaccination, and Reyes could not help scowling in momentary irritation at the injection, which was more painful than he was used to feeling. The odd sensation continued for several seconds, and he had to force himself not to reach up to rub his jaw as Fisher turned back to the table.

"Ryetalyn is the only known antidote for Rigelian fever," the doctor said as he returned the hypospray to his medical kit. "Given the similarities between the two strains of contagion, somebody at Starfleet Medical figured it made sense that their respective antidotes would also be related." When he turned once more to face his escort, Fisher noted that the Orion's expression was one of complete befuddlement. "Get all that, sport, or are you still worried about body parts falling off?"

That, coupled with the guard's worried look, almost made Reyes laugh. Though he had not been privy to specifics, he had heard assorted scuttlebutt about Admiral Nogura ordering some kind of medical inspections for all Starfleet and civilian vessels moored at the station. According to the gossip mill running rampant through the *Omari-Ekon*'s bar and gaming deck, teams of Starbase 47 medical personnel were crawling in and through the six docked ships, looking for who only knew what. Reyes had suspected a ruse from the outset, and he was sure Ganz, if not Neera herself, would also doubt the sincerity of any such action on Nogura's part. For the scheme to succeed, it meant Fisher and his people pushing a hard sell with inspections, examinations, and even vaccinations of supposedly "infected" people aboard any of the targeted vessels.

"Had to quarantine anyone yet?" Reyes asked.

Fisher nodded. "Two from one of those low-warp freighters. I've got them down in the hospital in an isolation ward. So far they're not showing anything serious, but the regs state we observe them for forty-eight hours." Casting a look in the guard's direction, he added, "Nothing's fallen off yet, but I suppose we'll see."

"*Mister Reyes,*" a voice, low and soft, echoed in Reyes's mind, and he grunted in surprise at the unexpected intrusion. "*This is Lieutenant T'Prynn.*"

Studying him warily, Fisher asked, "You all right?"

In his head, Reyes heard T'Prynn's voice say, "*If you can hear me, tell Doctor Fisher that you have a cramp in your lower leg.*"

Reyes reached down to rub his left calf. "Sorry. I guess I've been sitting here too long. Got a cramp." He cleared his throat as he adjusted his position in the chair, using the opportunity to glance at the guard, who showed no apparent signs of suspecting that anything untoward was taking place.

"You need to watch those," Fisher replied. "Probably not getting enough potassium in your diet. I'll have the quartermaster send over a crate of bananas."

"*Doctor Fisher has implanted a subcutaneous, subaural transceiver along your jaw,*" T'Prynn said. "*It operates on an encrypted, low-power frequency well below the range of scanning equipment employed by Ganz's people. We will now be able to communicate without detection.*"

Reyes had already guessed that much, as well as figuring that Fisher must also be outfitted with a similar device. Since receiving the initial communication from his former intelligence officer and agreeing to assist her if and when she was able to call upon him, Reyes had been waiting for some sign or signal that she was ready to proceed. Were he able to do so without attracting undue attention from Fisher's escort, he would have smiled in unabashed admiration at T'Prynn's seemingly never-ending resourcefulness.

"*I will ask you a series of questions,*" T'Prynn continued. "*At the same time, Doctor Fisher will also be asking you medical-related questions. The answers you provide to me should also be appropriate for his queries. If you understand, please tell Doctor Fisher that you've been having trouble sleeping.*"

"Since you're pumping me full of this and that," Reyes said, "I don't suppose you've got anything that might help me sleep?"

Fisher nodded. "I can probably help you with that. What's the matter? All that craziness in the casino keeping you up nights?"

At the same time, T'Prynn said, "*We require someone to access the* Omari-Ekon's *navigational logs and extract information. I cannot elaborate as to the nature of the data, but I can tell you the matter is of extreme importance. Are you willing to make such an attempt?*"

It took Reyes a moment to sort both questions in his head, during which he covered the lag with a small chuckle for the benefit of Fisher as well as the guard. Whatever T'Prynn was planning, he was certain she would not ask him to place himself at such extreme risk unless she believed it to be important. If he were caught while attempting to retrieve information of the sort T'Prynn was seeking, Reyes harbored no doubts that it would mean a death sentence at the hands of Ganz's people.

Finally, he answered, "You could say that."

"*Excellent,*" T'Prynn replied.

"I think I've got something here with me that will work," Fisher said, as he appeared to inspect the contents of his medical kit. "According to your files, you have no allergies. Is that still true?"

On the heels of the doctor's question, T'Prynn asked, "*Do you think you will be able to access a computer terminal? I should be able to guide you through the process of locating and extracting any relevant data.*"

"Yes, that's right," Reyes replied, nodding.

Extracting another vial of dark blue liquid from his medical kit, Fisher attached it to the receptor on the end of his hypospray before turning back to Reyes. "This is a vitamin supplement that should help regulate your melatonin levels. Might take a day or two to kick in fully, but you should notice a difference starting tonight." He placed the hypo against Reyes's left arm and once more triggered its injector.

Reyes felt the compound entering his bloodstream as T'Prynn

said, "*I will contact you later tonight to work out the details of our operation. I suspect your quarters are being monitored, so partake of your evening meal in a public venue, such as one of the restaurants on the gaming deck. I'll be able to hear you even if you whisper.*"

"I like the sound of that," Reyes replied, to Fisher as well as T'Prynn.

The doctor nodded in apparent satisfaction. "In that case, I think we're done here." He said nothing else as he returned his equipment to the satchel he had brought with him. Slinging the bag over his left shoulder, he turned to regard Reyes. "Anything else I can do for you?"

"Bring me some decent coffee?" Reyes answered. "The stuff they serve over here tastes like sweat running off a rhino's ass."

Pausing as though considering the image that description evoked, Fisher chuckled and shook his head. "Well, so much for *my* dinner plans." He held out his right hand. "Good to see you again, Diego. Take care of yourself."

Reyes gripped his friend's hand an extra moment. He considered attempting to convey a message to the doctor or T'Prynn that might in turn be delivered to Rana Desai, wherever she might be. He had learned of her rather sudden departure from the station, but she had not attempted to contact him prior to her leaving. Though he was certain she must have had her reasons for this abrupt decision, Reyes could not help but feel a pang of regret that she had chosen not to share any such rationale with him. While he figured Admiral Nogura knew where she had gone, Reyes was worried that any attempt by him to pass on a message might be exploited by the guard or someone else in Ganz's organization, such as whoever doubtless was monitoring the conversations right now taking place in this room. Deciding it was not worth the risk, Reyes offered only a simple reply. "You, too, Zeke."

"Okay, sport," Fisher said to his escort as he moved toward the door, "let's get a move on. Still plenty of ship to inspect before my day's over."

The sentry scowled as he stepped aside to allow the doctor to exit the room. Looking back at Reyes, he said, "You can go now, human."

"Thanks, buddy," Reyes said, offering a mock salute. "I was worried I might miss my spa appointment."

He waited until Fisher and the guard disappeared from sight before releasing a slow sigh, shaking his head in wonderment at what had just transpired. Had Fisher and T'Prynn truly managed to succeed where others before them—by all verifiable accounts—had failed, and embedded a spy aboard the *Omari-Ekon*? Reyes had to believe that other covert agents had operated at one time or another while working among the Orion vessel's crew and passengers. Likewise, he was sure most if not all of those spies ultimately had been discovered and disposed of by Ganz or members of his organization.

Well, let's hope we can buck that trend, shall we? The thought continued to rattle around in his head even as he left the room and made his way toward one of the turbolifts that would return him to the gaming deck. It was not until he emerged from the lift and was greeted by the raucous sounds and sights of the casino that T'Prynn's voice returned.

"I will be in contact with you soon, Mister Reyes, but I will be monitoring this frequency in a passive scan mode, should you have need to call for assistance. On behalf of Admiral Nogura and Commander ch'Nayla, I wish to thank you for agreeing to help us in this endeavor."

Glancing around to make sure no one was paying him any extra attention as he headed for the bar at the center of the gaming floor, Reyes could not help releasing a small chuckle as he considered his current situation.

"I just hope I don't talk in my sleep."

10

As he had every day for the past three weeks, Lieutenant Ming Xiong made a circuit of the containment chamber. Just as he had done on those prior occasions during the unit's construction and installation, he studied every detail and allowed nothing to escape his notice. He inspected each setting on every control panel, eyed every joint and seam where duranium metal plates had come together to form the compartment's outer shell. Even the conduits connecting the container to its source of power were subjected to his unflinching scrutiny. When he came abreast of the first control panel to be inspected during this latest assessment, Xiong without a moment's hesitation began the process all over again, only this time, he turned and began to circle the container in the opposite direction.

"Well, would you look at that," a male voice said from somewhere to his right. "I think he's finally snapped."

Another voice, also male though possessing a slightly higher pitch, replied, "What do you mean snapped? He seems perfectly normal to me."

"Can't you see?" the first man asked, his tone now clearly one of jest. "He's walking the wrong way." Then, his voice rising in volume, he said, "Lieutenant, if you keep that up, you're going to wear through the deck plating."

Unable to keep from smiling as he halted his inspection, Xiong turned to look at the two men standing at the entrance to the *U.S.S. Lovell*'s secondary cargo bay. "Mister Anderson. Mister O'Halloran. Glad you could make it."

"Wouldn't miss it," replied Anderson as he and O'Halloran made their way into the cargo bay.

"Says you," O'Halloran countered. "This was supposed to be my day off."

Anderson shook his head. "You big baby."

The verbal banter helped to ease Xiong's mood as the engineers approached. Both wore Starfleet uniforms with red tunics bearing a lieutenant's stripes, though neither officer appeared old enough to be more than a week out of the Academy. Xiong figured that their apparent youth in large part could be attributed to the jocular, almost irreverent manner in which they engaged nearly every conversation that was not directly related to their assigned duties. He was aware that such behavior was a hallmark of nearly every member of the *Lovell*'s crew, in particular the contingent of specialists assigned to the ship's detachment from the Corps of Engineers. However, having seen the crew work on several occasions, Xiong knew from experience that any unconventional antics they might exhibit disappeared when duty or necessity called. In this regard, he likened the men and women assigned to the *Lovell* to Captain Adelard Nassir and his crew aboard the *U.S.S. Sagittarius*. That eclectic, tight-knit group also was rather unorthodox in its methods, but no one could argue the results they achieved.

The same could be said for the *Lovell* itself, being an all but ancient *Daedalus*-class vessel. A relic of the previous century, it and two sister ships had been pulled from deep storage at the Qualor II shipyards and refurbished for use by the Corps of Engineers, offering its crew of specialists and miracle workers ample opportunity to tinker with every onboard system to the point where the *Lovell* now performed almost as well as any ship built within the past three decades. Given the irregular nature of what Xiong and this vessel's crew were about to attempt, "unorthodox" was just the sort of character trait that was needed here and now.

"Well," Xiong said, offering a wry grin, "I appreciate you being here, even if you're not supposed to be here today."

"No problem, Lieutenant," Anderson said. "Commander al-Khaled prefers to have us on hand when there's a possibility of something blowing up, or ripping open the fabric of space-time."

O'Halloran's eyes narrowed. "That's not going to happen today, though. Right?"

"I can't predict what might result from this test," Xiong replied, "but I'm fairly confident the space-time continuum is secure, at least for the moment." Even as he spoke the words, Xiong considered his answer. If Operation Vanguard had taught him anything, it was to anticipate the unexpected, the unlikely, or even the impossible.

"Good," Anderson said, making his way toward the row of workstations that had been installed in the cargo bay and configured to act as the center of operations for the forthcoming series of tests. "I hate to mess with that kind of stuff, at least before lunch." Settling into one of the seats positioned before the consoles, he ran his hand along one set of controls and nodded. "Everything shows green." Gesturing toward the container, he asked, "I take it our guest is behaving itself?"

Xiong replied, "So far." Moving to stand next to where O'Halloran had seated himself at another of the consoles, he tapped a control, and one of the workstation's monitors flickered to life before settling on the image of a now quite familiar crystalline polyhedron. Somewhat larger than a human head, the Mirdonyae Artifact—one of two currently held by Xiong and his team of researchers on Starbase 47—emitted a pulsing, violet glow, just as it had since he had used the mysterious crystal to capture the Shedai entity that had attacked the station months earlier. Whether the energy emitted by the crystal originated from the object itself or the mysterious being it now held within its confines, Xiong did not know. Weeks of intensive sensor scans of the artifact as well as its companion, which remained in its own secure containment facility within the Vault aboard the station, had yielded nothing in the way of tangible information.

"Is it me," O'Halloran said, "or does that thing just look pissed off?"

Anderson leaned back in his chair. "I think you'd be feeling the same way if somebody stuffed you into a fishbowl." Then, he asked Xiong, "We're sure this thing is safe?"

"As safe as it's going to be," Xiong replied. Given the awesome power already demonstrated by the Shedai entities since his first encounter with them on the planet Erilon, the young archeology and anthropology officer had his doubts that there existed one place or containment system that would render the artifact and the being it held "safe." The last attempt even to connect either of the artifacts to an external power source in order to affect sensor scans had evoked the wrath of a Shedai entity, presumably attracted by some signal or other energy emission from the mysterious crystals. That attack had been halted, but not before the entity had inflicted massive damage upon the station. Since that near-disastrous day, the artifacts had been held in isolation, first in the cargo hold of a Starfleet support craft while the station underwent repairs from the Shedai attack, and later within a special chamber installed in the Vault and constructed for the specific purpose of housing the alien objects. However, the protective measures had done nothing to ease the concerns of Admiral Nogura with respect to station safety, prompting this latest course of action. Even this isolation chamber—a twin of the one in the Vault devised by Xiong with the assistance of the *Lovell*'s Corps of Engineers team leader, Lieutenant Commander Mahmud al-Khaled—offered no guarantees.

"Once we activate the damping fields," Xiong said, "the chamber will be completely self-contained." Even the couplings connecting the unit to the *Lovell*'s power systems would be deactivated, and the chamber would rely on its own compact impulse generator, which al-Khaled and his team had taken from one of the ship's shuttlecraft. "In theory, at least, the chamber can remain active for a year without interruption."

"I should've taken bets," Anderson said.

Xiong ignored the remark as he studied the status displays before him. All power readings were nominal. All that remained would be to activate the additional layer of damping force fields al-Khaled and his team had designed to act as a buffer for the series of sensor and communications scans to which the artifact would soon be subjected. If they were lucky, they would be able to examine the enigmatic object, and perhaps even the equally mystifying entity it contained, without threat of another attack.

And if we're not lucky, Xiong mused, *it could be a bad day for everyone.*

The sound of the cargo bay's hatch opening drew his attention, and Xiong turned to see al-Khaled entering the room. The commander was followed by Doctor Carol Marcus, the civilian supervisor of Starbase 47's Operation Vanguard research team.

"Good morning, everyone," Marcus said as she and al-Khaled approached. Exchanging smiles with Xiong, she added, "Lieutenant, I trust everything is ready here?"

Nodding, Xiong replied, "Just about, Doctor." He paused, offering a small smile. "I just wish Nezrene was here." Operation Vanguard's Tholian benefactor, Nezrene, had defected and sought asylum aboard the station, and her knowledge and assistance had helped Xiong and the Vault research team to better understand the artifacts of Shedai technology they had encountered and acquired on a handful of planets throughout the Taurus Reach. Nezrene had also helped Xiong and his people to better comprehend the Shedai themselves, offering a much-needed yet terrifying perspective on the ancient race and the incredible power it commanded. Present at the time of the Shedai's attack on Starbase 47, the Tholian had been killed when the powerful entity tore its way through the station and penetrated the Vault in search of the Mirdonyae Artifacts to which it had been drawn.

Marcus reached out to place a hand on Xiong's shoulder. "Me, too, but I like to think she's here, after a fashion."

Comforted by her words, Xiong smiled before turning his attention to al-Khaled. "Are we in position?"

"Yes," said the head of the *Lovell*'s Corps of Engineers detachment. "We've established orbit at the limits of Vanguard's weapons range. If anything goes wrong, they'll be ready."

"Why don't I find that comforting?" O'Halloran asked.

Marcus replied, "Relax, Lieutenant. We may not be the Corps of Engineers, but we have a few tricks up our sleeve."

"Exactly," Xiong replied. "The damping fields may not be able to fully block any signals or energy the artifact might emit, but they should at least weaken and scatter them, thereby preventing a repeat of the last time we tried this." Eyeing Marcus, he added, "After all, I really don't think we want *another* of those things coming after us."

"I can certainly live without it," the doctor said. "What about sensors and communications?"

Al-Khaled answered, "That's where we're still shooting a bit in the dark. Since we've had no apparent success contacting the Shedai entities within the artifacts, we've decided to go back and start from scratch. We'll begin with low-intensity scans and work our way back to the levels that triggered your prior . . . incident. At each step, we'll reexamine the findings and see how they measure up so far as this new setup is concerned, and make the appropriate adjustments before continuing."

"Even after all of that," Xiong said, "there's still no guarantee we'll learn anything new, much less make actual contact with the Shedai entity."

"And we might just irritate it all over again," Marcus added.

Nodding, Xiong said, "That is a possibility, Doctor." It was this scenario, above everything else, that was behind the extraordinary lengths to which he, al-Khaled, and their teams had gone to prepare for this round of experiments. Despite all the precautions, Admiral Nogura had been reluctant to see the research continue, but had relented when offered the idea of using the *Lovell* as the test bed rather than the station itself. That the suggestion had been presented by the ship's captain, Daniel Okagawa, after he had explained the situation to his crew and they all—to a person—had supported the plan, had convinced Nogura to allow the effort to proceed.

"Well," Marcus said after a moment, "if there's one thing I've learned from working with Starfleet, it's that risk is part of the game. Let's do this."

As al-Khaled oversaw the chamber's final preparations, Xiong moved to the console that had been configured for monitoring the artifact. On the workstation's main monitor, the image of the crystalline artifact continued to emit its purple-white glow. Despite the physical distance and the very real barriers separating him from the object, Xiong could not help thinking he had still felt the odd tingle across his entire body when he had held the artifact in his bare hands. He tried to dismiss the strange sensation as a figment of his imagination, concentrating instead on the cold, precise data being fed to him by the container's network of internal sensors.

"Baryonic array, chroniton gauges, and tachyon scanners are all online and standing by," he said. "How are we looking?"

"All containment field readings are green, Ming," al-Khaled replied from where he had taken up station at an adjacent console. "Disabling main power and switching to internal systems."

Another of Xiong's console screens indicated the transfer to the containment chamber's independent power source. All of the other status indicators remained steady, and he nodded in approval. "Transfer complete. Everything looks good." Turning in his seat, he regarded his companions. "Only one thing left to do."

Al-Khaled nodded. "Initiating scans."

"All systems reporting active," Anderson noted, pointing to one of the screens at his console. "Internal sensors at optimum, and the telemetry's already coming fast and furious. Look at it."

Returning his attention to his workstation, Xiong glanced over the various status gauges and graphics as the chamber's internal sensor feeds sprang to life. Three of his screens began to cascade data at a rate too fast for his eyes to follow, but the lieutenant knew everything they were seeing was being recorded and stored within the *Lovell*'s main computer. He would have plenty of time later to review the information they were collecting.

"Commander," O'Halloran called out, "I'm getting some unusual readings here."

"Prepare to power down," Marcus said.

"Stand by to abort," Xiong ordered, a split second after the doctor. As they exchanged knowing glances, the lieutenant wondered if the tension he felt mirrored whatever feelings of anxiety she might be experiencing. To her credit, Marcus appeared calm and controlled, though he noted the slight tightening of her jaw line as she kept her attention focused on the scene before her.

Shaking his head, O'Halloran said, "No, wait. This doesn't look threatening. It's just . . . *unusual*."

"Feel free to elaborate," al-Khaled said.

O'Halloran, already hunched over his console, frowned. "It's just that . . . okay, now there's nothing."

"What do you mean, nothing?" Xiong asked. "You're not receiving?"

"I *am* receiving," O'Halloran replied, "but the artifact seems completely unresponsive to any external stimuli. There's no signal wave response, no high-energy particles, no communications signal. Nothing."

"Is it dead?" Marcus asked. "Could the intensity of the scans have killed the Shedai inside the crystal?"

"No, Doctor," Anderson replied. "We're at least getting that much. It's still very much alive in there."

"And the scans are reaching it?" al-Khaled asked, frowning in confusion.

Leaning forward in his seat, Xiong pressed a sequence of controls that allowed him to scroll through the data collected during the past few moments. He noted that the sensor arrays recorded the scans' penetration of the artifact's crystal surface, and even their examination of whatever it was that lurked inside. The Shedai was, in essence, noncorporeal energy even though it had demonstrated the ability to assume physical form, particularly when angered. It also had shown a propensity for occupying and controlling physical objects of massive size and power, such as the beings that Xiong had encountered more than once.

"According to this," he said, "the scans are hitting it, as are the communications signals."

"Maybe it doesn't know how to respond?" Marcus said.

Reclining in his chair, Xiong released a small, tired sigh. "That, or maybe it just doesn't give a damn."

11

Something intruded upon the Shedai Wanderer's slumber and she awoke with a start, confused and irritated at the disruption. How long had she been sleeping? It seemed to her as though time had ceased to have any meaning within this gulf of energy in which she languished.

What was it? Reaching out with her consciousness, she listened for whatever unidentified presence had sought to make itself known to her. She was convinced it was an attempt at communication, though she was unable to locate its source. The signal, if indeed that was what she had detected, was brief and weak, though still sufficient to upset the energy fields contained within her crystal prison. What was the signal's origin, and what was its purpose? For a moment she considered offering some form of response, but restrained herself. The fields gripping her had sapped her strength, leaving her all but defenseless. Though the Wanderer loathed the very idea of refusing to stand before an enemy, the simple reality was that here, she held no power.

Her own anger and lack of discipline had brought her to this place, this pocket of existence fashioned specifically to contain those of her kind. There were tremendous energies in play here, and she knew they were not natural phenomena. It had not taken her long after becoming ensnared within these odd fields to discern the artificial nature of their ebbs and flows, a product of the crystal that contained such unbridled chaos. Who could possess the power to create such a construct? Could it possibly be a creation of some long-dead species of *Telinaruul*? She had, after some time and reflection, dismissed such an unlikely possibility, though she forced herself to admit that the particular parasites that she had confronted with increasing frequency prior to her capture had succeeded in surprising her during their past encounters. However, she attributed that more to their adaptability and innovation rather than any real power they might command. She might even find them amusing, if not for the nuisance and—yes—the threat they had become.

As for the enigmatic crystal that held her, the Wanderer had probed and examined her surroundings and found no flaw or other sign of vulnerability that might be exploited. Not that it mattered, as what little strength and abilities remained to her had proven insufficient for making any real escape attempt. Her every effort on that front had failed, leaving her even more weakened and frustrated. She was at the mercy of her captors, whoever they were and for however long they saw fit to keep her in this place.

Wait.

Again, something seemed to summon her from the depths of the rift that held her prisoner, and once more she listened. Unlike the previous call, this one carried with it an element of familiarity. It, like her, was Shedai, but older—much older—than the Wanderer herself.

Where are you? Who are you?

The other consciousness, which the Wanderer had detected for but the briefest of moments, was gone, but in that infinitesimal interval she had sensed its power. When she had attacked the *Telinaruul* and their fragile habitat, she had believed one of the ancient crystals in their possession to be harboring one of the enumerated—one of the *Serataal*. There had been no time to verify that before she had been taken captive. As the other mind she had sensed began to coalesce into existence a second time, she reached out with whatever feeble wisps of perception she still commanded. Now, there was a connection. It was faint, but there, and once again she detected the extreme age and greater power of the other mind. She also sensed something else. Anger? Exhaustion? Then, realization dawned. This other, unknown Shedai seemed to be undergoing the same stresses of captivity that the Wanderer currently endured. Focusing her mind, she stretched across the abyss separating her from this new presence, searching for a stronger link. Was the other entity too weak to respond, or simply unwilling? Was it enemy, or ally?

Then, the connection was broken and the other mind faded once more into the maelstrom of energies, returning the Wanderer to her prison of solitude.

No!

Once more, there was nothing for her to do but wait. All she could bring to bear was her patience while preserving her limited strength and watching for an opportunity to act. She was certain that, sooner or later, her captors would have to reveal themselves.

Whoever or whatever they were, the Wanderer would destroy them.

12

Thomas Blair stopped himself from trying to force the turbolift doors to open faster, willing himself to stand still until they parted enough for him to exit the car and step onto the *Defiant*'s bridge. The first thing he noted was that the entire room was bathed in the harsh crimson lights that signified a Red Alert status. In keeping with Blair's personal preferences, the audible alarm had been muted on the bridge as well as in turbolifts.

"Status report," he called out, nodding to Commander Mbugua as the first officer vacated the captain's chair. Rather than head for the center seat himself, Blair made his way around the upper bridge deck toward the science station.

"We're approaching the coordinates of the sensor contact," Mbugua replied, moving to stand in front of the helm and navigation consoles at the center of the bridge's command well. Leaning back against the joint console, the muscled officer crossed his arms and nodded toward the main viewscreen. "Whatever was happening here before, it's over."

"Anything new with the sensor contacts?" Blair asked as he stopped behind Lieutenant Commander Nyn at the science station.

Without turning from her workstation, the science officer replied, "Nothing active now, sir, though I'm still picking up residual energy readings from what look to be particle weapons, Klingon disruptors in particular, along with something that could be Tholian."

Blair frowned. "Could be?"

"It's hard to be sure, sir," Nyn said. "The Klingon energy

signatures are pretty easy to pick out, and the readings I'm seeing as Tholian aren't entirely consistent with what we have on record for the particle weapons normally installed aboard their ships."

Perching himself on the railing opposite her station, Blair positioned himself so that he could divide his attention between Nyn and the viewscreen. "What about the ships themselves? Did everybody just bug out of here?"

The science officer replied, "Hard to say, sir. The area's saturated with residual energy readings, making things tougher for long-range scans to make sense of it all. Whatever happened here, it at least included what looks to be one hell of a firefight, but if I had to guess? Whoever was doing the fighting is long gone, assuming their ship wasn't destroyed."

"But you're not sure," Blair said.

Nyn shook her head. "Not at all, sir."

"Which is why we're at Red Alert with shields up and weapons hot," Mbugua added.

Nodding in approval at his first officer's decisions and actions, Blair said, "Works for me. Restore normal bridge lighting, but let's leave everything else as is for the time being." He sighed. "Looks like we're showing up late to the party again." He had known that would probably be the case from the moment Nyn contacted him in his quarters to report her initial long-range sensor contacts of what she had described as a likely combat action taking place. The *Defiant* had been too far away for its scanning systems to record anything detailed, but Nyn still had acquired enough information to make an educated guess that Klingon and Tholian vessels looked to be taking part in the action. Her suspicions were only strengthened after Blair ordered a course change to investigate, since the fight—if indeed it was a fight—while taking place in an area of space that at present was not claimed by either the Klingons or the Tholians, was close enough to the Tholian border that the *Defiant*'s captain had to wonder whether the Klingons finally had rubbed someone the wrong way.

Blair's attention was caught by an alert tone coming from the helm, and he turned as Lieutenant T'Lehr looked up from her console and reported, "We will be in visual range in less than ninety seconds, Captain."

"Slow to impulse," Blair ordered, rising from his perch on the red railing and stepping down into the command well to take his place in the center seat. Beneath his feet, he felt the reverberation in the deck plates as the *Defiant* dropped out of warp and the starship's powerful impulse engines took over.

A string of indicator tones sounded from Nyn's workstation, and the science officer turned to regard Blair, "Captain, I'm picking up four distinct signatures, all consistent with Tholian propulsion systems, heading away from this location on a direct course for their border."

"Maintain alert status," Mbugua said, as he moved from in front of the helm and took up a position to Blair's left. "Just in case they decided to double back, or they have friends out there somewhere."

Her attention once more on her console, Nyn called over her shoulder, "Definitely picking up traces of at least one vessel now, probably two. Configuration doesn't look right, but the metallurgy suggests Klingon construction."

"Let's have it on screen, Nyn," Blair ordered. As the image on the main viewscreen shifted, he saw a pair of indistinct shapes that might have been space vessels, though their silhouettes did not look familiar. At least, not at first.

"What the hell?" Blair asked, more to himself than anyone else as he pushed himself out of his chair. "Magnify that." An instant later, the image shifted to bring the unidentified objects into sharp relief, and the captain could not help the gasp of surprise that escaped his lips.

"Oh my god," Mbugua said, his voice low enough that Blair almost did not hear him. "Those are supposed to be . . . *Klingon ships?*"

Turning from her station, Nyn said, "According to our sensors, that's what they *were,* sir."

The pair of derelicts drifted in an expanding cloud of debris, one wreck tumbling end over end while the other was trapped in an endless roll. Despite the incredible damage inflicted upon the pair of vessels, Blair was able to make out the crushed shell of what had been the primary hull of one Klingon battle cruiser, its distinctive bulb-shape design still recognizable despite massive buckling and a number of missing hull plates. He was able to identify the other ship by the shape of one of its warp nacelles and the section of secondary hull still attached to it and bearing the bold trefoil of the Klingon military. There was very little beyond that to distinguish either vessel, which to Blair looked more like oversized fusions of scrap metal than spacefaring ships of any kind.

"What happened to them?" Blair asked, his gaze still transfixed by the ghastly image on the viewscreen. "Some kind of collision? Maybe an internal explosion?" Even as he posed the questions he knew that those were not valid explanations. Neither event was consistent with the type of destruction now on display before him, and it was an opinion that was only strengthened by his science officer.

Nyn replied, "I'm not detecting any residual energy traces that would be consistent with an engine overload, sir. Besides, given their proximity, if either of the ships' warp cores had breached, the resultant matter/antimatter explosion would have been more than sufficient to vaporize both vessels."

"What about collision?" Mbugua asked. "As crazy as I know it sounds, could this be the result of some kind of huge accident?"

Again, Nyn shook her head. "Doubtful, Commander. Such an event would require extreme neglect not only on the part of each vessel's helm officer, but also in automatic evasion protocols and the ships' deflector and shield systems." She paused, nodding her head in the direction of her workstation. "There's also one other thing, thanks to the computer having more time to chew on the sensor data we've been collecting. According to the readings I'm getting, something looks to have crushed the hulls of these ships. Stress fractures and buckling all along both vessels' spaceframes indicate a massive force enveloping the entire ship and drawing inward. It's almost as if they were squeezed by a giant vise."

"Or the hand of a god," Mbugua muttered, and it was only when he noticed Blair looking at him that he seemed to realize he had spoken the comment aloud. Clearing his throat, the first officer added, "Sorry, Skipper. It's just that Nyn's description made me think of a report I read last year, about the *Enterprise* encountering an alien who once passed himself off as one of the Greek gods on ancient Earth. He stopped the *Enterprise* dead in space with an energy field shaped to resemble a giant hand."

Blair nodded, recalling the report, one of many odd mission logs recorded by the *Enterprise*'s current commanding officer, James Kirk. "Commander Nyn, please don't tell me we're dealing with something like that here."

"I don't think so, sir," the science officer replied, unable to keep the hint of a smile from playing at the corners of her mouth. "For one thing, the energy signatures our sensors are picking up didn't match against anything on file in the computer banks, which would include anything the *Enterprise* scanners recorded during its encounter with . . . whatever that was supposed to be."

"Well," Mbugua said, "I suppose we can give thanks for small favors, then."

Nyn answered, "That might be the end of the good news, sir." She gestured to the array of eight status monitors positioned above her console, then waited until Blair and Mbugua returned to stand behind her before pointing to one of the monitors. "While the residual energy readings I'm finding here don't match anything exactly, there's still a hint of something similar to Tholian energy weapons."

"How could a Tholian vessel do that?" Blair asked, waving toward the viewscreen. "Everything we know about their ships tells us they're outmatched by Klingon D7s, as well as our *Constitution*-class ships. The only way they have a chance in a stand-up fight is if they bring enough ships to the fight in the first place." He had read the report of the *U.S.S. Bombay*'s destruction more than three years ago at the hands of six Tholian ships. The enemy vessels had employed their greater numbers and maneuverability to overcome the Starfleet ship's greater size and more powerful weapons. They had inflicted sufficient damage that the *Bombay*'s captain, Hallie Gannon, had ordered the ship's destruction in a last-ditch attempt to take some of her ship's attackers with it.

Mbugua said, "Maybe it's a new weapon—something they've managed to keep secret from us. If the Tholians excel at anything, it's playing their cards close to their vest."

"Well, we know they've got some of the best poker faces around, at any rate," Blair replied, punctuating his indiscreet observation with a humorless chuckle. "Okay, enough of that. Nyn, prep a briefing packet for Admiral Nogura and his intelligence people back on Vanguard. Include all of your relevant sensor data about the energy readings. Let's see if they can't connect some of these new dots."

Turning from the science station, Blair made his way around the bridge until he stood in front of the main viewscreen. He shook his head as he took in the sight of the destroyed Klingon ships, marveling at the power it must have taken to inflict such damage on the vessels. What might such a weapon, whatever it was and however it might work, do to the *Defiant*?

Not that I'm in any hurry to find out.

One thing Blair knew—and it was a fact that definitely would be playing into the ever-evolving and always fragile nature of the Taurus Reach's interstellar diplomatic situation—was that the Tholians appeared to have had quite enough of the Klingons or anyone else pushing them around. Certainly the Klingons would argue that any tolerance the Tholians had shown in the past would seem to be coming to an end. Might the simmering yet still deteriorating relations between the two powers finally be coming to a full boil? Sooner or later, the Federation would be forced to act, if for no other reason than to protect its own interests.

Blair sighed, knowing that when the time for such action finally came, it probably would not be good for anyone involved.

I wonder if it's too late to retire?

13

Feeling more than a bit exposed, Diego Reyes tried not to look too curious or nervous about the number of patrons inhabiting the bar of the *Omari-Ekon*'s gaming deck. Though the ship had its slack periods—so far as visitors to its casino, bar, and even its bordello were concerned—it was never truly empty of passengers and other guests, even at this hour in the middle of the day.

"Are you sure this is going to work?" he whispered, covering the act of speaking by rubbing his nose and trying to move his mouth as little as possible. The deception was easy to carry off, mostly due to the noxious odor of cigar smoke coming from a portly Tellarite sitting in an adjacent booth.

Thanks to the subcutaneous transceiver supplied to him by Doctor Fisher, he heard T'Prynn's voice in his mind as she replied, *"Given the nature of your current environment, this is our best option for making a covert entry into the* Omari-Ekon's *central computer in order to gain access to the ship's navigational logs."*

"But you didn't say whether you thought it was going to work," Reyes said as he regarded the gaming console set into the table at which he sat in one of the booths along the bar's rear wall. Like most of the other tables, the system before him allowed a customer to play computerized versions of the various games of chance available in the *Omari-Ekon*'s casino, either alone against the computer's simulated dealer or against players sitting at other stations in the bar. The interface was a simple, graphics-driven affair that allowed some customization with respect to presentation, such as the player's native language. "I don't see how playing blackjack is going to help us here."

"*I have created a method of infiltrating the central computer via the gaming subsystems,*" T'Prynn replied. "*A shell program will be running at the same time, providing cover for your activities and appearing to anyone who might be remotely monitoring you that you are simply partaking of one of the games.*"

This entire scheme had been of T'Prynn's devising. Reyes knew that attempting to access any of the regular computer terminals aboard ship carried far too much risk, and using the terminal in his quarters for anything short of ordering room service was suicide. Ganz had him under almost constant surveillance, affording Reyes little privacy. What T'Prynn had proposed—accessing the Orion vessel's computer system via an otherwise innocuous entry point in full view of anyone and everyone in the *Omari-Ekon*'s bar—was just brash enough to work, Reyes decided, provided he did not do anything to attract unwanted attention.

Wonder if T'Prynn's computed the odds of that *happening?*

"I suppose this is as good a time as any to say that I don't read or speak Orion," he said after a moment.

T'Prynn replied, "*There is no one single Orion language, Mister Reyes, but that should not present a problem. The gaming interface we will be exploiting contains an automated translation matrix, in order to provide patrons with simulations in their native language. It is my intention to utilize this feature as we transfer to other parts of the system.*"

Her use of "Mister" when addressing him bothered Reyes, though he knew it was not anything the Vulcan was doing as a deliberate attempt to insult him. Her professional demeanor and sense of decorum required her to refer to him in nothing less than a formal manner. Still, every time he heard the title it only served to remind him of what he had lost—what he had given up, and what had been taken from him. He harbored no ill feelings for anyone with respect to the decisions he had made and the actions he had taken which had brought him to this point, and held no one accountable save himself. That included the person now acting as his guide and perhaps even his guardian angel of sorts.

"T'Prynn," he said, making a show of scanning the selection of games offered by the tabletop console, "I'm glad you're okay. I've heard bits and pieces about what you went through, and I know how much that had to be affecting you while you were working for me. I'm sorry I couldn't do more to help." Tim Pennington had offered him some of the details regarding his journey with Doctor Jabilo M'Benga and the comatose Vulcan to her home planet, where she had been treated for her neurological issues. M'Benga had later received orders assigning him to starship duty as the assistant chief medical officer aboard the *U.S.S. Enterprise*, whereas Pennington had accompanied T'Prynn on what could only be described as a circuitous voyage back to Vanguard. It was during that journey that the former intelligence officer, operating on her own, had determined Reyes's status as a "guest" of the Klingons aboard the *I.K.S. Zin'za*, and had relayed that information to Starbase 47, perhaps even setting into motion the events that had brought him here, working with her.

"No apologies are necessary, Mister Reyes," T'Prynn said. *"Your detention and subsequent confinement while awaiting court-martial made you unable to render any assistance, not that there was anything you could have done. Ultimately, the course of action taken by Doctor M'Benga was the only means of treating my condition."*

Clearing his throat as he made a surreptitious visual scan of the bar to ensure no one at least appeared to be paying him undue attention, Reyes said, "Well, I guess I meant before all of that happened. I understand you felt you had to keep your condition a secret, and I can't imagine what it must have been like to carry the burden you endured all those years."

"I understand and appreciate the emotional sentiment you are attempting to convey," T'Prynn replied, *"but rest assured that there is nothing for which you need to apologize. The mental trauma I suffered is no longer an issue, and I have been held to account for concealing my condition as well as the illegal actions I took while acting as your intelligence officer. Those events are in the past, and my only desire is to carry out my du-*

ties, which now include completing a mission that could prove very dangerous. I would prefer to concentrate on that for the moment."

Seeing her point and agreeing with it, Reyes started to reply, but checked himself when one of the bar's exotic and rather scantily clad servers chose that moment to approach his table. Though she was Orion and quite beautiful, Reyes did not for one moment believe that she was a lowly employee—not when she eyed him with an openly solicitous expression, and certainly not when she bent forward and allowed him an unfettered view of her ample cleavage.

"Something to drink?" she asked, her tone soft and alluring.

Nodding, Reyes said, "I'll have a brandy, whatever brand you recommend." In actuality, he had no real desire for the drink, but had decided that acting as much like a regular bar patron as possible would only help to mask his deception.

The server smiled at that. "Are you sure? Some of the labels are rather expensive."

"I've been lucky at the tables," Reyes replied, forcing a grin. "So, I figure why not celebrate a little?"

His answer seemed to please the Orion even further, as she leaned closer and lowered her voice almost to a whisper. "Well, if you're looking to spoil yourself, I think I can help with that. Of course, I'm rather expensive, too."

T'Prynn's voice rang in his head. *"The server is undoubtedly a spy working for Ganz."*

"I don't doubt it," Reyes said, smiling again for the Orion's benefit. "Let's just start with the drink, and see where things go from there."

Affecting a mock pout, the Orion pursed her lips. "Well, if that's the way you want to play it. I can be patient, but not for *too* long." When she turned to leave, presumably to fetch his drink, she made a show of swinging her hips as she headed toward the bar, and punctuated the less than subtle invitation with a seductive glance over her shoulder.

"Though I cannot hear what anyone is saying to you,"

T'Prynn said, "*I can infer meanings based on your half of a given conversation. Beware that the myriad ways in which Ganz and Neera will seek to extract information from you know no bounds, Mister Reyes.*"

Reyes grunted in agreement. "You have no idea." During his stay aboard the *Omari-Ekon,* he had been confronted with all manner of attempts by various persons looking to befriend him or even to engage him in simple conversation. Someone might get chatty while sitting in an adjacent seat at one of the gaming tables, or while waiting at the bar for a drink or browsing in one of the shops on the merchant vessel's small yet well-appointed esplanade. Then there were the women, of course, no doubt aimed at him by Neera, Ganz's employer. Seeing through most of these attempts was easy enough, but there was the occasional sly effort that almost succeeded in catching him off guard. Though he kept almost everyone at the proverbial arm's length just as a matter of general principle, Reyes had decided the best approach was simply to treat anyone he encountered aboard Ganz's ship as a spy or other threat. In that regard, he had been most grateful when familiar faces like Tim Pennington and Zeke Fisher had found reasons to come aboard, just as he now appreciated the welcome voice of T'Prynn.

"Listen," he said after a moment, "can we get on with this? I feel naked out here." He began tapping selections on the gaming console, calling up an Orion variant of poker he had come to enjoy during his stay aboard ship. "I don't know how long I can sit here before someone starts getting suspicious."

"*Understood,*" T'Prynn replied. "*Insert your credit chip into the console's payment slot, and stand by.*" Reyes occupied his time by playing a poker hand dealt to him by the gaming program's computer-directed dealer, which he lost. As he watched his credit account reduced by the amount of his wager, he noted the screen's graphics shift for the slightest of moments before returning to normal.

"Was that you?"

"*Affirmative. I have forged a connection with the* Omari-

Ekon's *subnet. From here, I will be able to remotely monitor your actions and guide you accordingly."*

Frowning at the explanation, Reyes said, "I don't understand. If you can see what I'm doing, why can't you access the logs directly?"

"Such activity likely would trigger security alerts," T'Prynn said. *"So far, my actions have not been detected, but there may well be protective measures in place of which I am unaware."*

"Well, that's encouraging," Reyes said, looking once more about the bar. If T'Prynn was right and there were other, more covert monitoring schemes in place to detect any unauthorized access to the *Omari-Ekon's* central computer system, he figured his life expectancy after being discovered would be measured in minutes. The only real question was whether Ganz would have his people exercise any modicum of discretion and have Reyes removed from public view before his execution, or simply shoot him on sight.

Suddenly, that drink he had ordered was sounding pretty good.

"I am ready to proceed," T'Prynn said a moment later. *"Press the controls that allow you to place a wager."*

Without answering, Reyes did as instructed and entered a bet for the next poker hand. In the screen's lower left corner, a new window appeared. Unlike the rest of the screen, it contained only a prompt and a blinking cursor. He was able to hide that portion of the screen from casual view by resting his left arm on the table. "Okay, now what?"

"Using the manual interface," T'Prynn replied, *"enter the following command string."* She began reciting a sequence of seven alphanumeric characters, which Reyes typed using one finger on the gaming console's touch-screen keyboard he had already configured for Federation Standard. T'Prynn followed with three more such codes, though at her direction Reyes paused between entering each one, in the hopes of maintaining the illusion that his interaction with the console was for nothing more than playing a game.

By the time the fourth string of characters was entered, Reyes could feel sweat beneath his arms and down his back, and his anxiety only worsened when he detected movement to his left and looked up to see the Orion server once more approaching his table. She was carrying a tray on which sat a glass of dark liquid, which she set down on the table before him. Doing his best to present a casual demeanor, Reyes smiled as he rested his left forearm across the table, concealing most of the gaming console's screen.

"Will there be anything else?" she asked, leering at him.

Shrugging, Reyes replied, "I'm thinking about dinner. Check back with me in a few minutes, after I have another look at the menu."

In response, the Orion bent closer to him and whispered in his ear, "The best selections aren't on the menu, you know."

Despite himself, Reyes could not help clearing his throat as he once more forced a smile. "Well, that's certainly something to think about."

When the server left to see to other customers, Reyes blinked and exhaled audibly. The effects of Orion women on male humanoids were legendary, but certainly not fictitious. It had been a concern of his since first stepping aboard Ganz's vessel, knowing that the merchant prince would use every means at his disposal to trip him up and force him to reveal valuable information or otherwise compromise himself. The women were part of that equation, and while he figured a few of the solicitation attempts he had received were no more than those extended to other patrons of the *Omari-Ekon*'s various "services," he was certain Ganz and Neera were behind most of the attention being paid to him. For all he knew, his server was at this moment reporting to a superior whatever she might have seen or overheard while at or near his table.

Moving his arm, he noted that a series of messages now appeared on the screen's inset window. The text was some variant of written Orion—he could not identify the variant—and none of it made any sense to him. "Are you seeing this?"

"*Yes,*" T'Prynn replied. "*It is a standard message for accessing the subnet. We have exited the gaming subsystem and are now in a direct path to the central computer, using a utility program normally used by software technicians for maintenance purposes. Such programs are not normally subjected to intense scrutiny, due to their very nature and the need to have full access to the computer's operating system and application software.*"

The last thing Reyes needed at the moment was a computer technology lecture. Sighing, he reached for his drink and was ready to down a large swallow when he stopped himself. Paranoia was starting to kick in, and he wondered if the glass in his hand might contain something other than brandy.

"Okay, I'm really wanting to get out of here now," he said, placing the drink back on the table. Following T'Prynn's instructions, Reyes entered another string of commands and watched as a block of indecipherable text began to scroll within the small window. Unlike the first set of data, he was not certain what he now saw was even rendered in Orion text. "What is that?"

"*I do not know,*" T'Prynn replied.

His feelings of anxiety beginning to escalate, Reyes tried to appear casual as he cast another furtive glance about the bar. "What do you mean, you don't know?" he asked, catching himself as he realized he had vocalized the question at a volume slightly louder than the whisper he had been using. It was all but impossible to shake the nagging sensation that everyone in the room was watching him and knew exactly what he was doing. He forced himself to remain seated at his table when every instinct was screaming at him to run. For a moment, he imagined a hot ache between his shoulder blades, as though someone were aiming a disruptor at his back, and tried to convince himself that the heavy boots he heard thudding against the deck did not belong to one of Ganz's goons, marching their way toward him.

Her voice retaining its usual calm, quiet, and controlled tone, T'Prynn said, "*We have entered an area of the system which appears to be using some form of language override protocols for its user interfaces. Standard translation subroutines are being rendered ineffective, and the native language being employed is not one I recognize.*"

"Can you run it through the universal translation program on the station's computer?" Reyes asked.

"*I can,*" the Vulcan replied, "*but not directly. I have copied some of the information to my workstation and I am having it analyzed. It looks to be an obscure Orion dialect which has fallen out of common use. According to the library computer, it was utilized between three and four hundred years ago, mostly by a sect of Orion migrants who founded a colony in the—*"

Reyes grunted in growing irritation. "I don't care, T'Prynn. What can you do about translating it so we can get on with this?" As an additional protective measure complementing the computer system's existing security protocols, the language trick was elegant in its simplicity. Reyes did not figure on Ganz possessing the level of ingenuity needed to put such a scheme into play. Neera was likely the culprit.

"*At this time? Nothing,*" T'Prynn said. "*It would take too long for me to translate the information we access in this manner so that I can guide you through each successive step of the operation. What is required is a real-time translation protocol which you can use directly.*"

"You've got to be kidding," Reyes hissed, his feelings of exposure mounting with each passing moment. "Are you saying all of this was a waste of time?"

T'Prynn replied, "*Our efforts have yielded important information with regard to the* Omari-Ekon'*s computer security features. This will aid in refining our infiltration strategy and better enable us to conceal our presence in the system.*"

"What the hell is this all about, T'Prynn?" he asked. "What's so damned important that we have to jump through these hoops?"

"*I cannot elaborate as to the nature of the data,*" the Vulcan replied, "*but I can tell you that it involves the Shedai, and locat-*"

ing a world which might possess technology capable of defeating them. We believe Ganz's ship, or a ship in his employ, either traveled to this world or obtained artifacts from it."

"The orb," Reyes whispered.

T'Prynn said, *"That is correct. So, you should now understand the delicate and pressing nature of our assignment."*

Following her instructions, Reyes backed out of the system subnet, terminating the interface and returning the gaming console to its normal state. For good measure, he placed a bet and forced himself to play two hands of poker without acknowledging T'Prynn's queries, in full view of anyone who happened past his table. Satisfied that no one was going to walk up and jam the muzzle of a disruptor in his face, he closed out the gaming session and reached for the drink he had almost forgotten. He eyed the liquid and weighed his chances of surviving whatever toxic substance might have been added to the brandy.

Take your best shot, Ganz, he mused before tossing back his head and downing the drink in a single swallow. He relished the burn of the brandy as it made its way down his throat, grunting in momentary satisfaction as the liquid hit his stomach. If he was going to die, there certainly were worse ways to go.

"Mister Reyes," T'Prynn called, for the eighth or ninth time.

"Listen," he said as he placed the now empty glass on the table, "given the likelihood that I'll be dead by this time tomorrow, why don't you just call me Diego?"

There was a brief pause before the intelligence officer replied, *"Diego, my scans indicate that our efforts escaped detection."*

"Lucky us," Reyes said. "Now what?" He figured that whatever T'Prynn was planning as a countermeasure to the security they had detected in the system would require time to implement before they could attempt another covert access of the *Omari-Ekon*'s computer. This assumed, of course, that such a scheme could be devised at all.

It may have been his imagination, but Reyes swore he heard the indecision in the Vulcan's voice when she offered her answer.

"Stand by. I will contact you shortly."

14

Standing before the large viewscreen that dominated his office's port-side bulkhead, Admiral Nogura studied the image of open space presented to him. Doing so had always served to relax him, as he was able to lose himself—if only for a moment—amid the immense, absolute wonder that was the universe. How many stars were visible just in his field of vision at this exact moment, and how many of them had already died out, millions of years before their light reached him? Beholding such a vista never failed to remind Nogura just how insignificant he was in the grand scheme of all that surrounded him, and yet it also never ceased to energize him as he considered its vast, untapped potential. In the centuries to come, the boundaries of knowledge would push outward to encompass those stars, and still others beyond them, and what would be found? The very question filled Nogura with yearning, and even a small bit of envy for those who would be making such journeys long after he was gone.

That said, I plan to be here for at least a while longer.

Turning to face his visitors, Nogura indicated the viewscreen with a gesture. "Do you know what this place needs? A window. Viewscreens are nice, but I like looking out the real thing."

Seated in the two chairs positioned before the admiral's desk, Commander ch'Nayla said nothing, whereas Lieutenant T'Prynn regarded Nogura with a cocked eyebrow.

"A viewscreen affords you many options that a window cannot provide."

Despite the serious nature of the meeting for which the trio had assembled, Nogura regarded the Vulcan with mild amusement. "It's just not the same, T'Prynn." While it was true that the screen could be configured to display an image at any angle as supplied by the station's external sensor array, Nogura had grown accustomed to the large window at the rear of his offices on Earth. One of his habits—time and circumstances permitting, of course—had been to sit before that window, sipping from a cup of his favorite herbal tea, and look across San Francisco Bay and out toward the Pacific Ocean, watching as the sun, framed by the Golden Gate Bridge, slipped below the horizon. It was the perfect complement to the other half of his daily ritual, when he greeted sunrise from the porch of his mountaintop home in the Colorado Rockies and observed a small interval of tranquillity before transporting to Starfleet Headquarters to face whatever duties, tasks, and demands awaited him. Since arriving at Starbase 47, he had made do with the simulated dawn and dusk as presented within the terrestrial enclosure that occupied a significant portion of the station's primary hull and offered Vanguard's residents an illusion of being on a planet. It was a serviceable substitute, but it did not diminish his desire to return home one day.

One day, Nogura mused, *but not today.*

Making his way to the rear of his office, the admiral moved to the food slot set into the wall behind his desk. He retrieved one of the half-dozen data cards held in a small alcove next to the slot and inserted it into the reader below the device's door before pressing three of the unit's selection keys in a predetermined sequence. While he waited for the computer to process his order, he turned to ch'Nayla and T'Prynn. "I take it from your lack of a status report from Mister Reyes that you've encountered some difficulty accessing the *Omari-Ekon*'s navigation logs?"

"That's correct, Admiral," T'Prynn replied. Nogura retrieved and held his tea, waiting for it to cool a bit, as the Vulcan recounted the first attempt to infiltrate the Orion vessel's computer system, along with the current obstacles preventing her and Diego Reyes from extracting the required data.

"Using an outmoded variation of one of the older Orion languages is a simple yet effective security measure. While our computer's translation protocols are sufficient to render the proper conversions, doing so via a remote connection between the *Omari-Ekon* and the station would increase the likelihood of our infiltration being detected."

Nodding in understanding, Nogura moved to the chair behind his desk and sat. "But you're sure that neither your nor Mister Reyes's activities were discovered?"

Commander ch'Nayla replied, "Not so far as we can tell, Admiral. A scan of the computer system while the link was established picked up no traces of monitoring. No alerts were issued, and civilian spotters aboard the *Omari-Ekon* report that Mister Reyes has not been approached or subjected to any unusual scrutiny."

"Well," Nogura said as he held his cup to his nose and savored the tea's faint, soothing aroma, "no more than was already in place, at any rate." He paused to sip from the tea before asking, "All right, so a direct connection from here is out of the question. What other options are available to us?"

T'Prynn looked to ch'Nayla as though seeking approval before answering, "The option with the least amount of variables from a security standpoint is to provide Mister Reyes with a translation device which can be interfaced with the *Omari-Ekon*'s central computer. Once engaged, he will have the freedom to navigate the system and retrieve the information we seek."

Clearing his throat, Nogura said, "And do so without tripping any of those alerts and alarms you've so far managed to avoid. I'm going to hazard a guess that such an item can't be obtained from the station quartermaster."

"No, sir," ch'Nayla replied. "We would have to program the device for this specific task, using the information we've gathered about the *Omari-Ekon*'s computer system."

"Even with such preparation," T'Prynn added, "there remains a risk of detection, as we might still trigger a security protocol of which we are not yet aware."

Nogura could not help offering a small chuckle. "Those are

the best kind, Lieutenant." Not for the first time, the admiral was beginning to question the wisdom of undertaking this risky bit of espionage. While the importance of the data locked in the Orion vessel's navigation system could not be ignored, was there no other way to obtain it without resorting to these sorts of clandestine schemes? Although he understood the necessity for conducting such operations, Nogura had always preferred a more direct approach to solving problems of this type. Given time, he was certain he could find something—some price—that Ganz or even his superior, Neera, would be willing to accept in exchange for the information he sought. The problem with such an aboveboard tactic was that it required Nogura to trust the Orions, which was something he had no intention of doing. "Okay, so you're going to prepare something for Reyes to use. What then?"

"As before," T'Prynn replied, "I will guide Mister Reyes through another infiltration of the system. With the translation device in place, doing so should facilitate our efforts and allow us to retrieve the data in short order."

Already envisioning the worst-case scenario should Reyes be found out by any of Ganz's men, Nogura sighed. "And you're sure this is the best option available to us?"

T'Prynn nodded. "It is if we wish to obtain the navigational data quickly, sir."

"And we do," the admiral conceded. Locating the possible origin point for the Mirdonyae Artifact Ganz had surrendered to Nogura in exchange for Starfleet's continued good favor was of paramount importance, if for no other reason than to ensure no one else—the Klingons, Tholians, Romulans, or even some other as yet unnamed power who might get curious—found it first. So far, the Shedai who had so rudely been awakened from their millennia-long sleep had seemed content to lay dormant in whatever celestial hideaway they had fashioned for themselves. They had inflicted colossal damage and destruction before their mysterious disappearance, along with the destruction of the entire Jinoteur system, which apparently was their home. Considering what they might do if roused once again was something that had cost Nogura more than one night's sound sleep. If the displays of the ancient race's power he had witnessed were any indication, such as when the Shedai entity had attacked the station, a concentrated assault—even by as few as two or three of the beings— likely would prove disastrous for the confronted party.

Shaking his head, Nogura said, "I have to wonder how much longer we can keep sticking fingers in this particular dam and hope it continues to hold." Though Starfleet had done an admirable job containing the most sensitive aspects of the mysteries surrounding the Shedai and the Taurus Meta-Genome, some information had already become public. Even the explosive news features written by Tim Pennington for the Federation News Service—and whose authorization for release by Diego Reyes had ended the man's Starfleet career—had been limited in the amount of damage they had caused. The journalist's lack of direct knowledge about the meta-genome and the potential it carried had prevented any revelation of the Shedai's true origins, or any detailed insight into the awesome power they commanded.

How much longer could Starfleet hope to keep this information hidden? The Klingons, though lacking in-depth knowledge as to the true nature of the meta-genome, still had acquired sufficient information about the Shedai and their technology that they too sought artifacts or weapons for their own use. According to the latest intelligence reports, the Romulans, while understandably interested in the concentrated Federation activities in this part of space, appeared to harbor no direct information about the Shedai. As for the Tholians, there was no way to know what knowledge they possessed, or wanted to possess. Whatever public face the reticent, xenophobic race deigned to present to its interstellar neighbors offered no clues to their real agenda. The discovery that the Tholians were genetically linked to the Shedai and that their ancestors once had been slaves to the immensely powerful civilization had served only to make them withdraw further. Their isolationism was only intensified by the nightmarish possibility of the Shedai returning and using their influence to once more subjugate the Tholians, along with anyone else who stood in their way. Despite any token diplomatic overtures the Assembly might put forth, Nogura held no illusions that the Tholians would soon forgive the Federation for the strife it had unwittingly provoked when it stumbled into this part of space and disturbed the sleeping giant that was the Shedai.

"I am aware of efforts which have been under way for some time to perhaps secure possible allies in the event it becomes necessary to defend against a Shedai offensive," T'Prynn said. "Has there been any progress made in that regard?"

At first, Nogura said nothing. Following her court-martial, the Vulcan had been reduced two steps in rank and her security clearance had been downgraded so that she no longer had access to the volumes of sensitive intelligence information pertaining not only to Operation Vanguard but also to any number of classified subjects. Limiting her ability to obtain such information did nothing to erase the knowledge she already possessed, of course, nor could it prevent her from extrapolating any developments arising from the continued use and updating of that information as various operations continued.

One such effort involved those few persons in the Starfleet command hierarchy who possessed full knowledge of Operation Vanguard and the truth behind the Shedai and the Taurus Reach. At the behest of Diego Reyes while he was still in command of Starbase 47, those individuals had formed a small, top-secret task force with a single objective: sifting through and analyzing information from myriad sources in the hope of finding something that might prove useful in the event a battle with the Shedai seemed inevitable. Records from first-contact missions with advanced cultures, reports of any weapons or other artifacts found on planets that might once have been home to a civilization with a high level of technological advancement—all of it was being scrutinized. While starships on extended exploration missions had come across any number of societies that were on a par with or below that of the Federation, it was only on rare occasions that a civilization possessing superior technology was encountered.

In several of those instances, the meetings had been less than peaceful, although those cases were exceptions.

Reaching for a data slate on his desk, Nogura held it up for T'Prynn and ch'Nayla's benefit. "There hasn't been the kind of progress we'd all like to hear about," he said, "though every so often a promising lead presents itself. For example, I was just reading this report of the *Enterprise*'s mission to make contact with the Melkotian homeworld. Bit of a rocky start there, but Captain Kirk was able to open a dialogue with Melkot's leadership."

"Their level of technology is more advanced than ours in some areas," ch'Nayla added, "and the captain's report states that they're also extremely powerful telepaths."

Nogura nodded. "It's very possible they might have a trick or two up their sleeve that could come in handy."

Her right eyebrow cocking again, T'Prynn said, "I have read the report in question, Admiral, and according to the descriptions included in Captain Kirk's brief, the Melkotians possess no extremities on their upper bodies."

Vulcans, Nogura reminded himself. "T'Prynn . . ." he began.

"I apologize, Admiral," the lieutenant said. "I was under the impression that this was the point in our conversation in which a humorous observation might be welcomed, as a means of defusing any stress or discomfort generated by discussions involving unpleasant topics."

There was no stopping the chuckle that provoked, and Nogura leaned back in his chair, allowing himself to set aside, if only for a moment, the weight of responsibility and the current issues on his table. "Well played, Lieutenant." After another moment, he returned his attention to the matters at hand. "All right, back to business. Reyes: your first shot at having him hack the *Omari-Ekon*'s computer was rather bold on your part. I'm amazed he wasn't caught, trying that out in the open like he did, and it seems naïve to think you'd have that kind of luck again."

"Agreed," T'Prynn replied. "To that end, I have examined a technical schematic of the *Omari-Ekon* and have selected four possible locations for accessing the computer while still affording Mister Reyes some measure of privacy."

Nogura was not sure he liked the implications of that. "To me, that sounds very much like something that could get Reyes killed if he's discovered."

"There's certainly a risk," ch'Nayla said, shifting in his seat, "but we believe that with the translator device to assist him, Reyes will have an easier time accessing and navigating the computer system, and the actual time spent performing the data retrieval task should be much less than had he proceeded according to the original plan."

Seeing no other viable, timely alternative, Nogura nodded his approval of the plan. "Let's hope so, and let's hope he doesn't get caught this time." There had already been enough good fortune expended to this point with respect to Diego Reyes, as evidenced by the fact that he was still alive. Believing that condition to be anything but temporary was foolhardy, Nogura knew, just as he knew that, for the moment, there was precious little he could do to affect the situation.

Of course, if it all goes bad, he reminded himself, *you'll have plenty to do.*

15

Reyes sensed he was not alone in his quarters the instant he stepped into the room.

Waiting until the door slid closed behind him and without looking, he pivoted to his left and ducked his head, driving forward with his left shoulder until he collided with the person lurking against the bulkhead just inside the door. His action caught his unknown visitor in the chest, and Reyes heard a grunt of surprise at the sudden action. No sooner did he connect with his shoulder than he lashed out with his arm, looking to land a strike with the edge of his hand against the intruder's face. He was fast, but the other person was faster, and Reyes felt his arm's motion arrested as a tight, unforgiving grip closed around his wrist. Trying to pull back, Reyes got his first good look at the intruder, who was dressed in beige coveralls and appeared to be slight of build, and he realized he was facing off against a human female.

What the hell? It was all he had time to think as he felt another pair of arms wrap around him and lift him off his feet in order to pull him away from his opponent. Whoever it was, he also was human, with muscled arms partially exposed thanks to beige sleeves rolled to a point just below the elbow. Reyes tried to squirm free or at least loosen the new attacker's grip, but the effort was fruitless. He managed to kick his holder's shin, eliciting another grunt of pain, though the grip on him did not weaken.

"Commodore Reyes!"

Hearing his name and former rank caught him off guard, and Reyes jerked his head around to regard the first intruder, who was stepping closer to him. She looked to be in her late twenties or perhaps early thirties, with short brown hair and dark brown eyes. The woman held up her hand, open and empty, while the other pressed against her chest where Reyes had struck her.

"Commodore Reyes," she repeated. At the same time Reyes felt the arms around his chest release him, and he dropped several centimeters to the deck. "It's okay. You're safe."

"Who the hell are you?" Reyes growled, reaching up to rub his left shoulder where it still stung from his earlier actions. "Room service?"

Shaking her head, the woman replied, "No, sir. Lieutenant Mary Jane Hetzlein." She gestured over Reyes's shoulder. "My valet is Chief Petty Officer Joe Gianetti. We're part of Starbase 47's security detail. Lieutenant Jackson sent us."

Reyes turned to regard the other man, whose hair was black and shorter than Hetzlein's. The man held up his hands in a gesture of surrender.

"Sorry for the rough treatment, Commodore," Gianetti said.

Waving away the apology, Reyes snapped, "I'm not a damned commodore anymore. Is Jackson out of his mind, sending you over here? Are you *trying* to ignite an interstellar incident with the Orions?" He wondered about Ganz's first reaction should he or any of his people get wind of the presence of Starfleet personnel sneaking around his ship. Would he start the process of covering his tracks or hiding whatever needed to be hidden or destroyed, or would he jump straight to the part where Reyes and his two visitors ended up somewhere with the muzzles of disruptor pistols jammed in their mouths?

"I don't know all the details," Hetzlein said, reaching up to wipe her brow, "but Lieutenant Jackson told us he was operating with direct authority from Starfleet Command. Our orders are to extradite you back to the station, by any means necessary."

Reyes frowned. "Well, then you have a problem, Lieutenant, because I'm not going anywhere."

"Jackson warned us that'd be your answer, sir," Hetzlein replied, "which is why he added that 'by any means necessary' bit at the end."

Shaking his head, Reyes said, "You realize I'm here because the Orions granted me asylum, right? Theoretically, I could walk out of here any time I want; why do you think I haven't done that before now?"

"I'm guessing it has something to do with not wanting to go back to a Starfleet brig," Gianetti said.

"Bingo." Reyes knew that the only thing his extraction, peaceful or otherwise, would accomplish would be to see him returned to a Starfleet brig. That likely was his ultimate destination, assuming Ganz or one of his goons did not kill him, but if there was a chance that he could help T'Prynn to obtain the data she needed from the *Omari-Ekon*'s navigational logs, then he had to risk staying here a bit longer.

Hetzlein asked, "Do you really think Ganz would just let you walk off this ship? Not so long as he thinks you've got some value."

"You're not here because you're worried about me," Reyes said. "Starfleet's worried that I've turned traitor, and they want me out of here before I can do any more damage. Does Admiral Nogura know about this?"

"Admiral Nogura and the station's senior staff have been insulated from this operation, sir," Gianetti replied, "in order to shield him with plausible deniability should anything go wrong."

Reyes opted not to mention the covert communications link he shared with T'Prynn, reasoning that if she was aware of the operation, she would have alerted him to be on the lookout for Hetzlein and Gianetti. It also was probable that neither of them had any knowledge of the mission she was overseeing, and likewise did not know of his subcutaneous transceiver. The device was his lifeline, he decided, not to be shared with anyone except as a last resort.

Which could be any minute now.

"From what I know of Nogura," Reyes said, "when he finds out about this, you're going to wish the Orions had captured you." Regardless of whether the operation was successful, Reyes could see no means by which its execution and details might be kept secret. This extraction, successful or not, would become evident in short order, at which point the Orion government would without doubt dispatch the first in a series of harshly worded complaints to Starfleet Headquarters and the Federation Council. Given the already precarious state of relations between the two powers, there was no telling how the Orions might react to this incident, or what sort of recompense they could demand.

Looking to his would-be kidnappers, Reyes asked, "Okay, so you're here to extradite me. Why are you talking to me, instead of stuffing me in a duffel bag and trying to carry me out of here?"

"We considered it," Gianetti said.

Hetzlein cast a scowl in her companion's direction before adding, "If we could've beamed you out of your quarters, we would've done that by now."

"Which raises another question," Reyes said. "How the hell did you even get aboard in the first place?"

She tapped the patch above her left pocket. "We just walked in the front door. So far as anyone else knows, we're freight-haulers, from one of the civilian ships docked at the station, just looking to drink, lose some money, and have a good time." Their coveralls were of a type Reyes recognized as being in common use aboard civilian merchant freighters. Above each of their left pockets was a patch denoting a shipping company that Reyes knew contracted with Starfleet as well as private sector construction and colonization organizations to transport matériel to worlds throughout the Federation. Below the patch was a tape with the name *Tai' Shan* inscribed upon it in black letters. Reyes thought he recognized the name from various colony status reports and docking clearance requests during his tenure as commander of Starbase 47.

Skeptical of this idea, he asked, "And you guys have the sort of credits that can get you aboard a gaming vessel like this?"

Gianetti said, "We do if we've been on a long-haul run to a remote colony and back for seven months."

"Then you should probably go and enjoy yourselves," Reyes

said, "or, better yet, get the hell off this ship before Ganz or his people find out you're here."

"Mister Reyes," Hetzlein replied, "our orders are to get you off this ship, one way or another. It'd be a hell of a lot easier to stun your ass and have Gianetti throw you over his shoulder, but to be honest . . ." She paused, and Reyes saw the struggle in her face. "To be honest, I have too much respect for you, sir. So, I guess I'm asking you not to make me do anything I don't want to do."

Reyes shrugged. "Sorry, Lieutenant. Not interested."

Behind him, Gianetti said, "Sir, it's because we respect you that we're also disobeying orders and telling you now that our worst-case scenario is to kill you."

Deciding that he would rather be conscious, and not dead, for the next few minutes, Reyes offered a reluctant nod. "Well, since you're asking so nicely, have it your way, but good luck getting me out of here. The whole damned ship's covered with transporter inhibitors."

Hetzlein answered, "Well, it's not as though we're old pals or anything, but there's nothing that says we couldn't have struck up a conversation, say, in the bar, in about thirty or forty minutes, after Joe and I have had a chance to venture to the bar and have a drink or two and work at blending in with the crowd. We'll have a few drinks, maybe play a few games, and then make our way off the gaming floor to the private suites. We've identified a maintenance compartment in that section of the ship where the shielding is weaker than the surrounding areas. A transporter beam can get through, but only there and only one person at a time. That'll be you. You'll be beamed to a secure area aboard the station. Meanwhile, Joe here and I will return to the bar, and eventually make a casual exit from the ship by walking right out the front door."

"That plan sounds so stupid, it just might work," Reyes observed.

Rather than take offense, Hetzlein smiled. "My father always liked the K.I.S.S. principle: Keep It Simple, Starfleet. It's not the flashiest plan, but it doesn't have a lot of moving parts. Fewer things to screw up."

"Uh-huh," Reyes replied, already considering different possibilities for gaining an advantage at some point before they could beam him off the ship. "And what happens if Ganz or one of his goons makes you, or us? What's the plan then?"

Hetzlein and Gianetti exchanged glances before Gianetti lifted his left leg so that he could reach for the sole of the boots he wore. Unlike Starfleet-issue boots, their footwear lacked defined heels, and Gianetti simply flipped the entire sole of his boot down, revealing a hidden compartment within. Resting in the padded niche was what Reyes recognized as a compact phaser not unlike the standard-issue Starfleet type-1 model. Gianetti's concealed phaser was a civilian counterpart to that weapon, no doubt a deliberate choice so as to further hinder his and Hetzlein's identification as Starfleet personnel.

"Then we revise the plan," Hetzlein said.

Reyes did not have to wait long for opportunity to present itself.

Following Hetzlein down a stretch of corridor and with Gianetti behind him and holding on to his right arm, Reyes watched as the lieutenant came to a T-intersection in the passageway. The doorway at the head of the junction was one he recognized as being the entrance to the maintenance area.

"Sure you want to be caught doing that?" he asked, adopting a slight mocking tone as Hetzlein began to press keys on the pad set into the wall next to the hatch. His question earned him a squeeze on his arm from Gianetti.

Hetzlein ignored him, instead focusing her attention on the keypad. She began pressing keys in what looked to be a random pattern, and Reyes heard her curse just under her breath as whatever she tried failed to open the door. "Something's wrong," she said after a moment. "The code's not working."

"Are you sure you entered it right?" Gianetti asked, moving to get a closer look at the pad. His movements brought him abreast of Reyes, who took prompt advantage of the other man's momentary lapse and punched him in the side of the head. Gianetti grunted from the force of the strike, staggering forward and falling into Hetzlein.

"Son of a bitch!"

Ignoring Hetzlein's cry of surprise, Reyes was already sprinting down the corridor, scrambling to put distance between him and his would-be captors. He turned a corner, but already he could hear the sound of boots running across the metal hull plating behind him. He looked over his shoulder in time to see Hetzlein and Gianetti rounding the corner and running after him. Gianetti held his civilian phaser in his hand, and he wasted no time firing. The blast screamed past Reyes's head and slammed into the wall ahead of him, and Reyes brought himself to a halt, holding up his empty hands.

"Do that again," Gianetti growled through gritted teeth as he closed the distance, pointing the phaser at Reyes's face to emphasize his threat.

Reyes eyed the other man. "If you don't do it, Ganz or his people will if they find us."

"Move," Hetzlein said, pulling Reyes by his arm and indicating for him to follow along. "We're heading to the secondary extraction point."

Before Reyes could say anything in reply, a new voice entered the conversation: T'Prynn's.

"*Mister Reyes,*" the Vulcan said, her voice sounding small and distant due to a faint crackle of background static, "*I am attempting to monitor the situation from my position, but I am still working to acquire information. Do not acknowledge this transmission, as these agents are unaware of our communications link.*"

Reyes was about to say something regardless of the Vulcan's instructions, but the words died in his throat as two Orion males emerged from around a corner at the far end of the passageway. They were less than twenty meters away, which made it easy for him to identify the squat, short-barreled disruptor pistol each of them carried. He flinched at the howl of energy in the narrow corridor and the almost electrical sensation playing across his exposed skin an instant before realizing that the source was the weapon in Gianetti's hand. The security officer had fired his own phaser over Reyes's shoulder while standing directly behind him, with the blue-white beam striking the lead Orion in the chest. No sooner was he falling than Hetzlein followed with her own phaser, dispatching the other Orion with ease. Within seconds, the two security officers had released their hold on Reyes and were kneeling next to the fallen guards, retrieving their weapons and, to Reyes at least, looking for anything else of possible value. From one point, Hetzlein pulled what he recognized as a magnetic key.

"Our cover's blown," Hetzlein said, dividing her attention between her immediate task and the corridor behind and ahead of them.

Gianetti said, "They know we're here, and they know why we're here, but they don't know that you know anything about it. Just play dumb."

Shrugging, Reyes replied, "Not much point to that. You know this ship has internal sensors, right? It's not going to be hard for them to find us, even if they didn't keep tabs on me every second of every day." There was no turning back now, he realized; if this extraction failed and he ended up remaining on the *Omari-Ekon,* his death at Ganz's hands was all but certain.

"It's been factored in," Hetzlein said. "Right now, the station's chief engineer is testing the main deflector array after it experienced an unexplained malfunction last night. The effects of these tests are that there's all sorts of feedback and interference being thrown off by the thing."

"A malfunctioning deflector array," Reyes repeated, for T'Prynn's benefit. "Interesting. I suppose it's affecting communications and maybe the sensors, at least for any non-Starfleet ship in close proximity."

In his head, Reyes heard T'Prynn add, "*That would seem to be correct, Mister Reyes.*" As before, static accompanied her voice, though Reyes could still hear her without too much trouble.

"This is also the cause of our communications disruption, but our sensors are able to overcome the interference. I can track your movements, but it appears Ganz and his people cannot. You should keep moving."

"Why are we standing around, then?" Gianetti asked, a hint of anxiety in his voice. "Let's get the hell out of here before they send everybody with a weapon after us."

Reyes felt the larger man grab his arm again as the trio once more set off through the winding corridors, and he could not help shaking the anxiety he was feeling at the thought of moving away from the ship's more populated areas. Recalling what he knew of the vessel's internal configuration, he knew that this section comprised living quarters, storage, and maintenance access points. The omnipresent hum of the *Omari-Ekon*'s engines was even more noticeable here, reverberating off the bare metal deck plates and bulkheads. The doors on either side of the passageway were unadorned save for a single small plaque set into the metal at eye level and providing its compartment designation. Reyes had taken the time to learn how the designators were assigned, so he was able to discern that they were on a lower level and nearing the aft third of the ship.

Dark and isolated. Perfect for a nice, quiet execution.

Turning one more bend in the hallway, Hetzlein stopped before a reinforced hatch set into the bulkhead at the end of a short corridor spur. A hexagonal keypad with a magnetic reader was set into the wall next to the door, with three rows of four keys highlighted in blue and featuring characters in Orion text. Without hesitation, Hetzlein swiped the card she had taken from the Orion, and this time was rewarded with the sound of the oversized door's lock disengaging.

"Where are we?" Reyes asked, for himself as well as T'Prynn.

As the hatch slid aside, Hetzlein replied, "Maintenance passage. This'll take us to the utility compartment."

"Maintenance passage," Reyes said, hoping T'Prynn was still listening. "Sounds cozy."

Something bright flashed in the corridor an instant before the crackle of energy assaulted Reyes's ears, and he cringed as a disruptor bolt slammed into the wall just to the right of his head. He felt Gianetti's meaty hand on his arm just before the man pulled him aside and pushed him to the deck inside the maintenance hatch. Rolling onto his side, Reyes caught his first look back up the passageway and saw three more Orions at the intersection, firing from cover. Hetzlein, in the open, aimed her own weapon and snapped off several shots, which only added to the cacophony filling the corridor. The Orions ducked back around the corner to avoid being hit, giving her the opportunity she needed to get out of the line of fire. She jumped through the hatchway, vaulting over Reyes.

"Let's go," she said, reaching down to pull Reyes to his feet.

Gianetti, bringing up the rear, back-stepped toward the door, aiming his phaser back up the corridor. Reyes saw movement at the intersection just before one of the Orions ducked into sight, taking aim and firing his disruptor. The blast caught Gianetti in the thigh and the man grunted in pain as he fell to one knee.

"Get off me!" Reyes said, but by then it was too late. Though he was able to get off a few more shots, the Orions were like feeding sharks at this point, all three of them taking aim at the wounded man and unleashing the full force of their weapons. Gianetti was struck by half a dozen blasts in rapid succession, each shot pushing him back until he slammed into the bulkhead behind him. He fell limp to the deck, coming to rest with his head facing Reyes, who saw the man's lifeless eyes.

"Move!" Hetzlein said, taking aim at the keypad set inside the hatchway and shooting it with her phaser. This had the effect of forcing the hatch to close and preventing the Orions from chasing after them. Without another word, Hetzlein pushed Reyes down the narrow, darkened passageway, their boots clanging on the metal grating that served as deck plating in this part of the ship while covering all manner of conduits along with power and other optical cabling. Never having been in this area of the *Omari-Ekon,* Reyes had no points of reference for determining his present location as they navigated the passageway's numerous turns, though Hetzlein seemed to know with utmost precision just where they were going. Perhaps seeing the questioning expression on Reyes's face, she said, "Almost there."

"*Mister Reyes,*" T'Prynn said. "*Your current position appears to be in an area of the ship that is shielded from sensors. I am unable to isolate your exact location.*"

"Wonderful," Reyes replied, a response that drew a quizzical look from Hetzlein.

They reached another maintenance hatch, similar to the one they had accessed at the other end of the corridor, and once more Hetzlein entered a sequence of commands on the door's keypad. The door slid aside, revealing what Reyes at first took to be some kind of storage compartment. Tables lined the bulkheads at this end of the room, accompanied by equipment lockers, packing crates, and an assortment of tools and other items strewn around the room. Hetzlein led the way into the room, inspecting its interior while sighting down the length of her right arm and the phaser she still held in her hand.

"You need to get out of here before you get us both killed!" Reyes snapped. This was getting ridiculous. So far as he could tell, Hetzlein had led them into whatever passed for a mousetrap on this ship.

"With all due respect, Mister Reyes," Hetzlein said, her voice low and tight, "shut up or I'll shoot you myself." Taking a knee, she reached for the sole of her right boot and twisted it so that it dropped downward, revealing a small rectangle of burnished metal. Extracting the object from the boot's concealed compartment, she turned it over to reveal a single, recessed button in the item's metal casing. "Burst transmitter," she said, holding up the device. "Single-use, tight-beam focused transmission. It'll punch through any jamming field they might have up around the—"

Something bumped into something else at the room's far end, and Reyes and Hetzlein turned in that direction, each searching for the source of the odd noise. Reyes felt a knot form in his gut at the same time Hetzlein was retrieving her phaser from the deck next to her right foot. She managed to pick up the weapon before a burst of energy exploded from somewhere in the darkness and zipped across the room, striking her in the chest. Her face a mask of agony, Hetzlein crumpled to the deck even as a second disruptor bolt hit her.

Something clanked against the metal near the fallen woman and Reyes saw that Hetzlein had dropped the transmitter. For a fleeting instant, he considered diving for the device, but at the last second he kicked at it with his boot, sending it sliding across the deck away from him. He held up his hands to the approaching Orions, showing them that he was unarmed, but that was all he could do before something struck him in the back and he lurched as though touched by a live power conduit. His muscles jerked, racked by spasms, and his jaw clenched as the effects of whatever had hit him coursed over and through his body. Then, everything around him faded to black.

16

Heihachiro Nogura prided himself on not being a man given to negative displays of emotion. It was a rare event for him to raise his voice above a conversational tone, much less yell at anyone. Even more uncommon was his use of anything other than mild obscenities, and he preferred to avoid other abusive invective. He was confident enough in his position and in the authority he commanded that it was an infrequent occasion when he felt the need to make known his displeasure with anything other than a calm, professional demeanor.

Today felt as though it might just be shaping up to be one of those occasions.

His hands clasped behind his back so that they would not form fists of their own accord, Nogura stalked back and forth across the width of his office, pacing the section of deck between his desk and the silent, unmoving figure of Lieutenant Haniff Jackson. With the simple act of standing still and not saying a word, Nogura figured that Starbase 47's chief of security was doing perhaps the smartest thing he had ever done in his young life. Though he might well have been content to let the younger man sweat for the next hour or so while pondering his fate, Nogura had no time for such distractions, satisfying though they might appear to be at the moment. With that in mind, he halted his pacing as he came abreast of the lieutenant, turning to face him from a distance of less than one meter.

"Mister Jackson," he said, his voice low and controlled even though he permitted a hint of menace, "perhaps you'd be so kind as to tell me just what the hell's been going on aboard my station, and why I'm just now finding out about it?"

Holding himself at attention, Jackson stood more than a head taller than Nogura, but rather than looking down, the muscular security chief's gaze instead was focused on a spot somewhere on the office's rear wall. Beads of perspiration had broken out on the man's bald head, and one droplet already was working its way down the side of his face. Nogura watched him swallow whatever lump had formed in his throat before drawing a deep breath.

"I'm sorry, Admiral," Jackson said, and Nogura was certain that he heard a slight tremble in the lieutenant's voice. "I was operating under direct orders from Admiral Komack not to discuss the operation with anyone, including you, sir. In fact, he specifically ordered me not to brief you."

Komack. Nogura felt his teeth beginning to grate. While he was acquainted with his fellow flag officer, he had never worked with James Komack. The admiral was a recent addition to the senior staff at Starfleet Headquarters on Earth after being transferred from his previous posting as the head of the command element overseeing Sector 9. There, Komack had built a solid reputation as a no-nonsense officer who got results, and tolerated little in the way of deviations from established or accepted policies and procedures. Nogura also recalled that Komack had, years earlier, served for a time at Starfleet Academy, overseeing the institution's ethics review board, where he also was known as being unforgiving with regard to discipline, particularly if it involved cheating or other dishonorable behavior on the part of a cadet. In Nogura's opinion, Komack was a "rules person" rather than a "people person," meaning he was the sort of officer who preferred the letter of the law rather than its spirit and intentions. He seemed disposed to view the universe around him from a stark, black-and-white perspective, rather than learning to appreciate the myriad shades of gray to be found in the broad spectrum between those two extremes.

Nogura had little patience for people like that, and that was *before* such individuals chose to interfere with him and his responsibilities.

"Admiral Komack," he said, considering this revelation and not liking any of the scenarios conjured by his imagination. "Did he happen to offer any particular reasoning for that directive?"

Swallowing another lump, Jackson nodded. "Yes, sir. The admiral said he wanted to protect you and the station's senior staff from any recriminations should the operation fail."

"And what if you'd succeeded?" Nogura asked, allowing some of his anger to seep into his voice. "Was I to receive all the credit for a job well done? A ticker-tape parade across Fontana Meadow? Would the *Orions* have presided over the festivities, offering me a medal or perhaps a nice selection of pastries?" Turning from Jackson, he resumed his pacing. "Do you have *any* idea what this idiotic scheme will do to our relations with the Orions? It's bad enough we have to smile and nod our heads when we *know* their pirate ships are raiding our freighters and other civilian craft, even though we have no hard evidence to hold over their heads. Now, I have to find a way to kowtow to that jackass Ganz, in the hope he doesn't flush Diego Reyes down a waste extraction vent, or grind him up and serve him to his pet . . . *whatever* the hell he has for pets over there." His irritation continuing its slow boil, Nogura once again stopped before Jackson and eyed the security chief. "How long has this plan been in motion?"

"Admiral Komack contacted me three days ago, sir," the lieutenant replied. "We started making our preparations immediately upon receiving his orders."

"Three *whole* days?" Nogura asked, making no effort to contain his sarcasm. "Well, I can't imagine why the mission wasn't a resounding success, with that sort of in-depth advance planning." Then, regretting his words, he forced himself to draw a deep, calming breath before shaking his head in irritation. If there was one thing he never had been able to stomach, it was waste, and above all, he loathed the notion of wasted lives.

"This entire affair has been a mess from the beginning," he

said, turning from Jackson and moving to stand before his office's main viewscreen. "Admiral Komack should have gotten my input for any such mission. I probably should have apprised him of our efforts to utilize Diego Reyes. You should have come to me, Lieutenant, but I can respect that you were given direct orders by a superior, which you had to obey." Nogura held little regard for the practice of placing subordinates in positions where they were forced to lie to their commanding officers or otherwise keep information from them, and even less tolerance for officers who utilized the tactic. There would be a conversation with Admiral James Komack on this topic, Nogura decided, but for now it would have to wait.

"None of that matters," he continued. "All that matters is that two of my people are dead. No matter who takes the blame for this idiocy, that won't change." The best he could do now was to take steps to see that such an incident was not repeated. With a tired sigh, he turned his attention back to Jackson. "Lieutenant, please ensure that both Hetzlein's and Gianetti's families have been notified, and begin preparing their personal effects for transport to whatever destination they have listed in their records. I would also appreciate a personal letter to each of the families by you, to accompany the letters I'll be sending."

Jackson nodded. "Aye, aye, sir."

Before Nogura could say anything else, the intercom on his desk beeped for attention, followed by the voice of his assistant, Ensign Toby Greenfield. *"Admiral, Commander Moyer is here and wishes to see you, if you're available."*

"Send her in, Ensign," Nogura replied, then nodded to Jackson. "That will be all, Lieutenant. Dismissed." His office doors parted to allow the security chief's exit, and Nogura watched as the burly man maneuvered his large frame to one side in order to make room for Lieutenant Commander Holly Moyer, who stood just outside the office, holding a data slate next to her right thigh. Her expression was one of uncertainty, and Nogura could see that she was taking steps to maintain her poise. Without acknowledging Jackson's greeting, she waited until he was out of her way before proceeding into Nogura's office, then paused as the doors slid shut behind her.

"Commander," Nogura said by way of greeting. "What can I do for you?"

Moyer replied, "Good evening, Admiral. I've just been informed about the failed rescue mission aboard the *Omari-Ekon*. Sir, with all due respect, what the hell was Starfleet thinking, authorizing a covert operation onto an Orion ship? Do they want to start a war?"

"Don't get me started on Starfleet," Nogura said, shaking his head. "I didn't know about the rescue mission until after it failed. Starfleet Command is worried about how much damage Reyes can do if he's interrogated and broken by the Orions or whoever else they hire to work on him." He shrugged. "I don't think that's a real threat, because they have to know we're watching, and if we catch wind of anything like that taking place, they also have to know that I won't hesitate to flush every regulation down the toilet before sending an armed boarding party to that ship and running our flag up the mast." He paused, offering a small, humorless smile. "Figuratively speaking, of course. Regardless, you can be sure I'll be getting answers from Headquarters about all of this, and damned soon."

Appearing not to be comforted by that declaration, Moyer said, "This is just the latest addition to a very long list of things which have happened since we established a presence here. Diego Reyes sacrificed his career because he felt much of what was going on here was wrong. Not everything, but *some* things." She shook her head. "I don't know if I agree with his choices, and we can argue all day about whether this action or that decision was necessary, but some things *can't* be argued."

Struck by the passion behind her words, Nogura was forced to nod in agreement. "You're right, Commander. Some things can't be argued. History will have to judge whether the steps we took here were the right ones, but for now, all we can do is follow our orders, and our conscience. When those two are in conflict, then we simply must do the best we can, and hope that we're guided by sound principles and the best interests of everyone who stands to be affected by what we allow—or don't allow—to happen here."

Moyer frowned. "I'll be honest, Admiral; I don't see that happening. Instead, I see a lot of sneaking around, trying to get the drop on the Orions or the Klingons or whoever stands in our way. I understand that we need to keep the Klingons from getting their hands on Shedai technology, but if we end up in a war against the Empire, then what have we saved? How many people have died since that first meta-genome sample was found? How many more have to die to preserve this secret?"

"Hopefully none," Nogura said, "but we both know how unlikely that is. Instead, all we can hope for is that those who die don't do so in vain. I don't believe that's been the case, despite the best of intentions and efforts. Regardless, the stakes are simply too high to stop now. We have to keep pushing forward, and doing our best to make sure that everything that's come before hasn't been for nothing."

Shaking her head, Moyer released a long, slow sigh. "I don't know if I can do this, sir. My world is the law, and when we sidestep or push aside the law for expediency, even if we believe it's for a just cause, then we lose just a little bit more of what it is about us that's supposed to make all of this effort worthwhile."

"And that's precisely why I need you where you are, Commander," Nogura replied, "doing exactly what you're doing. I need someone to observe everything that goes on here through the very prism your position affords. I like to think I always know when I get close to stepping over some line, but I also like having someone else point it out to me when that's necessary."

Moyer said, "And what if I disagree with something you decide to do, sir?"

"I'll give you every opportunity to set me straight," Nogura answered. "If I still decide to go a certain way, you'll be free to file any protest or report you deem appropriate. You'll be able to carry out your duties with autonomy. On that, Commander, you have my word."

Appearing to be comforted by Nogura's words, Moyer nodded. "Thank you, sir. I appreciate your confidence."

Nogura smiled. "Don't worry, Commander. Considering everything we've faced to this point, and given what might still happen before it's all over, I expect we'll be having a lot of these conversations."

17

His fist clenched and poised above his head, Ganz paused in mid-swing as he took notice of Neera entering his office. Dressed in a dark maroon shift that was cut high on the thigh and that left little to the imagination as she passed beneath the room's recessed lighting, she regarded him with an expression of amused exasperation.

"Don't," she said, making her way past his desk toward the bar. "It's brand-new, and you've already gone through your ration of inanimate objects for this accounting cycle."

Ganz regarded the computer interface terminal on his desk, which was the intended target of his rage. It sat before him, defenseless, waiting for him to mete out a punishment it did not deserve. Though destroying the terminal would provide a fleeting moment's consolation, it would do nothing to solve the actual problems still requiring his attention.

"Well," he said, relaxing his fist and lowering himself back into the chair behind his desk, "I need to hit something. Or someone."

Standing at the bar, Neera cast a knowing, amused glance over her shoulder as she fixed herself a drink. "There's a vase in the bedroom I never liked. Feel free to hit that."

"Too easy. I prefer a challenge," Ganz replied, though he was already feeling his initial anger beginning to ebb. When the mood struck her, Neera could be a very astute caregiver, knowing just what to say or do in order to calm him at times like these, when all he wanted was to vent his frustrations on anyone or anything within reach.

He shook his head as he considered the report displayed on the computer terminal. Submitted by his head of security, Tonzak, it detailed the skirmish involving the two Starfleet officers who had come aboard the *Omari-Ekon* in a bid to extradite Diego Reyes. Though their attempt had not been successful, the true ramifications of the incident were yet to be felt, and it was this aspect of the unfortunate situation that unsettled him.

"I didn't think Starfleet had the *naghs* to send somebody to snatch Reyes," he said.

Neera turned from the bar, drink in hand, and eyed him with a quizzical expression. "Klingon slang?"

"I like the way it rolls off the tongue," Ganz replied without looking away from the screen. "Nogura must be out of his mind, authorizing something like this."

Pausing while she sipped from her glass, Neera said, "I don't think it was Nogura. While I wouldn't put it past him, he doesn't strike me as someone who would have authorized such an ill-conceived and poorly executed plan."

Ganz considered the wisdom of his lover's observation, nodding in agreement. "When you say it out loud, it makes sense. So, somebody ordered an extraction attempt over Nogura's head?" He smiled at that thought as he leaned back in his chair. "I'm guessing he didn't like that." From his few dealings with the Starfleet admiral, Ganz had concluded that Nogura was a man who would not appreciate anyone undermining his authority. He would be angry at the events that had transpired without his knowledge, even more so for the resulting deaths. Ganz could understand how the admiral might feel, though he did so for different reasons.

"Idiots," he said, gritting his teeth as he once more reviewed the report. "If they'd stunned the humans, we could have used them as leverage against Nogura." The prospect of holding two Starfleet officers, captured while in the midst of an illegal intrusion into Orion sovereign territory, might well have been all Ganz needed to extract some form of concession from the admiral as a means of avoiding an interstellar incident. Despite the attitude

Nogura had shown toward Ganz from the moment he had arrived to take command of Starbase 47, he would not have been able to refuse such an offer. Even if to do so was his personal preference, the admiral still had to answer to his masters at Starfleet Command, who would want an expedient resolution to what still held the potential to become an embarrassment not just to Starfleet, but to Ganz and even Neera, as well. If Neera's superiors within the Orion Syndicate were to learn of the problems being experienced aboard the *Omari-Ekon,* they might also decide that cutting their own losses was the prudent course of action in order to prevent the possibility of greater attention being cast in their direction. Such a decision likely would not be in favor of any continued breathing Neera, Ganz, or anyone in their employ might wish to do.

"Have you disposed of the bodies?" Neera asked.

Ganz nodded. "Tonzak took care of it."

"Well, at least he's showing some promise." Taking another sip from her glass, Neera swirled its remaining contents before adding, "Have you considered promoting him? You've been saying you need someone to replace Zett for months now."

Frowning, Ganz shook his head. "I may have had issues with some of Zett's choices, and it was his own bad judgment that got him killed, but that doesn't mean just anyone can replace him. He had skills, I'll give him that." Zett Nilric, his former "business manager," had numbered covert assassination among his many formidable talents. The Nalori had taken care of several delicate tasks for Ganz in recent years, and the Orion had valued Zett's ability to act quickly with precision and discretion. If he had possessed one failing, it was an overdeveloped sense of pride, and it was that pride, wounded by Cervantes Quinn, which led to his eventual death at Quinn's hands. In the months that had passed since then, Ganz had been without someone in the position Zett had once occupied. He had considered several members of his staff, but found each of them wanting. Tonzak was the most promising from a rather shallow pool of uninspiring candidates.

"I don't think I'm ready to make that kind of commitment

with Tonzak just yet," Ganz said, "but for now, he'll do, just so long as nothing truly delicate is required. He did well enough cleaning up this mess. Now all we can do is wait to see what Nogura does." Though the admiral had made no attempts at contact in the wake of the incident, Ganz figured some sort of Starfleet reprisal had to be in the offing. Indeed, some steps already appeared to be taking place. As he had expected would happen, the armed security presence near the docking port where the *Omari-Ekon* was moored had been increased, and Ganz did not doubt that every measure of covert sensor scan and communications monitoring available to the station was at this very moment trained on his ship, searching for any point of access or vulnerability that might be exploited. "Even if they don't plan to storm the ship, they should have evicted us by now, at the very least." Even as he spoke the words, he knew the lone reason why such actions had not yet been taken: Diego Reyes.

As though reading his mind, Neera said, "They won't do that, not so long as we have Reyes." Making her way across the office, she perched atop one corner of Ganz's desk. "At least your people didn't kill him, too,"

Ganz grunted. "That's the only reason Tonzak's still alive." After the incident with Reyes and Lekkar on the gaming floor, the *Omari-Ekon*'s head of security had adopted a no-tolerance policy with respect to any severe harm or "accident" anyone aboard ship might wish to inflict upon the human. He saw to Reyes's safety with the same dedication a mother watched over her children, no doubt worried about any repercussions that might fall to him should anything happen to the fugitive former commodore. That attitude had filtered down to his security officers, who had only incapacitated Reyes during the firefight with the two Starfleet officers. Rather than shoot him, the subordinate who had restrained Reyes—and possibly prevented him from being transported off the ship—had used a stun baton on him. Ganz smiled at the thought of the discomfort from such a weapon being inflicted on the human he so loathed. "At least Reyes will have a reminder of the affair, for the rest of the day, anyway."

Every time he moved, or ate, or even wanted to empty his bladder, Diego Reyes would feel the lingering effects of the baton, and that made Ganz happy. It still was not so satisfying as the notion of simply killing the man, but for now, it was sufficient.

Soon, he promised himself.

"I talked to Tonzak," Neera said, her tone turning more serious. "He said Reyes appeared to be resisting the escape attempt. He had a chance to get away, but didn't take it."

Frowning, Ganz regarded his confidante, his eyes narrowing in confusion. "The instant he steps foot on that station, he goes back to prison. Seems like an easy choice to me."

"Maybe," Neera said. "Then again, maybe not."

"What are you thinking?" Ganz asked. He had been hoping for Reyes to somehow reveal his true motives for requesting asylum aboard the *Omari-Ekon.* So far, the former Starfleet officer had managed to avoid making such an egregious error.

"He may be a spy, after all," Neera said.

"If he is," Ganz countered, then he has to be the most useless spy in the history of espionage. We've had him under almost constant surveillance. He can't get to any controlled areas of the ship, and his computer access is curtailed even further than for regular guests. If he's spying, then he has to be working largely on his own, without a handler to guide his movements. The only contact he's had with anyone from the station is that reporter, Pennington, and the doctor." While there existed the possibility, however remote, of Reyes having found some other, covert means of communicating with someone on the station, Ganz could not bring himself to believe it.

Neera nodded. "And if he's been under cover all this time, it doesn't make sense that they'd risk compromising him with such a sloppy rescue attempt." Tapping one fingernail along the edge of her glass, she shook her head. "Something's out of place here."

"So," Ganz said, not understanding why this had to be so complicated, "let's get rid of him, before he does manage to do some real damage."

Neera's expression turned to one of disapproval. "You do that, then you'd better be ready to warp out of here, because the second Nogura finds out Reyes is dead, he'll send every armed security guard he can find swarming onto this ship, and he'll worry about any political fallout tomorrow."

Although his current, strained relationship with Starbase 47 chafed him, there was no way Ganz could afford to leave the safety net afforded by being docked with the station. "And if Reyes stays alive?"

"Then Starfleet likely will be happy to keep things quiet, at least for now. The attempt to retrieve Reyes was illegal, and they won't want to admit to it. I don't think you want to admit that those two Starfleet officers were killed aboard my ship, and Starfleet won't press that issue, either, if for no other reason than to keep us from taking action against Reyes.

Considering what he had just heard, Ganz could only shake his head in admiration. "There's a reason I don't like playing chess with you."

"Just one of my many talents," Neera replied.

Everything she had just outlined, reduced to its essentials, equated to one thing so far as Ganz was concerned. "So, we wait, to see what Reyes does?"

Neera nodded. "Yes."

"I have to say, I don't like it. Reyes is no idiot. He's liable to figure out we're on to him at some point. Besides, with the luck he's had avoiding trouble, I'm beginning to think he's blessed with divine assistance."

Moving herself off the desk, Neera turned so that she was close enough to stroke Ganz's cheek. "Luck always runs out. Reyes's day is coming, but for now, we keep him alive." When her fingers reached his chin, she guided his face so that his eyes locked with hers. "Understood?"

"Yes," Ganz replied, and Neera bent forward to kiss the top of his bald head.

"Excellent," she said before turning and moving around the desk on her way to the bedroom. Looking back over her shoulder at him, she smiled. "Coming?"

"I'll be right there," Ganz replied. He waited until Neera disappeared through the doorway into his private bedchamber before reaching out to the computer interface and tapping its control pad.

Despite the confidence with which she had just outlined the situation, Ganz could not shake the nagging feeling that this entire affair was becoming too convoluted. To him, it seemed only a matter of time before something he could not control upset the entire fragile balance currently holding Starfleet—and Nogura—at the proverbial arm's length. Even with as keen an insight as she possessed, how could Neera not see that?

The time for action, Ganz decided, was now.

He opened a communications frequency and waited until the face of his head of security, Tonzak, filled the computer screen. The muscled Orion's large head sat atop a squat neck, and his broad torso, bare save for the pair of bandoliers he liked to wear across his chest, featured several scars and piercings, all bearing mute testimony to the demanding life he had lived as an underling within the syndicate.

"*Yes?*" Tonzak asked, staring out from the screen with a furrowed brow.

"Come and see me after your shift tonight," Ganz replied, keeping his voice low. "I have a special job for you." Even allowing for the occasional setback, the young Orion had proven valuable on more than one occasion. He, along with one or two others in Ganz's organization, were more than capable of utilizing the proper amounts of discretion and initiative which would be required to kill Diego Reyes.

Neera will be upset, Ganz mused, but for now he elected to set aside such concerns. Besides, if he ended up resolving the Reyes matter in such a way that it moved any unwanted scrutiny away from her superiors, they in turn might feel grateful to him to such an extent that Neera was no longer an issue, either. Perhaps they would see fit to grant him a measure of autonomy, something offered with great infrequency to other male Orions at his station within the syndicate hierarchy. Rather than having to stand idle as Neera took the larger share of credit for his work, he might begin to enjoy rewards more commensurate with the risk and responsibility he undertook.

That notion, Ganz decided, held definite appeal, though all of that could come later.

For now? It was time to put an end to the irritant known as Diego Reyes.

18

Storming through the large double doors to the building that now served as the chancery for the Federation's ambassadorial delegation, Jetanien locked eyes with his assistant, Sergio Moreno, who rose from behind his reception desk near the rear of the lobby. "How long have they been here?" The query was loud enough to echo off the prefabricated stone walls that were a common facet of nearly every structure in Paradise City.

"They just arrived, Ambassador," Moreno said as Jetanien strode past. "I was unaware you had scheduled a meeting for this morning."

"That is because I did not," Jetanien replied, moving for the stairwell that would take him to his office. It had taken him nearly ten minutes to make the transit from where he had been walking near the retail district, during his morning stroll through the streets of Paradise City. The daily ritual was one he had observed since first occupying the chancery despite the constabulary's reports and warnings about the increased yet still isolated incidents of disturbances scattered across the colony. That was when he had received the alert message on the private channel reserved for communications between him, Lugok, and D'tran. The summons had come from the Romulan senator, asking that the trio meet at Jetanien's offices as soon as possible. As he reached the stairs, he called out over his shoulder to Moreno, "Be ready in case I call you up to assist."

"Of course, sir," the assistant replied. "Is everything all right, Ambassador?"

"We'll see about that soon enough, won't we?" Jetanien replied, his words echoing off the stairwell as he ascended to the third floor of the chancery, which served as both work space and living quarters for him and his staff. His mind racing through the numerous possible reasons his colleagues would need to meet so urgently, he climbed the last few stairs and crossed the landing toward his office. When the door slid aside, he saw D'tran and Lugok standing together before his desk, their backs to him.

"Gentlemen, I got back as soon as I could," Jetanien said, noting that he sounded more than a bit out of breath. "What brings you to my humble abode, and how may I be of assistance?"

The Klingon and Romulan diplomats turned to face Jetanien, and he noticed their hands were filled—with bottles of drink.

"You can assist by getting yourself a glass," Lugok replied, laughing as he brandished a square-bodied silver bottle by its neck with such enthusiasm that some of its contents spewed from its open top and fell to the floor.

Jetanien eyed his counterparts with no small amount of confusion. "It seems a bit early for bloodwine, Ambassador."

His comment evoked a deep laugh from the Klingon. "Not today, my friend," he replied before bringing the bottle to his lips and taking a lengthy pull from the vessel.

Offering his own satisfied if comparatively restrained smile, D'tran held up his own bottle, which was clear and perhaps three-quarters filled with a bright blue liquid. "I suppose it's possible that our perception of time is no longer synchronous with yours. We have just concluded a lengthy subspace communication with members of the Klingon High Council and the Romulan Senate."

Clicking his beak, Jetanein replied, "Your appreciation for Romulan ale seems rather out of sorts this morning, as well."

"An infrequent indulgence," D'tran said, bowing his head in mock salute. "I'm obliging my fellow negotiator only to satisfy his desire for ceremony. After all, this is an occasion well worth recognizing and celebrating."

Realizing now what had so excited his two companions, Jetanien allowed himself a small chuckle. "I take it you have reached some sort of accord?"

"Rather more than that, I should think," D'tran replied, reaching for the glass he had left atop Jetanien's desk and refreshing it from the bottle of ale in his withered hand.

Lugok added, "Indeed. The Klingon and Romulan empires have finally agreed to an actual, mutually beneficial alliance—one created out of joint need and cooperation, rather than duplicity and one-upmanship."

"So, tell me," Jetanien said, "what was the big breakthrough?"

D'tran settled himself in one of the armchairs positioned before Jetanien's desk. "Each side was finally able to help the other understand the benefits of working together from their own point of view." He sipped from his glass before adding, "I like to think the success is owed more to the process itself, rather than any one particular point."

"And I can't even take full credit for it," Lugok added.

"I see," Jetanien replied, then paused, shaking his head. "Actually, that is a lie. I haven't the first clue what you mean, D'tran. Is this your way of telling me that you bamboozled them into accepting an agreement with a flurry of obtuse rhetoric?"

This evoked a laugh from Lugok, just as the Klingon was tipping his bloodwine bottle to his lips, and he nearly choked on his drink. "That is precisely what happened," he said, wiping his mouth. "I spoke with the High Council and explained that what the Romulans sought from us was relatively minor. However, I said that I had already told D'tran that their requests would be difficult to obtain, and that the Romulans needed to make substantial concessions to ensure an agreement. So, my people thought the Romulans were foolishly offering a lot for an accord that could have come at much less than they agreed to concede."

"And I convinced the Senate of the same," D'tran added. "So long as each side was able to believe it had received the better benefit, everyone seems happy."

Now Jetanien laughed, appreciating his comrades' shrewd if unorthodox tactics. "Given how previous attempts at consensus always seemed to be fueled by one side working to deceive or defraud the other, it's amusing to think that a reverse of such thinking is actually what brings about agreement." He shook his head. "Gentlemen, it's quite possible that interstellar diplomacy is well and truly doomed." In truth, the news was welcome, no matter how the arrangement itself had been reached, and could not have come at a better time—after what could only be described as "escalating tensions" between Klingon and Romulan forces near the outer boundary of the Taurus Reach in recent weeks. Lugok and D'tran, along with Jetanien, had also been involved in negotiations dedicated to defusing that situation. That those earlier efforts might now have yielded additional, tangential results would be well worth celebrating. "Dare I ask what each side conceded to the other?"

"Technology rights," D'tran replied. "The Klingons once again have asked for further insights into our cloaking systems, for which they offer heartfelt assurances that it will not be turned against us as an instrument of aggression."

Lugok said, "Whereas the Romulans have requested safe passage using agreed-upon lanes of travel through Klingon space so that they might have greater access to areas of space beyond their own borders and which in turn are in proximity to imperial territory." He turned to regard Jetanien before adding, "Including the Gonmog Sector."

"The Gonmog Sector?" the Chelon asked, schooling his reaction so as not to appear too concerned about this new development. "Really?"

Grinning, the Klingon ambassador nodded. "Come, Jetanien, don't be so coy. You know full well my people are aware of the ancient technology to be found there. After all, your Starfleet has done an exceptionally horrid job keeping that secret."

Despite a fervent desire to dispel his companion's claims, Jetanien knew Lugok was correct. Though intelligence reports showed that Klingon operatives working in the Taurus Reach were aware of the Shedai and the technology they commanded, there was almost no evidence suggesting the Empire held any real knowledge regarding the Taurus Meta-Genome itself or the potential it contained. It was a slim distinction, but an important one. At present, the only access to Shedai artifacts was through the use of specialized equipment developed by Doctor Carol Marcus, Lieutenant Ming Xiong, and their team of research scientists aboard Starbase 47. So far as had been determined, the Klingons possessed nothing approaching that level of sophistication.

So far, Jetanien reminded himself.

"For one capable of so few expressions, yours is a face that is easy to read," D'tran said, picking up on the unspoken conversation around which Jetanien and Lugok were dancing. "If our three governments can demonstrate an ability to cooperate here, within the confines of our little experiment, then surely such mutual respect can be extended beyond this worthless dustball of a planet. Wouldn't you say, Jetanien?"

Nodding, the Chelon replied, "Of course."

"Don't fret, Jetanien," Lugok said, holding up his bottle of bloodwine. "We look upon this as an opportunity to build trust between our peoples. After all, the trust we foster with this agreement can't help but influence goodwill toward the next one."

"Just as our efforts here perhaps played a role in reaching compromise with the accord you forged today," Jetanien replied. "So, no one ended up with—as my human friends are prone to say—the short end of the stick?"

"Only the Federation," was all Lugok managed to say before erupting with booming laughter. "That is what's most glorious of all."

Perhaps sensing Jetanien's wariness, D'tran said, "Our Klingon friend overstates the ramifications of what was accomplished here today. While it's true to say that at least some of the agreement's appeal lies in how it might serve to frustrate or concern certain Federation officials. That is not to say we remain closed to talks with you and your leaders, my friend."

Jetanien certainly had considered what a Klingon-Romulan alliance might mean for the Federation on any number of fronts. He had given the matter serious thought upon learning of the original pact the two powers had fostered nearly a year earlier, which had resulted in the Romulans' sharing some of their cloaking technology in exchange for a small fleet of Klingon battle cruisers. What had begun as a seemingly legitimate exchange of information and ideas had soured when it was learned the Klingon officer responsible for brokering the deal had engaged in duplicity and deception to tip the agreement in his favor. The ruse had even involved a spy embedded within the ranks of support staff attached to the Romulan Senate itself. Though the covert agent had been discovered and eliminated, the arrangement itself had fallen apart, leaving both sides to eye one another with renewed suspicion and resentment. At first, that accord's failure seemed be fortunate happenstance so far as the Federation was concerned. If the efforts of Lugok and D'tran were to be believed, however, then it seemed obvious to Jetanien that—eventually—the Klingons and Romulans might well achieve some form of permanent, formidable partnership.

And what then? It was a question for which Jetanien possessed no answer.

"Your unease is evident," D'tran said. "Remember that this treaty between the Klingon and Romulan empires has been a long time coming, and has suffered from the machinations of a shortsighted few." He gestured with both hands, indicating not only Jetanien's office but also—presumably—the rest of Paradise City. "Surely you, more so than anyone, can see that what we've managed to achieve here is too great for us to stand by and let it be squandered, much less take active steps to sabotage our own efforts."

Lugok nodded. "He speaks the truth. I for one did not spend all those months sitting on this cursed ball of dirt just to throw away all of that time, energy, and work."

"Of course not," Jetanien said. On the other hand, he knew from experience that Lugok was more than capable of engaging in deception, as he had done early on during his assignment as part of the Klingon diplomatic delegation to Starbase 47. One of his numerous duties had been overseeing the activities of Anna Sandesjo, a covert Klingon agent surgically altered to pass as a human female. For a time, she had been a member of Jetanien's staff, at least until he and the station's intelligence officer, T'Prynn, had uncovered her real identity. Sandesjo had later been killed in a mishap involving an explosion aboard a cargo ship docked at the station, and Jetanien had never been convinced that her death was anything other than murder, perhaps at the hands of an agent dispatched by Lugok. Jetanien, naturally, had never shared his knowledge or feelings of the situation with the Klingon, but he knew it could be argued that Lugok merely was doing the bidding of a superior, at least then. But now? Jetanien had spent a great deal of time with the Klingon as they waited for D'tran to arrive on Nimbus III, after which the trio set to the task of laying the groundwork for what had become the joint colony. Was it possible that Lugok could still be working to deceive him?

All things are possible, Jetanien reminded himself, then tried to recall something he once had read from an ancient human text given to him by a former assistant. The book had contained anecdotal passages about warfare, which the Chelon quickly had learned could be translated to diplomacy as well as any other competitive endeavor. It took him an additional moment to retrieve the passage from the depths of his memory: *Keep your friends close, and your enemies closer.*

"What our friend requires," D'tran said, shifting in his seat to reach for an empty glass sitting atop Jetanien's desk, "is to join us in our celebration. There will be time later for political maneuvering, posturing, and brinksmanship."

Lugok nodded. "Agreed," he said, hoisting his bottle. "Come, Jetanien, and learn why bloodwine is a most excellent substitute for any breakfast beverage you might otherwise choose to imbibe."

"Very well, my friends," Jetanien said, moving around his companions to the seat behind his desk. His movements were halted as a low rumble rattled his office windows and even the artwork hanging on his walls. The overhead light flickered, and there was a noticeable interruption in the bulb's audible hum.

"What was that?" D'tran asked, rising from his seat as Lugok did the same.

Frowning, Jetanien turned toward the doors leading to his balcony. "That sounded like a crash of some kind." Had an accident occurred, either on one of the nearby streets or even outside Paradise City's perimeter wall? Even before he reached for the control to open the door, he now could hear the faint sounds of alarm sirens wailing in the early morning air from some distance away.

But not that far.

"No," Lugok said, moving in the direction of the balcony. "That was an explosion."

Jetanien opened the door and stepped onto the balcony, where it took him no time to locate the origin point of the crash, explosion, or whatever had happened. A plume of dark smoke was rising into the sky from south of the city, where the colony's rudimentary spaceport resided.

"Some kind of accident?" Jetanien asked.

"Or sabotage," D'tran replied.

From behind them, the intercom on Jetanien's desk beeped for attention, followed by Sergio Moreno's voice. *"Ambassador, you have an urgent call from the spaceport administrator's office. It's Constable Schiappacasse."*

"Route it to my viewer," Jetanien called out, walking back into the office and taking a position behind his desk so that he could see his computer display. The unit's compact viewscreen activated, providing an image of Carla Schiappacasse, her eyes wide with concern and her hair tucked under a white brimmed cap that distinguished her as a member of the colony's security force.

"Ambassador Jetanien, I was told Senator D'tran was with you this morning. As you're no doubt aware by now, we've had an incident here at the spaceport involving the Romulan senator's private shuttle."

"This is D'tran," the elder Romulan called to the viewer as he moved to stand next to Jetanian. "What has happened?"

"I'm relieved to see you, Senator," the security liaison said. *"I was unable to raise you on your personal communicator."*

"I apologize," D'tran replied, reaching into the folds of his robes to produce the compact communications device. "I had deactivated it."

"As long as you're safe," Schiappacasse said, frowning as she lowered her head as though studying something off-screen. *"I'm afraid the same can't be said for your shuttle, sir. It's been destroyed."*

D'tran's expression showed his alarm at the news. "Was anyone hurt?"

"Not so far as we've been able to determine, sir," Schiappacasse replied. *"We've had several injuries among our security staff, and they're being treated at the infirmary."*

Standing to Jetanien's right, Lugok grunted in disapproval at the report. "Do you know what happened?"

The image, which jostled enough for Jetanien to realize they were seeing the view as transmitted from a handheld device, shifted to move Schiappacasse out of frame and focus on the tarmac. There was now a clear view of the smoldering wreckage of what Jetanien recognized as the Romulan transport. The smoke streaming from the ruined craft matched what he had seen from his balcony, and the ship itself was continuing to burn.

"We're still waiting on a detachment from the fire brigade to arrive on scene," Schiappacasse said after a moment. *"We were attacked, Ambassador. Our best estimates count a dozen colonists who infiltrated the port's secure area. All of them were angry and demanding access to a spacecraft so that they could leave the planet."*

"What?" Jetanien asked, stunned by what he was hearing. While pockets of unrest had continued to be trouble for the constabulary almost since the colony's first day, none of the incidents so far had risen to the level of deliberate, malicious attacks on private property. More troubling than the assault itself was its apparent motivation.

Schiappacasse's face returned to the viewer. *"I admit we didn't consider how serious they were. I thought it was something we could get under control, but they weren't being very receptive."*

"Who was it?" D'tran asked.

Clearing her throat, the security liaison replied, *"Klingons, sir. They said they were tired of being lied to about the situation here. There was something about their farming work being doomed before they could even start, and that they refused to stay here. When my staff and I tried to get them under control, they stormed the tarmac."*

Lugok said, "Consider yourself fortunate, Constable. They might just as easily have killed you and your staff." Turning his attention to Jetanien, he added, "It sounds as though this group is among our newer arrivals, brought here specifically for the task of assisting with our agricultural needs." He frowned, shaking his head. "I was told they had a warrior's drive to help us, but I found them to be less than motivated from the moment they arrived. I should have known they would cause trouble."

"Constable," D'tran said, "you indicated they were seeking transport off-world?"

On the screen, Schiappacasse nodded. *"Yes, Senator. Your transport was among those vessels they were able to access after reaching the tarmac. Though we were able to keep them from hijacking the ship, once it was clear they wouldn't succeed, one of the colonists—a female, according to the initial report by security teams at the scene—broke away from the group and threw some sort of explosive underneath it. After that, it was too late to do anything else. I must stress that we won't know more until we've had time to conduct an investigation."* She paused, reaching up to cover her mouth as she coughed, perhaps from inhaling smoke. *"Obviously, we need to find out where they got the explosive, and if they have any more."*

Jetanien asked, "Are you worried they may have smuggled contraband weapons to the colony, Constable?"

"They would have no need to do that," Lugok countered. "I suspect the components for building an improvised explosive are in abundance here, despite the colony's standing directives against weapons."

D'tran grunted. "Now, there's a comforting thought." To the

viewscreen, he said, "Have the infiltrators been taken into custody?"

"*Yes, Ambassador,*" the liaison replied. "*They're being held here until we can secure transport to the brig.*"

"I'll question them myself," Lugok said, almost growling the words.

Jetanien nodded. "We need to know if this is an isolated incident, or the symptom of a larger problem."

"Indeed," the Klingon said, before setting the bottle of bloodwine on Jetanien's desk and making his way from the office.

Turning his attention back to Schiappacasse, Jetanien said, "Thank you for your report, Constable. Please keep us informed of your findings as you are able."

"*Of course, sir. Schiappacasse out.*"

As the viewer deactivated, Jetanien looked to D'tran. "Well, for the moment, I think we can assume that your ship was not deliberately targeted."

"Perhaps it was coincidental," the aged Romulan replied, "but I cannot help but be troubled by this. Taken with the other incidents of unrest, I am beginning to fear that a pattern is emerging." Sighing, he added, "Jetanien, have you considered the possibility that there might be some form of organized, united effort being brought to bear against our mission here?"

In point of fact, Jetanien had lost count of the occasions on which he had pondered that very notion. "If that is the case, then we do not have the resources to combat it."

More troubling than that unfortunate reality, he knew, was the greater concern that anyone planning such action was also well aware of the colony's vulnerability.

19

It was with no small amount of satisfaction that Ja'tesh guided the Sporak all-terrain vehicle along the broken, uneven ground, steering it over and around rocks, vegetation, ditches, and other depressions with practiced ease. She had been piloting such vehicles since childhood, having been taught by her father almost from the time she had been able to walk.

"You drive as though you are possessed by a demon escaped from *Gre'thor*," said her mate, Kraloq, from where he sat in the Sporak's front passenger seat to Ja'tesh's left.

She laughed, keeping one hand on the wheel while reaching with the other to poke her mate's muscled arm. "Be thankful the ground's dry," she said, making no effort to quell the mischievous pleasure she was deriving from Kraloq's discomfort. "There's nothing like driving one of these through the mud after a good rainfall. That's the sort of terrain these Sporaks were built to conquer." Kraloq's only reaction was to roll his eyes, a response that prompted another laugh from Ja'tesh.

She knew that, like most males, Kraloq preferred to pilot the vehicle rather than subjugate himself to his mate's desires, but he endured this affront to his ego with silence, at least most of the time. As for her, the comfortable whine of the Sporak's engine as its vibrations permeated the vehicle's every surface never failed to soothe her. Likewise, they always elicited recollections of traveling with her father to his favorite hunting grounds on *Qo'noS*. The journey took almost an entire day from their home, with the travel time spent singing songs or listening to her father tell all manner of stories. Such tales often received increasing levels of embellishment during each subsequent trip, which only served to heighten their charm and embed themselves in Ja'tesh's vast catalog of fond memories.

"Next time, we use the transporters," Kraloq said, bouncing in his seat as the three tires on the Sporak's left side rolled over a large rock.

"Where's the adventure in that?" Ja'tesh asked, navigating the vehicle around an even larger rock. "The point of a trip like this isn't the destination, my lover; it's the journey we enjoy along the way." In addition to the many skills her father had taught her, most of which served little practical purpose in modern Klingon society while being well suited to life on a remote colony world such as Traelus II, he also had imparted to her an appreciation for enjoying life, rather than simply living it. She loved eschewing the trappings of contemporary life and instead plunging headlong into nature. It was this desire to love and understand whatever world on which she found herself that had guided her to her present career as a horticultural specialist, and made her a prime candidate for membership in a colonization effort. Though not as respected as a career in the military, the work of settlements like this one also was of service to the Empire, inasmuch as it allowed her people to extend their reach that much farther into the galaxy. The Traelus system was among those regions which were at the most extreme edges of Klingon territory and influence, and Ja'tesh knew that, in generations to come, it might well provide a point from which the Empire would again seek to push its borders outward.

Besides, if she had not opted to volunteer for the colony assignment on Traelus II, she would never have met Kraloq. Though a farmer himself, he had served as an enlisted soldier in the military before an injury during training cut short whatever glorious career he might have enjoyed. Having never faced an enemy in battle, Kraloq instead left the service with feelings of shame and failure. Ja'tesh had never given much credence to the popularization of military service as a cornerstone of Klingon culture. Yes, she believed a strong force capable of defending the Empire and its interests was important, but the glamorization of "honor above all" and the casual sacrifice of lives in the name of glory and conquest were attitudes with which she always had taken fervent issue. Though she had been involved with one or two soldiers during her young life and at one point even had seen herself as a willing, loving, military wife, Ja'tesh had long ago decided that she much preferred her lover in her bed rather than his medals on her wall. It had not taken long for her to convince Kraloq of the virtues her line of reasoning embraced.

"You're smiling," Kraloq said, reaching for a support handle as Ja'tesh navigated the Sporak around a hole in the ground.

"Am I?" she asked, opting to share nothing further, though when she reached for him this time it was to stroke his long, black hair. Glancing to the far horizon, she saw how far the sun had traveled, and she looked at the chronometer set into the driver's console. "It will be dark soon, but we should be home before that."

Kraloq grunted. "Or, we could spend one more night under the stars."

"That does carry a certain appeal," Ja'tesh conceded, her smile widening. Twelve days spent camping and touring the remote highlands located more than two hundred kilometers to the south of the colony had served as a welcome change of pace from the activities that all but consumed their days. It had been the first extended respite she and Kraloq had enjoyed since arriving at Traelus II, and they had done their best to savor every moment of the time spent away from their fellow colonists. Ja'tesh had been anxious to see areas of the planet that had not yet been disturbed or even explored as a consequence of the outpost's presence. For his part, Kraloq had spent a good portion of their getaway content to watch his mate bathing nude in the river that ran past their campsite, or lying on the small beach and allowing the warmth of the Traelan sun to dry her bare skin. And what of the nights? As Ja'tesh had expected, the open air, warm fire, and utter solitude had affected her mate's desires and attentions in other areas, much to her satisfaction.

Males, she mused. *So predictable.* Perhaps one last night before returning to their demanding duties was not the worst idea, after all.

"What is that?"

Kraloq's question broke through Ja'tesh's reverie, and she turned her head to see that he was pointing out of the Sporak's open passenger-side window at something in the distance. Her eyes tracked across the open terrain until she saw . . . something sitting atop a small rise. Whatever it was, its straight lines and reflective surface were very much out of place in the middle of open ground.

"Some kind of equipment from the colony?" Ja'tesh asked as she brought the Sporak to a stop. "I don't recognize it."

"It appears too small to be farm or excavation equipment," Kraloq said. "And even if it was, what's it doing all the way out here?"

Ja'tesh shrugged. "Maybe somebody else decided to camp tonight." She smiled, but it had no effect on Kraloq, whose expression had turned dour. "What?"

"We should see what it is."

"What do you think it is?" she asked, placing her hand on his shoulder.

Shaking his head, Kraloq replied, "I don't know. That's why I think we should look."

For the first time, Ja'tesh realized her mate was displaying actual concern. "You're serious."

"Yes," Kraloq said, nodding before pointing to the communications panel on the Sporak's console. "We should notify the colony."

Frowning, Ja'tesh said, "This is the soldier in you, isn't it?"

Rather than replying, Kraloq had shifted his position in his seat in order to reach behind him and pull a small satchel from the floorboard of the rear passenger area. Ja'tesh said nothing as he reached into the heavy, woven bag and extracted from it a disruptor pistol. "We're on an isolated planet near enemy territory. Yes, this is the soldier in me."

Ja'tesh released a sigh of concession. "Fine."

Shifting the Sporak into gear, Ja'tesh guided the vehicle toward the strange object as Kraloq made contact with the colony administrator and advised him of their discovery and current location, and that they were investigating the situation. Ja'tesh brought the vehicle to a halt at the base of the rise, and after refusing the disruptor pistol Kraloq offered her in favor of the knife she had already strapped to her right leg, the pair made short work of ascending the hill.

"It's not ours," Kraloq said, his brow furrowing as he studied the object sitting atop the plateau. Ja'tesh nodded in agreement as she regarded the odd construct. It was as high as her neck, and perhaps somewhat smaller than a typical shipping container. Rather than sitting on the ground, it stood on six short, thick legs. Its shell appeared to be constructed from some kind of metal or metallic composite material, though Ja'tesh saw nothing resembling seams, joints, or rivets. The thing looked to have been cast as a single piece, rather than assembled from plates or other components. Its black surface reflected the heat of the midday sun, though when Ja'tesh held her hand close to one side she felt no warmth.

"I've never seen anything like it," she said. "Is it some kind of generator?"

Kraloq replied, "Perhaps, but for what purpose? For all I know, it could be a bomb."

The object, whatever it was, emitted an abrupt hum, causing both Ja'tesh and Kraloq to take several steps backward. Before Ja'tesh could say anything, Kraloq had drawn his disruptor and aimed it at one side of the construct's flat, black shell.

"Wait!" she cried, holding out her hands. Then, unable to suppress a small grin, she added, "Don't kill it just yet." She cursed herself for neglecting to bring with her a portable scanner from the Sporak. "We should get some readings."

She jerked at the sound of weapons fire, realizing only after an extra instant that the report had not come from Kraloq's disruptor. A bright orange flash screamed past her and from the corner of her eye she caught sight of Kraloq dropping out of her field of vision just as something slammed into the side of the object. She felt bits of fire peppering her exposed skin as she dropped to the ground and rolled away from the object, trying to keep Kraloq in sight. She realized that the hum coming from the mechanism had died, but then her ears were filled with more disruptor fire, and Ja'tesh saw Kraloq kneeling on the ground, firing his weapon down the side of the rise. Jerking her head in that direction, she was startled to see a thin silhouette, maneuvering on a quartet of long, spindly legs as it held something in another, smaller extremity.

It was a Tholian, encased in what Ja'tesh recognized as the species' version of an environmental suit, and carrying what could only be a weapon.

"Kraloq!"

Her lover said nothing but instead continued firing. One of his shots struck the Tholian in its narrow chest and Ja'tesh watched as it shuddered from the force of the impact but remained standing. Rising to his feet, Kraloq uttered a low growl of irritation as he fired again. Another energy bolt drove itself into the Tholian, and this time Ja'tesh saw bits of the alien's environmental suit as well as its crystal body flying in different directions. The disgusting, insectlike creature emitted a high-pitched shriek Ja'tesh hoped was a cry of pain as Kraloq fired yet again, and this time the shot took the Tholian in the center of the hooded cowl obscuring the alien's face. Whatever wail of agony it was unleashing came to an abrupt end as the Tholian's body fell backward, stirring up dust and dirt as it tumbled down the slight slope.

His weapon held out in front of him, Kraloq made his way to the edge of the plateau and looked down, and Ja'tesh saw him nod in satisfaction at what he had just done. Looking over his shoulder, he said, "We need to warn the colony. If the Tholians are here, they're planning something." He was about to say something, but then Ja'tesh saw his eyes shift to look at something behind her just before he began to turn in her direction. Bringing his weapon around his body, Kraloq took aim at something Ja'tesh could not see before she heard the sound of another disruptor bolt, and a bright orange streak whined past her head and tore into Kraloq's chest.

20

Wait!

Festrene called out to his companion, Hazthrene, cautioning him not to give hasty chase as the large Klingon with the weapon fell over the edge of the plateau and out of sight. Its mate—a female, if Festrene was not mistaken—lunged toward the other Klingon, disappearing down the slope. Hazthrene, young and impulsive and caught up in the stresses of the moment, followed after his prey, his weapon held up as he searched for a target. The third member of their triad, Tozhene, had already paid the price for his impatience, if what had happened to him at the hands of the Klingon was any indication. Why had he not remained hidden at the Klingons' approach, which they had detected upon picking up the transmission from their vehicle to their settlement? Festrene had preferred to hide rather than directly confront the Klingons, waiting for an opportunity to neutralize the intruders without killing them. He could only reason that his younger companion had viewed the Klingons as a threat to the generator. However, his rash actions had now placed the entire mission at risk.

This was not supposed to happen! Festrene's orders for this mission were simple: install the network of web generators and deploy them, without engaging any of the local Klingon population. This mission had taken a great deal of planning and coordination to conceive and carry out, not just because of the stealth required to operate without detection on the Klingon-held world but also because of the new, experimental technology with which Festrene had been charged. He had expended substantial time and effort learning the system and its operation. According to his superiors, if the experiment failed to be carried out here, it likely would be some time before another opportunity to test the weapon presented itself. This, of course, did not even take into consideration the political ramifications should the Klingons learn what was taking place on their planet.

And now, it appeared to Festrene that the entire scheme was unraveling.

He was angry that Tozhene's impetuous actions had already caused two deaths. The whole purpose of the pacification field was to prevent unnecessary loss of life. After all, dead prisoners were of no use, and an intact infrastructure like a city or other installation was infinitely more valuable than vast swaths of irradiated rubble. Occupying such territory became easier, and those captured could in turn be added to the workforces the Tholians required to carry out all manner of tasks ill-suited to their delicate physiques. Festrene applauded the pacification field's concept as well as the attitude that had driven its creation, as he had always been reluctant to kill, even in battle, unless circumstances offered no other alternative. There were those who had argued that such measures and mercy were wasted on the Klingons, a warrior culture that prided itself on conquest and domination with little regard to the lives of those they fought. Thankfully, several of Festrene's colleagues shared his own views, in that such conduct on the part of an enemy did not justify compromising or discarding one's own morality.

It was his hope that this weapon, which he had championed, would demonstrate how easy it was to uphold such principles. The network of web generators had been established; the only thing that remained was to activate the field, but fate had conspired to bring the two interlopers into their midst, and now one of them was dead, and at the cost of one of Festrene's subordinates. He wanted no more casualties.

Be cautious, he said as Hazthrene approached the edge of the rise, and recoiled as a new onslaught of weapons fire echoed across the plateau. His warning to Hazthrene had been for naught as the air was filled with the frenzy of several flashes of harsh crimson energy. Hazthrene was caught in the barrage and Festrene could only watch as his underling's body absorbed the force of multiple strikes. A tortured chorus of agonized cries echoed off the nearby rocks as the subordinate collapsed to the ground, where he remained still.

No!

Pivoting on his hind legs, Festrene turned and skittered over the broken, uneven ground, lunging across the plateau to where he had placed the control console that would oversee the field's deployment. All of the coordinates and power settings had been input; the only thing left to do was initiate the activation sequence. If he could get to the console, it would be a simple task to execute, provided the Klingon female did not reach him first.

He heard footsteps as he reached the console and looked up to see the Klingon running, but not in his direction. His first impulse was to raise his weapon and shoot her, until he realized she was using the terrain for cover, protecting herself by denying him a clear sightline. *What was she doing?* Looking in the general direction of where she seemed to be running, Festrene now understood that she was heading for the ground vehicle in which the Klingons had arrived.

A disruptor bolt struck the ground near the console and he turned to see the Klingon firing at him. She did so while running and dodging, and Festrene surmised that she was doing so more as a means of providing cover than with the hope of actually striking a target. She was attempting to shield herself as she broke onto the expanse of open ground separating her from her vehicle. Her tactic was successful, preventing Festrene from bringing himself up to a suitable firing position. At first he was confused about the Klingon's actions; it was not typical of her people to run from a fight, or even to engage in such guerrilla-style strike-and-evade tactics. From everything he knew of Klingon society, they much preferred face-to-face battles in the open, staring down their enemies. Perhaps this Klingon was not a soldier, and was seeking escape.

No, you fool! Comprehension dawned as he saw her reach the vehicle. Instead of attempting escape, she reached for something, and Festrene remembered what had prompted this entire incident: the Klingons' transmission to the colony. *She's trying to warn them!*

Reaching for the console with his free appendage, Festrene struck the controls to initiate the pacification field. The Klingon was within the field's targeted zone of influence, so she would be among the first to be subjected to its effects. The console emitted several strings of melodic tones, which told Festrene the protocol was under way, and a moment later he heard the web generator on the nearby plateau began to produce an ominous, resonating hum. In moments the hum grew louder, and Festrene watched the power indicators for all twenty-four generators glow bright yellow. He silently counted down the intervals until the generators would deploy their portion of the field.

Something hot punched him in his upper torso and he fell back from the console. He heard his weapon bouncing off a rock somewhere behind his head as he collapsed to the ground, a wave of agony radiating outward from the center of his body. His limbs, as though possessed of their own will, twitched and jerked as he rolled onto his back, and every movement sent new spikes of pain shooting through him. Lolling his head to one side, he saw the Klingon female running from her vehicle and toward him from beyond the generator, her weapon tracking him as she readied another shot. The expression on her face was one Festrene recognized as unrestrained fury, communicating her intent: vengeance.

Then, the generator fired.

From his vantage point lying flat on his back, Festrene had an unobstructed view as a pulse of orange energy erupted from the top of the mechanism, accompanied by a shrill whine as it described an arc across the clear blue Traelan sky. As it traveled, the pulse began to expand, flattening and stretching with each passing moment. In the distance, Festrene could see the pulses fired from other generators in the network following similar courses, each doing their part to weave their portion of the web as they converged on a point Festrene had calculated as being above the center of the Klingon colony.

It is working! The thought pushed past the torment gripping Festrene as the pain from his wound mounted. He could not be sure, but he thought the Klingon's attack may well have damaged at least one vital organ in his torso. It was almost certain that he required medical attention, but there was none to be found in this place.

The field's effect on the Klingon was immediate, who staggered to a stop in midstride and dropped her weapon as she reached with both hands to grip the sides of her head. There was no mistaking the distress she obviously was experiencing as she fell to her knees. Blood was running from her nose, and Festrene saw now that it also was coming out of her mouth. She released a gurgling, anguished howl before falling forward and landing face-first in the dirt. Her body continued to twitch as Festrene watched in horror.

What was happening?

The device had been designed to be used as a neurological attack, so the field's effects on humanoids should not be this severe, and it certainly should not be killing anyone, as it appeared now to be doing.

What have I done?

Unable to move and feeling his strength ebbing, Festrene reached with one feeble appendage toward the console, willing it to deactivate itself. The mechanism was out of reach, and though it would deactivate itself after a prescribed interval, he knew by then it would be too late. Every Klingon at the colony would be dead, quite possibly along with every other specimen of animal life in the targeted area.

He had killed them.

With supreme effort as he fought through the pain racking his body, Festrene maneuvered himself so that he could crawl along the ground. Accompanied by the incessant hum of the web generator, he pulled himself through the dirt and dust until he felt the console's warm smooth surface. Once activated, the field could not be aborted until it completed its programmed duration, but there remained a single option for disabling it. Festrene's phalanges moved across the rows of controls and indicators until he found the familiar, octagonal switch that sat by itself in the center of the panel. It was intended for use only in the most dire of circumstances, which to Festrene seemed appropriate just now.

Despite his injuries and even as he felt consciousness beginning to slip away from him, Festrene was still awake and aware of his surroundings when the self-destruct protocol was triggered.

21

"What the hell are you doing here?"

His eyes wide with surprise as he regarded the welcoming, smiling face of Ezekiel Fisher, Reyes had to raise his voice to be heard over the background noise of the restaurant situated on the fringe of the *Omari-Ekon*'s gaming deck. All around him, patrons, servers, and other employees bustled past on their way into and out of the restaurant. Fisher himself seemed immune to the minor chaos unfolding around them, just as he appeared oblivious to the pair of Orions who had accompanied him this far into the casino. The burly security guards were going out of their way not to look obvious as they stood several meters away, pointedly looking anywhere except to where Fisher and Reyes stood.

Amateurs.

Hooking a thumb over one shoulder at the two guards, Fisher replied, "It's like I told Thick and Thicker over there: I'm here for the buffet."

Reyes resisted questioning the statement, knowing that for every guard he could see failing in his attempts to keep them under covert surveillance, there was another pair of eyes or ears keeping tabs on him from another, better vantage point. Instead, he said, "There's nothing in there that's good for you."

"Exactly," Fisher replied, smiling again. "I get tired of Starfleet dietary menus. Sometimes I just want to feel my arteries harden while I eat."

"This place'll do it," Reyes said, following Fisher as the other man led the way into the restaurant. "I'm surprised Nogura didn't declare this place off-limits to station personnel."

Looking around before answering, Fisher regarded Reyes with a neutral expression. "Why would he do that? It's not as though anything odd or bad has happened over here. At least, there's nothing on any of the news feeds or daily briefing reports."

It was more than just a casual statement, Reyes knew, thanks to the information T'Prynn had supplied him. The failed attempt to extract him, and the deaths of the two officers who had been involved, was being kept under wraps, at least for the time being. This had come as no great shock to Reyes, who could understand all the various reasons why Starfleet and Admiral Nogura, to say nothing of Ganz and Neera, would want to keep things quiet. It was just the sort of incident that could touch off all manner of headaches for the Federation. As for the Orions, while Neera seemed content to observe the status quo for the moment, Ganz was getting edgy. T'Prynn, having somehow managed to infiltrate the *Omari-Ekon*'s communications system, had overheard Ganz's instructions to his underling to begin plotting Reyes's "accidental demise." She had passed that information on to Reyes, with the advisory that he be even more aware of his surroundings and the very real danger he now faced, and that steps were being readied to extract him from the Orion ship, sanctioned this time by Admiral Nogura. Despite this, Reyes had volunteered to remain in place long enough to take another crack at the *Omari-Ekon*'s navigational logs, knowing that whether he succeeded or failed, it likely would be his last attempt to secure the information.

Meanwhile, Reyes mused as he tried to keep up with Fisher, who was working his way farther into the restaurant like a man possessed, *might as well eat.* He was only somewhat surprised to see Tim Pennington, sitting alone at one of the tables with several small plates and bowls arrayed before him. The journalist smiled, lifting a fork to his temple in mock salute as Reyes approached.

"Mister Reyes," Pennington said. "Fancy meeting you here, mate."

Returning the greeting, Reyes noted that neither Pennington nor Fisher so much as acknowledged each other as the doctor walked past. A casual observer might not pick up on this, but Reyes knew the men were acquainted if not actual friends, so the lack of greeting was more than a bit odd.

What are you up to, Zeke?

The pair navigated a path around tables, patrons, and servers bearing plates and bowls of various substances Reyes had learned over time was food of one sort or another. Reaching the start of the buffet line, he let his eyes wander over the dual aisles with their stations containing all manner of cuisines. Markings on placards next to each station indicated which foods were suitable for one species or another, and Reyes had learned during his first days aboard the *Omari-Ekon* which stations to avoid. Most of the selections were self-service, and patrons took advantage of the setup to load their plates with whatever particular foodstuff tickled their fancy.

"What's with you and Pennington?" Reyes asked, keeping his voice low.

The doctor turned and regarded him with a flat expression. "Pennington? He's here? Imagine that. He probably likes the buffet, too." He moved toward the serving line. "They make a pretty good Kohlanese stew, as I recall, but it's been a while, and I heard they changed chefs."

What the hell is he babbling about? The question teased Reyes, though he forced himself to play along. "They fired the last guy. Too many weird spices in the meat or something. Sent some poor bastard to the infirmary with a hole in his gut. Guess he didn't read the menu cards."

Fisher nodded. "That'll teach him." The line continued to move forward, and as he drew abreast of the first station along the buffet, he reached to where a stack of hexagonal plates sat waiting for customers. Retrieving two plates, he held one face up and offered it to Reyes. "Kind of reminds me of chow time at the Academy."

There was something about the way he made the statement, coupled with the way he held the plate for an extra heartbeat as Reyes took it, that set off an alarm bell in his head. He scrambled to search long-buried memories of his days at Starfleet Academy, trying to connect anything to what Fisher had just said. Then, as he watched his friend take his place at the end of the serving line that ran the length of the buffet and past each of the stations on this side of the restaurant, something about the doctor's movements triggered a response.

Fisher was holding his plate level, parallel to the floor, with his elbows tucked in tight at his sides, just as Academy cadets once had been required to do when navigating the dining facility during their meals. It had seemed silly at the time, he recalled, particularly given the emphasis with which his instructors had enforced the rule along with a host of others that, on their face, made no sense whatsoever. As it turned out, the rigid, formal movement through the cafeteria line, complete with facing movements and the proper positioning of arms and feet, had been one of numerous ways in which Academy instructors reinforced the various components of marching in formation during close-order drill. In hindsight, Reyes considered the practice as overkill, and indeed such policies and practices had been relaxed over the years, but for old-school Starfleet types like him and Fisher, it was just one more outdated practice from a bygone era.

So why the hell is he doing it now?

Instinct told Reyes to follow his friend's movements, though he opted to do so while attempting to appear relaxed as he made his way through the buffet procession. After several moments spent perusing the various selections, both men made their choices. Fisher stood silent, an amused expression gracing his weathered features as he waited for Reyes to pay for both meals using his own credit chip.

"No, really. I got it," Reyes said, his voice dripping sarcasm as he handed his chip to the cashier.

Finding an empty table along one wall of the restaurant's dining area, the next few moments were spent in silence as they ate their meals. Reyes had not even put the first spoonful of Kohlanese stew in his mouth when a server, a lithe, striking Andorian woman whose outfit consisted of less material than the napkin in

Reyes's lap, approached their table and asked if they wanted anything to drink. As she left, Fisher turned to watch her as she disappeared into the depths of the crowded restaurant.

"You think she gets cold, walking around dressed like that?" he asked.

Reyes shrugged. "I think she'll kick your ass if you don't stop looking at her like that." Taking another bite of his stew, he asked around a rather large chunk of spiced meat, "So, you want to tell me what you're doing here?"

"Can't I come and visit an old friend once in a while?" Fisher asked, offering a wan smile as he picked at his salad. "Besides, after that inoculation I gave you, I wanted to make sure you weren't suffering any adverse side effects." His expression betrayed nothing, as though the doctor had been carrying out covert conversations in public his entire life. At least Fisher's first visit had served a purpose: providing Reyes with the subcutaneous transceiver that allowed him to communicate with T'Prynn.

"Well, I'm still having trouble sleeping," Reyes said. He paused to glance around, checking to see if anyone might be eavesdropping on their conversation, "but I don't think there's anything you can do about it. Just too much racket around here, is all."

Nodding, Fisher offered another wry grin. "Well, maybe what you need is a change of venue. You're overdue for a vacation, aren't you?"

"For a couple of years now," Reyes replied. "Got any suggestions?"

The doctor shrugged as he turned his attention from his salad to a bowl of soup he had selected. "I'll see what I can dig up."

Taking a few more bites of his stew, Reyes cast a casual glance about the bar. No one seemed close enough to be eavesdropping, but he kept his voice low as he asked, "What happened with Hetzlein and Gianetti?"

It was obvious from Fisher's expression that the doctor was uncomfortable discussing this topic, particularly given his present surroundings. Without looking up from his plate, he replied, "Their bodies weren't recovered, but one of T'Prynn's informants reported that Ganz had his people make them disappear, if you know what I mean. Starfleet's not acknowledging their actions, and their families have been told they died in an accident during training. Nogura can't press Ganz about it, and there's no way Ganz is going to cop to murdering two Starfleet officers."

Reyes forced himself not to react to the news. It was not an unexpected development, given the clandestine nature of the extraction attempt. Why Ganz had not taken advantage of the situation by capturing the two covert operatives and using them as leverage against Admiral Nogura, he did not know. All that was certain was that the two officers' deaths were now added to the list of acts for which Reyes hoped the Orion merchant prince would be held accountable one day.

Movement in his peripheral vision made Reyes turn to see an Orion male—one of the two security guards who had been shadowing Fisher outside the restaurant—heading toward the table. Reyes felt his muscles tense in anticipation, not liking what he was seeing. The guard brushed past a server and two patrons on his way in their direction, and when he came to a stop at their table, he stood in silence, glaring at them. After several seconds, during which Fisher continued to work on his soup, Reyes decided he would be the one to break the ice.

"We're not ready for the dessert menu just yet, sport. Come back in about fifteen minutes." The remark was enough to make the Orion turn his smoldering gaze upon Reyes, though the guard said nothing to him. Instead, another moment passed in odd silence before he turned his attention to Fisher.

"Come with me. I've been ordered to escort you to the main entrance."

"I'm not finished with my lunch," the doctor replied.

As if to emphasize his point, the Orion leaned across the table toward Fisher. "Yes, you are. Come with me, now."

"What's this about?" Reyes snapped, scowling and deciding that he did not care how the guard chose to interpret his question or tone.

The guard turned to glower once more at Reyes. "I've been

ordered to escort this human off the ship. I don't know the reason, and I don't care." To Fisher, he said, "Let's go."

Shrugging, the doctor wiped his mouth with a napkin before pushing back his chair and rising to his feet. "Food was cold, anyway." He sighed, offering Reyes another small, knowing smile. "See you around, Diego," he said, before looking back to the guard and nodding toward the restaurant's exit. "After you."

Reyes was certain he heard the Orion growl in irritation as he gestured for Fisher to move along. He watched the unlikely pair work their way through the crowded restaurant, with the guard retrieving what Reyes knew to be a communications device from his belt and holding it up to his mouth. No doubt he was alerting whoever was on duty for the *Omari-Ekon*'s security detail that he had his charge in custody and was escorting him to the exit, where Reyes guessed Fisher would be shown without ceremony to the docking ring leading back to Vanguard.

See you around, Zeke.

Looking down at his meal, Reyes decided that Fisher's dismissal and the prospect of eating yet another meal in solitude had removed what remained of his appetite. He was contemplating an attempt to annoy Ganz and his cronies by winning at the gaming tables when his thoughts were interrupted by the voice of T'Prynn echoing in his head.

"Mister Reyes."

"I thought you were going to call me Diego?" Reyes asked, masking his mouth with his water glass, from which he then sipped.

The Vulcan seemed to ignore that. *"I have just been informed that Doctor Fisher has left the* Omari-Ekon. *As you have likely surmised, his visit was a pretense."*

"No kidding," Reyes mumbled. "I'm assuming Pennington's part of the plan, too?"

T'Prynn said, *"That's correct, but he's there only to serve as a distraction. His last visit attracted some scrutiny, but I do not believe they know anything about the messages he helped you to pass to us. However, he volunteered to take his evening meal aboard the* Omari-Ekon *simply as an exercise in diverting the attention of any security guards who might be watching Doctor Fisher."*

Reyes wiped his mouth with his napkin. "Okay, but if Zeke was supposed to tell me something, he either didn't get a chance to say it, or I'm too stupid to have understood it."

T'Prynn replied, *"Doctor Fisher's task was to leave you something. Please check the underside of your plate."*

Trying to affect as casual a demeanor as possible while not making it appear too obvious that he was looking about to see if he was being observed, Reyes took the better part of a minute to inspect the underside of each of the plate's eight edges with his fingers. On the left side of the plate, close to the edge nearest his side of the table, his fingertips brushed over something thin and smooth. It required only the smallest amount of force to move the object, and it fell from the plate into his palm. He left his hand in place for an extra moment as he forced himself to take another bite of his stew. Around the meat in his mouth, he mumbled, *"What is it?"*

"A transceiver, fitted with an additional translator module," T'Prynn replied. *"You will use it during your next attempt to access the* Omari-Ekon's *navigational logs."*

Reyes suspected as much. The device was small enough that he could conceal it in his hand, and he covered the movement by reaching up with that same hand to rub his nose. "I was wondering if you'd forgotten about me." It might have been his imagination, but he swore he heard T'Prynn sigh before answering.

"Hardly. It took some time to program the module to be able to access all known spoken and written Orion languages, including those which have fallen out of common use. You should encounter no further linguistic difficulty when you make your next attempt."

"Excellent," Reyes said, reaching up to scratch his chin. "When do we go for it?"

"If you have no objections," T'Prynn replied, *"I was thinking we might try later this evening."*

That suited Reyes just fine. He was tiring of this entire affair, and there was a part of him that wanted it to be over, one way or the other.

Of course, he mused as he considered the transceiver still secreted in his palm as he strolled out of the restaurant, *I definitely prefer one way over the other.*

22

Ming Xiong heard the footsteps crossing the open deck of the *Lovell*'s cargo bay, only then realizing that he had missed the sound of the room's access hatch opening. Had he been dozing? Jerking himself upright in his seat, he reached up to wipe his face while turning his seat in the direction of his visitor, uncertain as to whether he should expect a dressing down or merciless ribbing for his apparent nap.

"What in the name of all that's holy are you doing here at oh-whatever hundred hours time it is?" asked Lieutenant Kurt Davis, Mahmud al-Khaled's second in command for the *Lovell*'s Corps of Engineers team. Tall and thin, with long arms that seemed much too small for the sleeves of his uniform tunic, when Davis smiled his mouth seemed capable of devouring the rest of his face, and Xiong was certain the man possessed the whitest teeth he had ever seen.

"I could ask you the same question," Xiong said, rising from his chair and making his way toward the food slot set into the nearby bulkhead.

Davis shrugged. "Just making the rounds. It's my shift. Commander al-Khaled and I usually work opposite each other, and I like the night shift. It's quieter—most of the time, anyway. Besides, it gives me time and space to sort through a tough project without all of the interruptions that come with working on prime shift. There's also never a line in the mess hall, either." He glanced toward the isolation chamber. "If I'd known you were down here, I'd have dropped by sooner."

Rubbing his chin, which he now realized had grown fuzzy

with very fine beard stubble, Xiong reached for one of the data cards lying on a nearby shelf and inserted it into the food slot's reader. He entered a sequence on the row of buttons below the reader, and the slot's door opened to reveal a cup of hot coffee. As he retrieved the steaming beverage, he held it up to Davis, who shook his head at the silent offer.

"So," the engineer said, "what's the matter? Can't sleep?"

Xiong nodded. "Something like that." After a sleepless turn in the bunk he had been provided in what laughingly passed as guest quarters aboard the *Lovell*, he had opted to return to the cargo bay and review the data that had been collected during their previous attempts to scan the Mirdonyae Artifact. Still ensconced within the isolation chamber, the artifact appeared dormant save for the constant muted violet hue emanating from within its crystalline heart.

"I've reviewed some of the data," Davis said as Xiong returned to his seat and sipped his coffee. "No new progress, I see."

Xiong shook his head. "Nothing. We've repeated some of the more intensive scan cycles a few times, but there's been no response of any kind, or any other indication that the Shedai wants anything to do with us."

"I'm guessing you've run diagnostics on the chamber itself," Davis said.

"Until my fingers were numb," Xiong replied before taking another sip of his coffee. "Everything checks out; we're just not getting a response." Shaking his head, he reached up to brush hair from his eyes. "I'm considering resetting all of the scan procedures and starting over, just to see if I'm missing something stupid."

Davis frowned. "I don't think that's it. For one thing, Anderson and O'Halloran might like to clown around, but they also don't miss much. If there was something wrong with the equipment, or if a scanner frequency was off by the smallest degree, one of those two would've found it. I swear their DNA was crossed with a bloodhound's at some point."

Rather than instill confidence that he was on the right track, the engineer's words only served to heighten Xiong's concern that he had done something wrong. It had to be something so obvious or innocuous that it was easy to miss. To reverse a popular idiom, it felt to him as though he was missing the lone tree that lurked in plain sight at the forefront of the forest commanding his attention.

Xiong sighed. "This sounds foolish to say out loud, but part of my frustration is that every advance we've made to this point has been almost by accident. We hypothesize and test and record data and draw conclusions from the results, and then we start the process all over again. It's very slow, even when there's progress. The only time there seems to be a significant development is when we happen across a Shedai artifact, or somehow back into getting some of their technology to work." He shook his head. "We're supposed to be smarter than this, especially considering how long we've been buying this stuff."

"Maybe we should take that as a hint then," Davis said. "After all, it seems that whenever we try to kick-start Shedai technology, it turns around and bites us on the ass."

When Xiong turned to regard the engineer, he saw from the expression on the other man's face that he was not at all serious with his suggestion, and it made him realize how negative he was sounding. "Okay, point taken. Besides, I really have no intention of waiting around for the next happy accident." Eyeing the isolation chamber, he frowned. "I just feel like we're poking a stick into a cage sometimes. I know I don't like being poked. I like to be asked. Nicely."

"So if I ask you nicely," Davis said, "you'll bring me breakfast?"

That made Xiong laugh, which in turn helped to dispel at least some of his somber mood. "I think not," he said, leaning back in his chair and lifting his feet to rest on the edge of the console as he let his gaze wander across the set of status monitors at his station. The patterns of energy readings fed to the screens by the isolation chamber's internal sensor network were almost hypnotic, and as his mind began to wander, he considered how the sensor probes might be received within the body of the artifact. He knew from previous scans that it was a complex latticework imbued with energy, even though the source of that power remained a mystery. As for the Shedai entity held within the artifact, of course it was present in a noncorporeal state, but beyond that? How did the Shedai's energy—its life force, he allowed—exist within its crystalline prison? He doubted this bizarre incarceration was comfortable for the entity, but what else might be in play here? Could the sensor scans to which Xiong and his companions were subjecting the artifact be having some kind of detrimental effect on the Shedai? Was it possible that the life-form was in pain?

"I know that look," he heard Davis say. "I see it on faces all over this ship. What are you thinking?"

Removing his feet from the console, Xiong pushed himself closer to the workstation and began entering a string of commands. "We're telling the artifact what we want," he said, more to himself than the engineer.

"Excuse me?" Davis asked.

Xiong did not look away from his console as he replied, "We're scanning the hell out of that thing. We're bombarding it with the most intensive data-gathering sensor probes we can throw at it. We're practically screaming at the Shedai trapped inside, telling it what we want to know about it." Pausing, he turned and offered a wry grin to his companion. "We're not *asking* it."

His eyes widening in surprise, Davis then nodded in appreciation. "Okay, that's a bit out of left field, but everybody on this ship owns property out there. I see where you're going. By subjecting the artifact to the intensive sensor sweeps and rudimentary linguacode hailing messages, we're essentially trying to force the Shedai to talk to us."

"Exactly," Xiong said, feeling renewed excitement beginning to well up from within him. "We've known all along that we're dealing with a life-form, but all our efforts have been directed at penetrating the artifact itself. The communications attempts have been secondary—almost an afterthought. We should instead be focusing on trying to *talk to it*."

Davis's brow furrowed as he considered the notion. "Can we do that? I mean, we've been hailing it, even if we've been clumsy about it." Moving closer to one of the operations hub's adjacent consoles, he began tapping a series of colored buttons. "We could try transmitting a standard hail using a tight-beam directional broadcast, like we would a message sent via subspace."

Realizing what the engineer intended to do, Xiong held up a hand. "Wait. You want to try this right now?"

"Why not?" Davis asked. "You worried we might wake it up or something?"

Despite himself, Xiong chuckled. "No, of course not. It's just that we haven't discussed it or anything."

Davis eyed him. "You want to wait until morning?"

It would be the prudent thing to do, Xiong knew. Even with the containment procedures in place, and given that this experiment would not even approach the level of intensity of the previous sensor scans inflicted upon the artifact, there was the omnipresent concern of some unexpected consequence of their action. However, days of sensor telemetry indicated such a development was unlikely.

When he saw the smile on Xiong's face, Davis laughed. "Now you're thinking like an engineer." Reaching for the console, he input another string of commands. "We'll use the same standard linguacode messages that are employed for first-contact scenarios. After all, when in doubt, go with what works."

"We probably shouldn't expect any sort of meaningful response," Xiong said. "Then again, we don't know anything about how the Shedai communicate with other life-forms."

"One thing at a time, Lieutenant," Davis said, his attention fixed on his workstation. "Activate the isolation protocols."

Xiong carried out that task, nodding in satisfaction at the status indicators telling him the chamber was in full isolation mode. "Everything shows green. Transmit whenever you're ready."

"Here goes nothing," Davis said as he pressed a final control.

"Hailing frequency open; transmitting linguacode greeting." Drawing a deep breath, the engineer looked to Xiong before adding, "Knock, knock."

Pointing to a new set of data scrolling on one of his display screens, Xiong said, "I'm seeing indications that the beam's scattering once it penetrates the artifact's outer shell."

"I can try changing frequencies," Davis suggested, entering the necessary commands to his console. A moment later, he shook his head. "I've set the transmission to repeat on a rapid cycle through the frequency bands, but it doesn't seem to be having any effect."

"What about increasing power?" Xiong asked.

Pausing to consider that, Davis tapped the edge of his console. "This system isn't all that powerful, but we can still kick it up a few notches and see what happens. If we really wanted some juice, we could pump the signal through a subspace relay."

Xiong shrugged. "Got any of those lying around?"

"Sure," Davis replied, "but they weigh about four hundred kilos and are around the size of a photon torpedo. Bring two, if you're going." Holding up a finger as though arriving at another idea, he said, "On the other hand, if we reroute through the *Lovell*'s communications array, that would almost certainly be more than enough power to get the job done."

"And it would violate the isolation protocols," Xiong countered. "I'm not ready to take that kind of risk just yet."

Davis nodded. "Agreed. Let's just see what we can do with what we've got, then." Tapping a sequence of controls at a speed that almost made Xiong's eyes hurt as he tried to follow, Davis entered another set of commands. "We're at full power, and I've got the hailing message cycling through every frequency, including several that are out of range of most regular communications equipment." When he saw Xiong's questioning look, he said, "We like to tinker on this ship, remember?"

Ignoring the question, Xiong moved back to his own workstation, noting the new readings on his monitors. "The transmission beam is holding together a bit better now, but I think it's still scattering." Once again, he could only marvel at the construction of the inscrutable Mirdonyae Artifact. How had its creators managed to forge such a brilliant feat of engineering prowess and even artistry?

"Damn, but that thing's stubborn," Davis said, shaking his head in wonder.

"Wait." When the engineer looked in his direction, Xiong pointed to one of his monitors. "There's a new reading here."

"What?" Davis all but jumped from his chair, moving to stand behind Xiong. He leaned over the lieutenant's shoulder, angling for a better look at the screen. "I'll be a son of a bitch. It's working?"

"To a degree," Xiong replied, reaching out to tap the monitor. "The signal's still degrading before it penetrates too far, but at least it's making it in there."

"By the time it gets through the outer shell and into the crystal's interior latticework," Davis said, closing his eyes while he spoke, as if envisioning the artifact's internal construction in his mind, "the signal's so fragmented and diluted, it's probably not much more powerful than whatever background noise is being put out by the artifact's own energy source." Opening his eyes, he added, "I speak euphemistically, of course."

"Of course," Xiong repeated.

"Our signal may be like one voice in a crowd of thousands," Davis continued, holding up his hands to emphasize his point. "We know we're getting in there, but there may simply be just too much else going on for us to be heard."

Glancing back to the monitor that depicted the image of the artifact as it rested in its cradle inside the isolation chamber, Xiong considered the engineer's hypothesis. "So, what do you suggest we do in order to be heard?"

Davis smiled. "We pump up the volume."

23

Tendrils of energy punched through the storm gripping the Shedai Wanderer, feeling to her as though spikes of agony were being driven through every molecule of her being. In her weakened state, she was unable to deflect or mitigate the probe. Adrift within the nebulous void that was her prison, her only defense was to force her consciousness to fold in on itself and wait for the assault to subside. It took several moments to erect the necessary barriers, and even then she still felt the effects of whatever was being directed against her.

Now able to focus on the new contact, she turned her attention to the wave pushing through the cacophony surrounding her, and the Wanderer realized this new presence was very similar to the pathetic, disjointed drone that had earlier punctuated the constant, unwavering dissonance.

What do you want of me?

Continuing to listen to the odd, plaintive call, the Wanderer realized that it seemed to be repeating the same sequences in rapid succession. Some of it was familiar, while other parts seemed to be little more than hollow imitations of structured communication. As the signal persisted, she began to decipher and comprehend fragments.

We call to you.

It took most of her flagging strength even to grasp the meaning. Who was attempting to make contact? Surely not one of her own people. No, the Wanderer decided, this was something else. *Telinaruul.* Yes, that made sense, as she detected hints of the signals they had transmitted between one another, entwined with those bits she recognized as Shedai. She had experienced their efforts at understanding the technology of her people on more than one occasion. At first their attempts seemed clumsy and inadequate, but the Wanderer had recognized the perseverance driving their endeavors. They had acquired a pair of the reviled crystals—the storied orbs that were believed capable of harnessing the very power commanded by the Shedai. That the *Telinaruul* were motivated by a greedy self-interest and the hope of plundering the resources and power commanded by her people was a given. Such audacity could not be tolerated, and she vowed the *Telinaruul* would pay for their insolence.

Whatever they might be doing, it was having an effect. Her awareness of her surroundings seemed to be gaining greater clarity. The energies working to hold her hostage within the crystal seemed to subside, if only by the slightest of degrees. Her link to the signal was growing in intensity, and the Wanderer realized now that in addition to what she was already hearing, there was something else—something far more formidable—lurking somewhere beyond the fringes of her perceptions. She had sensed this presence earlier, during the last disruption of the energy fields ensnaring her. In addition to carrying with it a recognizable timbre possessed by others of her kind, it was more prominent this time, and the Wanderer now felt it with greater force as it reached out to her.

Who are you?

I am Shedai. Who are you?

I too am Shedai.

The Wanderer was at once struck with a range of visceral emotional reactions, chief among which was surprise, given her enforced solitude, that she was hearing what purported to be a member of her race, all of whom had been dispersed by the Apostate when he extinguished the First World. At first she thought it might well be the Apostate who had somehow found her here, in this cursed abyss, and fear manifested itself. Would she now have to face off against one of the oldest and most powerful of all Shedai? Though the Apostate had taunted her on infrequent occasions, the Wanderer had not heard his thoughts since her incarceration. She quickly realized that the voice was not that of the Apostate, nor any other Shedai she had ever encountered, and yet there was something familiar about this new presence. She began to feel hope that the second crystal stolen by the *Telinaruul* might well contain one of the Enumerated Ones. If that was true, then she might finally have an ally, one to whom she had pledged eternal loyalty.

Where are you? Are you here?

I am alone. I am within nothingness. I long to be free, though I am powerless to act.

Extending her thoughts, the Wanderer tried to locate this other Shedai. Despite a profound sensation that he must be somewhere nearby, so far as she could tell, she was alone within her realm of exile. So, where was this potential compatriot of hers? Was he a friend or an adversary? To what or to whom did he vow allegiance?

Though we appear to be separated, we may be able to achieve liberation by working together.

No. I have been held here for uncounted generations. Escape is not possible. If freedom is to be gained, it will come at the hands and whims of our captors. Anything else is a waste of effort and energy. Of this I am certain.

Despite what the Wanderer at first perceived as defeatism, the other's words contained another, unidentified quality. *How do you know this?*

Because I have tried, many times. Countless times, likely since before you came to be.

But perhaps we can combine our strength, the Wanderer implored, *channel it together, and present a more powerful front to that which holds us.*

Your power is insignificant compared to that which I possess.

There was no use expending energy or time debating that observation. The Wanderer, just from the thoughts offered by the other, could discern that her counterpart spoke the truth. Echoes and hints of a power far greater than she would ever command brushed her consciousness.

I sense great age, and wisdom, older than the Apostate, and perhaps even the Maker. How is that possible?

I am the First Shedai. I am the Progenitor.

The Wanderer was dumbstruck. Could it be true? Stories— myths—of the Progenitor were among her earliest memories, to say nothing of the collected recollections of those Shedai with whom she had linked over the course of her existence. Legends told of this, the First, most powerful and revered of all Shedai and greater than all the other *Serataal,* being captured by an ancient enemy. Such rumors persisted through the ages, the story expanding and becoming more exaggerated with each successive telling. No proof, either of the Progenitor's capture by some unknown rival or even of his very existence, had ever been found. Older Shedai who subscribed to such tales held to the belief that it was the Progenitor's defeat at the hands of this mysterious adversary that had set into motion the series of events that ultimately forced the Shedai into their long sleep. The Wanderer had never subscribed to such outlandish notions, until now.

You are the first of my kind I have encountered since my imprisonment. Do our people thrive? Are we the masters of all the stars?

No. The Wanderer's reply was tinged with sadness. *Our once-great civilization has fallen; it is no more, and what was there before its demise was something less than your great vision.* She sensed the Progenitor's disappointment, though another emotion was there, as well: determination. It had not been there before, she thought, but now there was no mistaking its presence.

Then perhaps we will remake it. After all, my vision remains clear.

Doing so requires us to escape our confinement, does it not?

Yes, the Progenitor replied. **For this, we must be patient. Our time will come. Of this, I also am certain.**

24

Reyes waited for an alarm to sound, or for secret doors to open and hordes of Orions or whoever else Ganz might have on his payroll to come storming out of the walls, each of them wielding a disruptor or blade. He wondered if and when a hidden airlock hatch might open, blowing him out of the ship and into open space.

Despite his mounting anxiety and paranoia as seconds seemed to pass at a glacial pace, none of that happened. Instead, the computer terminal before him emitted a simple, innocent beep before a single line of text appeared on its display screen: "Transfer Complete. Original Data File Purged."

"Okay, that's got it," he said, reaching for the terminal and retrieving from one of its peripheral slots a red hexagonal data card. The card was similar to those used with Starfleet computers, and T'Prynn assured him that bridging any compatibility gaps between the media formats would not present a problem. Reyes would have preferred to transfer the data directly from the *Omari-Ekon*'s computer to T'Prynn over on Vanguard, but the Vulcan had assured him that such activity would almost without fail be detected by the Orion vessel's security measures. "They're going to be pretty pissed when they find out we've deleted their navigational data. Are you sure we got it all?"

In the utter quiet of the small maintenance office that had been selected for this last iteration of Reyes's covert activities, the voice of T'Prynn in his mind seemed loud enough to rattle the walls. *"My search protocols found no duplicates of the data. It is possible the data was copied to secondary storage, but there is nothing we can do about that now.* "It is now time to bring you to safety, Diego."

Though he had known this was going to be the end result of this little game of espionage, Reyes still was not sure how to feel about it. He knew that, despite what he had done here with T'Prynn's assistance, he was still a convicted felon who had been court-martialed and dismissed from Starfleet. The time he had spent in the custody of the Klingons and the Orions also made him a fugitive. Though he wanted to believe that his decisions and actions while in such questionable company had been in keeping with the best interests of Starfleet and the Federation, he knew that others would see him as nothing more than a traitor.

Time for that later, he reminded himself. *Maybe.*

"All right, then," he said, moving the data card and the transceiver supplied to him by Ezekiel Fisher to an inside pocket of his jacket. "What's the plan?"

"I have identified two areas of the ship where the shielding can be penetrated by the station's transporters," T'Prynn replied. *"I have designated these as primary and secondary extraction points. The first location is closest to your present position. I suggest we begin moving you in that direction with all due haste."*

"Show me the way to go home, Lieutenant," Reyes said, feeling a rush of adrenaline and anticipation. After so much time living aboard the *Omari-Ekon,* the thought of finally being freed from his pseudo-prison was almost too much to believe. Of course, it was easy to temper his mixed feelings of enthusiasm and apprehension, just by thinking about all of the things that could still go wrong before he once more set foot aboard Starbase 47.

Following T'Prynn's instructions, Reyes exited the small office, emerging into a dark, narrow corridor. He knew from his studies of the *Omari-Ekon*'s layout that T'Prynn had directed him to one of the lower levels near the port-side impulse vents along the vessel's aft section. Chosen by the intelligence officer for its relative isolation, this part of the ship was free of most foot traffic, save for the occasional maintenance employee and, on more unfortunate occasions, a member of Ganz's security staff.

Such occasions were even less pleasant when there was more than one guard, as there was now.

"Well, look who it is," said one of two goons Reyes saw in the passageway as he stepped from the office. To his surprise, this thug was a Tellarite he did not recognize, stocky and sporting a large belly that lapped over the wide leather belt he wore. His prodigious midsection almost, but not quite, succeeded in hiding from view the sizable disruptor pistol resting in a holster along his right hip. As for his companion, he was an Orion whom Reyes had seen on occasion, working in the bar or wandering the gaming deck. Unlike other members of the ship's security staff, this Orion, Nakaal, seemed content to wear form-fitting tunics rather than walking about with a bare chest and sporting his assortment of tattoos and piercings. There was something about the way the pair carried themselves that told Reyes this was not to be one of the frequent harassment calls paid to him by members of Ganz's organization who were feeling brave and looking to stir up some kind of confrontation.

No, Reyes decided, *this is definitely different.*

"And wandering around all alone," Nakaal said, his voice low and carrying more than a hint of menace. "It's dangerous down here. A person could get hurt if they're not careful."

"Your concern is touching," Reyes replied, working to keep his own tone neutral, even casual. "That's what I like about everybody on this ship. Always looking out for everybody's welfare. Somebody should tell Ganz how conscientious you are. That's the sort of thing that looks good on personnel reviews when the time for pay raises comes around."

"*Mister Reyes?*" T'Prynn prompted, though Reyes did not acknowledge her.

Predictably, neither Nakaal nor the Tellarite seemed amused by his observations. "You need to come with us," the Orion said, his expression turning to one of irritation as he reached for his belt and retrieved a long, sharp knife from a scabbard on his left hip.

"Where are we going?" Reyes asked, unable to keep his eyes from watching the knife as light from the overhead fixtures reflected off the blade's polished surface.

Stepping forward, the Tellarite reached toward him with one beefy arm. "We don't want to spoil the surprise." At the same time, his other hand was moving to a knife on his own belt. Reyes figured that meant the goons were trying not to attract too much attention, even down here and well away from the ship's more populated areas. No doubt their plan was to hustle him away to a more private chamber and carry out whatever plan they had in mind.

Well, screw that.

In the close quarters, Reyes decided he had the advantage over the burly Tellarite, who now blocked Nakaal as he moved closer. Without pausing to consider what might happen next, he lashed out with one leg, his foot connecting with the Tellarite's right knee. The thug grunted in pain and staggered, trying to keep his balance. Behind him, Nakaal was already moving, but Reyes kept his focus on the Tellarite. Closing the distance, Reyes struck with his right fist, catching the guard along his left temple. He heard the knife fall from the Tellarite's hand and clatter to the deck, and instinct guided his foot as he kicked the weapon out of reach. He shoved the goon backward, blocking Nakaal's advance and clogging the narrow passageway so neither guard could maneuver. This gave him the opportunity he needed to reach for the Tellarite's holstered disruptor.

In response, the Tellarite twisted his considerable bulk in a bid to block him, and Reyes responded by punching him a second time, this blow landing on the guard's sizable nose. The reaction to the attack was immediate: the Tellarite howled, reaching for his face with both hands and providing Reyes the opening he needed to land another strike, this time driving his fist into the thug's groin. The Tellarite responded by sagging forward, offering his defenseless chin to Reyes, who promptly grabbed the guard's head while driving his knee into his face. He felt the cartilage of the Tellarite's nose breaking, and the goon fell back, unconscious before his limp body dropped in a heap to the deck.

"Damn you, Reyes!"

Hearing the words at the same instant light glinted off something metal and shiny in his peripheral vision, Reyes pulled back his head just as Nakaal's arm slashed forward, the knife in his hand slicing the air between them. Reyes jerked to one side, struggling for maneuvering room in the cramped hallway and almost tripping over the Tellarite's body. Nakaal kept coming, stepping over his companion and waving his knife before him as he advanced. Backpedaling, Reyes tried to avoid getting forced into the corner he knew was behind him as the passageway made a turn to his left. He watched the Orion's hand as it waved the blade before him, trying to determine from the movements if Nakaal was really all that skilled with the weapon. Reyes decided he was good enough.

Nakaal, perhaps sensing his opponent's hesitation, seemed to decide he had the advantage and was looking to press it. His knife held before him, he stepped forward, and Reyes noted the look of satisfaction that seemed to brighten the Orion's face.

Then, his expression went blank and his eyes widened before his entire body went slack and he sank forward, dropping to the deck in a disjointed heap.

Standing behind Nakaal, her arm extended to where she had applied a nerve pinch at the junction of the Orion's neck and shoulder, was T'Prynn, dressed from neck to feet in a black, nondescript, and very form-fitting jumpsuit, over which she wore a black belt with several small pouches. Unlike Nakaal's, her expression was all but unreadable as she beheld Reyes.

"Son of a bitch," Reyes hissed, blowing out his breath in a relieved sigh.

T'Prynn's right eyebrow arched. "It is agreeable to see you again, as well, Mister Reyes."

Sparing a glance to the fallen Nakaal, Reyes checked the corridor in both directions, searching for more of Ganz's men. "Not that I'm ungrateful, Lieutenant, but what the hell are you doing here?"

As she turned and set about searching the fallen guards,

T'Prynn replied, "Ganz has ordered your assassination. These two were sent to carry out that directive." Moving the unconscious Nakaal's right arm, she retrieved the disruptor from its holster on the Orion's hip.

"He ordered the hit on me for tonight?" Reyes asked, holding out his hand as the Vulcan passed the purloined weapon to him. "That sounds a bit too coincidental." He tried to backtrack his movements during the evening, searching for whatever it was he had said or done to arouse Ganz's suspicion about his activities and push the Orion toward ordering his men to take action.

"Not at all," T'Prynn said as she moved to the fallen Tellarite still lying like a lump in the corridor. "As I told you, I've been monitoring Ganz's communications. When I learned he had put the assassination order into motion, I moved up my own timetable so that you could make another attempt to access the ship's navigational logs tonight, rather than two days from now."

His eyes narrowing as he parsed her comments and realization hit him, Reyes glared at his former intelligence officer. "Wait, so you *knew* they were coming after me tonight, and *didn't tell me*? What the hell is *that* about?"

"I did not wish to alarm you," T'Prynn replied. Her search of the Tellarite completed, she now held his disruptor pistol in her right hand. "At least, not while you needed to focus on your task. Once that was accomplished, it was my intention to update you on the current situation and guide you to a safe haven. What I failed to anticipate was that any of Ganz's men would find you so quickly. I therefore employed an impromptu deviation to my strategy for your extraction."

Reyes shook his head, giving up on translating any of that. "And your big backup plan was to come and get me? Basically, you're just making this up as you go along, right?"

"That is essentially correct," the Vulcan said.

Noting the weapons they each carried, Reyes asked, "You didn't bring any weapons?"

T'Prynn nodded. "I have a type-1 phaser in my belt, but I think it prudent to limit the use of Starfleet-issue weapons until no other options remain available." She held up her disruptor. "These should prove sufficient for our needs."

The observation was enough to make Reyes check the power gauge on the disruptor she had given him. It offered no stun option, and even the lowest setting would still be sufficient to inflict serious injury on his intended target. He resigned himself to what that might mean should he and T'Prynn encounter further resistance while attempting to escape the ship.

Them or you, ace.

"Okay," he said, "what's your plan?"

Moving to step over the Tellarite, T'Prynn replied, "We will proceed to my designated extraction point and request an emergency transport to the station. Lieutenant Jackson is standing by, awaiting our signal." She then said, "Lieutenant Jackson, do you read?"

Reyes was startled by the sound of the security chief's voice inside his head as Jackson answered, "*Right here, Lieutenant, and it's good to be hearing your voice again, Commodore.*"

"Didn't anybody get the memo about my court-martial?" Reyes asked, scowling, though it was good to know that T'Prynn also carried a subcutaneous transceiver within her own body. It would make communication that much easier should they become separated during the escape attempt. "And what about Ganz? You can bet he's looking for us."

T'Prynn shook her head. "The ship's internal sensors are offline. I was able to effect that while you were logged into its computer network. They won't be able to track us except for handheld scanners, and such devices are already blocked by the ship's internal security measures. I simply executed an instruction which will prevent the protocol from being terminated."

"I'm not even going to pretend I understood any of that," Reyes said. "Whatever. With sensors offline, that just means Ganz will send more goons out to find us. So, what do you say we get the hell out of here?"

"*Hang on,*" Jackson said. "*We've got a problem. It looks like somebody just activated a transport inhibitor shield around the* Omari-Ekon."

Reyes replied, "That means he knows somebody's here, trying to help me."

"A logical conclusion," T'Prynn said, "though it's also possible Ganz is simply anticipating a transporter as our means of escape. Either way, it does not appear that we'll be beaming off this ship."

Reyes took another look at the disruptor in his hand. "You said internal sensors were offline? I'm thinking that means we might have another card to play."

25

Ganz was more than ready to kill someone. Diego Reyes was his preferred target of choice, but at the moment, anyone would do.

"Where is he?" Turning from the railing of his balcony, which overlooked the *Omari-Ekon*'s gaming deck, Ganz moved back into his office and regarded Tonzak. To his credit, the head of security seemed appropriately terrified, which did little to alleviate Ganz's increasingly foul mood.

Clearing his throat, Tonzak replied, "I don't know. I had three teams following his movements. The last time I heard from Nakaal and Drev, they had spotted Reyes heading away from the gaming deck and into the service passageways. They tracked him to a maintenance compartment in section six, but they don't know what he was doing."

Ganz knew what Reyes had been doing, though it alarmed him that he had acquired this knowledge only after the troublesome human had completed whatever task had taken him to the maintenance section. "He was accessing the ship's computer," he said, feeling his jaw clench.

"How could he do that?" Tonzak asked, his brow furrowing in confusion.

"He had help, obviously." Moving to his desk, Ganz settled his muscled physique into his oversized padded chair. "He would have needed it to get past our security safeguards." Though he held no doubts that Diego Reyes possessed no small number of skills in his own right, the security measures implemented to protect the *Omari-Ekon*'s computer system were such that the human would not have been able to bypass them all from the interface terminal he had utilized in the maintenance office. Navigating through the maze of protocols and oversight subroutines required a level of knowledge about the system Reyes could not have acquired on his own. At least, that should have been the case, unless Ganz's security staff was even more incompetent than this latest failure would seem to indicate. What concerned Ganz now was what information Reyes might have accessed or taken from the computer once he found a pathway into the system, as the human had done a remarkable job covering his tracks.

I'll just have to ask him myself, then.

Finding some momentary satisfaction at the thought of how such a discussion might proceed once Reyes was brought before him, Ganz asked, "Where are Nakaal and Drev now?"

Tonzak said, "In the infirmary. Neither of them was injured that severely, though Drev took the worst of it."

"Make sure I never see either of them again. Anywhere." Ganz chose not to elaborate, leaving it to his subordinate to exercise whatever initiative and action he thought best. "And no one else has seen Reyes?"

Shaking his head, Tonzak replied, "No. He has to be hiding somewhere on one of the maintenance levels or in the service crawlways. With sensors offline, we're having to conduct a section-by-section search with handheld scanners."

Ganz released an irritated grunt. Disabling the ship's internal sensors was a shrewd play on the part of Reyes or whoever had helped him. The hand-carried units Tonzak's people would be using to conduct their search would be helpful, but it would still take time, perhaps long enough for Reyes to find a way off the ship. Whoever was assisting him had to have a plan for extracting him, which Ganz hoped had at least been disrupted by his decision to activate transporter inhibitor fields throughout the vessel.

"Have security round up every human and send them to the exit," he said. "I don't care who they're with or what they're doing. I want them off the ship, now." That, he decided, would at least simplify trying to find one lone human among a ship full of

Orions and representatives of the other nonhuman species currently on board.

"That will take time," Tonzak said.

"Then the faster you get started," Ganz snapped, "the happier I'll be." Walking back to the balcony, he looked down at the gaming deck and let his eyes wander over the mass of patrons standing around the gambling kiosks and tables or the bar, or occupying tables or booths in the restaurant and the smaller, satellite bars situated around the casino's perimeter. There were more humans among the crowd than he could count, and he also saw more than a few Starfleet uniforms.

"We'll have to notify the station that we're doing this," Tonzak said.

"You can notify them after they're off the ship," Ganz replied. "Make up a story. Something about a contaminant that's dangerous to humans, but get it done. *Now*." He knew that such a deception would not hold up under scrutiny, and without question would bring with it Admiral Nogura's unwanted attention. There would be time to deal with that later, he decided. For now, the priority was capturing Reyes and finding out what information he had retrieved from the ship's computer.

From behind him, he heard Neera's soft yet still questioning voice. "Ganz? What are you doing?"

"Trying to find Reyes," Ganz answered, turning from the railing to see Neera regarding him with an expression of questioning disapproval. "He got into the computer and probably took something, though I have no idea what that might be. If he's managed to copy something, then he's probably looking for a way off the ship."

Neera gestured toward the balcony. "And your response is to eject every human? Do you honestly think Nogura will let that pass unchallenged?"

"It doesn't matter what I think," Ganz replied, feeling his mounting anger beginning to seep around the edges of his self-control. "If Reyes gets off the ship with whatever he's stolen, Nogura won't have any reason to let us stay here." Indeed, he expected the admiral's order for the *Omari-Ekon* to disembark from the station would come within minutes after Reyes's successful escape.

"He can't beam off the ship," Neera said, sounding now like a mother attempting to lecture a recalcitrant child, "and your people are working to restore the internal sensors. Once that's done, finding him will be much simpler. There's no need to rush headlong through this situation. Patience is our best ally now."

Ganz's response was interrupted by the sounds of disruptor fire, accompanied by shouts of alarm and shock from the gaming deck, drifting over the balcony and into his office.

"What's going on?" Neera asked, moving toward the balcony, but Ganz stepped in front of her as he caught sight of disruptor bolts flashing upward toward the ceiling above the gaming floor. Moving to where he could look out from his office without exposing himself, he realized he also could hear the intermittent yet unmistakable whine of a Starfleet phaser in between the more frequent reports from disruptors. He peered over the balcony railing and saw people running in all directions for the gaming area's various exits. Several of his security staff—some with disruptor pistols drawn—were scrambling to move in and around the scattering patrons. A few had taken up positions behind the bar or various gaming tables, aiming their weapons and searching for something at which to shoot. Ganz followed their gaze into the mob of people moving toward one of the casino exits, and his eyes widened in surprise and anger as he recognized two people in the crowd: Diego Reyes and the Vulcan who at one time had been the former commodore's intelligence officer, T'Prynn.

"Reyes!" Ganz shouted, incredulous. Reyes, hearing him, looked up from where he was seeking cover amid the gaggle of patrons. The two men made eye contact, and each saw the hatred in the other's eyes.

Then Reyes lifted his arm, aimed the disruptor in his hand at Ganz, and fired.

26

"Damn it!"

Reyes saw his shot miss its mark, but only by a small measure as Ganz ducked back from the balcony at the last possible instant. *Stick that big head of yours out there again,* he thought. *I dare you.*

"I'm thinking they're on to us," he said, raising his voice so that T'Prynn could hear him over the chaos of patrons fleeing in all directions from the gaming deck. The strategy had been a simple one, calling for Reyes and T'Prynn—after donning dingy gray coveralls of the sort worn by members of the *Omari-Ekon*'s maintenance staff—to make an attempt at blending with the mass of civilians and Starfleet officers crowding the ship's more populated areas. Reyes had banked on Ganz thinking he might try to hide somewhere in the vessel's bowels after thwarting the attempt on his life by Nakaal and the Tellarite. If the tactic bought them enough time to make it to the passageway leading to the station, both Reyes and T'Prynn had decided that would be close enough, and the weapons in their hands would help them get the rest of the way. They had briefed Haniff Jackson on the plan via their subcutaneous transceivers, and the lieutenant had assured them that security teams would be standing by at the docking area.

Their idea lasted long enough for Reyes and T'Prynn to make it most of the way across the casino, less than a dozen paces from the exit leading toward the corridor that would take them to the docking hatch, when it was foiled by at least one attentive member of the ship's security contingent. That was when they heard the first shouts of warning and alarm, and people began to look and move around in response to the added security guards rushing toward the casino as well as the neighboring bar and restaurants. It was at that point that someone, perhaps feeling lucky and thinking of the rewards to be had from Ganz after capturing or killing the would-be escapees, opened fire. Then all hell broke loose on the gaming deck.

"Lieutenant Jackson," T'Prynn said, "we are making our way to the docking port."

In his head, Reyes heard the security chief reply, "*Copy that, Lieutenant. We're here.*"

Reyes knew that Starfleet security teams could not board the Orion vessel uninvited, and he had to wonder just how far Jackson and even Admiral Nogura might push things if he and T'Prynn got close enough to the docking hatch that the decision to render assistance became a very real issue.

I guess we're about to find out.

"Watch out," T'Prynn said from Reyes's right, and he turned in time to see the Vulcan raising her arm to aim her phaser at two hulking Orion security guards attempting to make their way through the crowd toward her and Reyes. She waited until the guards stepped into the open before putting them both down with a pair of well-aimed shots from her phaser. Though he knew there was little chance of making it off the ship without being forced to kill at least some of the Orions who would be standing between them and the exit, Reyes had pressed for nonlethal force during their escape attempt if at all possible. Perhaps the gesture, small though it was, might at least reduce the amount of interstellar wailing and gnashing of teeth his escape would generate once Ganz reported the incident to his superiors. The Orion had to know Reyes was not operating alone. Accusations of Starfleet collusion during his time as a "guest" aboard the *Omari-Ekon* would provide no small amount of ammunition for whatever passed for an Orion diplomat airing grievances to the Federation Council.

None of which I'll get to enjoy if we don't get the hell out of here.

"You know where you're going, right?" he asked as he followed T'Prynn out of the casino and into the main passageway leading to the docking port that connected the *Omari-Ekon* to the station.

She nodded. "Affirmative." Reyes nearly ran into her as she stopped and once more took aim with her phaser. Another security guard had emerged from the concealment of a support stanchion and was coming at them, but T'Prynn dispatched him with her phaser. A disruptor bolt flashed past Reyes's right ear and he turned in that direction, instinct guiding his arm up and letting him take aim at the approaching Orion. He felt his finger on the weapon's firing stud before the movement even registered in his mind, by which time a harsh flash of energy caught the guard in his muscled green torso. Reyes cursed the weapon in his hand, seeing the flesh on the Orion's chest marred as he was struck and knocked backward, his mouth contorting in agony.

"Tell me you have another phaser on you?" he asked, reaching up to wipe sweat from his forehead.

"Negative," T'Prynn replied. "We must keep moving. It is likely that more security personnel are converging on our position."

"*We're blind here,*" Jackson said. "*They've activated shields that block our scans. You're on your own getting to the exit.*"

Using various groups of evacuating patrons for cover while at the same time praying that none of the security guards would see fit to start firing into the crowd, Reyes and T'Prynn ran from the casino. Ahead of them lay the entrance to the gangway that would take them to the docking port and—Reyes hoped—freedom.

He flinched as a disruptor blast chewed into the wall ahead of T'Prynn, and they both ducked while turning to face the new threat. Reyes saw a group of six Orions emerging from the casino, and his eyes widened in recognition as he saw who was at the front of the group: Ganz, carrying a disruptor pistol in his hand. One of his subordinates was talking into what had to be a communications device, no doubt calling for reinforcements, but Ganz's eyes were locked on Reyes, and the burly Orion raised his weapon.

Without thinking, Reyes brought up his own weapon and fired. The shot was wide, passing just to the right of Ganz's head but close enough that all six Orions ducked for cover. Reyes grunted in renewed irritation at his latest miss even as T'Prynn pushed him through the hatch. Stepping over the doorway's threshold, she slammed her fist against the control panel set into the bulkhead to the hatch's left side. She dropped to one knee as the door began to close, firing through the narrowing gap to keep the guards at bay until the entryway sealed itself. Then, before Reyes could offer any sort of protest, she fired her weapon at the panel, sending a blue streak of energy into it and destroying it.

"There are still people on board!" Reyes exclaimed.

T'Prynn moved past him. "This will offer us only momentary protection, and even Ganz is not so stupid as to fire on innocent civilians. We must hurry." As the pair set off down the gangway, Reyes could hear the sounds of fists pummeling the hatch from the other side, followed by the unmistakable reports of weapons fire. How long would it take them to force the locking mechanism, or simply burn a hole through the door itself?

The gangway led them to an intersection with two options. To the left, the passageway quickly terminated at a reinforced hatch that, if Reyes could trust his memory, led to a maintenance area and an airlock providing access to the docking port's exterior. The entrance to the station was to the right, and as he and T'Prynn ran in that direction, they saw that the portal beyond which lay their liberation from the *Omari-Ekon* was blocked by a quartet of Orions, each already wielding a disruptor pistol. One of the guards, standing behind a small workstation, reached for something and the corridor filled with the sounds of an alarm Klaxon.

"Aw, shit!" was all Reyes had time to utter before the first guard fired. His shot missed and T'Prynn's aim was better, catching him in the chest. With no other choice available to him, Reyes lunged to his left, kneeling near the bulkhead as he opened fire with his own weapon. He tried to ignore the other Orions shooting at him as he popped off shot after shot down the narrow corridor, and tried not to think of just how many years had passed since his last foray into close-quarters battle.

Something hot punched him in the right thigh and Reyes dropped his disruptor as he sagged against the bulkhead. He smelled the stench of singed clothing and flesh and looked down to see the small scorched area on the side of his leg. Though it looked to have been only a glancing blow, the disruptor bolt had still burned through the material of the coveralls he had appropriated as well as his own skin and muscle tissue. His eyes watered from the pain of his injury even as more phaser fire filled the corridor, but the cacophony died and he looked up to see T'Prynn running to him.

"It does not appear to be serious," she said, raising her voice to be heard over the alarm as she inspected his wound. Reyes managed to retrieve his fallen disruptor as she helped him to his feet, before looking up to see all four Orions lying on the deck, victims of T'Prynn's formidable marksmanship. "We have to go. Now."

Even with the siren blaring in the corridor, Reyes still heard the sounds of heavy, running footsteps echoing over deck plates and growing louder. Gritting his teeth against the pain in his thigh, he favored his injured leg and allowed T'Prynn to assist him down the passageway as he looked back the way they had come, waiting for Ganz and his minions to appear.

Come on, you big green son of a . . .

He felt cool air on his sweat-dampened skin at the same instant his feet all but tripped over the raised threshold of what he knew was the docking port's pressure hatch. T'Prynn guided him through the entryway, and Reyes looked down to see the familiar gleam of polished duranium deck plating. How long had it been since he had last set foot on the station? How long had he stared at it from one of the *Omari-Ekon*'s viewing ports?

"Watch out!" he warned, feeling his heart race at the sight of Ganz and at least a dozen followers—only some of whom were Orion—turning the corner in the passageway leading back to the merchant vessel. He felt T'Prynn starting to turn in that direction even as she kept carrying him farther into the station's service corridor, and her motion allowed him to raise the disruptor in his left hand.

"Reyes!" Ganz bellowed, his face a mask of unrestrained fury. The Orion, rather than stopping at the threshold separating his ship from the station, seemed to have no intention of giving up the chase. Less than ten meters away and still pressing ahead toward the hatchway, he raised the disruptor pistol in his massive green hand and aimed it at Reyes's face.

Then, everything dissolved into chaos.

Phaser fire pierced the air all around him as Reyes felt himself pulled downward. Streaks of blue-white light flashed over his head, interspersed with the deep howls emitted by disruptor pistols coming from the other direction. T'Prynn lowered him to the deck before scrambling to return fire, though her efforts seemed not to be needed, as Reyes caught sight of at least half a dozen men and women in Starfleet uniforms. He felt a hand on his shoulder and looked up into the face of a male Andorian officer he at first did not recognize. Then he realized that this must be Commander ch'Nayla, T'Prynn's replacement as the station's intelligence officer.

"Mister Reyes," he said, adjusting his hold on Reyes so that he might help him move out of the line of fire, "come with me."

Feeling a fresh twinge of pain in his thigh, Reyes allowed himself to be maneuvered backward by the Andorian even as T'Prynn and other station personnel retreated to positions of nominal cover at the first corridor intersection leading into the station. The Orions appeared to outnumber the Starfleet security detachment and were using their advantage to press their attack, moving forward while laying down a vicious string of covering fire. For his part, Ganz had taken momentary refuge behind the entrance to the docking gangway, leaning out every few seconds to take a shot with his own disruptor.

"Is he out of his mind?" Reyes asked of no one in particular as he shifted his weight off his injured thigh and leaned against the bulkhead for support.

Ch'Nayla, leaning into the corridor to return fire, replied, "It certainly seems that way."

A shadow fell across the deck plating near Reyes and he turned to see Tim Pennington standing behind him, wielding the portable audiovisual recorder he had seen the man use on several occasions.

"What the hell are you doing here?" Reyes asked.

Appearing slightly out of breath, Pennington offered a knowing grin. "Right place at the wrong time. Story of my life, mate."

"Mister Pennington," T'Prynn said from Reyes's right. "I should have known you would somehow find your way here."

"Nice to see you, too, Lieutenant," Pennington replied, before jerking himself back as a disruptor blast tore into the bulkhead behind him.

Another bolt of weapons fire screamed past, much too close, and Reyes recoiled as it struck ch'Nayla where he knelt next to the bulkhead while trying to return fire. Hit in the chest, he was knocked backward and off his feet, collapsing on the deck. One of his teammates rushed to pull him back to cover even as more disruptor bolts filled the narrow passageway.

"Damn it!" Reyes shouted above the din. "It wasn't supposed to be like this!" Looking to where the security guard—Reyes did not recognize the young ensign—knelt over ch'Nayla, he asked, "Is he all right?"

The ensign shook his head, ducking as more weapons fire sailed overhead. "No, sir. He's dead."

From where he stood next to Reyes, trying to lean forward with his recorder in order to capture the firefight, Pennington said, "What the . . . is that *Ganz*?"

Angling for a better view, Reyes leaned around the corner to see the muscled Orion advancing from the relative safety of the docking port, his disruptor held up and firing at any target that presented itself. He seemed not to care about the hailstorm of phaser fire hunting him and his men, some of whom were falling victim to the hasty defense being staged by the Starfleet security force.

T'Prynn turned her head toward the journalist, gesturing with her free hand for him to stay behind her. "Mister Pennington, you are in the way. Please—"

"Look out!" the reporter shouted, reaching forward and grabbing the Vulcan's extended arm and pulling her toward him just as a disruptor bolt slammed into the wall next to her head. Pennington's movements sent her past him and back around the corner, making him pivot to his left as his momentum carried her after him, and Reyes heard another report as energy once more howled in the corridor. He heard the impact of the shot against soft flesh at the same instant Pennington cried out, the force of the shot sending him tumbling forward into T'Prynn. Something metal or plastic clattered on the deck, and Reyes looked down to see Pennington's recorder where it had fallen from the journalist's grip.

Then he cringed again when new weapons fire blasted away a chunk of the bulkhead to his right. He looked up to see Ganz firing at him from the other end of the short passageway. Some of his men lay unmoving on the deck behind him, and still others were running for the docking port and supposed safety aboard the *Omari-Ekon,* but Ganz was standing his ground. The expression on his face made Reyes wonder if the Orion had taken actual leave of his senses.

Then their eyes met, and any lingering skepticism vanished as Ganz released an enraged snarl and stepped into the corridor, moving forward with menacing purpose. "I've been waiting a long time to do this, Reyes," he said, bringing up his weapon to take aim.

"Me, too," Reyes replied, pulling his own disruptor into view and firing the instant he could sight down its length and see nothing but the Orion's face. The energy bolt, discharged at the weapon's highest setting from a distance of less than twenty meters, took Ganz's head and most of his torso on its way into the wall behind him. Soft, bloody shrapnel painted the bulkhead around the point of impact, and what little remained of his body lingered upright for an additional few seconds. It then fell backward, dropping to the floor with a sickening, heavy thud.

Seconds later, Lieutenant Jackson and two of his security officers rushed forward, covering the other fallen Orions and verifying that no threats remained. Jackson was speaking into a communicator, and Reyes heard something about reinforcements, sealing off access to the *Omari-Ekon,* and requesting an emergency medical team for the injured personnel. Hearing that, Reyes turned to where T'Prynn was huddling over Pennington, who lay unconscious on the deck with a ghastly wound covering most of his right arm and shoulder.

"T'Prynn," he said, "is he all right?"

The Vulcan shook her head, and Reyes thought he heard the note of concern in her voice. "I do not know."

Sagging until his back rested against the bulkhead, Reyes allowed himself to slide to a sitting position on the deck. He bit back the pain from his own injury, at the same time allowing the first wave of relief to wash over him. After his long exile with the Klingons and the Orions, he was free, at least in a relative sense. There was no way to know what might next be in store for him, but at the moment he did not care.

A moment later, he looked up to see Lieutenant Jackson walking toward him, pulling his attention from his fallen crewmates long enough to offer a small, grim smile as he nodded in greeting.

"Welcome aboard, Mister Reyes."

27

Amid the hive of perpetual activity that was Starbase 47's operations center, Admiral Nogura watched the image of the *Omari-Ekon* as displayed on one of the room's oversized viewscreens. The Orion vessel had just disconnected from its docking port along the station's secondary hull and was now maneuvering away, rotating on its axis as it took up a course for open space.

"Good riddance," Nogura said. Turning away from the viewer, he looked to where the station's executive officer, Commander Jon Cooper, stood at a nearby workstation. "Commander, keep an eye on that ship until it's out of sensor range. I don't really care where they're going, just so long as they go."

Smiling at the comment, Cooper nodded. "Aye, aye, sir. Do you think that's the last we'll be seeing of them?"

"I highly doubt it," Nogura replied. "They found a way to ingratiate themselves to me once before. Something tells me they're not above trying it again." It would have to be something spectacular, he decided, for him to consider allowing the Orion ship to regain the favored status it once had enjoyed. With T'Prynn having seen to the deletion from the *Omari-Ekon*'s navigational logs of any useful information pertaining to the possible location of the Mirdonyae artifacts, Nogura could conceive of no reason he might entertain the idea of allowing the Orion ship to return.

But, he reminded himself, *you said that once before.*

"There's always the chance they'll come looking for me," said a voice from behind him, and Nogura looked over his shoulder to where Diego Reyes stood, flanked by two members of the station's security detail. "But something tells me they'll probably just cut their losses and call it a day."

Nogura nodded as he turned to face Reyes. "Were I in their position, I'd likely do the same thing. Neera has an easy scapegoat in Ganz, and you did her a favor when you tied off that particular loose end."

"Happy to be of service," Reyes replied, his expression flat and unreadable.

Nogura gestured for Reyes and his security escort to accompany him as he began walking toward his office. "Given that the Federation now has every reason and justification to make life absolute hell for every Orion vessel in the quadrant, I'm thinking Neera and her bosses are more than happy to lay everything at Ganz's feet." In addition to Ganz being killed, several of his subordinates had been stunned and taken into custody by members of Lieutenant Jackson's security detail. They had languished in the brig for more than a day while Nogura decided what to do with them. It had been his first impulse to have them all tried under Federation law for Commander ch'Nayla's death as well as those of two security officers, along with the injuries to Reyes, Tim Pennington, and other members of the detail.

The reality of the situation, Nogura knew, was that such a trial would only serve to shed unwanted light on the reasons for the incident in the first place, including the acts of subterfuge and espionage Reyes had conducted with Starfleet authorization aboard the *Omari-Ekon*. After consulting with Lieutenant Commander Holly Moyer in order to get the Starfleet JAG view of the situation, Nogura had come to the reluctant conclusion that the best for all involved parties was to see to it that the matter was handled as quickly and quietly as possible. The Orion Syndicate would also want to avoid public attention, so attributing everything to Ganz, his wounded pride, and his insatiable need for vengeance against Reyes in response to any perceived slights made for a nice, tidy end to the entire odious affair. Starfleet's position was that it was easier to accept such a premise knowing that Reyes had been successful in obtaining the navigational log information from the *Omari-Ekon*'s computer.

Reyes said, "I don't think it's a simple case of blame game. If Neera really was pulling Ganz's strings, then there's no way she would have sanctioned sending an armed boarding party to the station after me." He paused, frowning as though recalling a memory. "You should have seen the look on Ganz's face there at the end. He was livid, and wanted my head on a plate, right then and there, and by any means necessary."

"That's pretty much what Neera said when Lieutenant Jackson questioned her," Nogura replied. "According to her, she laid on the tears and came across as little more than the helpless moll, forced to do his bidding. She had no idea that we suspected the truth about her relationship with Ganz." There had been isolated reports—some dating back more than a century—of other female Orions holding positions of power within criminal organizations similar to the one supposedly run by Ganz. In several of those examples, the females chose to downplay their role, allowing a subordinate—almost always a male—to be the group's public face. This carried with it the obvious benefit of allowing the figurehead manager to be the target of competition, ridicule, and even the odd assassination attempt. The dynamic also was useful for situations where blame needed to be shifted away from the organization's true leader.

"You mean Neera didn't try any of those tricks on Jackson that Orion women do so well?" Reyes asked. "I've experienced that sort of thing firsthand, and I can tell you that resisting their charms is harder than you might think."

"I can imagine," Nogura said. "I observed Jackson's interview with her, and she did try to wile him with her charms. She played up how grateful she was that we'd taken care of Ganz for her, as she'd been scared of him and all sorts of other nonsense." He shook his head. "There was a minute there when I thought I'd have to intervene, but Jackson kept everything under control. Her little secret's safe, though I expect she'll have a tough time finding a dependable replacement for Ganz, given the fate he suffered and how quickly Neera and everyone else threw him to the lions." He shook his head. "Her problem, not ours."

Nogura led the way into his office, instructing the two security guards that they could wait outside before indicating that Reyes should follow him. Clasping his hands behind his back, he waited until the doors closed before saying, "By the way, I haven't yet had a chance to thank you for what you did over there. I know how much danger you were in just by being there, but helping us placed you at even greater risk. I appreciate that you accepted that risk on our behalf."

Reyes shrugged. "Old habits die hard, I suppose. I just hope it's worth it, for ch'Nayla's sake, and Pennington, Hetzlein, and Gianetti, and everyone else who's died or been hurt since we found that damned meta-genome."

"With any luck," Nogura replied, "we'll know something soon." Even as he stood here with Reyes, Lieutenants T'Prynn and Xiong were working with the navigational data Reyes had secured from the *Omari-Ekon*.

"I can hardly wait," Reyes said, and Nogura heard the tinge of sarcasm in the other man's voice. "By the way, I want to thank you for simply confining me to guest quarters. You'd have been right to just toss me in the brig until someone's ready to take me to Earth."

Though he had considered doing exactly that, Nogura had decided such treatment was not needed. He did not believe Reyes to be any sort of flight risk, and keeping him under guard in guest quarters would be sufficient to contain him until such time as his final disposition—be it transport to the New Zealand penal colony on Earth as per the original sentence from his court-martial, or something else—was determined. "It seemed the least we could do, given the circumstances. I trust you're comfortable in your new quarters?"

"Best sleep I've had in months," Reyes replied. "It's nice, being able to go to bed and not have to worry about maybe being dead before you wake up."

Nogura chuckled at that. "I can imagine." Gesturing to where Reyes had been injured during the firefight that climaxed his escape from the *Omari-Ekon,* he asked, "How are you feeling?"

"Zeke—that is, Doctor Fisher—fixed me up. It's nothing to worry about. I'll be sore for a few days, but that's about it." Reyes's expression changed to one of concern. "Don't know if I can say the same about Pennington."

Nodding, Nogura released a sigh. "What happened to him is unfortunate, but I have every faith in Doctor Fisher." Unlike Reyes and others who had been injured during the firefight, Pennington had been wounded much more severely. According to Fisher's last report, the damage to the journalist's arm and shoulder were such that the doctor was still considering amputation and prosthetic replacement. "I've also recommended to Starfleet that he be awarded a civilian citation for valor. What he did probably saved your life, and T'Prynn's."

"If I know Pennington," Reyes said, "he'll likely offer a polite refusal. He's a journalist, through and through. He'd rather report the story than be a part of it, even if the last couple of years make it seem the opposite's true." Pausing to look around the office, he asked, "I guess I have to wonder what's next for me?"

Nogura had of course been considering the question since receiving the report from Jackson that T'Prynn and Reyes had made it off the *Omari-Ekon.* "There are a lot of questions, of course. You'll be debriefed in full about your time with the Klingons and the Orions. Your association with the Klingons in particular has a lot of people at Headquarters calling for your head. Many of them don't buy that you were acting to protect Starfleet and this station as much as possible given your situation, rather than actively colluding with the Klingons."

"Anybody who wants to call me a traitor is going to have to come out here and tell me to my face," Reyes snapped, the first hint of bitterness or anger over his current status Nogura had seen since the disgraced officer's return. "Everything I did was to protect as many lives as possible. That's all I've ever done. I even got court-martialed and convicted for it, if you recall."

"You were court-martialed for disobeying orders and violating your Starfleet oath," Nogura countered, allowing a slight edge to creep into his voice.

Reyes stood his ground. "My oath was to protect Federation citizens and obey all lawful orders from my superiors and our duly elected civilian leaders. There's nothing in there about safeguarding dirty little secrets or acting out of political expediency to cover my or anyone else's ass. I said basically the same thing at my trial, and I stand by it."

Saying nothing for a moment, Nogura regarded the former commodore before offering a slow nod of appreciation. "I know you do. While I can't officially condone your actions, I can respect them, because I believe you always were acting with noble purpose. Whether anyone agrees with either of us is something we'll have to wait to find out." He sighed. "I'm sorry I didn't take the time to tell you this before."

He had chosen to refrain from interacting with Reyes during his pretrial confinement and court-martial, to avoid even the perception of attempting in any way to influence the proceedings. The result was that he had not been afforded the opportunity to simply talk to the man. He had never suspected Reyes of being a traitor, or even of acting with malicious intent when deciding to disobey orders and allow Pennington to publish the story that had brought the Shedai—if not the truth behind the secrets and power they possessed—to the public's attention. Likewise, Nogura believed him still to be a man of character and honor, as demonstrated by his prompt decision to assist T'Prynn with the espionage she had conducted. The question now was whether anyone else stalking the halls of power at Starfleet Command would see things in similar fashion.

I probably shouldn't hold my breath.

"The debriefings are liable to take a while," Nogura said. "We'll do our best to see to it that you're as comfortable as possible. Is there anything in particular you need?"

Reyes shook his head. "No, Admiral, thank you. I appreciate everything you've already done for me." He stopped, his eyes turning downward to stare at the floor for a moment. When he spoke again it was without raising his head to meet Nogura's gaze. "Can you assist me with getting in touch with Captain Desai?"

Having expected that query, Nogura nevertheless was uncomfortable now that Reyes had given it voice. "Of course. We'll get word to her that you're no longer with the Orions, but you understand that you're still technically a prisoner. There's nothing I can do about that until after you've been properly debriefed."

His expression once more growing impassive, Reyes drew himself up before nodding. "I understand." Then, as if deciding there was nothing more to be said, he added, "Thank you for your time, Admiral."

Nogura said nothing as Reyes turned and exited the office, waiting for his security detail to take up positions in front of and behind him as they escorted him back to his quarters. For the first time, the admiral realized he felt sorrow for the former commodore, who at one time may well have been fueled by the knowledge that Rana Desai, the woman he loved, might still be waiting for him once he navigated the obstacles separating them. That this appeared no longer to be the case probably had done nothing but increase Reyes's sense of isolation. His life and career already in virtual ruin, he had no one but a handful of steadfast friends on whom to lean. Otherwise, Diego Reyes, without doubt, had to feel utterly alone.

And for that, Nogura thought, *I'm truly sorry.*

28

"My arm hurts."

The persistent, throbbing ache Tim Pennington sensed in his right arm flared enough to rouse him yet again from fitful sleep. Lying flat on his back, he grunted in irritation at his inability to do little more than doze, rather than enjoying anything resembling restful slumber. Even beyond the pain in his arm, there was the simple matter that the hospital bed was anything but comfortable. He was unable to shift onto his right side and slide his arm beneath his pillow, situating himself as he had since childhood. His current position was likely to be the best he could manage for a while.

Wonderful.

Closing his eyes as the dull pain continued to nag him, Pennington became more aware of the ambient sounds permeating his hospital room: conversations held in hushed tones drifting from the corridor, the low hum of passing antigrav carts, even the dull, two-stroke tone of his own pulse as interpreted and amplified by his biobed's array of sensors and status indicators. Listening to the melodic chorus of the machines overseeing his care, he began to sense his own body mocking him, as each beat of his heart seemed to pulse in rhythm with the pain from his arm.

Well, that's just damned annoying.

The sound of his room door sliding open was followed by a shift in the light beyond his closed eyelids, and Pennington blinked as he raised his head, squinting to clear his vision. Beyond the foot of his bed, a silhouette moved against a curtain of white illumination, which disappeared as the door closed once more. The room returned to its dim scales of gray, though he still could discern the figure as it moved toward him.

"Hello?" Pennington called out, noting how raspy his voice sounded.

"So, you're awake," replied a deep voice he recognized as belonging to Ezekiel Fisher even before the physician moved closer to the right side of his bed. "Take a drink. You've been asleep for quite a while."

"Doesn't feel like it." Pennington leaned toward Fisher and the small cup the doctor held in his hand, grasping the tip of its thin straw between his teeth. The water flooded his mouth with cool relief, prompting him to take several gulps of it before releasing the straw. Leaning back, he felt the liquid's chill as it coursed down his throat.

"How are you feeling?" Fisher asked, an almost paternal expression gracing his weathered features as he set the cup on a stand next to the bed.

"My arm hurts," Pennington replied.

Fisher smiled. "I heard you the first time. That's why I came in." He paused, glancing toward the middle of the bed. "Which arm?"

"That's not very damn funny," Pennington said, scowling.

Holding up a hand, the doctor shook his head. "I'm not trying to be, son. It's a legitimate question given your situation. Do you remember our last conversation?"

Pennington paused for a moment, attempting to sift through his grogginess and pain in order to recall when he might last have spoken to the physician. "I think so. It was after I was shot."

"Yes, it was," Fisher said, nodding. "You were brought to the hospital from the docking platform, near the Orion ship."

Memories came flooding back into Pennington's consciousness, accompanied by another series of dull throbs in his shoulder. "You took my arm."

"I did," Fisher said, his eyes now betraying a hint of sadness. "I took your arm."

Closing his eyes, Pennington swallowed as his throat once

more felt dry. "I remember." He turned his head, opening his eyes again as he looked to his shoulder. The arm, which had been in enough discomfort to awaken him—and in which he still felt that odd, constant ache—was gone. His shoulder seemed oddly mis-shapen to him, a sensation enhanced by the fact that the empty right sleeve of his blue hospital tunic appeared to have been tucked neatly behind his back.

"The disruptor bolt damn near destroyed your shoulder," Fisher said after a moment, "and damaged a great deal of the sur-rounding tissue. There was no way I could regenerate or repair what you would've needed fast enough to save your arm. I had to make a choice. I'm very sorry."

"No, Doctor," Pennington said, perhaps a bit too quickly. "No apologies needed. I'm sure you did everything you could to patch me up." He shrugged. "This will just take some . . . getting used to, is all." As he spoke the words, he realized his gaze remained fixated on his right shoulder, and the space where his arm should be resting beside him on the mattress.

"This doesn't have to be permanent, you know," the doctor said. "Despite the damage, you're a perfect candidate for a bio-synthetic replacement. After some extended sessions with our dermal and muscle tissue regenerators, it'll definitely be an op-tion worth exploring."

"Of course," Pennington said, his voice drifting as his thoughts turned to the memory of a veteran reporter he had known at the start of his Federation News Service career. Despite the elder journalist's byline of Garold Hicks, the news staff had called him "Old Dane" for reasons Pennington never did learn. Old Dane had been as spry and resourceful as reporters one-third his age, and among the tales he heard Hicks relate time and again was how the man had lost his left arm and leg while covering a conflict on a planet being considered for Federation member-ship—an application that subsequently was denied once Old Dane's reports went live on FNS feeds. He regaled every new member of the bureau staff with his account, ending it each time by saying, "That piece cost me an arm and a leg—but it cost that planet a hell of a lot more!" Pennington never noticed Old Dane's replacement limbs slowing him down, and that remembrance now seemed to offer a measure of emotional comfort, if only for a moment.

As for physical comfort, Pennington admitted to himself that he could use that, too. "Right now, Doc, I'd be happy for something to ease this pain."

Fisher offered a knowing nod. "I understand, but the best I can do is to give you something to help you sleep. The pain you're feeling isn't real. It's all in your head."

Wincing at the words, Pennington lolled his head back on his pillow. "You think I'm just imagining this? It hurts like hell."

"That's not what I meant," the doctor replied, his tone one that Pennington recognized as intended to soothe him. "Your neurological circuitry is adapting to your loss. It's attempting to rewire itself—to work around what it can no longer control. Now, we can try a few sessions with a neural neutralizer, or I can go in there with a cortical stimulator and desensitize a region of your thalamus, but I don't want to try any of those solutions before you decide whether you want to try biosynthesis. You might feel better, but you need all the synaptic activity you can get if you want that new arm to work."

Despite a momentary wave of disappointment he felt sweeping across him, Pennington accepted the explanation. "Okay, you got me." Then, forcing a smile, he added, "I mean, I can't bloody well type with just one arm, can I?"

Fisher chuckled at that. "You input your stories manually?"

"Sometimes," Pennington replied, shrugging again. "When the mood strikes, or I'm not in too much of a hurry."

"Well, don't be in too much of a hurry here, either," Fisher said. "It'll take a little time, but not as much as you might think. We can begin some of the scanning work as soon as you feel up to it, and when you want to sleep some more, I can give you more for that, too."

Pennington once more glanced down at his arm, or where his arm should have been. Was it odd that he seemed to feel no re-sentiment at having lost the limb, either as a consequence of the firefight or due to Fisher's inability to treat the injuries he had suffered? Part of him felt as though he should be angry and should be wanting to lash out at something or someone, but as quickly as such thoughts manifested themselves, they seemed to dissolve of their own volition. Was he in denial about what had happened to him, or had he already begun to accept it without so much as a token protest or outburst at the unfairness of his current situation?

Beats being dead, I suppose, he conceded. *At least now, the doc can fix me. Most of me, anyway.*

"Any chance I could get something to eat?" he asked, almost without thinking as he felt a rumbling in his stomach. How long had it been since his last solid meal?

"Done," Fisher said. "Also, do you feel up to visitors? Strictly your decision."

Pennington was somewhat taken aback by the question. "Really? Somebody's come to see me?"

"They've actually been waiting quite a while," the doctor replied. "Hang on a minute." He left the room, leaving Pennington to wonder who might be calling on him. Admiral Nogura? Vanguard's commanding officer would be too busy. Perhaps T'Prynn had—against all of her Vulcan logic—taken pity upon him and opted to drop in? Maybe Allie from Tom Walker's place? There was always Lieutenant Ginther from station security, he supposed.

And don't forget . . .

His thoughts were interrupted by his room door sliding open once again, followed by a gruff voice.

"Um, hi, Tim."

"I'll be damned," Pennington said, feeling a surge of satisfaction at the sight of Cervantes Quinn standing in his doorway. Unable to resist, he offered a small smile. " '*Tim*'? I get a bloody 'Tim' from you? I must look a hell of a lot worse than I thought." He watched as the haggard-looking trader entered the room without any actual invitation being extended, shuffling more than walking as he made his way to the side of the biobed. To Pennington's sleep-weary and drug-hazed eyes, Quinn still appeared unkempt and downtrodden, and appeared to be battling all manner of inner demons even as he put on a brave face.

"I hear you've had a rough go," Quinn said, his voice low and sounding as tired and drained of spirit as the man himself.

Pennington nodded. "I'd say you can *see* I've had a rough go. Might as well talk about it, I suppose."

"Okay, then," Quinn said, seeming to relax a bit. "So, how are you feeling?"

"Like an idiot," Pennington replied. "I guess I was due, right? Running around, getting the story, doing what I do. I shouldn't be that surprised to wake up one day and see this. Could've been worse, the more I think about it."

"It's not your fault," Quinn said. "You got shot. From what I hear, you kept other people from getting hurt, too."

Frowning, Pennington tried to remember details of the firefight, and was surprised to realize that some of the memories were still refusing to present themselves. "I'll have to take your word for it. Maybe it'll come back to me."

"Maybe," Quinn replied. "Then again, maybe it's a good thing you can't remember."

Pennington nodded. "Do me a favor? Pass me a drink? I'm not that steady."

His expression turning to one of confusion, Quinn blinked several times before answering, "I'm not carrying anything on me at the moment."

That's a damned lie. Pennington almost said the words aloud, but caught himself at the last moment. There was nothing to be gained from going down that path. Not now, at least. Instead, he nodded to the stand next to his bed. "Over there. The cup."

Quinn lifted the cup and maneuvered it to Pennington's lips, and the reporter sipped from the straw. Once he had done so, he tried once more to find a comfortable position in the bed.

"Believe it or not, it's good to see you, Quinn."

"Yeah," his friend replied, averting his gaze to stare at something on the wall behind Pennington's head. "I wasn't sure that would happen again."

"What," Pennington said, nodding toward his right shoulder. "This changed your mind?"

Quinn nodded. "Got me thinking, yeah."

"Thinking that the last time we spoke, you acted like a complete bastard?"

To Pennington's surprise, Quinn smiled at that. "There's the newsboy I know."

"And where's the Cervantes Quinn that I know?" Pennington let the question hang in the air a moment before pressing ahead. "You're standing there worried about me? Hell, mate, I'm worried about *you*."

"Well, don't," Quinn snapped. "I'm the one standing on the good side of a hospital bed, not you."

"This time, anyway," Pennington said. "Maybe next time I'll be standing on the good side of a slab in the morgue." No sooner did the words leave his mouth than he felt regret wash over him. *Bloody hell.*

Quinn's features darkened, his brow furrowing and his lips pressing together as he backed away from the bed. "Well, just look at the time. I'll tell the doctor you're ready for your next hypospray." As he walked to the door, he added without turning his head, "See you around. *Tim.*"

Angry at himself and his own stupidity, Pennington called out, "Damn it, Quinn, don't go. I'm sorry. I'm not my—" He sighed when he saw that he was speaking to a closing door. "Damn it."

Releasing a sigh of exasperation, Pennington shifted in the bed, hoping he might grow accustomed to reclining just enough that he could doze off again. He knew that was unlikely, at least in the short term, as his mind no doubt would continue to torture him with replays of the disastrous conversation that had just transpired. Despite that, he closed his eyes and drew several deep breaths, trying to force himself to relax, but his thoughts turned once more to his friend, whom Pennington suspected might be nearing his limit. How much further could he descend, spiraling ever more out of control? Quinn seemed content to commit slow self-destruction, and it angered Pennington that he would probably be forced to watch the final act of his friend's deterioration from a hospital bed.

Damn you, Quinn.

The sound of his door opening yet again startled him from his reverie, and he looked up to see yet another unexpected visitor.

"T'Prynn?" Despite his earlier musing about her, part of him had hoped she might see fit to pay him a visit.

Just outside the doorway, dressed in her familiar red Starfleet uniform and with her hair pulled back into a functional, regulation bun, the Vulcan stood with her hands clasped behind her back. "May I enter without disturbing you?"

"Probably not," Pennington said as he squinted into the light from the room's open door. "But please enter anyway."

T'Prynn moved far enough into the room for the doors to close behind her. "May I approach?"

Pennington laughed for what he imagined was the first time in a while. "You're being awfully formal, considering we used to be married. I mean, even though it was a sham marriage that you insisted on so that you could use me for personal gain and all."

Her right eyebrow arching, T'Prynn replied, "I would never presume that our rather odd venture into temporary matrimony afforded me any special privileges, particularly now that our marital contract has long since been voided."

"Of course not," Pennington said, punctuating the reply with another small chuckle. "Please . . . approach. I promise that losing an arm isn't contagious."

Stepping closer, T'Prynn countered, "Not unless you had lost it as a result of contracting Arcturan limb-specific necrosis."

"Wait, they actually have such a thing?" When T'Prynn said nothing, Pennington's eyes narrowed. "Wait. Did I survive all this just so I could see you crack a joke?"

"I understand how your recent trauma might alter your perceptions," T'Prynn said, "so I will keep my visit brief. I trust that you are recuperating according to Doctor Fisher's expectations."

Pennington nodded. "Looks that way. As illogical as I'm sure this will sound, my missing arm hurts quite a bit. Other than that, I seem to be coming along fine."

"Excellent," T'Prynn said. After a moment, she brought her right hand from behind her back. "I also have come to deliver something." Reaching toward his bedside table, she placed atop it a slim, silver-bodied device.

"Ah," Pennington said, recognizing the object as she withdrew her hand. "You've found my recorder."

"It is not your recorder," T'Prynn corrected. "Yours was damaged to the point of necessitating a replacement. I was able to acquire an identical model. You will find that it contains all of your original audio and visual files, in case you need them for review."

It took Pennington an extra moment to comprehend what he had just heard. When realization dawned, he lifted his head to regard T'Prynn with skepticism. "Wait a minute. *All* of them? Including what I was recording at the time I—"

"Your files are complete," T'Prynn replied. "Admiral Nogura was initially disinclined to return the recordings, but I explained that your traumatic injury likely resulted in some short-term memory lapses, and that your files might offer restorative benefits should you choose to view them."

"I suppose they could," Pennington said, nodding in agreement as he studied the device before him. "And what did he say about their journalistic value? I recorded an armed assault by Orion pirates aboard a Starfleet installation, which was incited by the legally questionable extradition of a former Starfleet officer who had requested asylum within protected Orion property. That's news."

T'Prynn replied, "Your predilection for discerning what information better serves the citizens of the Federation by being kept from public dissemination was successfully argued by Mister Reyes. He may be your strongest advocate aboard the station."

"But not my only one," Pennington said, shifting his gaze from his recorder to her. "Thank you, T'Prynn." Nodding toward the device, he added, "Don't get me wrong; it's a tremendous story, but not for the news feeds. I'll archive it along with the rest of my Vanguard recordings and when I'm ready, I'll give it a look."

Maybe I can write a book or three about all of this one day.

"As you wish," T'Prynn said.

She said nothing else for a moment, and when that moment began to lengthen to the point of awkwardness, Pennington shifted his position once again, his discomfort now existing on multiple levels. "Was there something else?" he finally asked.

T'Prynn seemed to be experiencing her own bout of uneasiness. "There is another matter. I have come to acknowledge the circumstances which led to your injury. Your actions prevented harm to me, and I . . . thank you, Tim."

Thanks, from a Vulcan? Pennington could not help the odd tinge of humility he now felt as he contemplated what T'Prynn must have mustered within herself to share those words. Sensing her anxiety despite her best efforts to maintain her cool, composed demeanor, he said, "T'Prynn, please. I did what anyone else would have done in the same situation."

"You have shown me much kindness," T'Prynn said. "I realize this is a normal, if illogical, practice of your species, and one from which I have encouraged you to refrain on multiple occasions. And yet, you persist."

"Call me stubborn," Pennington replied, now feeling more than a bit anxious in his own right, and seeking a way to ease the tension they both seemed to be experiencing.

T'Prynn's eyebrow arched once again. "*Mister* Pennington, with your permission, I would like to reciprocate."

"Permission?" Pennington puzzled a bit over his own question. *Reciprocate? What the hell is she saying?* "I suppose, but what do you need permission for?"

Without replying, T'Prynn stepped closer to his side, reaching up to rest her fingers along the sides of his face. Pennington felt the gentle pressure of her fingertips against his temples and at points just below his eyes.

"Tim Pennington," she said, her voice barely a whisper, "my mind to your mind. Our minds are merging. Our minds are one, and together."

"Wait, what are you . . ." There was an initial rush of uncertainty at what was happening, but Pennington forced himself to relax, knowing T'Prynn was not attempting to harm him. He tried to speak further, but the words only thickened in his mouth. Then, a preternatural calm overtook him, and though he could not hear her words, he felt her presence in his mind. Soothing warmth washed over him like a thick, inviting blanket, and he felt the tension in his body melt away, and a sensation of euphoria began to overtake him. T'Prynn was there, but just beyond the perimeter of his perception, and he comprehended he was slipping away into the welcoming embrace of sleep, no doubt brought on by T'Prynn's mind-meld and whatever passive instructions she was feeding to his subconscious.

As he drifted away, content to let whatever spell T'Prynn had cast upon him soothe his overtaxed mind and body, Pennington realized she also had given him one additional gift.

The pain from his nonexistent arm was gone.

29

Standing on a rise that afforded him an unobstructed view of the valley below, Thomas Blair studied the settlement through the viewfinder of the field binoculars. The structures, all of obvious Klingon design, appeared to be intact. He saw no signs of attack or even a natural disaster that might have been misconstrued as an attack. To his eyes, nothing about the colony appeared amiss.

Except for the bodies, of course.

"Good God," Blair said, his voice barely louder than a whisper. His mouth had gone dry, and he swallowed several times in an effort to work up some spit. Panning the binoculars across the colony center, he opted to stop counting the number of Klingon bodies scattered along the open streets and courtyards. Other corpses were draped over balconies, or slumped over the consoles of land vehicles or other equipment. From somewhere, probably within one or more of the structures, Blair heard the low, constant hum of machinery still in operation. Generators, he thought, or environmental control or refrigeration units. He saw no sign of weapons or other military apparatus. "No life signs. You're sure about that?"

Standing next to him, his security chief, Lieutenant Commander Trethishavu th'Vlene, replied, "None, Captain. At least, none within the target area."

"Eight kilometers across," Blair said, repeating that nugget of information from the briefing his science officer had given to him prior to his decision to beam down. "And almost a perfect circle. There's no way this was a natural phenomenon, so what the hell happened? An attack, or maybe some kind of accident?"

Magnifying the image being fed to him through the binoculars, he focused on a section of one of the streets where three bodies were strewn across the ground. The expressions fixed on the Klingons' faces and the dried blood running from their mouths, noses, and ears told Blair that whatever had caused their deaths, it had been anything but pleasant.

"Perhaps some sort of chemical or biological agent was deployed," th'Vlene said. The Andorian *thaan* was holding up a tricorder, its sensors aimed toward the settlement. "Though it would have to be something we've never encountered. I'm not picking up any traces of contaminants in the atmosphere."

"That's probably a good thing," Blair said, "especially considering we're standing out here in the open, with no sort of protective equipment." Sensor scans of the planet from orbit had shown no trace of anything untoward, which was the main reason he had opted for a firsthand look at the colony site.

Th'Vlene frowned, adjusting the tricorder's settings. "However, I am detecting a residual energy signature. It's like nothing I've seen before."

Blair lowered the binoculars and turned to look as th'Vlene angled the tricorder so that he could see its display. "Send your readings back to the ship. We'll get the computer chewing on it." Sighing, he reached up to wipe the light sheen of perspiration that had formed on his forehead. "This is a farming colony. Would the Tholians resort to attacking civilians?"

"There are unconfirmed reports that the Klingons have a military installation hidden somewhere on this planet," th'Vlene replied.

"I've read those reports," Blair said, "but according to Commander Nyn, there's nothing here to suggest a military presence. According to every scan she ran, this is a farming colony, which makes absolutely no sense, considering everything else this planet has to offer."

Frowning, th'Vlene replied, "Maybe they got what they wanted simply by laying claim to the planet. If they're here, then we can't be, and we can't conduct mining operations."

"But you'd think they *would* be," Blair countered. He then paused as he realized what his security chief was inferring. "You mean they're just holding on to this rock for now—saving it for a rainy day."

Th'Vlene said, "I don't know why the weather should factor into whatever strategy the Klingons might have for exploiting this planet's resources."

His eyes narrowing, Blair chuckled despite the situation and his surroundings, and shook his head. "Are you *sure* you're not a Vulcan?"

By all accounts, the Traelus system had been of interest to the Empire even before their first forays into the Taurus Reach. Traelus II, the world on which Blair and his landing party now stood, was rich in natural resources valued both by the Federation as well as the Klingons. Deposits of dilithium, pergium, rodinium—minerals essential to the operation of modern starships as well as starbases and other land-based facilities—were present across the planet. The system's proximity to the Tholian border also made it attractive from a strategic point of view, as it was one of a handful of such systems from which military action could be supported in the event of a conflict with Tholian forces. It was these same interests that had motivated the Klingons to stake a claim to Traelus II ahead of the Federation.

According to the latest version of whatever fluid diplomatic agreement governed the two powers' activities in the Taurus Reach, simply by beaming down to the planet, Blair may well have triggered an interstellar incident, even though his reasons were straightforward. The distress call his communications officer had intercepted, broadcast without benefit of any encryption, had not expressly forbidden any non-Klingon vessels from answering the plea for help. On the other hand, it had been a generic, all-purpose distress signal transmitted on a repeating loop, the sort of pre-recorded summons often designed to be dispatched quickly, such as when some kind of massive accident or disaster had occurred. Whether that was sufficient to absolve Blair of any wrongdoing so far as answering the call was concerned, he did not know.

All that's for the politicians to worry about, he mused as he once more raised the binoculars to his face and took another survey of the devastated settlement. He had come here with the intentions of answering the distress call—detected two days earlier as the *Defiant* continued its patrol of the sector—and making a good-faith effort to render whatever assistance might be needed. As that was no longer necessary, his first instinct was to send Doctor Hamilton and her team to search for clues and answers as to what might have wiped out the colony.

An autopsy of one of the victims was out of the question, of course, and not just because his chief medical officer—so far as he knew, at least—possessed no in-depth knowledge of Klingon anatomy. While he was certain Hamilton could conduct at least some cursory examinations using whatever records might be on file in the *Defiant's* library computer, even that would take more time than Blair knew remained to him. What if the settlers had fallen prey to some as yet unknown, perhaps even infectious disease that defied detection by sensor scans? Was that not important enough to secure as much information as possible? A full science team was what really was needed here, but the likelihood of the Empire allowing such an excursion was small, no matter how noble or innocuous the purpose. Despite whatever pretense of peace imposed upon the Federation and the Empire by the Organian Peace Treaty, tensions remained strained between the two powers, and events that had transpired in the Taurus Reach in recent months had only exacerbated the situation. The last thing Blair wanted was a confrontation with a Klingon battle cruiser here. Not now, when there remained far too many questions about what happened here.

"There's nothing we can do now," he said, shaking his head in disgust, "and our being here's only going to upset whoever comes to check on the colony." The best Blair could do now would be to compose a detailed report and transmit it back to Starbase 47, where Admiral Nogura would see to it that it was forwarded to the appropriate parties on the Federation as well as the Klingon side of whatever negotiating table the governments' respective diplomats currently graced.

"Commander Mbugua did order me to make sure you returned to the ship within one hour, sir," th'Vlene said.

Eyeing the Andorian, Blair replied, "Has it been that long?" He then heard the telltale beep of his communicator, and he offered a small smile. "Well, it looks like the commander's been keeping at least one eye on the clock." Reaching for the device at the small of his back, he flipped open the communicator's antenna grid. "Blair here." Expecting Mbugua, he was surprised to hear the voice of his science officer.

"It's Commander Nyn, sir," the young woman replied. *"Captain, we've found something you need to see."*

The first thought that occurred to Thomas Blair as he studied the object before him was that it was the product of a science experiment gone wrong in some horrific manner.

"What the hell is it?" he asked as he walked a circuit around the odd device, which sat alone atop a small plateau no more than twenty meters across at its widest point. "Some kind of probe?"

From where she stood to one side, tricorder in hand, Lieutenant Commander Nyn said, "I don't think so, sir. I'm picking up components of what looks to be some kind of sensor apparatus, but it seems to be fairly limited in scope."

"A weapon of some kind?" Blair frowned, and for a worried moment, he wondered if it might be some kind of mine. *Now's a hell of a time to think of that.*

Nyn shook her head. "That'd make sense, sir, particularly given what else we've found." She gestured first to where the bodies of two Tholians lay a short distance from the object, near the edge of the rise, before pointing to the body of a Klingon female. "That said, I don't see how." Pausing, she continued to consult her tricorder. "I mean, I'm picking up what looks to be some kind of particle beam generator, but there's nothing else that makes me think it's part of a weapons system. No targeting array, and it doesn't seem to have any sort of propulsion or flight control systems. It pretty much just sits here, and whatever beam it's supposed to generate goes in one direction, though from what I can tell the beam is meant to disperse as it travels from its origin point, rather than focusing on a single target."

"And this is the only one we've found that's intact?" Blair asked.

"That's correct, sir," Nyn replied. "Though our sensors found twenty-three other sites, arrayed in an equidistant perimeter around the colony, every one of those sites has nothing but a small crater and some residual materials that are obviously artificial in origin."

His gaze still fixed on the object, Blair said, "Let me guess. The perimeter is eight kilometers wide." He heard Nyn clear her throat before replying.

"That's right, sir."

Blair ran his hand along the object's flank. "And what's that sound like to you, Commander?"

"Whatever these things are," the science officer said, "they formed a kill zone, with the colony in the middle. Afterward, they initiated some kind of self-destruct protocol." Turning, she pointed to another, smaller crater. "Something was over there, too, but beats me what it might've been. My tricorder picked up traces of Tholian remains from that site, sir. Whatever blew up, it took at least one Tholian with it."

His fingers brushing over a series of scorch marks blemishing the object's otherwise flawless black surface, Blair said, "Somebody took a shot at it. These look like disruptor burns."

Nyn replied, "Judging by the damage and residual energy reading. I don't think it's from a Klingon weapon, though."

Bending closer, Blair saw that the object's outer casing had been penetrated. "Whatever hit it managed to punch through the shell."

"There appears to be some internal damage," Nyn said. "Some kind of computer component, I think, but without tearing it apart, I can't be sure."

Blair always liked a good puzzle, even if he knew he would not like the picture it would form. "I'll bet a month's pay this is the reason we have twenty-three craters instead of twenty-four." He pointed to the damaged section. "The shot damaged whatever self-destruct mechanism this thing contains."

"It's certainly a possibility, sir," the science officer replied.

Turning from the still unidentified object, Blair said, "What the hell were the Tholians doing here?"

"Upsetting the natives, I think," another voice answered, and Blair turned to see th'Vlene making his way up one angled face of the rise toward them. The Andorian stopped before pointing back the way he had come. "I found another Klingon down there."

Blair walked to the edge of the plateau and directed his gaze down the slope until he caught sight of the unmoving form lying at the bottom of the ravine th'Vlene had been investigating. The body was partially obscured by boulders and vegetation, but there was no mistaking the rather large burn mark on the Klingon male's chest. Clothing along with skin and muscle tissue had been burned away, probably from a particle beam weapon at close range.

Pointing to another area of the ravine, th'Vlene replied, "As for the other Klingon, she didn't have any obvious signs of trauma, but she looked like what we saw at the colony, sir."

"Interesting," Blair said, his attention shifting between where th'Vlene had pointed and the general direction of the settlement. Nodding toward the mysterious, drone-like object, he said, "She's between this thing and the colony." That seemed to lend some additional weight to his idea that the drone, along with its twenty-three destroyed counterparts, might well be some kind of broad-based antipersonnel weapon. How had they gotten here undetected? Were they moved into position by hand, or dropped from orbit? Without a more detailed examination of the drone, there would be no way to answer such a question, along with the hundred or so others Blair was contemplating, such as how the Tholians, however many there might have been, had kept their presence a secret. Where was their ship? Not in orbit, or it would have been detected by the *Defiant*'s sensors. Was it here, hidden? That made more sense. If the Klingon colony here was in truth just an actual agricultural outpost and not part of a larger, clandestine military operation, then the inhabitants likely would not have had access to the same levels of sensor and weapons technology used by the imperial forces. A party with sufficient skill, particularly if they were employing covert infiltration tactics, could very easily exploit such a shortcoming.

Maybe the colony was targeted for exactly that reason. The thought at once saddened and angered Blair, for the devastation that had been wreaked as well as the idea that the Tholians had with deliberate calculation targeted civilians with whatever weapon they had created. Such an overt, unjustifiable act would only serve to further deteriorate the already fragile political situation in this part of the Taurus Reach. *And here we are, stuck right in the middle.*

"Get this thing ready for transport," he said. "We're taking it with us. You'll start your investigation on our way back to Vanguard. Meanwhile, I want every sensor scan you can throw at this planet. The Tholians had to have a ship. I want it found."

Nyn nodded. "Aye, sir."

His communicator beeped for attention, and Blair reached for the device and activated it. "Blair here."

"Defiant *here, sir,*" replied the voice of Commander Mbugua. "*It's time for you to call it a day, Skipper. We've got company.*"

Uh-oh, Blair thought. "Klingons?"

"*No, sir,*" the first officer replied. "*Long-range sensors are picking up three Tholian ships, heading this way at high warp. They'll be here within the hour.*"

Th'Vlene said, "It seems someone else heard the colony's distress call."

"That, or the Tholians sent their own," Blair countered, then nodded toward the drone. "Or one of these things fired off a call for help before self-destructing. Doesn't matter now." He was gripped by the sudden thought that everything they had seen of the mysterious Tholian technology here had smacked of tracks being covered. Perhaps the devices had self-destructed so as to give the Tholian government plausible deniability for what had happened here?

"Nyn, get this thing back to the ship, now." For all Blair knew, this was the lone remaining piece of evidence implicating the Tholian Assembly as instigators of interstellar war with the Klingons.

If that was the case, and with more Tholian vessels fast approaching, Blair was certain of only one thing: The best place to be right at the moment was anywhere but here.

30

As the doors to his office slid aside, Admiral Nogura was greeted by the sight of T'Prynn and Ming Xiong. The duo was standing in the open area between his desk and the door, obviously waiting for him to arrive.

"I've never really liked it when my own meetings start without me," Nogura said, eyeing his charges as he passed them on his way to the food slot set into the rear wall of his office.

"We hadn't started, Admiral," Xiong said, the expression on his face one of such concern and sincerity that Nogura almost felt a small pang of guilt for making what he had intended to be a mood-lightening remark.

Almost, but not quite.

"I directed that at myself, Lieutenant," he said, waiting until the food slot's door slid upward to reveal a cup of green tea resting in a saucer. "Flag officers make comments such as those in order to avoid offering a proper apology when they're running late. Stick around Starfleet long enough, and you'll one day be able to keep people waiting, too." Retrieving the tea, Nogura made his way to his desk and lowered himself into his high-backed chair. Gesturing toward the pair of chairs in front of him, he said, "Those aren't decorative. Somebody use them." As Xiong settled into one of the chairs, leaving T'Prynn to stand behind him, Nogura lifted his teacup from its saucer. "So, I take it we have some sort of new development?"

Turning to walk to the wall-mounted viewscreen on the left side of the admiral's office, T'Prynn replied, "Yes, Admiral. We have completed our analysis of the navigational data obtained by

Mister Reyes from the *Omari-Ekon*." Without waiting for further instructions, she took the square blue data card she had been carrying in her right hand and inserted it into a reader slot situated next to the screen. She then pressed a sequence of keys on the control pad next to the reader, and the screen flared to life. A wash of computer data coalesced into the image of what Nogura recognized as a standard Federation star chart. Moving to the side of the screen so as to offer an unobstructed view, T'Prynn clasped her hands behind her back.

"Based on navigational and chronological data recorded by the *Omari-Ekon*'s main computer," she said, "we believe that the Mirdonyae Artifacts originated in this star system. Federation stellar cartography databases currently list this system as FGC PSR 0108+143."

Shifting in his seat, Xiong said, "It's a pulsar, sir, estimated to be two hundred million years old. As you can tell by the database, we haven't given it much attention in terms of exploratory research."

"But the Vulcans have," Nogura countered.

T'Prynn nodded. "Indeed. Our star charts refer to it as Eremar. The only information we possess was provided by automated survey probes, dispatched centuries ago. As with much of the Taurus Reach, Vulcan never sent crewed vessels to that region."

"So, where is this Eremar system?" Nogura asked, leaning back in his chair as he sipped his tea.

"Approximately thirty-five light-years from our present position," T'Prynn replied, tapping the control pad again. In response to her command, the star chart magnified, this time highlighting and bringing into sharp relief one section of the Taurus Reach with which Nogura was becoming increasingly familiar.

"In the center of this . . . what did you call it? Tkon Empire?" he asked.

"We believe this to be the center of what once was the Tkon civilization, Admiral," Xiong replied. "At least, according to the information we've so far been able to obtain on that area, including information supplied to us by Cervantes Quinn and Bridget McLellan from their mission to retrieve the stolen Mirdonyae Artifact."

Nogura said, "Yes, of course. Their encounter with the Shedai . . . Apostate?"

"Yes, Admiral," Xiong replied.

Offering a nod of thanks, Nogura eyed the image on the viewscreen. "That looks to be a bit of a hop from here," he said. "Do we know why the *Omari-Ekon* was in that vicinity in the first place?"

T'Prynn shook her head. "We do not believe the vessel actually traveled to the region, sir, but rather obtained the relevant navigational data as part of the business deal that gave the Orions the artifact itself. According to the intelligence data we've been able to gather, we believe that neither Ganz nor any member of his crew possessed knowledge of the artifact's specific origin or properties." Stepping closer to the viewscreen, she placed one hand on the highlighted area. "Mister Quinn reported the Apostate's mention of an alliance with factions from the Tkon Empire, one that resulted in the creation of a great weapon capable of imprisoning individual Shedai and neutralizing any threat posed by their activities."

"Which we believe to be the Mirdonyae Artifacts," Xiong said. "Quinn's descriptions match the crystals in physical characteristics and function. Given that we have two Shedai contained within a pair of the things, it seems to me we're barking up the right tree."

"It certainly seems that way," Nogura said, setting aside his tea, which had cooled rather more quickly than he had anticipated. "Mister Xiong, what do we know about the Tkon, and Eremar in particular?"

Drawing himself up, Xiong replied, "Unfortunately, much of what we do know—including what was given to us with the reports supplied by Quinn and McLellan based on their encounter with the Shedai Apostate—is more story than fact. We know that their civilization existed more than six hundred thousand years ago, and tales have been told and circulated for generations. Consistent details describe the Tkon as having controlled a vast region within what we now call the Taurus Reach. Their empire crossed the border we've since established as separating the Alpha and Beta Quadrants, and their territorial boundaries extended into what is now Klingon space, though they did not reach across to areas now under the control of the Tholians."

"According to these tales," T'Prynn said, "the Tkon civilization was quite advanced—well beyond our present technological level. Among their many unsubstantiated achievements, they are believed to have mastered terraforming, as well as traveling interstellar distances without benefit of faster-than-light spacecraft."

"The wildest stories involve the Tkon being able to literally relocate entire solar systems," Xiong said.

Nogura said, "Sounds a lot like our friends, the Shedai, and what happened to the Jinoteur system." His left hand resting on the desk, he began tapping its smooth surface with his forefinger. "Even taking into account gross exaggerations and embellishments of these stories, it's probably safe to say that the Tkon likely were a dominant power in this part of the galaxy, at least for a time."

"That's correct, sir," Xiong said. "Given their probable level of technological sophistication compared to surrounding civilizations, they would have seemed like gods to less-developed societies. According to the stories, some emerging cultures evidently worshipped the Tkon. That, or they simply feared Tkon power."

"At least, until their empire fell," Nogura said.

T'Prynn nodded. "Yes, Admiral. It is generally believed that the Tkon civilization all but died out after the star in their empire's core system went supernova."

"Eremar," Xiong said.

Reaching again for the viewer's control pad, T'Prynn pressed a key that further magnified the image, this time bringing into focus the Eremar pulsar and the lone planet orbiting it. "According to Mister Quinn's report, the Shedai Apostate alleged that the Shedai themselves detonated the star, thereby crippling the Tkon civilization before its apparent superweapon could be employed."

"Well, we know Shedai technology can destroy planets and make solar systems disappear," Nogura said, scarcely daring even to imagine what it might be like to control such power. "Forcing a star to go nova seems right up their alley. If they were responsible for Eremar, then they obviously viewed the Tkon as a threat."

"Absolutely," Xiong replied. "Rumors have persisted for generations that some survivors of the Tkon people remain, scattered to the various worlds that once fell under their empire's control. Given their supposed ability to transit between star systems as we've seen the Shedai do, it's unlikely their entire civilization was destroyed."

T'Prynn said, "Admiral, even if there are no living Tkon, artifacts of their technology might well remain."

Nogura sighed. "Why did I know you were going to say that? It was bad enough when we were working to keep the advanced weaponry from one dead empire out of our enemy's hands. Now you're thinking there's a second such civilization, with the power to have stood toe-to-toe with the Shedai?" He shook his head. "I should have retired and moved back to Fujiyama when I had the chance." Returning his attention to Xiong, he said, "What do you think, Lieutenant?"

Stepping closer, Xiong replied, "I think we need to go and have a look for ourselves, Admiral."

"I knew you were going to say that, too," Nogura said, softening his remark with a small, wan smile. "Any race that could construct those crystals probably has a few other tricks up their sleeves." No sooner did he speak the words than he glanced to where T'Prynn still stood by the viewscreen. Though she said nothing, her right eyebrow did rise a notch. "Quiet, you."

"Aye, sir," the Vulcan replied.

Eyeing Xiong, Nogura asked, "Lieutenant, are you still having trouble trying to communicate with the Shedai inside the artifact you have on board the *Lovell*?"

"We are making progress, sir," the younger officer replied. "Commander al-Khaled and his people have some new ideas, and we're working to implement them now."

Nogura nodded, satisfied if not overly enthused by the report. "Keep at it." Perhaps, if communication with the Shedai was successful, the imprisoned entity might even have information of some use to Xiong before he set out on the journey to Eremar.

Somehow, I don't think we're that lucky.

Pausing a moment to consider the plan he was about to put into motion, Nogura straightened in his chair. "Very well, then. I'm authorizing an exploratory mission to Eremar. Find out whatever you can—information, technology, whatever." Recalling the latest status reports from the station's dockmaster, Nogura said, "The *Endeavour* is on patrol and won't be back for more than a month." He looked to Xiong. "You've got the *Lovell* tied up with your current round of experiments, and she's not the ship for this kind of mission, anyway. That leaves the *Sagittarius,* which is undergoing some overdue maintenance on several key shipboard systems, and won't be ready for a long-haul trip like this for at least two more weeks."

Not for the first time, Nogura regretted his decision to allow the starships *Theseus, Akhiel,* and *Buenos Aires*—the other vessels assigned to Starbase 47 on an interim basis—to be spirited away by Starfleet Command for other missions they deemed to be of equal or greater importance than Operation Vanguard. The other vessel on temporary assignment to him, the *Defiant,* under the command of Captain Thomas Blair, also had been dispatched to a distant corner of the Taurus Reach, pursuing its own investigation of recent tensions between the Klingons and the Tholians. Though Nogura had full faith in Captain Nassir and the crew of the *Sagittarius,* the *Archer*-class scout just was not the type of vessel he preferred to send on the undertaking he was about to order. He considered waiting for one of the larger, more powerful ships to return before putting Xiong's plan into motion, but if he and T'Prynn were right, then time was of the essence.

"Two weeks, Lieutenant," Nogura said, tapping the top of his desk for emphasis. "You've got that long to prepare your mission profile and bring the *Sagittarius* crew up to speed."

Xiong nodded. "Understood, sir." Though he said nothing else, Nogura sensed the younger man's unease.

"Don't worry, Lieutenant. It's my intention to send the *Endeavour* or somebody in your direction as soon as I'm able." To T'Prynn, Nogura said, "Lieutenant, dispatch a message to Captain Khatami, and have her start hightailing it back this way. If we can reroute them to Eremar to assist the *Sagittarius,* that would make my year."

"Aye, sir," the Vulcan replied.

An authoritative tone from the communications panel on Nogura's desk interrupted the proceedings, and he reached for his desktop computer interface and tapped the key to activate it. Expecting a visual communication from his assistant or perhaps even Commander Cooper up in the station's operations center, the admiral instead was surprised to see the heading for an eyes-only encrypted communiqué indicating the need for his immediate attention.

"Thank you both," he said, calling an abrupt end to the meeting. "That'll be all. Dismissed."

He said nothing else, watching until the door slid closed behind the pair of junior officers, leaving him alone. Reaching for another control on his desk, he activated the door's lock, thereby preventing his assistant or anyone else from entering and interrupting what he was about to do. He then entered his authorization code on the computer terminal, unlocking the encrypted communication. He was surprised to see from the message's header that it had been sent by Captain Blair from the *Defiant,* which at this moment was supposed to be making its way back from the distant Traelus star system.

It was a distress call.

31

"Lies! Every word that comes out of your loathsome face *is a lie!*"

The Klingon, whom Jetanien recognized as a farmer named Kanjar, was one of the colony's more outspoken residents. He stood at the rear of Paradise City's Public Hall, dressed in a soiled set of coveralls, the cuffs of which were tucked into a pair of oversized, scuffed, and muddy boots. His hair, long and also covered with a film of dust, was pulled back from his face and secured at the back of his neck, though a few strands had freed themselves to hang before his eyes. His outburst had captured the attention of the several dozen colonists occupying seats in the hall, bringing to an abrupt end the candid yet calm discussion being guided by Jetanien with the help of Lugok and D'tran.

Rising from his seat at the center of the raised dais positioned at the front of the room, Jetanien gestured toward the Klingon. "Kanjar, please, join us. We'd be happy to address your concerns. Perhaps they are even shared by others in the audience." Even as he extended the offer, the ambassador knew he was on shaky ground. After spending the better part of the past two hours discussing the recent escalating displays of civil unrest within Paradise City and in several of the outlying camps, he had been pleased to see that many of the citizens who had chosen to attend the proceedings appeared mollified by the discourse as well as some of the proffered remedies. An outburst such as Kanjar's, if the renewed mumblings he heard from the crowd were any indication, carried with it the potential to tip the mood of the meeting back to one of uncertainty and discord.

"They are not merely my concerns," Kanjar snapped, his

voice echoing off the chamber's high, smooth rock walls, "nor are they even just the concerns of the people in this room. No, they apply to every Klingon and every colonist on this worthless planet!" Even if Jetanien had not already known that Kanjar—according to the constabulary—was among those suspected of being involved in a handful of acts of unrest in recent weeks, he could see that the Klingon's tone and stance were those of someone accustomed to influencing others. The ambassador had no doubt that, given sufficient motivation, Kanjar might well be capable of inciting even greater, more aggressive acts of resistance.

Jetanien turned to his right and regarded Lugok, who for the first time seemed at least somewhat interested in contributing more to the proceedings beyond the occasional scowl, grunt, and indifferent glare directed at the audience. "Perhaps you might weigh in on this, Ambassador?"

For his part, the Klingon diplomat shifted his position in his chair before emitting a disapproving groan. While Lugok had privately communicated to Jetanien his opinion that public forums such as this were futile and even stupid gestures with no conciliatory value, he had promised Jetanien not to share that opinion with the citizenry. Holding true to his word, the ambassador said nothing to that particular effect as he rose from his chair.

"*Qagh Sopbe'!*" he snapped, pointing to the Klingon farmer. "You've spent too much time in the sun, Kanjar. Sit down and learn something."

Though he said nothing, Jetanien still could not help the audible sigh that escaped his mouth. *This will not end well.* As the thought taunted him, he glanced to the rear of the meeting hall, where Constable Schiappacasse and two members of her security staff stood along the back wall, maintaining a discreet vigil over the proceedings. Schiappacasse offered him a subtle nod, reassuring him that she would, if necessary, step in and alleviate any problems before they got out of hand.

From where he sat to Jetanien's left, Senator D'tran said in a low voice, "Perhaps calling him a coward isn't the best choice for attempting to calm his temperament."

For his part, Kanjar waved away Lugok's suggestion. Instead, he stepped forward until he stood just in front of the raised dais before turning to regard the audience. "But, I will make certain that everyone in this colony learns something that will change their minds about the promise of Paradise City."

Jetanien stepped to the edge of the dais. "I ask you again, Kanjar," he said, keeping his voice low and level, "take a seat so that we can discuss these issues in an open and honest manner."

Turning to face Jetanien, Kanjar leveled an accusatory finger at the ambassador's broad chest. "Open and honest manner? Will you openly and honestly admit that your police force is at this moment holding as prisoners those who would make their voices heard regarding the truth of this colony?"

"Anyone currently in the custody of the constabulary has been suspected of violating codes of conduct," Jetanien replied. "Your right to protest has not been suppressed, but security has been ordered to step in when such protests become disorderly and a possible danger to other citizens."

Kanjar grunted in obvious dissatisfaction. "And the majority of your arrests have been Klingons!"

Renewed stirring from the crowd reached Jetanien's ears, and when he looked up to scan the faces of the audience he saw expressions of irritation and impatience. Accompanying those, however, were reactions of interest and even concern over what Kanjar was saying. The implications of the Klingon's words were obvious, and any public claims or allegations of inequitable treatment along racial lines, given the charged climate currently permeating the city, might add to an already tense situation.

"I do not have detention records to consult," Jetanien said, "but even if that is the case, I'm sure there must be some rational explanation." Even as he spoke the words, he knew they possessed a hollow ring. He had received enough reports from Constable Schiappacasse to know that many—though certainly not all—of the problems in recent weeks had involved several of the Klingon colonists. The main problem, as he saw it, was not that non-Klingons were more virtuous than Klingons—far from it.

There were plenty of accounts of bar fights, vandalism, and petty squabbles from other settlers to know that the problem was not so simple as blaming any one group. Instead, the evidence seemed to indicate that the Klingon colonists, on general principle if for no other reason, were predisposed to using aggressive means to resolve disputes.

As if you needed a report to tell you that. The thought was a disturbing one, though Jetanien could not dismiss it.

"Hah!"

The new voice of dissent came from the far left side of the room, and when Jetanien looked in that direction he saw a bulky Tellarite sitting among another group of colonists, his expression, like theirs, indicating equal parts of amusement and disdain. The brown jumpsuit he wore looked to be soiled with dirt and perhaps grease, leading Jetanien to wonder if the Tellarite was one of the mechanics tasked with servicing and repairing the multitudes of farming and other equipment upon which the Nimbus III colony relied.

"Of course there's a rational explanation," the Tellarite called out. "It's because the Klingons are the ones who start all the fights!" The comment was enough to elicit laughter from his companions, as well as several other members of the audience.

"All right," Jetanien said, raising both his voice and his arms in an attempt to reassert control of the meeting. "Let's all do our best to keep this dialogue productive for everyone, shall we?"

Ignoring the Chelon's plea, Kanjar turned to point toward his heckler. "Whereas fat, lazy Tellarites do nothing but start arguments they can't finish."

Springing to his feet with more speed and grace than Jetanien would have thought possible given his girth, the Tellarite grunted as he aimed his own pudgy digit at the Klingon. "By Kera and Phinda, I'll finish this one!" Several of his comrades also rose from their seats, each of them glowering at Kanjar as though daring him to attack all of them. In response, Kanjar squared his shoulders and clenched his fists, and Jetanien knew that there were perhaps a handful of seconds at best before the aggrieved

Klingon took matters into his own hands. As other members of the audience began standing up—some moving for a nearby exit while others stood their ground—another, unexpected voice made itself heard.

It was with no small amount of relief that Jetanien watched Constable Schiappacasse move from her place at the rear of the room and make her way through the crowd to where the Tellarite stood with his companions.

"Sir, if you'll come with me for just a moment?" she asked, her voice low and polite, but firm.

Eyeing her with suspicion, the Tellarite said, "What? Me? Why am I being singled out?"

Schiappacasse shook her head. "You're not, sir. I'm just trying to keep the peace here, is all. We're going to step to the back of the room for a minute while the ambassador gets the meeting back on schedule."

"Go, Tellarite!" Kanjar said, laughing. "Hide behind the Earther woman, though I suspect that will be a challenge, given your ponderous bulk." The comment evoked more laughter from the audience, though Jetanien was buoyed at the realization that it came only from a precious few observers.

"Friends!" said D'tran. The aged Romulan had risen to his feet and made his way to stand next to Jetanien, holding up one withered hand. "Let us not allow these proceedings to deteriorate. We are all tired, and we all have legitimate concerns, but no one can truly be heard unless we all agree to listen."

"Perhaps we should adjourn the meeting for this evening," Jetanien said, feeling his own anxiety increasing with each passing moment. Even as he made the suggestion, he wondered if that might be the best course. What would happen when the emotionally charged audience spilled into the city street? Without even the semblance of order offered by the public meeting hall, would this disagreement escalate into yet another fight? Would Schiappacasse and her people be able to contain such a situation?

If Kanjar heard D'tran's request, he seemed not to care. "No one here has anything to say that I wish to hear." He nodded to

Jetanien while addressing Lugok. "The Earthers and their pets like to stand around and talk, but I expected more from a Klingon, even one who resigns himself to futile pursuits such as this. Are you truly willing to look on while Klingons are subverted and oppressed, and do the bidding of Federation lapdogs such as this?" Gesturing to D'tran, he added, "Are we so weak that we must take orders from Romulans so feeble they can barely stand upright, let alone comport themselves in battle?"

"Enough!" Lugok snapped, lunging from his chair and launching himself from the dais before Jetanien or D'tran could say anything. He vaulted the distance separating him from Kanjar in a single leap, landing before the surprised farmer and seizing the other Klingon by the arm. Without preamble, he turned Kanjar toward the door and began advancing toward it. Schiappacasse looked to Jetanien for direction, but the Chelon shook his head.

"You heard Ambassador Jetanien, this meeting is over." Looking back over his shoulder, the Klingon called out in a louder voice, "That means everyone. Go home." Jetanien and everyone else in the room could only watch as Lugok disappeared through the doorway, all the while hoisting Kanjar high enough that his boots barely touched the ground.

"Leave it to Lugok to dispense with protocol," D'tran said as the crowd began to disperse.

Jetanien nodded. "It would seem that we're reaching a tipping point among the colonists. I can appreciate their frustrations, but if we lose the drive to work together, I fear all hope for this colony may be lost."

"We may have asked for too much too soon, my friend," D'tran replied. "A noble effort, yes, but perhaps one we are not yet ready to achieve."

Both diplomats turned at the sound of approaching footsteps as Constable Schiappacasse moved to stand before the dais. Her features were darkened by worry, and Jetanien could see the uncertainty in her eyes.

"Gentlemen," she said, "I think you should consider implementing the first stage of our contingency plan."

"Curfews?" Jetanien asked.

Schiappacasse nodded. "Just for the next night or two. I'd like to increase our security patrols, as well. By no means do I want this to be permanent—just until we can calm things down a bit. Based on some of the things we've been seeing the past few nights, along with what went on in here, it feels like people are looking for an excuse to fight. I'd like not to give them that."

Turning to D'tran, Jetanien asked, "What are your thoughts on this?"

The aged Romulan sighed. "I don't relish the notion of added restrictions and enforcements which might make us appear to be panicked ourselves. If anything, such action might serve only to solidify any resentment against us as the authorities of the colony. Any response we take needs to be measured, restrained, and explained to the public as thoroughly and honestly as possible."

"We also can't afford to seem indecisive," Schiappacasse countered. "There's still a significant number of the population who support the colony and what you're trying to achieve here. They need to know we're taking steps to protect them, as well."

D'tran nodded. "Agreed." To Jetanien, he said, "Very well, my friend."

"Constable," Jetanien said, "alert your security forces. I'll prepare a statement for the colony, and we'll broadcast it as soon as—"

A heavy thump resounded off the walls of the meeting hall, rattling windows as well as the arrangement of chairs occupying the chamber's main floor. The overhead lighting blinked several times before returning to its normal, steady state, and Jetanien flinched, recalling the incident at the spaceport from several evenings ago.

"Oh no," D'tran said, and when Jetanien looked to him he saw that his elderly friend's lined face had gone white with shock.

"That was just outside!" Schiappacasse yelled, already turning and running for the door.

D'tran said, "No, it wasn't, but it was close." From somewhere beyond the building, sirens could now be heard blaring in the streets. Jetanien recognized the alarm as the one designated for citywide emergencies calling for the security force to begin employing crowd control procedures.

"Come," Jetanien said, his voice fearful as he took his friend by the arm. "We need to see what's happened." After he assisted D'tran from the dais, both diplomats crossed the room toward the exit when the heavy door was flung open to reveal Lugok.

"Not this way," the Klingon said, pointing past Jetanien toward the room's opposite end. "Out the back, now!" He did not wait for a response as he pushed Jetanien and D'tran up the chamber's main aisle.

"What happened?" Jetanien asked.

"A bomb," the Klingon replied. "Just up the street. Two storefronts were destroyed just as the crowd left here. There are numerous casualties." When D'tran paused in response to this report, Lugok reasserted his grip on the Romulan's arm. "Keep moving!"

Jetanien was incredulous. "A bomb? Tonight? Of all nights?"

"It would seem that coincidence is unlikely," D'tran said. "The meeting was a public event, after all, and scheduled several days ago. Plenty of time to orchestrate an act of insurrection."

"You're saying this was planned?" Jetanien asked, his beak clicking at an increasing rate in keeping with his elevated anxiety.

Lugok hissed, "Don't be a fool, Jetanien. Someone wanted either to scare or to hurt anyone who might be viewed as being in support of making the colony work. I wouldn't be surprised if that *petaQ* Kanjar intentionally disrupted the meeting in order to force an early end and get people into the streets amid confusion before the explosive was triggered."

As they reached one of the building's rear exits, Jetanien paused, shaking his head. "I can't believe it. It's one thing to start a brawl, or cause a work stoppage, or protest overzealous law enforcement, but this? Causing deliberate injury and perhaps death?"

"Anyone with such grievances possibly feels their complaints haven't been heard," Lugok said, opening the door and casting a furtive look into the street beyond. "You're listening now, though, are you not?"

Running footsteps outside the door made Jetanien step back, and Lugok pushed forward, his fist raised and poised to strike. Then the door opened to reveal Constable Schiappacasse and one of her security officers, both with phasers drawn. Both officers looked worried, their concern only heightened by the constant wail of the alarm sirens permeating the outside air.

"Gentlemen," Schiappacasse said, gesturing for them to follow her. "Come with me, please. We're taking you to the Federation Consulate, as it's the most secure location that we can get to quickly."

The three diplomats followed on Schiappacasse's heels as the constable guided them from the building and into the narrow alley separating it from the neighboring structure. Her companion guarded their rear as they moved, while the sounds of chaos filled the air. Sirens blared their warbling tones, which rang sharply off the storefronts, and people shouted either from the streets or the open windows of nearby buildings. Schiappacasse seemed to move with practiced ease through the side streets, avoiding exposure on the main thoroughfares. Light from what Jetanien took to be fire flickered against nearby walls, and acrid smoke from an unknown source assailed his nostrils. Shadowy figures sprinted along intersecting streets, though no one seemed to be taking any notice of anyone other than themselves.

As Schiappacasse led them around a corner at one intersection, Jetanien was startled to see a ground transport belonging to the colony's security forces bearing down on them. Rather than stopping, the transport screamed past them on its way deeper into the city, and Jetanien offered silent thoughts for the safety of the officers inside the vehicle. After all, there was no way to know the severity of the situation into which they were traveling. Though security teams were the only persons allowed to carry weapons within the colony, that would not deter any would-be insurgents, particularly if they had greater numbers, which seemed likely.

"D'tran," Jetanien said, looking to his friend, who was showing visible strain in the face of the prolonged exertion. "We're almost there." He gestured ahead of them, where the familiar entrance to the Federation Consulate beckoned. Jetanien was relieved to see that a detachment of six security officers stood outside the structure's reinforced main doors. When one of them caught sight of Schiappacasse, he waved for her to bring her charges forward, and within a minute the group was inside the building's relatively safe environs.

"Ambassador!" called Sergio Moreno, who looked as if he'd been waiting for Jetanien to return. "Thank goodness you made it back safely. Are you all right?"

Jetanien shook his head. "I'm not injured, but Senator D'tran needs rest." Indicating his friend with a nod, he added, "Please tend to him."

As Moreno saw to D'tran, Jetanien turned to Schiappacasse. "Constable, I'm in your debt."

"Just part of the job, Ambassador," Schiappacasse replied, holding her communicator in her hand. "If you'll excuse me, I'm trying to get an update on the situation."

"Please keep me informed," Jetanien said, and the security officer nodded as she stepped away, already talking to someone else via her communicator and leaving the Chelon alone. Looking around the lobby, he saw Lugok making his way toward the door.

"Lugok," Jetanien called out, "where are you going?"

Pausing at the door, the Klingon turned and replied, "I must get back to my own consulate. I need to apprise my superiors of this situation, and advise that they send us assistance." He regarded Jetanien with a somber expression. "You should do the same, and so too should D'tran."

"Reinforcements?" Jetanien asked. "Do you think the situation will deteriorate that far?"

"I do not know," Lugok answered, "but my standing orders are to advise the High Council of any change in the status quo here, particularly if something occurs such as what we're now witnessing." Nodding toward the door, he added, "Face it, Jetanien, this may well be just the beginning of something far worse than what we've already seen."

Walking to a nearby window, Jetanien reached up to part the heavy drape so that he might gaze out at the street beyond the consulate grounds. He was able to see fire from at least three locations elsewhere in the city. The sounds of people shouting were only just audible over the cry of alarm klaxons and the sirens of security force ground transports. A few people ran between buildings, and when he looked toward the courtyard at the center of the city he saw a gathering of colonists, though from this distance he could not discern what they might be doing. Were they planning more disruption, or were they among those who might now need the assistance of the constabulary and anyone else not interested in rousing unrest and violence?

"I'm not ready to give up on this, Lugok," Jetanien said after a moment. "Not after everything we've invested in this effort."

Lugok sighed. "I know, my friend, but you must consider the possibility that all of this may well have given up on you."

32

Cup of coffee in hand, Reyes moved from the food slot along the interview room's rear wall and returned to his seat at the small, rectangular table. The table and its quartet of chairs were the room's only furnishings, constructed from the same sort of dull, depressing slate gray duranium composite materials often used in Starfleet facilities where comfort was not a primary concern. Similar furniture adorned the guest quarters to which Reyes had been assigned, so he did not mind the decor. It was a step up from his previous billeting, at any rate.

"Lieutenant Commander Moyer," Reyes said as he took his seat. "Congratulations on your promotion. It's well deserved."

Moyer nodded, though her demeanor remained professional as she used the stylus in her right hand to write something on the face of the data slate she had brought with her. "Thank you, sir. The rank is permanent, but the position is temporary. Starfleet is sending someone out to formally replace Captain Desai. I don't know who it is yet, but they should be here by the end of the month."

"Plenty of time for Starfleet to reconsider leaving you where you are," Reyes said before taking a sip of his coffee. "But I suspect we're not here to talk about you, are we?"

Clearing her throat, Moyer replied, "No, sir, I'm afraid not. I've been ordered to debrief you in full about your time in Klingon and Orion custody. Admiral Nogura has asked me to emphasize that this is not an interrogation. You are not being charged with anything, at least not yet. Any interviews that might go toward determining that will be held at a later time. For now, the purpose of this session and any that might follow is strictly for the gathering of information with respect to its relevance to Operation Vanguard."

Reyes regarded her with a quizzical expression. "I take it you've been read into the project?"

"Yes, sir," Moyer replied, her attention shifting between Reyes and her data slate. "Admiral Nogura briefed me himself." She paused, and Reyes noted the uncertainty she was trying to hide.

"I can imagine it was a lot to absorb and accept, even if you didn't agree with it all," Reyes said. "How'd that make you feel?"

Looking up from her data slate, Moyer said, "With all due respect, Mister Reyes, my feelings on the subject are irrelevant."

"They're relevant if they're affecting your judgment and how you plan to carry out these debriefing sessions," Reyes countered, and punctuated his statement with another sip of his coffee.

The commander's jaw tightened just the slightest bit, but Reyes saw it anyway. "If you're worried you won't be fairly represented," she said, "you can be assured that everything we say here is being recorded, and will be reviewed by Admiral Nogura as well as the Starfleet JAG. My job here is strictly obtaining answers to questions prepared by the admiral as well as Lieutenant T'Prynn, Doctor Marcus, and Lieutenant Xiong."

Reyes nodded in understanding. "All right, then."

"Now, you indicated to Admiral Nogura that you believed, at least during the time you were in their custody and based on your interactions with the Klingon ship commander, Kutal, that the Empire does not seem to possess our level of knowledge concerning the Shedai?"

"From what I could gather, no," Reyes replied. "They obviously know what the Shedai are, and were, and they've had their own run-ins with them as well as their technology. That said, everything I saw and heard points to them not having any real insight into the meta-genome and its potential. Oh, there may be, or have been, a few of their scientists who started putting the pieces together, but from what I know, most if not all of those people are dead now."

Moyer, jotting notes on her data slate, said, "Lieutenant Xiong reported something similar during his time in captivity on Mirdonyae V." She frowned. "Frankly, that surprises me. We know that the Klingons do employ scientists and engineers—if not their own, then others from species they've conquered. They're certainly not stupid."

"No, they're not," Reyes acknowledged, "but the priorities and focus of those in charge tend to lean more toward the military applications of any plundered technology or equipment. Waiting around for a scientist to figure out that a blob of mold pulled from a rock formation on some uninhabited planet actually contains the building blocks for an entire civilization, weapons included, isn't something they're liable to do. They want something that can be employed now, if not sooner."

"So, you're saying it's willful ignorance on the Klingons' part that they haven't pursued learning more about the meta-genome?"

Finishing his coffee, Reyes rose from his chair and made his way toward the food slot. "Not at all, Commander. They're simply looking for the upper hand. Given enough time and the diversion of sufficient resources to the effort, they're more than capable of figuring out on their own what the meta-genome represents, and what they can do with it if they can ever learn how to work with it. I don't see that happening any time soon, though. After all, we've been screwing with it for more than five years since we first discovered the damned thing, and look where we are."

"Where are we, exactly?" Moyer asked.

Reyes slid a card into the reader beneath the food slot's door and pressed a couple of the buttons in the proper sequence. "Assuming Admiral Nogura hasn't been lying to me, and based on the progress that had been made before I was—as they say—removed from my former position, I know that Xiong and his crew in the Vault have had limited success interfacing with Shedai technology, thanks mostly to the assistance of a Tholian expatriate named Nezrene. The artifact Xiong brought back with him from Mirdonyae V and the one Ganz handed over apparently represent the technology of another race, the Tkon, which might be able to stand toe-to-toe with the Shedai." Retrieving the fresh cup of coffee from the food slot, he turned and offered Moyer a smile. "How am I doing so far?"

"Not bad, actually," the commander replied. "Speaking of the Mirdonyae Artifacts, how much about the Shedai do you think Ganz and his people knew, so far as their properties or origin are concerned?"

Shaking his head as he returned to his seat, Reyes said, "Not much, I think. They saw the things as being of some intrinsic value to anyone willing to pay a good price. I'm certain they don't know anything about the Tkon, at least not beyond tall tales or space legends or whatever you want to call stories you tell at the bar." Thanks to Nogura—who likely had violated a handful of regulations and security protocols in order to update him on what had been happening while he was away—Reyes knew about the mission undertaken by Cervantes Quinn and Bridget McLellan to retrieve the artifact stolen from the station by one of Ganz's men on behalf of a Klingon client. He knew also of their journey to the unnamed planet that had emitted traces of the mysterious carrier wave signal Ming Xiong had dubbed the Jinoteur Pattern, and where Quinn and McLellan had come face-to-face with the Shedai entity that had made the entire Jinoteur system simply disappear as though it had never existed. Reyes had given up trying to imagine a race like the Tkon possessing technology that might be on a par with such an astounding display of power. The very idea made his head hurt.

"And what about the Klingons?" Moyer asked. "How much do you suppose they know about the artifacts?"

"I honestly don't know," Reyes answered. "They seemed to know that they could interface with Shedai technology, at least to some degree. I'm guessing that had to do with what they learned while Xiong was being held by Klingons on Mirdonyae V, and that's what motivated the covert mission to steal the artifact from the station."

Moyer nodded, saying nothing for a moment while she jotted more notes on her data slate. "The artifact you helped them to steal?"

Sipping his coffee, Reyes noted the look of accusation in the JAG officer's eyes, and smiled in approval. "Nicely played, Commander. I've already admitted to providing information that allowed the thief to bypass the station's security measures and get into the Vault. I told all of this to T'Prynn, but I don't mind repeating it: They were going after that thing, with or without my help. All I did was try and see to it that they didn't kill anybody along the way."

"You briefed them on our security codes, protocols, and procedures," Moyer said.

Reyes tapped a finger on the table. "And you changed all of that ten seconds after the heist was over, right?"

"You did everything but hold the front door open for them."

"It could just be my imagination," Reyes said, reaching for his coffee, "but this is starting to sound a little like an interrogation."

Shaking her head, Moyer replied, "That's not my intention, sir, but if you helped them to get onto the station and into the Vault, then we need to ascertain what other information you may have given them with respect to the Shedai."

"None," Reyes said. "First, because doing so would've increased the risk of harm to Starfleet and civilian personnel. Second, they never bothered to ask."

That gave Moyer pause, and her expression was one of skepticism. "Really?"

"Really. Now, what else do you have?" In truth, Reyes did not mind the line of questioning. It was expected, and Moyer would not be doing her job if she avoided putting forth the pointed queries. He trusted in her ability and willingness to weigh what she was hearing against established facts and find her own way to the objective truth. Rana Desai had always spoken in the highest complimentary terms about the bright young officer and the potential she exuded. If Rana trusted Moyer's judgment and commitment to carrying out her duties without being waylaid by personal views, that was more than sufficient for Reyes.

A faint metallic tone chirped from Moyer's data slate, one Reyes recognized as coming from the device's internal chronometer. She looked down at the unit, tapping her stylus across the slate's smooth surface.

"I'm sorry, Mister Reyes, but that's all the time I have for this at the moment. Would you mind if I scheduled a follow-up session for tomorrow at this same time?"

Reyes shrugged. "I'll check my calendar, but I think I'm free." As he watched Moyer collect her data slate and return it to the briefcase she lifted from the floor to lay atop the table, he added, "I appreciate you being so polite about all of this, Commander. I mean, it's not as though I can refuse requests like this, right?"

"I don't see a reason to create an air of animosity where none's required," Moyer said, closing her briefcase. "I tend to reserve the harsher tactics for those I deem deserving of them."

Comprehending the implicit meaning behind her words, Reyes offered a small smile of gratitude. "Thank you, Commander."

Nodding, Moyer said, "We'll likely be having a few of these sessions before I'm finished, during which we'll be delving into the more unpleasant aspects of your time with the Klingons and the Orions. There are many people in Starfleet who want to charge you with treason, or collusion at the very least."

"And what do you think about any of that?" Reyes asked.

Moyer's eyes shifted to the table for a moment before she returned her gaze to his. "I think I'd like to be your lawyer, should it become necessary for you to retain counsel."

"I appreciate the offer, but let's see what happens, first," Reyes said. "Nogura's main problem will be making sure that even with all that's happened, the secrecy surrounding the meta-genome can still be protected. For what it's worth, I think that can be done, but there are a few loose ends that need tying off."

"Including you?" Moyer asked.

Reyes sighed in agreement. Of all the threads dangling from the worn yet still intact quilt of security enveloping Operation Vanguard, he was perhaps the one requiring the most immediate—if not judicious—attention. With all that remained at stake, Nogura's choices so far as to what to do with the disgraced former commodore might come down to simple expediency, with the aim of defending the most valuable aspects of the project's clandestine status. Were his and the admiral's roles reversed, Reyes would view the matter in the same way.

"Yes," he said. "Even me."

33

On the bridge of the *Defiant,* Thomas Blair shifted in his seat in a futile effort to find a more comfortable position. No matter what he did, the ache in the small of his back continued unabated. Indeed, it had begun to radiate outward, across his hips and down into his thighs. His shoulders felt like little more than piles of knots, and hammers seemed to be pounding beneath his temples, driving spikes directly into his brain. For perhaps the sixth or seventh time in an hour—he had lost count—Blair swiveled the command chair to face the engineering station at the back of the bridge. As he had done during each previous iteration of this exercise, he asked the same question.

"So, how are we doing?"

Sitting at the console, Kamau Mbugua, who often filled in at the station while the *Defiant*'s chief engineer, Lieutenant Commander Stevok, toiled belowdecks, replied, "Holding steady at warp 8.1."

Blair nodded at the report, offering a small, sardonic smile. "I suppose there's no point asking if Stevok might coax just a little more juice out of the old girl?"

"I think we both know what he'd say to that, Skipper," Mbugua said.

Unlike many chief engineers with whom he had served over the course of his career, Stevok was never one to offer anything but exact answers for any queries posed to him. He did not inflate repair estimates and then complete his tasks in a time frame well within such forecasts in order to bolster his reputation as someone capable of extraordinary feats. Likewise, he did not underplay or exaggerate the abilities of the vessel in his care. When asked how well the *Defiant* might perform at a sustained rate of high warp speed, Stevok without embellishment or undue worry had answered that the ship's engines would be able to withstand such a demand for no less than 9.6 hours.

According to the chief engineer, those same engines also would be unable to handle the strain for anything more than 9.9 hours.

Rising from his chair and reaching behind him to rub the small of his back, Blair moved the railing separating him from the science station. "Any change in our pursuers?"

Clarissa Nyn turned in her seat. "No, sir. The Tholian ships are still gaining on us, if only slowly. According to our long-range sensors, they're giving chase at warp 8.3." She did not need to say anything else. Blair could do the math as well as she could, and he knew that even if the *Defiant* continued its evasive course, the trio of Tholian vessels would overtake his ship long before it could reach help, and perhaps even before any other starships might close the distance themselves and be in a position to render aid. Blair had already ordered a comprehensive report detailing their findings on Traelus II and their current situation to Starbase 47 along with a call for assistance, but the truth of the matter was that the *Defiant* was a long way from any sort of help. All of this had made him settle on a series of course corrections designed to change direction at irregular intervals when the ship came within proximity of other star systems and other interstellar phenomena. Much of the area they had been traversing during the past day had not previously been visited, at least not by any Starfleet vessels and—so far as the library computer's record tapes were able to confirm—not by any known civilian ships, either. The *Defiant*'s current heading was still largely linear, adjusted as needed to remain parallel to the border separating the Taurus Reach from Tholian space.

Tholian space, Blair mused. *That's funny.* One of the first things learned about the Tholian Assembly after the Federation's first contact with the reclusive, xenophobic race was their habit of taking over systems beyond their defined territorial boundaries. It was not unusual for a Tholian vessel to travel into an unclaimed region, after which the ship's commander would declare it an annex of the Assembly. Given their penchant for such actions, Blair had at first wondered why the Tholians seemed reluctant to conduct similar expansionist activities in the Taurus Reach. Upon learning of the race's apparent connection to the Shedai, Blair decided he could not fault the Tholians for wanting to give this region a wide berth.

Sounds like a pretty damned good idea, right about now.

Releasing a tired sigh, Blair turned away from the railing and made his way back to his chair. He glanced at the chronometer mounted just above the astrogator between the helm and navigator positions, and realized he had been on the bridge for nearly ten hours without any sort of respite save the cups of coffee brought to him by his yeoman at irregular intervals. In fact, it had been the last cup of coffee, brought to him by the young woman who served as his yeoman during gamma shift, that made Blair realize just how long he had remained here. Though most of his alpha shift crew had taken breaks at one point or another, each of them had, through unspoken agreement, elected to remain at their posts rather than surrender their stations to officers from the oncoming duty shift. He knew he could order his crew to their quarters for much needed and deserved rest, but what would be the point? Who could sleep now, with enemy ships chasing after them?

You need rest, Blair reminded himself. *Your people need rest. They need to be sharp if and when the Tholians catch up.* He was considering calling his yeoman for another cup of coffee, a thought that in turn elicited his latest lamentation about the notable lack of food slots on the bridge, when Ensign Sabapathy called out from the communications station.

"Captain, I'm picking up a distress call."

His eyes narrowing in suspicion and confusion, Blair turned back to his communications officer just as Mbugua crossed over from his station. "Distress call? Out here?" Blair noted that the commander's expression was one of skepticism, which Blair was sure mirrored his own.

Sabapathy nodded. "Yes, sir. It looks to be a civilian long-haul freighter, but their transponder codes don't match anything in the data banks."

That bit of information only served to heighten Blair's doubts. Looking to Nyn, he asked, "Is it showing up on sensors?"

Bent over the hooded viewer at her station, the scanner's view-finder bathing her face in its warm, blue glow, the science officer replied, "No, sir, though I'm able to track the distress signal to its point of origin." Looking up from her viewer, she tapped a series of commands across one of her console's banks of colored buttons, and one of the large monitors above her workstation shifted from an image of a planet to a star chart. Nyn tapped another control and a red blinking circle appeared, superimposed over a cluster of smaller white dots. "It's coming from this sector, near the Vintaak system."

"Never heard of it," Blair said.

"That's not surprising." Nyn pressed another control and the star chart began to rotate, offering a three-dimensional readout of the highlighted region. "It's not within Tholian boundaries. At least, not today. Like a lot of systems in this area, it's been charted by long-range reconnaissance probes, but we've never sent any ships there. Not yet, anyway."

"But you can't detect the ship itself?" Mbugua asked, frowning as he folded his arms across his broad chest.

Nyn shook her head. "No, sir. It could just be that it's too small for our sensors to pick up at this range." She shrugged, tapping another control, which had the effect of magnifying the portion of the star chart within the highlighted circle. "On the other hand, the sensor readings we're getting are coming back . . . the best way I can describe it is that they're scattering, as though running into some kind of energy field or other disruption."

Studying the star chart, Blair asked, "Is it a natural phenomenon, or something artificial?"

"It's hard to be conclusive, sir," the science officer said, "but from the readings I'm able to get, I'm leaning toward it being naturally occurring."

"What are you thinking, Skipper?" Mbugua asked, and Blair heard the tone of caution in his first officer's voice.

Blair gestured toward the screen. "I'm thinking a naturally occurring sensor blind is a good place to hide."

"It's also a nice place for an ambush," Mbugua countered.

Conceding the point, Blair sighed. "That, too, but we have to at least get close enough to determine whether the distress call is real." His gut told him the signal was a ruse, but if it turned out to be legitimate and he did nothing, he could be held responsible for whatever fate befell whichever troubled vessel and crew were out there. That did not matter so much to him as how his own conscience would torture him with the knowledge that he might have been able to do something had he chosen to act. Even without rules and regulations pertaining to the handling of ships in distress, there was no other option so far as he was concerned.

"The Tholians will know we're headed there, sir," Nyn said, the inflection behind her own words matching Mbugua's. Had she somehow sensed the debate he was having with himself?

Nodding, Blair replied, "Yeah, but that place is a dead spot for sensors, so that'll even the odds a bit. We might be able to stall long enough for help to find us before the Tholians do." Turning from the science station, he moved down the railing and said to Sabapathy, "Ensign, prepare an updated status report for transmission to Vanguard. Full encryption package—the works. Apprise them of our course change and immediate plan, and if they want to hurry the hell up with the cavalry, that'd be nice, too."

"Aye, sir," the ensign replied, then asked, "Should I attempt to hail the ship sending the distress call?"

Blair shook his head. "Not yet. Let's see what this is about, first." He reached up to rub the bridge of his nose. The area behind his eyeballs was beginning to protest his lack of rest. On the bright side, this new discomfort almost made him forget about the stiffness in his back and shoulders.

Well, not really.

"Make the course change, Kamau," he said to Mbugua. "And ask engineering to push the throttle through the wall if they have to, but get me some more speed."

Releasing a slight, humorless chuckle, the first officer replied, "You know what Stevok's going to say."

"Then tell him he can get out and push," Blair countered. "In the meantime, let's keep our ears open for anything new from that ship. Maintain sensor sweeps of that area, anyway. Maybe the readings will clear up, the closer we get. Besides, just because we don't see them doesn't mean they can't see us coming." Glancing to Mbugua, he offered a knowing look. "After all, it looks like a good place for an ambush, right?"

Returning to his command chair, Blair lowered himself into his seat, grunting at the pain in his tired back, wondering if he had not just directed his ship into the middle of a trap.

I guess we'll see what we'll see.

34

Something slammed into the wall behind Jetanien's head, startling the ambassador from sleep and causing him to sit up straight on the stone slab that served as the bed in his private quarters. Rising to his feet, he moved to the window at the rear of his room and pushed aside one of the drapes just enough to peer outside. He was in time for something small and fast to strike the window directly in front of his face.

The projectile—whatever it was—hit just as Jetanien stumbled back and bumped into his slab, impacting against the window's reinforced, shatterproof glass before falling to the street three stories below his room. His heart racing from the near miss—despite logic telling him he was never in any real danger—the Chelon reached for the large dressing gown lying atop a table next to his bed and donned it. No sooner had he secured it around his body than there was a knock on his door, followed by the worried voice of Sergio Moreno.

"Ambassador? Are you all right?"

Walking to the desk that occupied one corner of his private quarters, Jetanien reached for the control pad embedded into its surface and disengaged the door lock. As the door slid aside to admit Moreno, the ambassador said, "I'm fine, Sergio." He moved back to the window and pulled open the drapes, no longer content to hide behind the symbolic cover they offered. "They're back, I see."

"Yes, they are," his assistant replied, his voice betraying a hint of the anxiety he no doubt was feeling. "And they seem more agitated this time."

Gazing out the window, Jetanien peered into the predawn near-darkness, which was broken only by the sporadic illumination offered by those few street lamps that were still working. The streets were littered with the evidence of the previous night's riots. Chunks of artificial stone, singed and splintered wooden beams, and other debris lay scattered everywhere. Smoke emanated from open or broken windows, and the roofs and walls of at least three buildings Jetanien could see from his vantage point showed fire damage. He could only assume that the other streets and structures were in similar condition, all having fallen prey to the unruly mobs that seemed to be roaming the city at will.

"How many are there?" he asked, indicating the small assemblage on the street below them.

"Perhaps a dozen or so," Moreno said. "I recognize a few of them, Ambassador. I think they're all Federation colonists."

Several members of the group seemed content to lurk in the weakening shadows as sunrise approached. Most of them looked to be human, though Jetanien also discerned a pair of Tellarites and a Gallamite as well. To a person, they appeared dirty and disheveled; some of them even looked to be nursing injuries of one sort or another, and a few seemed barely able to stay on their feet. One of the humans, a woman, stepped out from a doorway leading into a building across the street, wielding something Jetanien did not at first recognize. Then she pulled the object to her shoulder, and the Chelon realized she was aiming some kind of weapon. Before he could react, the woman's body lurched as the rifle discharged and was followed by another impact against one of the room's other windows.

"What is that?" Moreno cried, his voice rising an octave, and when Jetanien looked at him, the assistant's fear was evident in his features.

The ambassador said, "Some kind of crude projectile weapon." He watched the woman run back across the street, her movements affording him a brief unobstructed view of her weapon. It was not like any rifle he had ever seen, looking as though it had been fashioned from a length of metal pipe and featuring what appeared to be a sort of canister or other container strapped to the end opposite its barrel. A length of tubing connected the canister to the pipe, and Jetanien wondered if the weapon might not be gas-operated after some fashion. Were the security forces aware of this development? Though they were armed with phasers, Jetanien was certain the crude projectiles being fired at his window could still inflict significant damage on unprotected flesh.

Returning his attention to the computer display screen, he saw that one man, the apparent leader, stood before the group in front of the now-barricaded steps and gates leading from the street to the consulate's front veranda. With his left arm held close to his chest in a makeshift sling, the man brandished a section of pipe in his free hand and seemed to be shouting toward the consulate. There was no way to hear him through the window thanks to the building's soundproofing, so Jetanien moved to his desk and activated his computer interface terminal. With a few touches of the unit's keypad, the Chelon activated the feed from the array of audiovisual pickups positioned around the building. The viewer finally settled on an image of the group standing near the consulate's main gate, and ambient sounds from outside began to filter through the computer's intercom, followed by the voice of the man at the head of the group.

"Open the gates and let us in!"

Jetanien listened to the reply from one of the consulate's security officers, imploring the man and his comrades to disperse, and he felt a pang of guilt. Should they not open the doors and give these people at least something resembling safety? Though he had been given the answer by his security chief, it was a response that had done nothing to assuage the remorse that gnawed at him. Constable Schiappacasse had informed him that the shelter the consulate afforded was not what these people sought. Instead, it was the transport shuttle sitting on the building's roof, and the promise of escape the vessel offered. After the events of the past two days, there were precious few such ships remaining, and not nearly enough room for the number of people wanting to leave. While a significant percentage of the colony population appeared content to stay on Nimbus III, most of those people had fled the city, waiting for help to arrive and for the situation to be brought under control. That still left a sizable number of disgruntled citizens looking for any means of fleeing the planet.

Overcome with his own regret, Jetanien reached for the control to activate the intercom system and open a channel to the conduit nearest the group's location. "Sir, please lead your people back to your homes. Assistance is on the way and will be here soon, I promise you."

"To hell with that," the man shouted, his voice sounding distant and hollow as transmitted through the speaker. *"We're not staying out here. Let us in, or we'll find our own way in!"*

Jetanien looked at Moreno. "I trust the building's entrances remain secure?"

"For the moment," his assistant replied. "The front gate's taken a pretty good beating but seems to be holding. The other doors were easier to fortify, but as Constable Schiappacasse has told us, this building wasn't equipped to withstand a siege, sir."

"Let's hope we can avoid that, shall we?" Jetanien said before returning his attention to the viewer and reopening the intercom circuit. "Sir, we are not equipped to assist you. Please take your injured comrades to the medical clinic, and return to your homes to wait for the arrival of Federation assistance."

"We're not leaving!" the man on the screen shouted, holding up for emphasis the length of pipe he carried. *"We want your shuttle!"*

Sighing, Jetanien shook his head. "It seems Schiappacasse was correct." During the previous day, rioters had succeeded in overrunning the spaceport and commandeering several civilian transport vessels and freighters as well as a handful of shuttles belonging to the Federation, Klingon, and Romulan consulates. At last count, more than three hundred colonists had left the planet, and the spaceport facility had been ransacked, according to reports provided by Schiappacasse. The security force was overextended, trying to maintain some semblance of control over other official facilities such as the constabulary, medical clinic, and the consulates themselves. Thanks to Schiappacasse's foresight, before the events of the prior day, each of the diplomatic cadres had secured one of their personnel shuttles atop their respective buildings, in the event the situation became so untenable that a hasty escape was required. The problem with this tactic was that each of the vessels was plainly visible from the street, and bound to attract the attention of anyone seeking any means of leaving the planet. Jetanien knew that even the small crowd now clamoring for entry into the consulate would be underserved and outraged. The small Class-F shuttlecraft was barely large enough to accommodate Jetanien and his staff, and even then not for a journey of any great length.

Sensing his words were being wasted, Jetanien nevertheless leaned once more toward the intercom. "Sir, we can discuss evacuation and relocation options as soon as Federation transports are—"

"You've been warned!" the man shouted, cutting him off. *"Whatever happens now is on* your *hands!"* Turning away from the video pickup, he and several of his companions moved to the far side of the street, huddling in a small circle.

"Sergio," Jetanien said, gesturing toward the image on the viewer, "what do you make of this?"

Moreno leaned closer, studying the video feed. "I'm not sure, but it can't be good. Given the surprises we've already seen, I think we should alert the constable."

"Agreed," Jetanien said. "See to that, please." As the assistant left the room to carry out his instructions, he was forced to step aside as the hunched, feeble form of Senator D'tran appeared in the doorway. The Romulan maneuvered to allow Moreno egress from the room before stepping inside.

"So," he said, "I see you're aware of the situation outside?"

Jetanien nodded. "Yes. It doesn't look good, my friend." Rising to his feet, he crossed the room and reached to open the standard-issue Starfleet equipment locker which—for the time being, at least—served as an armoire for his wardrobe.

"Have you heard from my consulate?" D'tran asked as he shuffled to the lone chair positioned before Jetanien's desk and lowered himself into it.

The Chelon replied, "No, not since S'anra's last report." D'tran's assistant had made contact with Sergio Moreno earlier the previous evening, ensuring him that the situation at the Romulan Consulate was similar, with the staff watching from the relative safety of the building as the rioting had unfolded in the streets around them. Further attempts at communication had gone unanswered, and Jetanien had begun to fear the worst.

"It's likely that their security was breached," D'tran said, as though reading his friend's thoughts. "The Klingon insurgents would have made my consulate a target. After all, they consider us even greater enemies than they do the Federation." He sighed, reaching up to rub the bridge of his thin, angular nose. "Young S'anra is lost. All of them are, and I am to blame."

"Please don't say that," Jetanien said as he selected a simple garment that would be comfortable while providing ease of movement. "There were many contributing factors to what we now face, and none of them are your doing."

Leaning back in his chair, D'tran said, "I'm afraid that's not completely accurate, my friend. My staff and I were under orders from my praetor to gather intelligence data not only on you but also Lugok and his staff by any means available. Though I did not agree with this action, there were those on my staff who acted of their own accord, working to breach your security systems as well as the Klingon Consulate in the hope of gleaning some sort of useful information."

Jetanien turned from his wardrobe to regard his friend, who seemed to have aged years just in the past few days, no doubt owing to lack of rest and the stresses of the current situation. "They were successful?"

"In part," D'tran replied. "S'anra came to me when she discovered the effort, and together we have been acting to keep their transgressions in check. While pretending to support their activities and receive regular status reports from them, S'anra saw to it that none of the data they collected—either from your or Lugok's staff—was transmitted to Romulus."

"Was Lugok aware of this?" Jetanien asked.

Nodding, D'tran replied, "I told him myself. We agreed to keep the incident between us, so as not to cause you concern or prompt you to lose faith in our efforts." He then offered a small, wistful smile. "Lugok and I were using this as an opportunity to strengthen the bonds of trust between us." He shook his head, and a tired chuckle escaped his lips. "Imagine, a Romulan and a Klingon working together to spare a Federation diplomat's feelings. What would our forebears have thought about that?"

"If they had imagined it themselves," Jetanien replied, "then countless lives might have been saved, and we would not need to be here today." Stepping closer to the aged Romulan, he placed one of his large manus on the senator's shoulders. "Of course that did not happen, and one of the few fortunate effects of that short-sightedness is that you and I were able to become friends."

"Thank you, Jetanien." D'tran reached out to place one weathered hand atop the Chelon's. "For longer than you have been alive, I have wanted nothing but to find some way for our peoples to live together; not necessarily in peace, but at least not at war. I have seen much that has given me cause for despair, tempered only by a few incidents that have brought hope. None of those measure up to the vision you hold for us, my friend."

Pulling back his manus, Jetanien drew himself up, feeling a sense of pride in the face of D'tran's words. "Not just my vision. If not for you and even Lugok, none of this would have been possible." He paused, sighing. "Though this can hardly be called our shining moment, I firmly believe it does not have to be our *defining* moment. We will get through this, and we will do so together." Would the Federation see things his way? Would any support his government might choose to show so far as this "great experiment" was concerned be reciprocated by its Klingon and Romulan counterparts? There would be no way to know that—at least, not until well after the crisis currently affecting Nimbus III was resolved.

A harsh buzz erupted from Jetanien's desktop computer terminal as its screen began to blink bright crimson. He and D'tran exchanged confused looks before a new voice burst from the intercom.

"*Attention, all personnel!*" shouted the voice of Constable Schiappacasse. "*The consulate is under direct attack. Move away from all doors and windows. Move away—*"

Everything in the room rattled around the two diplomats, and Jetanien even felt the floor shaking beneath his feet as something seemed to punch the entire building. The impact was followed by a new set of alarms ringing in the hallway outside the room. Even over the new commotion Jetanien was able to hear the shouts of nearby consulate staffers and security officers, the overall tone of which was one of confusion and fear.

"What was that?" he asked, moving toward the window.

"Jetanien!" D'tran snapped, and the Chelon stopped in mid-stride, realizing what he was doing. "That was an explosion. Get back!"

Aghast, Jetanien felt his pulse racing as he absorbed the significance of his friend's words. Rioters had for several days already been using explosive compounds and devices improvised from various materials. Their employment to this point had been isolated incidents, targeting buildings or vehicles that at the time of attack were not occupied. The makeshift contraptions had been utilized as statements of protest, not weapons, at least until now. This was different, and like the projectile rifles possessed by at least some of the remaining insurgents, the explosives signified a definite shift in motivation with respect to how far the protesters were willing to go.

"We have to stop this," he said, reaching to his desk in an effort to support himself as he felt his legs shake. "People will be hurt or killed, D'tran. We can't allow that to happen. Not now."

D'tran's expression was one of resignation. "We may not have a choice, my friend."

Footsteps sounded in the hallway beyond his quarters and then his door slid open. Jetanien flinched as a figure brandishing a weapon ran into the room. To the Chelon's great relief, it was Constable Schiappacasse, phaser held up and ready to fire. When she saw Jetanien she lowered her weapon, though her eyes remained wide with excitement.

"Ambassador," she said, then upon seeing D'tran, added, "Senator. Time to go, gentlemen." From somewhere behind her, shouts and the occasional burst of phaser fire echoed in the passageway.

"Where are we going?" Jetanien asked even as the constable gestured for him to join her at the door.

Schiappacasse pointed upward. "Roof. We're bugging out and moving to a secure location to wait for reinforcements to arrive."

There was more movement in the passageway, and Jetanien looked past Schiappacasse to see Sergio Moreno step into view. "They're through the outside gate, sir. They'll be inside any minute!"

"That's our cue, people," Schiappacasse snapped, her attention divided between the room and the hallway. "We're outnumbered at least three to one if they get in here."

With the constable leading the way, Jetanien, D'tran, and Moreno followed her from the room and down the corridor the Chelon knew would lead them to the building's center staircase and access to the roof. They had progressed less than ten meters from Jetanien's quarters when a flash from ahead of them illuminated the passageway just as another, louder explosion rocked the building. Dust cascaded from the ceiling, and Jetanien was certain he heard what had to be the sounds of debris falling somewhere ahead of them

"They're inside," Schiappacasse hissed, increasing the pace of her advance as she closed the distance toward the foyer leading to the staircase. "Come on! Move!"

The quartet reached the stairway landing, itself a balcony overlooking the open space that was the center of the entire building. Jetanien peered over the railing to see smoke and dust billowing up from below. Where the set of massive double doors forming the front entrance should have been was now a ragged, gaping hole. Figures obscured by the smoke were darting about, and Jetanien heard the thump of running footsteps on the stairs.

"All units, report in!" Schiappacasse called into her communicator as she moved to take up a defensive position near the stairs. Jetanien, hearing the muffled sounds of a voice replying to the constable through the communicator's speaker, began moving toward her, but he was stopped when she gestured upward with the muzzle of her phaser. "Get to the roof!"

Reaching back to take D'tran by the arm, Jetanien led the way to the stairs even as the footsteps from below continued to grow louder. The Chelon was startled by the howl of phaser energy in the narrow passageway, which was followed by the sound of something falling back down the stairs. Then a resounding snap echoed in the corridor and Jetanien heard Schiappacasse cry out in pain. He turned in time to see the security officer thrown backward and off her feet, her phaser sailing from her hand to disappear over the railing as she crashed to the floor. Jetanien stepped toward her, realizing as he drew closer that her face now was a mask of blood and shattered bone.

"No!" he shouted. Then, realizing his cry likely would draw attention, he turned and lumbered toward the stairs, where Moreno was assisting D'tran. Heavy footfalls clamored up the stairwell behind them just as the trio reached the security door leading to the rooftop. Moreno keyed a code into the pad set into the bulkhead and the hatch slid aside. He hustled D'tran through with a small yet firm shove from Jetanien. The Chelon stepped through the doorway and hit the keypad on the other side, and the last thing he saw as the door closed was the lifeless body of Carla Schiappacasse. The chaos of the moment would prevent him from offering her a proper acknowledgment of her sacrifice, and he vowed to rectify that at the earliest opportunity. For now, however, the only thing he had to give seemed woefully inadequate.

Thank you, Constable.

Turning from the door, Jetanien realized for the first time that they were not alone on the roof. Several members of his staff—two female humans, a male Rigellian, and two female representatives of his own race—stood near the shuttlecraft. Two others, both male humans, were absent.

"Where are Thies and Adinolfi?" Jetanien asked.

One of the human females, a short woman of medium build with close-cut brown hair named Tara Varney, was visibly upset as she shook her head. "We don't know. They were on the ground floor when the bomb went off." She said nothing else, leaving Jetanien to contemplate the dreadful possibility behind her words. Turning to look beyond the parapet surrounding the building's roof, he gazed upon Paradise City, evidence of the night's violence staining the brightening sky with a dozen columns of dark smoke. One such plume rose from the vicinity of the Romulan Consulate. Random shouts echoed above the ambient noise from the streets below, punctuating the single thought that now taunted Jetanien.

The Planet of Galactic Peace was a failure.

Beside him, visibly stressed from his exertions, D'tran said, "We can do nothing for them, my friend. Your responsibility now is to these people."

"You're right," Jetanien said, his voice low and tight. To the group, he added, "Get aboard the shuttle." Then something thumped against the other side of the door leading to the roof, and Jetanien realized the hatch would not withstand a prolonged assault. Whatever resistance it might provide would without doubt be nullified if the rioters had brought with them another explosive.

Standing near the shuttle's hatch, Moreno flipped open a communicator. "Code One alert to anyone receiving this message! We're being attacked at the Federation Consulate! Help us!"

"Get aboard the shuttle!" Jetanien repeated, all but shouting the command. "There's no one in range to hear you, anyway." How long until the first Starfleet support vessel was due to arrive? Hours, at last report. Even if they arrived ahead of schedule, it likely would be too late unless he and his charges acted to save themselves.

The shriek of rending metal pierced the air and Jetanien turned to see the control panel near the door explode in a shower of sparks just as the hatch slid aside, revealing at least a half dozen men and women, all of them dressed in utilitarian garb and brandishing some sort of weapon. The first one through the doorway was the man Jetanien had seen on the video feed, his left arm still in its sling and his right hand wielding that same length of metal pipe. He swung the improvised club at Jetanien the instant his eyes locked on the Chelon, but Jetanien was faster, shambling out of his attacker's reach. The man, his eyes wide with unchecked rage, lunged forward, swinging the pipe a second time even as the rest of his group followed him onto the roof. Jetanien stumbled as he tried to keep one hand on D'tran's arm, but the elderly Romulan staggered, unable to match his friend's pace. He twisted in an effort to keep his balance, but the motion cost him momentum, giving the man with the pipe an opening.

"*No!*"

The metal club struck D'tran's head with sufficient force to crack the Romulan's skull. His eyes rolled over white as green blood spilled out across his silver hair. Already dead, the senator crumpled to the rooftop as Jetanien rushed his killer, slamming into him and throwing him to the ground. The man landed on his wounded arm and cried out in pain, but Jetanien ignored him as he reached forward to wrench the pipe from the rioter's hand.

"I should kill you myself!" he barked, reaching for the man with his free hand. He stopped when he heard Moreno calling for help, and turned to see his assistant fighting with another of the rioters near the front of the shuttlecraft. As he moved to help, the other man, a large human male dressed in soiled coveralls, threw Moreno to the ground before turning and moving for the shuttlecraft's open hatch. Pulling himself to his feet, Moreno moved to follow the other man.

"Wait!" Jetanien shouted, and his assistant halted, looking to him for guidance. "Let them go! Just let them have it!" Turning back to the man who had just killed D'tran, he pointed the pipe at his face. "Go," he said, his attention drawn once more to D'tran's limp, lifeless body. A pool of bright green blood was spreading beneath the Romulan's head. "Go, before I change my mind."

He did not watch the man regain his feet and run for the shuttlecraft even as he heard the vessel's engines whine to life. His gaze instead remained fixed on D'tran. For more than a century, and often working in secret, the elder diplomat had broken ranks with his fellow senators and even his practor, devoting a significant portion of his adult life to pursuing peace between the Romulan Empire and its interstellar neighbors. A life's work, crushed with the same intensity as with the weapon that had ended his life.

Not if I can help it.

Dropping the pipe at his feet, Jetanien turned to look for Moreno even as he saw the shuttlecraft's hatch closing. His assistant was backing away from the ship as its engines increased their power output. Where would they go? The shuttle had no long-range capabilities, and the moment it was detected by an incoming starship, everyone aboard would be taken into custody.

Or maybe they'll just fly it into a mountain.

The thought echoed in his mind at the same instant Jetanien felt a tingle playing across his body. A whine filled his ears and a bright, white light washed out his vision, and for the briefest of moments there was the familiar sensation of limbo before the sound faded. When the light dissolved, he saw that he now stood along with Moreno on the transporter pad of a Klingon vessel.

"Welcome aboard, Ambassador," said Lugok from where he stood in front of a bulky console. "We received your distress signal, but the nearest Starfleet ship is still more than an hour away, so we intervened."

"Thank you," was all Jetanien could muster as he maneuvered himself to sit on the step leading down from the pad. Moreno, his face a mask of worry, moved toward him.

"Are you hurt, sir?"

Jetanien shook his head. "No."

Stepping closer, Lugok asked, "What of D'tran?"

"Dead," the Chelon answered, replaying the fresh memory of his friend's last awful moment. "He was killed just before you arrived."

"Then it is a tragic day," Lugok said, his voice softening. "Despite the many differences our peoples hold, I came to respect him."

"As did I." Shifting his bulk to a more comfortable position, Jetanien added, "It's a shame that his government sought to undermine what he was trying to accomplish here with more of the same deception and subterfuge that has defined the relationship between our societies for generations."

Lugok said, "He was not alone. My superiors sought something similar. Perhaps if I was stronger and endeavored to make my voice heard by the High Council, they may well have made an honest, honorable commitment to this initiative. Instead, I believe it was their lack of vision that ultimately doomed us to failure."

"What?" Jetanien asked.

Releasing a derisive snort, the Klingon replied, "Come, Jetanien. You saw those who would represent the Empire. Criminals, disgraced warriors, and even those deemed unfit to serve. Outcasts from our society, but possessing not the fraction of pride necessary to take their own lives and restore some measure of honor to their Houses. They did not come here of their own volition; they were banished here. I should have demanded more. I should have demanded better. I failed in that regard."

"I think we all failed," Jetanien countered. "Our failure here was one of imagination. Perhaps the concept we envisioned was flawed from the start, and our peoples are not yet ready for peaceful coexistence."

"So, we keep trying."

Surprised by the abrupt comment, Jetanien turned to see Moreno regarding him, conviction evident in his eyes. Then, the man blinked several times, as though reconsidering whether he should have spoken.

"Go on, Sergio," Jetanien prompted.

"It's wrong to just give up so easily," Moreno said. "Not after everything that's happened. So what if our governments choose to continue doing things as they always have. D'tran worked under that burden for more than a century. He didn't need or expect any assistance from his superiors, and yet for decades before any of us was born, he worked with his Federation contact to broker agreements and *keep the peace*. Now that he's gone, someone else will have to take up that mantle, otherwise his death truly will be a tragedy."

Jetanien sighed. "We can do that, but not here, and not today."

Frowning, Moreno asked, "Why not?" Before either Jetanien or Lugok could respond, he said, "Tell me, what do you think will become of Paradise City?"

"I suppose it will be evacuated and abandoned," Jetanien said, "a monument to what could have been."

Moreno said, "Or, we can petition for the colony to be restored. Let it be a distraction, rather than an attraction."

"A distraction," Lugok repeated. "It could end up appearing more like a mockery."

"And if it does," Jetanien said, beginning to comprehend what his assistant was suggesting, "then so much the better." When Lugok scowled in confusion, he held up one of his manus. "Think about it. There are colonists who would be content to stay on Nimbus III, so long as the situation is brought under control. We can convince our governments to let them stay here, particularly if the settlers are doing so on their own and not requesting much in the way of formal support. Let the 'experiment' continue, and let the detractors think it's a waste of time."

Lugok smiled. "And while everyone sees the very public failure on constant display, we in turn possess a haven where we might continue our work, away from the prying eyes of those who would seek to undermine real, open communication."

"Exactly," Moreno said.

Jetanien recalled the first clandestine meetings he had shared with Lugok and D'tran, there on the barren, unwelcoming surface of Nimbus III. From the shared insights and compromises reached during those first days had sprung Paradise City, with its promise of lasting peace forged between three interstellar neighbors. Despite the very real setbacks that had consumed the colony, Jetanien knew the situation could be remedied in short order, perhaps even within weeks after the arrival of support vessels. After that? There seemed now to be more reason than ever to revisit the strategy with which he and his companions had begun, only this time, there would be no spectacle, no pressure exerted from officious meddlers with no vested interest in the outcome. Removed from the spotlight, the peace process could, with proper nurturing, thrive.

"What do you think, Lugok?" Jetanien asked. "Is it worth pondering?"

The Klingon replied, "And what if someone takes notice of our little refuge of diplomacy?"

"Then we move it somewhere else," Jetanien countered. "Someplace even more remote, if that's what it takes. The location isn't important. What matters is that we preserve the peace, by any means necessary."

Lugok smiled. "D'tran would certainly approve. Come, let us find a bottle of bloodwine, and drink to the memory of that bothersome Romulan and all the work he will cause for us in the days to come."

35

Ming Xiong studied the status indicators on the communications panel, satisfied that everything was properly set. "I think we're ready to go."

"Excellent," replied Mahmud al-Khaled from where he sat at one of the half-dozen consoles that had been installed in the *Lovell*'s secondary cargo bay. "I've activated and synchronized the processor with the communications array. It should time out perfectly with the frequency rotation."

Nodding in satisfaction, Xiong could not help smiling. "I have to say, the idea of adding a harmonics resonance processor was genius, Commander."

"Tell that to my number two," al-Khaled replied, gesturing toward another console, which was manned by Lieutenant Kurt Davis, the executive officer of the *Lovell*'s Corps of Engineers detachment. "It was his idea. Isn't that right, Kurt?"

The tall, lean bald man was hunched over his console, engrossed in the data being fed to him by the workstation's array of status monitors. Al-Khaled had to repeat the question before Davis looked up to see who was talking to him. "What?"

"He said if this doesn't work, he's blaming you," called out a new voice, and Xiong turned to see the *Lovell*'s first officer, Araev zh'Rhun.

"Wow. There's a fresh idea," Davis replied, smiling. "Come down to keep an eye on us, Commander?"

Casting a sardonic look in the engineer's direction, zh'Rhun said, "Someone has to keep you honest." She turned her attention to al-Khaled. "So, where are we?"

The engineer replied, "I think we're ready, Commander. Kurt?"

"Levels are optimum, sir," Davis said, patting his console. "The subspace relay will draw power from the warp engines. That should help regulate the relay, the communications array, and the harmonics processor, and still provide enough juice to penetrate the crystals' internal power fields while keeping the signal focused."

"What about the universal translation matrix?" Xiong asked.

Tapping the console again, Davis replied, "Also ready to go. We know from the last run that the Shedai entity is likely receiving our signals. We think we were able to at least send a simple message through the translation protocols, but now that we're synchronizing the harmonics to work more effectively with the orb's interior crystalline structure, the translation should be more effective. Hopefully it'll be enough to coax a response."

Xiong nodded in approval at the report before turning to eye the self-contained chamber occupying the space at the center of the cargo bay. As before, all of its internal components had been activated and it now operated free of the *Lovell*'s other onboard systems. On one of the monitors at al-Khaled's workstation, Xiong saw an image being fed to them from inside the chamber, that of the crystal polyhedron sitting in its cradle, waiting. The orb emanated its omnipresent violet glow, radiating a quiet menace that Xiong thought reflected the entity it contained. How would the Shedai react when a connection finally was made? What would it want? What would it say? Was there a chance it could be reasoned with, and some mutual understanding reached? Xiong had no idea. Despite the setbacks the previous three years had brought and even considering the obstacles he had faced and the challenges he had endured, he remained optimistic, even if that hope now was balanced with no small amount of caution. There was no denying the Shedai commanded unmatched power; what remained to be seen was whether their intellect and wisdom rivaled their strength. He could not believe that a civilization capable of achieving so much could not be engaged in constructive dialogue.

What was needed was common ground, and a way for both sides to navigate their respective paths to that point of accord.

Will we find our path today? Only one way to find out.

"Okay," Xiong said, nodding to zh'Rhun. "I think we're ready to proceed, Commander."

Zh'Rhun nodded before moving to a wall-mounted intercom set into a nearby bulkhead and activating the unit. "Zh'Rhun to bridge. Captain, are you monitoring?"

"Affirmative, Commander," replied the voice of the *Lovell*'s captain, Daniel Okagawa. *"Commander al-Khaled and Lieutenant Xiong can proceed at their discretion. We'll leave this channel open."*

"Acknowledged," zh'Rhun said before looking to al-Khaled and Xiong. "It's your show, gentlemen."

With a gesture to Davis, al-Khaled turned back to his workstation and began pressing several of the console's multicolored buttons in a prearranged sequence.

"Activating the frequency rotation protocols," al-Khaled said, "and transmitting the first hailing message. Let's see what happens."

We call to you.

Another signal, this one of greater force and possessing a new level of clarity, now reverberated through the crystalline lattice that formed the Wanderer's prison. Amplified by the crystal itself as well as the energy fields surging within the enclosed environment, every syllable was a spear of pain driven through the Wanderer's mind.

Free me.

She pushed the message through the cacophony enveloping her, feeling the resistance of the protective fields holding her hostage. Who called to her? Not the Progenitor, of that she was certain. This did not feel like him, with its odd, maladroit rhythms and lack of sophistication. No, she decided, it must be *Telinaruul* who called to her.

The impudence. How dare they try to communicate with her as though considering themselves her equals.

We call to you. Do you understand?

That they had managed to effect a method of discourse that even resembled the high language of her people was an impressive feat, she conceded. It was not their apparent technical prowess that angered the Wanderer. Rather, it was their arrogance.

Free me. Free the Progenitor. Free us, and I may grant you continued existence.

She detected the shift in the energy fields surrounding her. What was happening? Something was having an effect on the crystal. A low drone was filling her mind, forcing aside her every thought as its intensity expanded.

We do not understand. Help us to understand.

Something else was happening to her. The Wanderer felt a renewed sense of strength welling up within her being. A vitality she had not felt since becoming a prisoner was beginning to pulse through her consciousness. Concentrating on the new sensations, she realized that the source of her returning vigor was somewhere beyond the confines of the crystal holding her. Whatever power was being used to drive the signals being directed at her was also disrupting the orb's crystalline fabric. Already she could feel its structure beginning to fluctuate, and she at once set to searching for any new points of weakness. Even the energy field that acted as her guardian seemed to be changing, and the Wanderer perceived a loosening of its perpetual grip on her. As her strength increased with each passing instant, so too did her anger and sense of determination.

You will understand.

A status indicator on al-Khaled's console changed from green to red, and Xiong pointed at it. "What's that?"

"Power fluctuation," the engineer replied, his fingers moving over the rows of buttons and other controls. "And sensors are picking up some kind of disturbance inside the crystal."

The intercom on al-Khaled's workstation whistled for attention, and was followed by the voice of Doctor Carol Marcus. *"Marcus to Xiong. What's going on over there? We're detecting all sorts of odd readings from the crystal."*

Reaching across the console to activate the intercom, Xiong replied, "We're picking up irregularities from inside the crystal, Doctor. Commander al-Khaled is diagnosing the problem now."

In front of him, al-Khaled leaned forward, and Xiong saw his friend's eyes narrow. "There are microfissures forming within the latticework. Kurt, reduce power to the subspace relay."

At his own workstation, Davis replied, "Aye, sir. Reducing power."

"Won't that affect the signal?" Xiong asked, casting a glance toward the isolation chamber.

Al-Khaled nodded. "Yes, but if we keep the power at its present level, it might make the microfissures worse."

"Is the crystal stable?" asked Commander zh'Rhun.

"For the moment," al-Khaled replied.

Damn it! Xiong shook his head, feeling his sense of apprehension beginning to rise. *It was working!* According to the computer, their initial message to the Shedai entity had been received and had been answered. The alien's next response had been garbled by the power fluctuations, rendering it indecipherable, but Xiong could not help but hope that some form of real connection might finally have been made.

Davis said, "Something's wrong." He waited until Xiong and al-Khaled moved to stand behind him before pointing to a pair of status monitors. "See this? Energy levels inside the crystal are rising. It's almost like . . ."

". . . a buildup to detonation?" zh'Rhun asked, completing the thought.

"Exactly," al-Khaled said, his voice low. He looked to Xiong, and both men shared a look of horrific understanding before the engineer moved back to his console and called up another status graphic. "The microfissures are increasing," he said, then reached for his station's intercom switch. "Al-Khaled to engineering. Cut all power to the subspace relay. Stand by to divert that power to the isolation chamber's containment field."

"Mister al-Khaled," said Captain Okagawa from the still-open channel to the bridge. *"What are you doing?"*

"Trying to keep the artifact from shattering, sir," al-Khaled said, his fingers almost a blur across his console as Xiong watched him work. "If we can't do that, then we'll have to eject the chamber."

The statement made Xiong look up toward the cargo bay's massive, reinforced hatch, the only thing separating the compartment from open space. If the crystal was unable to contain the Shedai entity it held, there would be no other option, and that likely would not be sufficient to protect them from attack if the creature broke free. Phaser strikes from the *Lovell* or Vanguard might work, but it was not an option Xiong was anxious to explore. "Can you halt the degradation?"

"I don't know." Al-Khaled said nothing else, so intent was he on his work, but Davis pointed to his own console.

"Power readings are spiking inside the crystal," he said, his face a mask of confusion. "How is that even possible? We've cut off everything."

Xiong knew the answer. "It's the Shedai. It must have found a way to refocus the energy we were expending to penetrate the crystal with our signal."

"The cracks are getting worse," al-Khaled said, his words now laced with tension. "I don't think there's anything we can do to stop it."

Over the intercom, Carol Marcus's voice had grown louder and more anxious. *"Ming, you need to jettison the chamber. Now."*

"She's right," zh'Rhun said as she moved to the still-active intercom panel on the bulkhead to her left. "Captain, are you hearing this? Move us away from the station and have ship's phasers on standby."

● ● ●

"Alert Vanguard that we're preparing to eject the containment chamber."

The voice of Commander zh'Rhun blared from the speakers around the *Lovell*'s bridge, and Daniel Okagawa wasted no time putting his first officer's directions into motion. Pointing to his helm officer, Lieutenant Sasha Rodriguez, he snapped, "Do it. Evasive course away from the station, any heading. Take us to a distance of fifty thousand kilometers and bring us to a full stop." Looking over his shoulder to the communications station, he added, "Pzial, notify Vanguard that we're going hot."

Ensign Folanir Pzial, a Rigellian and one of the *Lovell*'s junior communications officers, replied, "Aye, sir." Okagawa heard the anxiety in her voice, and tried not to dwell on how much it mirrored his own. After a moment, she said, "Captain, we're receiving an advisory from Vanguard's weapons control. Phasers and photon torpedoes are standing by." She paused before adding, "They want us to know that they're targeting the *Lovell*."

Nodding at the report, Okagawa said, "Not surprising. If that thing gets out of the cargo bay, it's likely to head right for the station." He knew that Admiral Nogura would be ready for this course of action, one that had been discussed when outlining the plan to attempt communication with the Shedai entity contained within the odd alien crystal. If the creature locked inside the mysterious orb managed to escape, Carol Marcus and her team believed it would target Starbase 47 itself, perhaps repeating its attempt to come after the Mirdonyae artifact contained within the station's top-secret research facility. The station had already felt the alien's wrath once, and Nogura was unlikely to want a repeat of that experience.

"Approaching fifty thousand kilometers from the station, sir," reported Rodriguez from the helm. "Preparing to answer full stop."

Pzial said, "Captain, Vanguard control reports the *Sagittarius* is powering up with orders to follow us."

"And do what?" Okagawa asked, then waved away the question. "Never mind." Though he had nothing but respect for Captain Nassir and the crew of the compact *Archer*-class scout, there would be precious little the ship could do if the situation became a shoot-out with an escaped Shedai entity.

Then the voice of Commander zh'Rhun erupted from the speakers. *"Bridge, the crystal is breaking down! We're losing containment!"*

"Jettison the container!" Okagawa ordered, but instead of a response from his first officer, he heard only the sounds of metal rending and twisting.

The Shedai was breaking free.

36

Alarm klaxons echoed in the cargo bay, and most of the status indicators on the various consoles overseeing the operation glowed and blinked red. Xiong felt sweat running down his back as he watched al-Khaled's and Davis's frantic efforts to keep the situation under control.

They were failing.

"Jettison the container!" shouted Captain Okagawa, his voice blasting through the intercom. Commander zh'Rhun started to reply, but then a new sound rang in the cargo bay: metal being stressed.

"The crystal's gone!" al-Khaled snapped, his attention split between his workstation and the isolation chamber, which was now shaking on the deck plates. Xiong looked at the monitor with its audiovisual feed from inside the chamber and saw that the Mirdonyac Artifact had disappeared, and in its place was a roiling, amorphous black mass. It appeared to be bouncing around the container's interior, and Xiong could see dents and other rends in the bulkhead panels. Outside the chamber, telltale blue flashes of energy sparked each time the container shifted its position and came into contact with the surrounding force field.

"Engineering!" Davis called out. "Full power to the containment system!"

Over the intercom, the voice of the *Lovell*'s chief engineer, Lieutenant Commander Moves-With-Burning-Grace, replied, *"You've got everything we can push through, Lieutenant. Anything more and the circuits will overheat."*

Davis growled in mounting frustration as he continued to work his console. "Son of a bitch! I don't think it's going to be enough."

"It's not," al-Khaled confirmed, before glancing over his shoulder to zh'Rhun. "Evacuate. Everybody out of the secondary hull. *Now.*"

"What the hell are you talking about?" Xiong asked, incredulous.

"Just do it!" al-Khaled snapped.

Beside him, Davis added, "The field might hold for a couple of minutes, but only if I can keep the power levels steady. That thing in there is siphoning the power at an exponential rate. If we jettison the chamber, the field drops and it'll be free."

"At which point," Xiong said, "it will likely attack the *Lovell.*"

"Exactly," Davis replied. "But if we hurry, we can get everybody out of the secondary hull, separate, and let Vanguard blow this section to hell." As though in response to the engineer's statement, the isolation chamber shuddered, eliciting another flash of energy as it bounced against the inside of the containment force field.

Xiong realized what was being proposed. "But someone has to stay back to maintain the field levels."

"Right," al-Khaled said. "Davis is rotating the field frequencies, trying to keep the Shedai from locking into it and drawing power that much faster. The longer we wait, the less that trick's going to matter."

Moving to the wall-mounted intercom, zh'Rhun slapped the activation control with the palm of her hand. "This is Commander zh'Rhun. Commence immediate emergency evacuation of the secondary hull. This is not a drill. Repeat: *This is not a drill.*" She punctuated her order by smacking the panel's Red Alert control, at which time a louder, more intense alarm siren began wailing in the cargo bay. She then turned back to Xiong and the others. "The three of you: out."

"I can't," Davis said, not taking his attention from his console.

"I'm making manual adjustments to the field settings. There's no time to teach you what needs to be done, Commander."

Zh'Rhun hesitated not one instant. "Fine. I'm staying with you in case you need help. Al-Khaled, Xiong, see to the evacuation of this section."

"*Commander,*" said Okagawa over the intercom, "*I'm not liking what I'm hearing.*"

Appearing to ignore the captain's comment, zh'Rhun pointed to Xiong and al-Khaled before gesturing to the cargo bay's exit. "Move!" Then, in a somewhat softer tone, she added, "Hold the door, and contact me when everyone's out. We'll come running."

Al-Khaled paused, sharing with the first officer a meaningful look that Xiong understood to be an unspoken exchange of mutual respect from two shipmates who together had seen and experienced their share of trials and challenges. "I'll be there."

"We'll be there," Xiong corrected.

Eyeing the two officers, zh'Rhun nodded in understanding and gratitude. "Go."

Xiong followed the engineer out of the cargo bay, stopping at the hatch long enough to turn back and see zh'Rhun and Davis now standing alone at the row of consoles, whatever they might be saying now completely drowned out by the alarm klaxons. The isolation chamber before them was in a constant state of movement, with dents clearly visible all across its surface. How much longer would it hold?

Long enough, I hope.

He had to run to catch up with al-Khaled, who had already traversed the short corridor leading from the cargo bay and made it to the wider passageway running the length of the *Lovell's* secondary hull. At the far end of the passage was another reinforced hatch, leading to the "access boom" that connected this part of the ship to the spherical primary hull. Essentially an oversized, reinforced cylinder, the boom contained a single passageway that allowed for transit between the vessel's two main sections. It also supported the warp nacelles, though if the secondary hull was jettisoned, the ship would only be capable of achieving sublight speeds—more than enough to return to Vanguard, assuming the *Lovell* survived the next few minutes.

Always the optimist.

Feeling something less than useless, Araev zh'Rhun watched as Kurt Davis continued his frantic work, his head bobbing between his console's rows of buttons and controls and their accompanying status monitors. Every few seconds, she spared a glance toward the isolation chamber, one side of which was now bulging outward and looking to zh'Rhun like a pregnant mother's swollen belly.

Considering what was about to happen, she decided the analogy was apt.

"What can I do?" she asked.

"Get out of here," Davis replied, not turning from the monitors.

Zh'Rhun shook her head. "You first." Each had already stated for the record—and in Davis's case that included a possible charge of insubordination and disobedience of lawful orders—that neither would leave without the other, and Davis was determined to remain on task as long as necessary. Staring at his face, illuminated as it was by the glow of viewscreens and status displays, zh'Rhun comprehended the man's resolve, seeing that he was prepared to sacrifice himself for his shipmates. There was no way she was going to leave him here to do that alone.

"How much time?" she asked.

Davis grimaced, squinting from droplets of sweat running from his bald head and into his eyes. "A minute. Maybe." As if on cue, another muffled impact of something against metal sounded in the cargo bay, and zh'Rhun looked up to see a new tear along the top of the isolation chamber's bulging side panel.

"I'm thinking less," she said.

She flinched at the sound of Mahmud al-Khaled's voice bursting from the wall-mounted intercom. *"Al-Khaled to zh'Rhun. Everybody's out, Commander!"*

"That's it!" zh'Rhun said, grabbing Davis by the shoulder and pulling him away from the console. "Time to go!"

"Wait!" Davis said, extending his arms as though stretching for the workstation. "We can't!"

Zh'Rhun heaved the lieutenant ahead of her and pushed him toward the exit. "It's over. Move!" She tried to ignore the sounds of metal coming apart behind her, concentrating instead on the sounds of her boots against the deck plates as she closed the distance to the hatch. Davis, running ahead of her, plunged through the opening and waited for her to follow him into the corridor before smacking a control panel set into the bulkhead next to the hatch. The reinforced door began cycling shut, allowing zh'Rhun one last look at the twisted, distended isolation chamber as a black, shapeless mass erupted from inside the wrecked container.

As the door sealed, Davis hit another control and a status indicator on the panel with the label BAY DECOMPRESSING illuminated. A deep rumble made its way through the bulkheads, and zh'Rhun felt a mild reverberation in the deck beneath her feet as the cargo bay's outer hatch was opened while the compartment still possessed an atmosphere. In her mind's eye she pictured the bay's contents being blasted toward the now open hatch as everything in the room was vented into space.

Then, something—the Shedai, of course—slammed into the hatch right in front of them.

No. She did not know why she should be surprised. After all, what was a decompressed cargo bay to an entity that had already demonstrated its ability to traverse interstellar distances without any known form of space vessel?

"I think our plan has a few holes in it," Davis said, seemingly an echo to zh'Rhun's own thoughts.

"*Bridge to zh'Rhun,*" echoed Captain Okagawa's voice over the intercom. "*Where the hell are you?*"

"Come on," zh'Rhun said, grabbing Davis by the arm and pulling him along with her as she began to sprint the length of corridor toward the access boom. Standing in the doorway, waving for them to hurry, were al-Khaled and Xiong.

"Move!" al-Khaled shouted.

Behind zh'Rhun, another impact against the bulkhead echoed in the hallway, and this time it was accompanied by the rush of escaping oxygen. Another alarm sounded in the corridor, and she recognized it as the alert for a hull rupture. They were less than ten meters from the hatch when it slid shut, blocking their escape and hiding al-Khaled and Xiong from view. Halting their advance, they turned in time to see a black mass ripping through the corridor's interior bulkheads before the pressure door ahead of it closed, sealing the two officers in a ten-meter section of passageway. Decompression protocols were in effect, with containment doors closing throughout the ship, sealing their respective compartments and preventing the entire vessel from being compromised.

"Shit!" Davis said, his eyes wide and his voice rising.

In response to his obscenity, something punctured the hatch leading back to the cargo bay, and a long, black spike thrust itself through the metal. Once again, zh'Rhun heard the hiss of air escaping into space.

From the control panel positioned next to the door that would have been their portal to escape, the intercom flared to life with Captain Okagawa's voice. *"We're picking up a hull breach. All containment hatches are in place. Is everyone out of there?"*

"No" was all zh'Rhun had time to say before the hiss became a roar.

The decompression alarm howled in the corridor just as the pressure hatch began to shift, and Xiong pulled al-Khaled back before the door could slice him in half.

"Watch it!" he said, yanking the engineer almost off balance before the hatch sealed with a resounding click. With the hull breach, Xiong knew the emergency doors spaced throughout the ship would be closed, which he recalled was normal operating procedure on older vessels like the *Lovell*. The ancient *Daedalus*-class ship was from another era, before emergency containment force fields and other protective measures had become standard equipment on modern starships.

Slamming his fist against the hatch, al-Khaled released a grunt of rage. "No!" Then, training and experience seemed to reassert themselves as he turned to the control panel set into the bulkhead beside the door. Xiong saw that the panel was more than a simple door or intercom panel, as it also contained controls for overseeing emergency protocols such as separating the hulls. There was an intercom, as well, and Captain Okagawa's voice erupted from it.

"We're picking up a hull breach. All containment hatches are in place. Is everyone out of there?"

Though he reached for the intercom to reply, al-Khaled was stopped when he and Xiong heard the simple response from Commander zh'Rhun.

"No."

The bulkheads and deck plates shuddered around them as the compartment was rocked by a series of muffled explosions, and instinct made Xiong reach toward the nearby wall for support. "What was that?" he asked, before realizing what it must be, and he looked to the control panel to see a large indicator glowing bright yellow and illuminating the words SEPARATION SEQUENCE INITIATED.

"Damn it!" al-Khaled said, looking from the console to the hatch and back again as he processed what was happening. "Bridge!" he called to the intercom, "zh'Rhun and Davis are still over there! Can you lock onto them with transporters?"

There was a pause—slight but there nonetheless—before Okagawa replied.

"It's too late."

Everyone on the *Lovell*'s compact bridge sat in stunned silence, watching the horrific scene on the main viewscreen play out before them. Okagawa, as startled by the vision as the rest of his crew, rose from his chair and felt his jaw slacken as he took in the horrific sight of the ship's engineering hull being torn apart.

"Dear God" was all the captain could muster as he stood, transfixed. On the screen was the image of the *Lovell*'s secondary hull, pushed away by the force of the explosive bolts responsible for separating it from the rest of the vessel. It had begun to tumble in response to other forces being inflicted upon it, and though the image offered no sound, it was not hard for Okagawa to imagine the shriek of twisted metal as strips and chunks of hull plating were ripped with stunning speed and violence from the hull's spaceframe. Whatever form the Shedai entity had adopted, it seemed well suited to the task of slicing the duranium sections with the same effort one might expect a knife to cut bread. A cloud of debris now surrounded the wreck, expanding in all directions as the Shedai continued its task of reducing the secondary hull to little more than shrapnel. Within seconds the hull had ceased to resemble anything that might ever have been a component of a space vessel, and at the heart of the flotsam was what Okagawa could only think of as a dark, undulating cloud.

"Shields up," he snapped, allowing his anger at what had been inflicted upon his ship and crew to seep into his voice. "Target all weapons on that thing and prepare to fire." Before his order was acknowledged, he saw the black mass on the screen lunge out of the debris field it had created. At the same time, another alarm wailed across the bridge.

"Proximity alert," reported his weapons officer, Lieutenant Jessica Diamond. "It's coming straight at us!"

The next instant, the *Lovell* trembled and the image on the main viewscreen scrambled and flashed blue as something impacted against the ship's deflector shields. This prompted yet another alarm, which Okagawa ordered silenced. "Fire!" he shouted.

"I can't get a lock," Diamond called out. "It's too close!" Then her voice seemed to raise an octave as she added, "Shields are failing!"

Feeling powerless as he watched the black form spread and

expand to fill the viewscreen, Okagawa felt the ship quake around him as the Shedai broke through the deflector shields and slammed itself into the *Lovell*'s hull. The deck lurched beneath his feet, and he stumbled backward and fell against the side of his chair. Multiple alarms erupted around the bridge and Okagawa saw status indicators at different stations begin to flash bright red. Somewhere beyond the ship's multiple layers of hull plating, he heard the unmistakable groans and shrieks of metal being torn asunder.

"Multiple breaches across the front of the hull!" Diamond shouted from where she was holding on to the edge of her console in order to remain on her feet.

"Evacuate those sections!" Okagawa ordered. As he tried to figure out how many seconds remained before the Shedai punctured the hull, the captain realized he had one last card to play: the self-destruct protocol. Would it be enough to take the Shedai with them? There was only one way to find out, but only if the alien granted him the time needed to carry out the last-ditch act.

One way to find that out, too.

Another indicator tone sounded from Diamond's station, and the weapons officer said, "Captain! It's the *Sagittarius*!"

Before Okagawa could respond to that, the image on the viewscreen shifted yet again, and this time the Shedai seemed to be reacting to something. It jerked violently, pulling itself away so that stars along with the wreckage of the *Lovell*'s engineering hull once again were visible. Then bright blue beams cut across the screen, striking the Shedai and sending it tumbling away from view.

"Track it!" Okagawa snapped, and the image shifted to maintain the Shedai at its center as it continued to writhe from the assault on it. The phaser beams were hitting it in rapid succession now, strike after strike, with each blow inflicting noticeable distress on the entity. "Fire all weapons!" he ordered. At the helm, Sasha Rodriguez stabbed at her weapons controls and the *Lovell*'s phasers joined the fray. Like those of the *Sagittarius,* the *Lovell*'s phasers had been retuned in accordance with specifications provided by the small scout vessel's chief engineer. According to Captain Nassir, the refinements had been developed after the *Sagittarius*'s encounter with a Shedai on Jinoteur IV. Whatever the engineer had devised, it seemed to be working.

"It's weakening!" Diamond shouted, but then added, "Some, that is, but the phasers are having an effect."

"Maintain firing," Okagawa ordered, taking a small bit of unwonted satisfaction each time a phaser strike impacted against the Shedai's body.

Then, the Shedai disappeared. There was no flash or explosion; it simply was gone.

"What the hell just happened?" Okagawa asked, not turning from the screen as he searched for some signs of the entity.

"I don't know, sir," Diamond replied, and the captain heard the confusion in her voice. "It's just gone." She tapped several controls on her console before looking up from her station. "I think it fled, sir."

Frowning, he turned to regard his science officer. "Fled?"

Diamond nodded. "Yes, sir. Sensors did detect its departure from the system, but it was moving so fast there was no way to track it." She glanced toward the viewscreen before returning her gaze to Okagawa. "I'm sorry, sir."

Waving away her apology, Okagawa returned his attention to the viewscreen. "Nothing you could have done, Lieutenant." After a moment, he glanced over his shoulder toward the communications station. "Ensign Pzial, hail the *Sagittarius* and offer Captain Nassir my thanks, and tell him to let his chief engineer know that he is one talented bastard. I'd love to have him if he wants to jump ship."

For whatever's left of this one.

The thought was enough to redirect his gaze to the screen, where the expanding cloud of debris that had been the *Lovell*'s secondary hull drifted. His mind turned to questions of the being that had caused such destruction. Where had the Shedai gone?

More important, when would it be back? Okagawa did not know, and answers likely would not be forthcoming today. For now, there were more important things to do, such as pausing to reflect and appreciate Araev zh'Rhun and Kurt Davis, who had given their lives in order to save their shipmates.

"Thank you," Okagawa whispered.

37

Free!

The Shedai Wanderer drove herself deeper into the void, away
from the *Telinaruul* and her cursed prison. She felt nothing but the
boundless energies of the cosmos itself. The weakness and pain
inflicted by the *Telinaruul* weapons was already beginning to
fade, further displaced with every passing moment by the power
she had longed to regain. Temptation surged within her, willing
her to reverse her course and continue the retribution she had only
just begun to inflict now that she was regaining her strength.

No, she decided. Despite their limitations, the *Telinaruul*
were never again to be underestimated. They had succeeded in
seizing some imperfect yet adequate control over technologies
that they would never possess the capability to fully understand,
and they still held the Progenitor captive, though the Wanderer
was certain the parasites were ignorant of the prize in their midst.
For that alone, they deserved annihilation. Even with their mea-
ger comprehension, the upstarts still posed a threat. Given sufficient time, they might well improve their awareness of the power
in their grasp. What then? Would they come after her, and those
Shedai that still remained? What had once seemed implausible
whimsy now carried a seed of possibility. That alone was sufficient not to risk further misjudgment of their intellect and ability.
After all, it was such arrogance and self-assurance that generations ago had forced the Shedai to seek their self-imposed exile.
Such mistakes could not be repeated, not if her people were to
return to their former glory. It was the destiny of the Shedai to
rule, to force the galaxy to bend to their will.

In order to succeed, the Wanderer knew from this point forward that she must cease thinking of these *Telinaruul* as minions, and embrace them for what they truly were: the enemy. The danger they posed was significant. They were adversaries to be respected, if not feared. They must be viewed as skilled, if not superior. Her options were few, but not exhausted, and victory would be difficult, but not impossible.

However, that victory would not come without aid. For this, she would have to trust others of her kind. She would have to find some way of convincing those whom she once opposed to set aside their own selfish interests, and instead align with her against their common enemy. Would they be willing to do that? The Wanderer did not know, but there was no choice but to try. Her only alternative was to stand by and do nothing, and perhaps wait for the Apostate to finish what he had started. Indeed, the bold action she now contemplated was sure to rouse her foremost adversary, and he would stop at nothing to see to her failure. The lingering question for which she at present had no answer was whether the Apostate had acquired any followers from among her people. He was formidable even while acting alone. With a group to support him, he might well be unstoppable.

Marshaling her increasing strength, she reached with her mind toward the distant stars, seeking any of her people who might come forward to act during this most grievous challenge without question. To anyone who might be listening, she put forth her plea.

There was no answer.

Not yet. For now, the Wanderer would be patient, continuing to broadcast her entreaties while fueled by comforting thoughts of final, merciless retribution.

38

When the door to Cervantes Quinn's apartment opened, it required physical effort on T'Prynn's part to maintain her expression and composure as a vile aroma assailed her nostrils. Thanks to her keen olfactory senses—a trait shared by most Vulcans which was even more pronounced in females of the species—she had detected Quinn's approach to the door even before it had opened, but now the combined stench of alcohol, old food, and his own unwashed body was almost too much to bear. Despite her best efforts to maintain her bearing, T'Prynn could not help blinking several times as her nose twitched in response to the malodorous assault.

"What the hell do you want?" Quinn barked. His voice, which was louder than necessary, echoed off the duranium plating of the nearby bulkheads and almost made T'Prynn wince. As it was, his words were slurred, and Quinn's features and general demeanor suggested that he was still under the influence of the intoxicating beverage with which he had seen fit to embalm himself.

"Mister Quinn," T'Prynn said, clasping her hands behind her back and maintaining a formal posture. "Is this a bad time?"

Quinn reached up to wipe his mouth with the back of his hand. "I don't know. What time is it?"

"Current station time is 0954 hours," T'Prynn replied. "I do not consider myself an expert on many human customs, particularly those involving the consumption of mood-altering substances such as alcohol. However, it is my understanding that imbibing such products at this time of day is considered unhealthy, and perhaps even indicative of addictive tendencies."

Blinking several times, Quinn frowned before shaking his head. "You lost me at 'current time,' lady. Think you can condense all of that down to something us non-Vulcan types can understand?"

T'Prynn arched one eyebrow. "You are drunk, Mister Quinn."

"No," Quinn said, holding up his hand and pointing one shaky finger at her for emphasis. "I was drunk last night. I'll probably be drunk again after lunch."

"And now?"

Shrugging, Quinn belched, his expression twisting as though even he was repulsed by his own breath. "I'm in a cooling-off period." He paused, his brow furrowing as though he was struggling to push past the fog enveloping his mind. Then his eyes widened and he regarded T'Prynn as though she had just appeared before him. "What?"

"I did not say anything," T'Prynn replied, now beginning to consider the wisdom of her decision to call on the trader. "Before you decide to embark on your latest bout of inebriation, I have come to . . . make a request of you."

That seemed to register with Quinn, as his eyes narrowed in suspicion. "I thought we were all even on the favors and debts I owed you."

T'Prynn nodded. "Indeed we are. I have not come to collect on any outstanding obligations, nor is this a formal request from Starfleet. This would be . . . a favor, one which I would expect to repay at some point."

"Really?" Quinn said, his tone one of surprise, though T'Prynn still sensed his wariness. "And what might this favor entail?"

Glancing in both directions to ensure they were alone in the corridor, she said, "We believe we have located a possible source for the Mirdonyae Artifacts. At the very least, it is possible it is a repository for such artifacts, and may contain other Tkon technology or clues which may prove useful as defenses against the Shedai. You are one of a very small group of people with any exposure to these objects, and one of even fewer people who have interacted directly with a representative of the Shedai. Your knowledge and expertise might prove valuable on the forthcoming reconnaissance mission to be conducted by the crew of the *Sagittarius*."

In truth, she had doubts about Quinn's usefulness on this mission, and not simply because of his current impaired state. While it was true that his firsthand experience with the Shedai made him an all but irreplaceable commodity, his state of depression over the loss of Commander McLellan would almost certainly affect his judgment. He might engage in some form of reckless behavior that could prove dangerous to the *Sagittarius* crew. Had McLellan's death so completely affected him that he would forsake all of the progress he had made regaining control over his life during the past year?

Judging by his reaction, T'Prynn decided this might well be the case. His demeanor turned even more belligerent, and he scowled at her. "You know who else had knowledge and expertise? Bridy Mac, and she died the last time we went out on one of your little missions. So, I'm done playing spy, sweetheart."

"I was sorry to hear about Commander McLellan, Mister Quinn," T'Prynn said. "Her death is regrettable, though she gave it in service to Starfleet, and to you." The mission reports submitted by Captain Khatami after the *Endeavour*'s rescue of Quinn from the mysterious, unnamed planet where he and McLellan had encountered the Shedai Apostate were quite thorough. By all accounts, Bridget McLellan had given her own life during a mission to find a possible origin point or other storehouse of Shedai technology and keep it from falling into the hands of the Klingons. The pair also had learned about the Tkon and how they had created the artifacts, and the other technology they had developed as defenses against the Shedai. "If not for her efforts, we would not have the information and opportunities we now possess, but our mission is not yet over. Do you wish her sacrifice to be in vain?"

The look of anger on Quinn's face deepened, and when he spoke this time, his voice was low and contained what T'Prynn recognized as a hint of menace. "Don't play that guilt game with me, lady," he said, and when he pointed a finger at her this time, T'Prynn noted that his hand did not shake. "I said I'm done. Whatever you're planning, I don't want any part of it. Now, would all of you damned do-gooder types kindly just leave me the hell alone?" He stepped back into his apartment without another word, and T'Prynn stood in silence as the door slid shut.

It was a waste, she decided—an illogical squandering of a useful resource, which was precisely what Cervantes Quinn had become. However, if he wished to throw aside everything he had accomplished toward reclaiming the sense of self-worth and respect that humans seemed to require, then that was his choice. Despite this conclusion, T'Prynn considered pressing the issue, confronting Quinn yet again and continuing to do so until he saw reason.

She discarded the notion. In his present state, there would be no persuading Quinn, at least not in the short term. There was insufficient time for him to dispel the effects of prolonged alcohol abuse and grief—not in the time she had available to her.

"So be it, Mister Quinn," T'Prynn said to the apartment door. With a final, protracted look at the unyielding barrier, she turned and walked away, leaving Quinn to his drink and his despair.

"You look tired, Admiral."

Standing before the viewscreen in his office, his arms folded across his chest, Nogura released a sigh that he figured would serve only to confirm the observations of his visitor. Turning from the screen, upon which were displayed several status reports—none containing anything he might consider positive or heartening updates—Nogura directed his attention to Daniel Okagawa, presently a captain without a ship to command.

"I'm better off than some," he said, moving away from the viewscreen. "I'm sorry about your people who were lost. I understand there will be a memorial service this evening?"

Okagawa nodded. "Yes, Admiral. I hope you can attend, and perhaps offer a few words."

"Absolutely," Nogura replied. "I think it's the least I can do."

"As tragic as their loss is," Okagawa said, "their sacrifice saved everyone else aboard the *Lovell*." His gaze shifted to the floor for a moment, and Nogura knew what the other man had to be thinking.

"I'm sorry about the *Lovell*, too," Nogura added. "She was a tough little ship." The sight of the vessel's secondary hull, torn literally to pieces by the Shedai entity, had been unnerving to say the least. He was, in all honesty, stunned that the ship had suffered so few casualties. Two crew members, Ensigns Frances Porter and Bernd Perplies, were lost when the alien attacked the *Lovell*'s primary hull. It was a credit to Areav zh'Rhun and Kurt Davis, their unwavering leadership and poise under tremendous pressure and chaos, that the remainder of the *Lovell*'s complement had survived. As for the vessel itself, it was far beyond any reasonable hope of repair. Though its primary hull remained largely intact despite the Shedai's best efforts, Starfleet had decided that restoration, which would have to include replacing the lost hull section and upgrading the vessel's systems, was not worth the effort.

"You have no idea," Okagawa replied. "She may not have been the slickest or best-looking, but she had heart." He paused, and a small chuckle escaped his lips. "I'll never forget the first time I saw her after my orders came through. She was six months off the scrap heap at Qualor II along with the other two *Daedalus*-class dinosaurs the Corps of Engineers had salvaged, and I was sure Command had to be yanking my chain." A small smile teased the corners of his mouth. "And the crew. Every one of them is really something special." Holding up a hand, he added, "I know, rare is the captain who says any member of his crew isn't less than a stellar performer, but I'm particularly proud of my people.

"They took an old rust bucket that was already decades beyond its expected operational lifetime," the proud captain continued, "and over the next year, they tore that thing practically down to the spaceframe before renovating, reconfiguring, or flat-out rebuilding every major system. And they did all that while we were carrying out our regular assignments, including a handful of missions that were anything but routine." When he smiled this time, it was an expression of unabashed smugness. "The *Lovell* may not have been much to look at, and she was a long way behind the sleeker, more modern ships Starfleet has these days, but she never let me down—not once." With another faint smile, he leaned back in his chair. "I'm going to miss that old girl."

"It's a shame she can't be salvaged," Nogura said, glancing at the viewscreen and one of the reports it displayed—a briefing submitted by Captain Okagawa on the *Lovell*'s condition and status of its personnel. With the vessel no longer serviceable, its contingent of specialists from the Corps of Engineers would be assigned to another ship, and the rest of the crew would probably receive orders to other starships or stations throughout Starfleet. "I've informed Command that I'd like to keep at least some members of your crew on hand for a while, namely Commander al-Khaled. He and Lieutenant Xiong make a good team, and if Xiong's theory about the Shedai is right, we're going to need all the help we can get." His attention lingering on the viewscreen, Nogura's gaze fell upon another report he had been disturbed to receive. "Especially if the *Defiant* didn't just get lost on its way home."

"You haven't heard anything new?" Okagawa asked.

Nogura shook his head. "They transmitted an encrypted message that said they had left the Traelus system and were being chased by Tholian ships. Captain Blair indicated he was setting an evasive course, and according to the star charts of that area, he took the *Defiant* into territory we haven't yet investigated. Who the hell knows what might be there?" During his many years of Starfleet service, Nogura had come to understand and accept that whenever he saw what he thought was the most startling revelation the universe had to offer, the universe would find a way to show him something even more remarkable. "Well, it won't remain unsurveyed for long; I've already asked Starfleet for a ship that I can send to look for the *Defiant*." He had been reluctant to do so, given the classified nature of Operation Vanguard, but with the *Endeavour* still on patrol and more than a month away and the *Sagittarius* preparing for its critical mission to the Eremar system, Nogura had been left with no other choice. Thankfully, there were one or two vessels whose captains were briefed into Starbase 47's top-secret mission, at least to varying degrees. Starfleet, understanding this, had dispatched the *Enterprise* to the Taurus Reach, and according to its captain the vessel was expected to reach the area of the *Defiant*'s last known position in three weeks.

Leaning forward in his chair, Okagawa rested his elbows on his knees. "Is it possible they've found a place to hide and they've just gone quiet, to reduce the chances of detection?"

"Maybe," Nogura conceded. He had waited for forty-eight hours from the time of Captain Blair's last message before declaring the *Defiant* missing in action, but he refused to change that status to "presumed lost" until such time as the *Enterprise* completed its search operation.

Of course, while ascertaining the *Defiant*'s fate was important, Nogura had another pressing concern. "Whatever they found on Traelus II, it's obviously something the Tholians don't want anyone to know about, particularly the Klingons."

Okagawa frowned. "Do we have anything more on what he was talking about?"

"Blair didn't go into specifics in his messages," Nogura replied, "but we can gather that he was talking about some kind of weapon, which the Tholians apparently used on the Klingon colony on Traelus II. If the Tholians wiped out that colony, then the Klingons will want payback." The Traelus system was close enough to Tholian territory that an imperial presence on the second planet had caused the Tholian government to launch a flurry of protests in the wake of the Klingon colonists' taking up residence there. It was but one of several aggressive actions the Empire had undertaken since first venturing into the Taurus Reach, to which the Tholians also had objected. Tensions between the two governments had only worsened during the past two years, with both sides becoming ever bolder toward one another, and Nogura was resigned to the inevitable confrontation he was sure would soon erupt. In his mind, it was not a question of if, but rather when. Of course, if the Tholians also were behind whatever fate had befallen the *Defiant,* then the Federation would find themselves with few options so far as confronting the Assembly was concerned.

And won't that be grand.

Clearing his throat, Okagawa said, "I'm guessing diplomacy isn't our best friend at the moment."

"Did working with those engineers give you a gift for understatement, Captain?" Nogura sighed, shaking his head.

"You become numb to that sort of thing after a while," Okagawa replied.

The report Nogura had received from Ambassador Jetanien on the collapse of the joint-venture colony on Nimbus III was not unexpected, but nonetheless disheartening. He knew that Jetanien, working in concert with Klingon Ambassador Lugok and Romulan Senator D'tran, had expended great effort to convince all three parties to cooperate in establishing the settlement on Nimbus III. Skeptics, Nogura among them, had doomed the undertaking to certain failure from the outset, but that had not dissuaded Jetanien. The multitude of external pressures being applied by the respective governments had not helped. Also contributing to the mix were the inherent problems that came from both the Federation's and the Klingon Empire's quest for a means of dealing with the Tholian Assembly, and doing so while each party fought not to appear vulnerable to the other. The simple truth was that the Klingons and even the Romulans were more interested in any intelligence avenues that might be exploited via Nimbus III, and Nogura was confident such an agenda had motivated the Federation, as well. No one from any of the three governments would ever admit to this, of course. Some political analysts were even conjecturing that the colony might actually continue in some form for a short while, if only to keep up the pretense of wanting to engage in constructive collaboration.

Nogura was curious to see how that might play out, and just how much support the colony received from any of its sponsors.

I'm betting not all that much.

"So, we've got the Tholians mad at the Klingons," Nogura said, "and the Klingons mad or getting ready to be mad at the Tholians, and the Klingons and the Romulans all mad at us. Pretty good, I'd say, for not even being lunchtime yet."

"What about the Tholians?" Okagawa asked.

Nogura waved away the question. "They were already mad at us. That just leaves the Shedai, and with the luck we've been having, they may be on their way here right now."

There was no way to know what had become of the Shedai entity that had escaped from confinement inside the Mirdonyae Artifact and wrecked the *Lovell*. The brief contact Xiong and Mahmud al-Khaled had achieved with the creature had yielded little in the way of useful information. The two officers, along with Doctor Carol Marcus, believed that with communication now possible with the entities and if some measure of control could be put in place, some sort of dialogue and negotiation might be feasible. If nothing else, the link at least provided one of the best new avenues of research into the mysterious Shedai that had been discovered since Operation Vanguard's inception.

All of which might not matter, Nogura reminded himself, given Xiong's other theory: that the escaped Shedai entity had fled somewhere to regroup, or regain whatever energy it had lost while being held prisoner. The lieutenant had also put forth the unpleasant hypothesis that the Shedai might well be seeking out others of its own kind.

"What if that thing decides to come back?" Okagawa asked. "What if, God help us, it decides to bring friends?"

Reminded of the power just one of these creatures possessed during its attack on the station and the *Lovell,* and knowing from mission reports what a group of the aliens could do if provoked, Nogura had only one answer. "If we don't or can't find anything useful in the Eremar system, then we're probably going to need God's help."

39

Hospitals. Reyes had always hated them.

He had avoided them as best he could throughout his life, and even on those few occasions where he had entered one as a patient, he had done his level best to ensure that his stay was as brief as possible. Although logic reminded him that he should know better and that hospitals generally were dedicated to the preservation of life, he still tended to think of them as places where people went to die, or at the very least to emerge as somehow worse off than when they entered. His dislike went back to one of the more unpleasant memories from his childhood, when his parents would take him to visit his maternal grandmother at a hospice where she had spent the final months of her life suffering from an incurable blood disease. Seeing her, withered and fading with each passing day, had become almost too much to bear, but young Diego Reyes had put on a brave front out of consideration for his mother, maintaining it throughout his grandmother's funeral and his mother's mourning. In the years that followed, his choice of career had seen to it that he had spent more than a bit of time calling on sick or injured loved ones and friends confined in such places, and one of Reyes's deepest regrets was that he had been unable to make the transit to the Sol system to be by his mother's side when she too had contracted a mortal illness.

Thankfully, his visit to Vanguard's hospital was with the knowledge that the person upon whom he was calling would soon walk out of here under his own power and one day resume the life that had been so harshly interrupted by one moment's selfless act.

"They told me you were coming for a visit," Tim Pennington said, looking up as he noticed Reyes, flanked by a pair of officers from the station's security detachment, entering the patient ward. He pressed a button on the control panel next to his bed, which raised him to a sitting position. The journalist shifted as though trying to make himself more comfortable. Offering what Reyes thought might be a forced grin, he added, "You're interrupting my beauty sleep, you know."

Reyes shrugged. "Doesn't seem to be doing much good, anyway. I thought Zeke was going to fix your face while he had you here."

"How do you improve on perfection?" Pennington asked, and Reyes watched him reach across his body with his left hand for a carafe situated atop the bureau next to his bed. As he poured himself a glass of water, he noticed Reyes studying him. "I've got a ways to go before I'm ready to try this with the other mitt."

Nodding in appreciation, Reyes replied, "You'll get there, Tim." Though the prosthetic was all but identical to the arm he had lost, Pennington still faced months of physical therapy before using the artificial limb became second nature to him.

"Damned right, I will," the journalist said as he returned the carafe to its place on the bureau. "I mean, I'm still bloody well right-handed, you know." Looking down at the replacement arm, most of which was concealed by the long sleeve of his hospital shirt, he held up the artificial hand, which to Reyes looked real enough. He noted that Pennington winced at the movement, and he massaged his shoulder with his left hand. "One good thing about this is that I'll be able to type a hell of a lot faster. I'll have to increase my word count goals, just to keep things challenging."

For some reason, Reyes found that funny, and allowed himself a smile and a small laugh. He did not know if Pennington's demeanor was born from an honest positive outlook, or if he might just be affecting bravado. If it was the latter, then Reyes decided that the man's performance was flawless.

Shifting again in the bed, Pennington swung his legs from

beneath the sheets and stood, using the opportunity to stretch. "I can't wait to get out of this place and into a proper bed. Doctor Fisher said if he liked what he saw during his next exam, he'd release me to my quarters, and I'd only have to come down for physical therapy." With a nod, he gestured past Reyes to the pair of security guards standing behind him. "Still not old enough to go to the loo on your own, I see."

Reyes glanced over his shoulder to confirm that the security officers were not amused by the remark. "They *do* have phasers, Tim."

"Yes, they do," Pennington said. "My apologies, boys. Blame it on the excellent pharmaceuticals Doctor Fisher has provided during my stay." Turning his attention back to Reyes, he asked, "So, rumor control has it you're leaving."

Nodding, Reyes replied, "That's right. Starfleet's finally figured out what they want to do with me."

"Bastards," Pennington said, his expression turning to one of disdain. "Even after everything you did to help Nogura and T'Prynn, they're still going to throw you in a hole."

"Nogura did everything he could," Reyes replied, choosing his words with care. "I can't say I disagree with Starfleet's decision."

It was not a lie so much as an artful navigation of the truth. Nogura had in fact been a staunch advocate for Reyes, convincing Starfleet Command to commute his sentence in recognition for the services he had provided while aboard the *Omari-Ekon*. However, the admiralty and JAG Headquarters had been unwilling to overturn Reyes's court-martial conviction. In exchange for the leniency they had decided to show by not sending him to the New Zealand Penal Settlement, Reyes had agreed to go into permanent exile. His life would be comfortable and he would be able to enjoy his retirement at some quiet, undisclosed location where every effort would be made to ensure his new identity afforded him a degree of freedom and anonymity. There would be no official record of his final disposition, save for a classified file at Starfleet Headquarters. Like most of the documentation pertaining to Operation Vanguard, it would be buried under multiple levels of security and all but impossible to retrieve save for those few individuals who would possess the necessary authorization and "need to know." So far as the rest of the galaxy was concerned, Diego Reyes would cease to exist.

I can live with that. After everything that had transpired since he was named Starbase 47's first commanding officer, retreating to some unnamed corner of the universe to live out the rest of his days had acquired a definite appeal.

For a moment, Reyes wondered if Pennington might be seeing through his small deception, but if the reporter suspected anything, he had opted not to raise the issue, at least in front of the security guards. Instead, he asked, "So, what brings you down here? I'm surprised Nogura even let you out of your house arrest at all."

"He's given me some time to wrap up a few loose ends," Reyes replied. "Say my good-byes—that sort of thing." Pausing, he considered the odd relationship he had shared with Pennington since their arrival on the station. They had begun as adversaries, with Pennington on the constant hunt for any information that might fuel his news stories, while Reyes was tasked with ensuring the journalist never got too close to the truth of the station's actual mission in the Taurus Reach.

"I came to say two things. First, thank you, again, for the things you did that saved the lives of people under my command. You took a lot of risks when you didn't have to, but those actions made all the difference when it came to those men and women. I'll never forget that."

Looking uncomfortable with the praise being heaped upon him, Pennington swallowed before replying, "You're welcome, I guess. I certainly hadn't planned on things going that way, but I'm glad it worked out, at least most of the time."

Reyes nodded. "Second, I'm pretty sure I never got around to saying I'm sorry. I'm sorry for the things done to you early on. T'Prynn was my intelligence officer when she did what she did, so that makes me responsible for her actions. I'll never forget that, either. I'm truly sorry, Tim, for everything." He held out his right hand, realizing only after doing so that it might not be the most appropriate gesture, given Pennington's condition.

For his part, Pennington grinned. "You probably want to forgo that for the time being." He held up his right hand again for emphasis. "I haven't quite gotten the knack of not crushing the pulp out of anything I touch with this thing. Maybe next time."

"Next time," Reyes repeated, his voice low. Gripped with a sudden bout of self-consciousness, he tried to ignore the sensation that the patient ward had grown cooler in the last few minutes. Drawing a deep breath, he said, "I should probably get going."

"Thanks for stopping by," Pennington replied, his gaze shifting around the room. Then, he unleashed another of his insufferable smiles. "Don't take this the wrong way, but I bloody well hope you get wherever you're supposed to be going this time."

Once more Reyes laughed. "I'll do my best. Take care of yourself, Tim."

"Same to you, Diego."

It was harder to leave the ward than he had anticipated, but any anxiety Reyes might have felt started to fade the moment he and his security detail emerged into the corridor and found Ezekiel Fisher standing in the passageway as though waiting for him. In his right hand he held what looked to be a large glass bottle filled with a golden brown liquid, and wrapped with a label he was sure he recognized.

"Is that Kentucky bourbon?"

Holding up the bottle, Fisher replied, "You planning to make me drink it by myself?"

"Not a chance in hell," Reyes said.

After asking the pair of security guards to wait outside his office, which required convincing them that there were no secret exits from his cramped, disheveled workspace, Fisher directed Reyes to one of two chairs positioned around a small conference table in the room's far corner. The doctor retrieved two glasses from a cabinet behind his chair and commenced dispensing generous portions of the bourbon into them.

"I suppose you can't even tell me where you're going," Fisher said, taking a seat.

Before replying, Reyes sipped from his glass, relishing the smooth, warming sensation as the alcohol worked its way down his throat. "After drinking the watered-down bug spray that passed for booze on that ship, you have no idea how good this tastes." He glanced over his shoulder to verify that the office doors were still closed before saying, "I'm not allowed to tell you or anyone else that I'm heading for Caldos II."

Fisher grunted. "Never been there, but I hear it's nice."

The colony world was one of five destinations Nogura had suggested as ideal locations for Reyes to "fade away" in compliance with his agreement. Though the original settlement was well established and continuing to grow, the colonists there prided themselves on adhering to the tenets of individuality and personal privacy. It was not uncommon for families to set out on their own and build homes far away from the colony center, either deep in one of the world's teeming forests or among the isolated mountain regions. "There's plenty of planet for anybody looking for a nice place to retire," Nogura had said. The offer was sweetened by the notion that in Reyes's case, exile did not mean total isolation. He would be given a new identity, so that he could live among the other colonists and not attract undue attention.

"I wasn't sold on the idea at first," Reyes said, "but the more I thought about it, the nicer it sounded. Besides, compared to prison, I think I can learn to live with anything. And who knows? I might even be happy there one day."

"Now there's something I'd like to see," Fisher replied, smiling as he took a belt from his glass. "How many people know about this?"

Reyes shrugged. "You, me, Nogura, and two or three of his friends at Starfleet Command who made the whole thing happen."

"Well, it's probably all recorded in a computer file somewhere, anyway," Fisher said. "They still have to get your retirement pay to you, after all."

"True." Nogura had also seen to it that Reyes would receive a small stipend. It was not a full restoration of the pay and benefits that would have been owed him had he officially retired from Starfleet, but it would be more than sufficient for living a quiet, anonymous life on a Federation colony world. "Other than that, though, and maybe checking up on me from time to time, they'll probably leave me well enough alone. Ten years from now, nobody will know or care who I am, or was, or whatever, and I'm okay with that." He had pledged to Nogura that he would accept and even embrace this generous revision of his sentence, and harbored no intentions of going back on his word, if for no other reason than to avoid dishonoring the admiral and the extraordinary effort Reyes knew he had expended on his behalf.

Taking another drink from his glass, Fisher asked, "So, what are you planning to do with all that free time?"

"Catch up on my leisure reading," Reyes replied. "Got any recommendations?"

Fisher nodded, playing his part. "I gave you a perfectly good selection of books, and you let them get blown up. I hope Caldos II has a decent library."

Chuckling at that, Reyes drained the contents of his glass, grimacing at the bourbon's sting as he swallowed. "Well, I haven't really gone fishing since I was a boy. Maybe I'll do that." As he poured himself another drink, a mischievous thought entered his mind. "I could buy myself some old boat, fix it up as a do-it-myself restoration project, then hire it out for fishing charters. That ought to drive some of those admirals at Starfleet nuts." He paused, considering another idea that had just occurred to him. "You know, taking on a job like that, I could use a partner."

"Yeah," Fisher said, leaning back in his chair and cradling his glass in both hands, "that's exactly where I see myself: cutting bait on the back of some shipwreck you've given a fresh coat of paint. Do you even know how to sail a boat? What could possibly go wrong?"

Both men shared a laugh, then said nothing for several moments, two old friends each so comfortable with the other that small talk to fill quiet air had long since become unnecessary. It was Reyes who finally broke the silence.

"Thanks, Zeke, for everything."

His gaze remaining on his glass, Fisher asked, "What did I do?"

"You were there," Reyes answered. "Always. You never doubted me, not for one damned second, and you looked after Rana after I left the first time. I know we haven't talked about it, but I'm betting it wasn't easy for her, first thinking I was dead, then wondering what I must've done to end up with the Klingons or the Orions." He sighed, at once both sad and angry that he had never been given the opportunity to talk to Desai before her abrupt departure from the station. "Thanks for taking care of her."

Fisher nodded, seemingly content to leave it at that. "How much time do you have?"

Glancing to the chronometer set into the computer workstation on the corner of the doctor's desk, Reyes replied, "Four or five hours. Nogura has a transport scheduled to take me to Caldos II, leaving in the dead of night so as to attract minimal attention." It would take three weeks to make the journey to his new home, even at the transport's high-warp speeds. Within a month, he would be settled into his role as just another colonist on the frontier of Federation space, making an honest go at a new, challenging life away from the buzz and static of fast-paced modern society.

Yes, Reyes decided, he could live with that.

"Well, then," Fisher said, reaching once more for the bottle, "as I remember it, we said our long good-byes the last time you left on a transport. I figure there's no reason to rehash all that again. Besides, it's just a waste of good drinking time."

Reyes smiled at his old friend's gentle yet unassailable wisdom. He could live with that, too.

EPILOGUE

April 2270

Pennington felt a shiver, and for the first time realized that the fire had died down to the point that it was nothing more than a bed of smoldering embers. The only other means of determining the length of his visit was the whiskey bottle on the nearby table. It was now less than half full, and Pennington noted the warm, comfortable glow enveloping his body from the homemade alcohol's effects.

"So," he said after a moment, "you told him, but not me? I don't know whether to be surprised or insulted." As he spoke the words, Pennington regretted them in the face of the long, close friendship Reyes had shared with Ezekiel Fisher.

"Be both," Reyes replied, his expression growing somber, and Pennington figured the other man's thoughts were lingering on his old friend. "Save yourself the burden of decisions."

Holding up his glass, Pennington eyed it with suspicion. "Has it occurred to you that a lot of your encounters with friends involve drinking in one form or another?"

"Call it a coping mechanism," Reyes said, rising from his chair. "How else are my visitors supposed to put up with me?" He reached for the metal poker and knelt before the fireplace, stirring the embers before adding two new logs to the withered remnants still sitting in the firebox's soot-covered cradle. "It's too late to call for a ride back to the mainland. I've got a spare bedroom. You can collapse in there if you want."

Lifting his glass to his lips, Pennington frowned upon noting that the vessel was empty. "Trying to run me off, are you? There's still a lot you haven't told me, like just what the hell you do to stay busy around here, of all the damned places. I mean, if nowhere really does have a middle, I'm pretty sure this planet sits squarely in its belly button."

Reyes, appearing satisfied that the fire soon would return to its former blazing glory, replaced the poker in its stand and returned to his seat, where he set about pouring more whiskey into his glass. "You know, it's amazing what you can buy when you've been saving for your retirement for thirty-odd years. One of the benefits of spending most of my adult life living in Starfleet billeting aboard starships and space stations is that I never had to pay rent. So, I just banked those credits for a rainy day." He gestured toward one wall and, presumably, the forest beyond the confines of his cabin. "Like I said before, we get a lot of rainy days here."

"So," Pennington said, reaching for the whiskey bottle, "you had this place already picked out?"

"Hardly," Reyes replied, his gaze returning once more to the fire. "Caldos II was number four on a list of five planets where Starfleet was willing to authorize my 'relocation,' with the proviso that once I picked a place, that's where I'd agree to stay until I died, the planet blew up, or Starfleet needed me—whichever came first."

Trying to imagine how that conversation might have played out, Pennington uttered a bemused grunt. "It must've been a hard choice."

"Not really," Reyes countered, sipping his drink, "not when you remember that the alternative at the bottom of the list was prison." He paused, glancing around the cabin. "Anyway, they helped smooth things over so far as my actually buying this place. I own the entire island, and my cover story is that I'm a retired civilian engineer who came looking for a nice, quiet corner of the galaxy to live out my golden years. It's enough to let me move around, interact with the locals, and so on. Everyone pretty much keeps to themselves here, so I don't get anyone nosing around looking for answers to questions that don't even come up, anyway." Pennington smiled as Reyes glared at him from the corner of his eye. "Well, most of the time, that is."

Pennington shook his head. "So this is it, then? A cabin in the woods on a lake, for the rest of your life?"

"There are worse ways to live," Reyes replied, shrugging. "Like I said, prison's still there, if this ends up not working out."

"And Starfleet's not worried that anyone else might come looking for you?" Pennington asked. Though he had no problem with the notion that he might be the first person to have successfully tracked down Reyes, it stood to reason that he also would not be the last.

Waving his free hand as though to swat away the suggestion, Reyes frowned. "Even if somebody does find me, there's nothing for me to tell that you probably haven't already written about, right?"

Pennington regarded him with an expression of bewilderment. "You mean you haven't read my reports for FNS? Thanks for the loyalty."

"Haven't had much use for news since I got here," Reyes said. "Besides, as I recall, there was a news blackout around the station for a long while after I left. I'll admit I was curious at first, and considered staying updated on the entire situation, but after a while, there didn't seem to be much point in keeping up with all of that, along with the goings-on in the rest of a galaxy I'll never again be a part of. Better to make a clean break from all of it, and get on with life." Raising his glass to his lips, he stopped in mid motion as his eyes met Pennington's. "But I can see from the look on your face that you've got a story you're dying to tell, and I'd be lying if I said I didn't want to hear it."

"You would, would you?" Pennington punctuated the question with a small, humorless smile. The events that had brought to an end the astonishing project known as Operation Vanguard were fresh enough that he imagined he still sensed a pain both physical and emotional. Several seconds passed before he realized he was recalling those events all while unconsciously rubbing his right arm at the point where his prosthetic limb joined his shoulder socket. Startled, he removed his hand and guided it back to resting in his lap, took another sip of his drink, and forced himself to enjoy the soothing warmth of the fire for an entire minute before returning his attention to Reyes. "Well, then. What do you want to know?"

Reyes hesitated, as though trying to decide how much of whatever Pennington might tell him he actually wanted to hear. Then, he answered, "How long did you stay on the station after I left?"

It was now Pennington's turn to consider his answer. He had quit counting after running out of fingers the number of nondisclosure agreements and letters of secrecy he had signed in the aftermath of Operation Vanguard. He knew that by simply being here, he had probably violated most if not all of those agreements. If he was discovered here, he faced the very real possibility of being sent to the very same penal colony Diego Reyes had managed to avoid.

And yet, he did not care. For the first and perhaps only time in whatever might remain of his life, Tim Pennington would get to tell another living person about his final, fateful days aboard Starbase 47.

"I was there until the end, mate," he said after a moment. "The bitter, bloody end."

The saga of

STAR TREK®
VANGUARD

will conclude in

STORMING HEAVEN

ACKNOWLEDGMENTS

Thanks of the first order are reserved for our editors, who exercised far more patience and compassion than we deserved. Their unwavering support and mentorship were instrumental in the completion of this book.

To Marco Palmieri and David Mack, co-creators of *Star Trek: Vanguard*, we're going to flout convention and repeat what we said in the dedication: Thanks for inviting us to the party. Writing for this series has been some of the most unqualified fun we've had working in the *Star Trek* "expanded universe," and much of that is owed to the drive and passion you both brought to the table. To say we're going to miss this is a criminal understatement.

A round of heartfelt applause is directed to Doug Drexler, Oscar- and Emmy-winning art wizard whose efforts have graced the covers of all the *Star Trek: Vanguard* titles. His love and enthusiasm for *Star Trek,* particularly the original series, is infectious. If you're reading this, Mister D., rest assured that you are a steely-eyed missile man.

Special thanks are sent out to Eric Kristiansen, fan and artist responsible for the "Starfleet Exploration Craft: *Duedalus*-class" blueprints he created as part of his *Jackill's Technical Readout Data Sheets* series. We purchased a set of these for six bucks years ago when we first were developing the *Lovell* crew for our *Star Trek: Corps of Engineers* stories. Though we took a few small liberties, plotting and details of the *Lovell*'s interior spaces were realized thanks to inspiration supplied by these data sheets. Check out a whole bunch of Eric's awesome work at www.jackill.com.

As this novel likely marks the last time we'll ever write for this particular set of characters, we'd like to give our final round of thanks to the readers and fans of the *Star Trek: Vanguard* series. It's been an absolute joy to work on these books over the past several years, and the response from the *Star Trek* fiction reader community has been nothing short of astounding. It was your enthusiasm and excitement for each new book that kept us motivated throughout our tenure on the series, and we hope we held up our end of the deal.

ABOUT THE AUTHORS

DAYTON WARD. Author. Trekkie. Writing his goofy little stories and searching for a way to tap into the hidden nerdity that all humans have. Then, an accidental overdose of Mountain Dew altered his body chemistry. Now, when Dayton Ward grows excited or just downright geeky, a startling metamorphosis occurs.

Driven by outlandish ideas and a pronounced lack of sleep, he is pursued by fans and editors as well as funny men in bright uniforms wielding stun guns, straitjackets, and medication. In addition to the numerous credits he shares with friend and co-writer Kevin Dilmore, Dayton is the author of the science fiction novels *The Last World War; Counterstrike: The Last World War—Book II*; and *The Genesis Protocol*; the *Star Trek* novels *In the Name of Honor, Open Secrets,* and *Paths of Disharmony*; as well as short stories in various anthologies and web-based publications. For Flying Pen Press, he was the editor of the science fiction anthology *Full-Throttle Space Tales #3: Space Grunts*.

Dayton is believed to be working on his next novel, and he must let the world think that he is working on it, until he can find a way to earn back the advance check he blew on strippers and booze. Though he currently lives in Kansas City with his wife and daughters, Dayton is a Florida native and maintains a torrid long-distance romance with his beloved Tampa Bay Buccaneers. Visit him on the web at www.daytonward.com.

KEVIN DILMORE is but one more proof of Dr. Hunter S. Thompson's assertion that when the going gets weird, the weird turn pro. It all started in 1998 with his eight-year run as a contributing writer to *Star Trek Communicator,* for which he wrote news stories and personality profiles for the bimonthly publication of the Official *Star Trek* Fan Club. Since that time, he also has contributed to publications including *Amazing Stories, Hallmark,* and *Star Trek* magazines. Look for his essay in the forthcoming anthology *Hey Kids, Comics—True Life Tales from the Spinner Rack,* edited by Rob Kelly.

Then he teamed with writing partner and heterosexual life mate Dayton Ward on *Interphase,* their first installment of the *Star Trek: S.C.E.* series in 2001. Since then, the pair has put more than one million words into print together. Among their most recent shared publications are the novella *The First Peer* in the anthology *Star Trek: Seven Deadly Sins* (March 2010) and the short story "Ill Winds" in the *Star Trek: Shards and Shadows* anthology (January 2009).

By day, Kevin works as a senior writer for Hallmark Cards in Kansas City, MO, doing about everything but writing greeting cards, including helping to design *Star Trek*–themed Keepsake Ornaments. His first children's book, *Superdad and His Daring Dadventures,* with illustrations by Tom Patrick, was published by Hallmark Gift Books in May 2009.

A graduate of the University of Kansas, Kevin lives in Overland Park, Kansas. Keep up with his shameful behavior and latest projects on Facebook and Twitter.